LITTLE GIRL BLUE

REBECCA GRIFFITHS

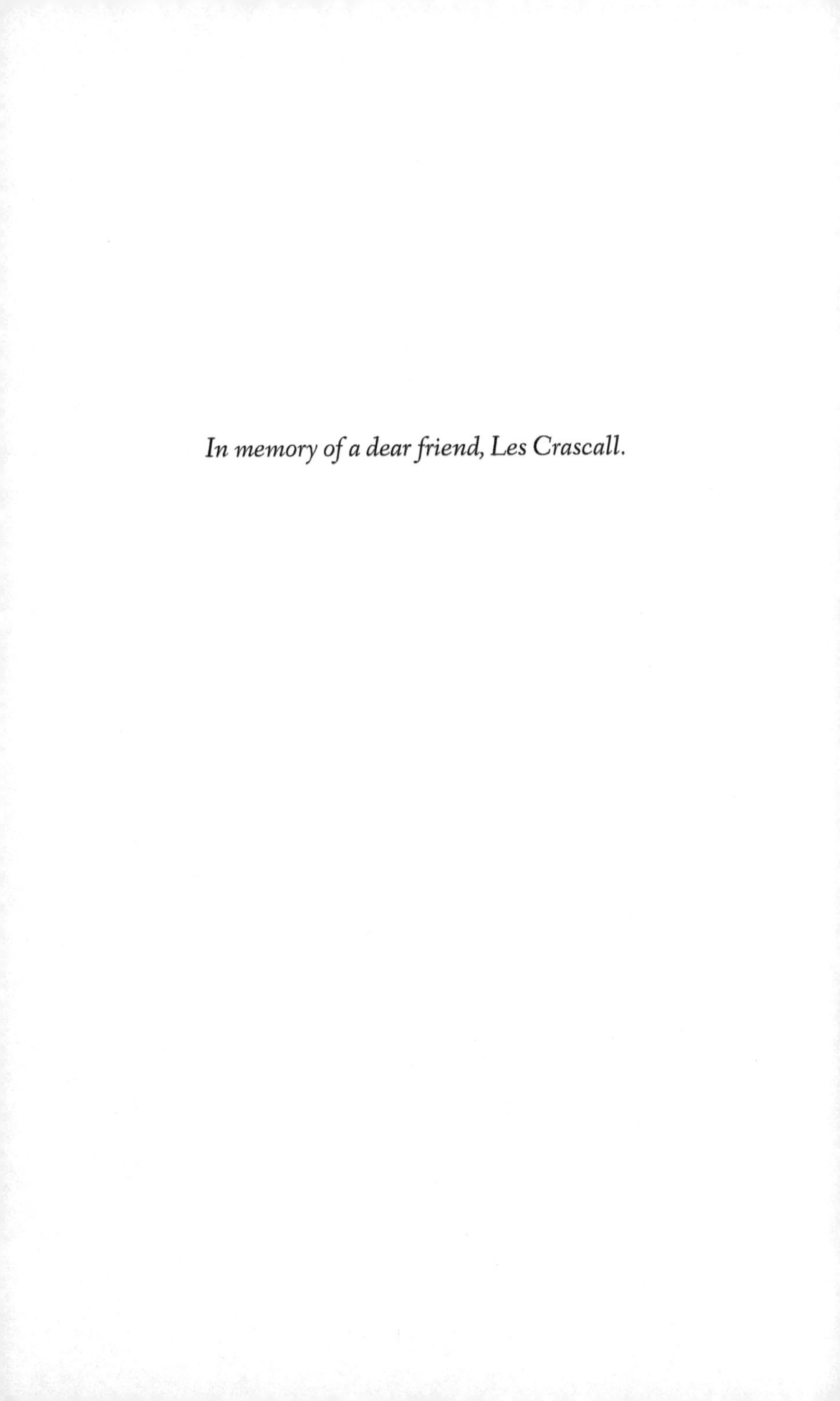

In memory of a dear friend, Les Crascall.

PROLOGUE

Tonight, in a part of Cardiff that was unaccustomed to violence, a black cat with yellow eyes looked down from the third-floor window of a Victorian terraced house. The only witness to a brutal knife attack that had left a man slumped on a pavement pitted with oily puddles.

The wounded man closed his eyes to the pervasive winter darkness. Exchanged it for another kind of darkness as his heartbeat weakened and he feared time was against him. Believing this was where he would die, he rolled heavily onto his side. Tasted grit along with blood in his mouth as the revving north-easterly wind pushed through the buttons of his smart overcoat.

ONE

TWENTY-ONE YEARS BEFORE

A thin, grey morning. Cold for May. The birds beyond the window of Julia Opie's top-floor consulting room were confused by it. Her next appointment wasn't due until quarter past, so she'd fetched a cup of coffee from the machine in the staffroom and lit a sneaky fag. Naughty, she knew the rules, and there was always the risk of setting off the fire alarms but sod it, she was gasping, and there wasn't time to nip downstairs to share it with the dead leaves and wheelie bins at the rear of the building.

She tugged up the louvre blinds and opened the window. Blew her expended smoke as far as she could over the hospital car park and the cloud-covered city beyond. She shivered as she watched it disperse. With the recurrent need to strip down to the bare necessities, Julia was reluctant to wear thicker layers. A dilemma for women her age: hot one minute, freezing the next; she considered it a miracle she could function at all.

Her thoughts, following the twirl of an abandoned plastic bag on the tarmac below, spun to her next patient: someone that was enough to bring her out in a sweat all on their own. The referral came through the family's GP over three months ago but CAMHS (the NHS child and adolescent mental health services), stretched to the max as usual, had sat on it. Even when the inevitable happened and someone got seriously hurt, Julia – one of four child psychologists working out of this Cardiff clinic – still dilly-dallied, unable to find room in her jam-packed schedule.

She had found room now though, hadn't she?

This one was an emergency.

A ticking bomb.

A glance at the clock had her extinguishing the cigarette and pinching out a mint from a tube she kept on her desk. Coffee finished, she dropped the cup into the bin and put the mint in her mouth, then felt the familiar creeping sense of dread before the customary prickle against her top lip, at the nape of her neck. Not now, she grimaced, bracing herself for another of her ferocious flushes. Returning to the window to flap the chilly air against her face with a hastily grabbed file, she trailed the roof of a new blue Ford Focus as it slid to a stop in the car park below. The driver, a large man in a sheepskin jacket, got out and closed the car door. She watched him rake a hand through his blond curls and throw a desperate look at the sky.

Julia flinched and stepped back from the window, fearful of being seen. But telling herself this was unlikely, that she would be invisible against the concrete and glass-sided hospital block, she peered down again and saw the man grappling with a boy of around seven or eight, dressed in what she supposed was his school uniform of red V-neck and grey trousers. Once wrestled from the car, the boy began to scream and kick the man she assumed was his father.

Could this be her next appointment? Very possible. The child she was scheduled to see was around this one's age. Dabbing away perspiration, Julia focused beyond the raging heat that surged through her body and scribbled... ***assess for Asperger's... borderline personality disorder...***

***antisocial personality disorder*...** on her writing pad. When she returned to the awful scene below, her mind curved to the case notes she read on her commute to work. The account provided by the boy's father to the family GP had unsettled her more than usual, referring as it did, to explosive episodes and terrifying outbursts, when the child would smash things and lash out against his father and grandparents. It also stated these destructive tantrums had intensified in severity and frequency over the past eight months, and that things at home had reached crisis point.

Her flush subsiding, Julia pressed an anxious hand to her mouth as the man knelt on the tarmac and hugged the now tearful boy. The abruptness with which the child's tantrum subsided was as surprising as his sudden submissiveness, as he allowed himself to be cuddled and soothed.

'Do you want to start by telling me what happened?' Julia asked the seven-year-old boy she had been watching in the car park only minutes before.

He eyed her. Wary as a wild animal.

'Would you like to draw something for me instead?' She gestured to the box of crayons and the pads of paper on the desk behind her. 'Sometimes it's easier to show rather than tell.'

Breathing in the remnants of her recent cigarette, Julia could also smell the freesias that had been a gift from a colleague for her birthday. A birthday that celebrated more than a fortnight ago meant they were past their best. Not unlike her, she thought, eyeing the dead petals littering the top of the metal cabinet of children's files. Something that, long before this office became hers, had been prettified with cartoon characters she doubted anyone would be able to remember the names of anymore.

Julia hated these awkward silences. Even with twenty-plus years of experience to draw on, she was still unsure how to fill them. She crossed and uncrossed her legs and listened to the rasp of nylon competing with the sounds of their breathing. She stared at the brown-speckled carpet and clicked the nib of her pen in and out, then added to the doodles of stars and fishes she'd made in the margins of her notepad.

'You can tell me anything.' She looked at the boy, at the muscle twitching along the smooth line of his jaw. The suggestion he draw something was obviously of no interest.

Don't do that. She wanted to smack his hand when she saw him pick at the large plaster on his neck. Her nerves were frayed enough. Something dark and heavy had filled the room, pressing down on her, and she looked up at the ceiling, half expecting to see it. She sniffed the dying freesias again and identified the reek of decay; she must remember to chuck them out before going home.

Feeling the need to avert her gaze, Julia scoured the pages of the GP's report for the account of the incident that happened at this child's home. *Violent. Aggressive. Frightening. The final straw.* The words had been underscored in a red ballpoint. This was why she'd found the time to see the child. Why she'd rescheduled inconsequential appointments and cancelled others. She read on, refreshing herself with details about how the boy's sister had inadvertently done something to provoke him and that by the time their father realised something was amiss, the child sitting opposite her had stabbed his sister with a fork. Narrowly missing her eye.

'Okay.' Julia, forcing a pseudo brightness, tried to ignore the hostility rippling beneath the boy's skin. 'If you don't want to talk about that, how about you tell me what happened to your neck?'

Rapid blinking was accompanied by some fierce leg kicking and, plaster forgotten, the boy began to nibble his nails. This was almost as bad as him picking the plaster but she let it pass. Told herself, as long as he was still in the room and not calling for his daddy, then part of him wanted her to know, wanted her to understand.

'Did something happen at school, is that it?'

What he'd done hadn't happened at school, she knew this. It said in his notes he loved school and that he behaved well for his teachers and had many friends, but she had to start somewhere.

'No,' he said, then mumbled something she couldn't hear. 'Didn't happen at school.' So quiet, Julia needed to lean forward to hear him. 'At home.'

At last, she smiled her relief. 'Good.' She drummed her biro against the notepad and took a deep breath. 'This is good.'

'No, it's not good!' The boy shot out a scream and pummelled his thighs with his fists, his face flushed and indignant.

Julia waited for him to speak again, but the minutes ticked by without a word. She watched the anger flicker behind his eyes and felt more than a little afraid of him.

Afraid? Really? She challenged herself. This was a child, a child who had lost his mother eight months ago. Yes, he was big for his age and within a few short years would be capable of grievous violence... or even to kill... but for now, he needed her empathy and help. Because, she reasoned, to lose your mother at such a crucial stage in your development was unbearably cruel and, in many ways, this boy's recent behaviour could be considered a justified response.

'Bang. Bang. Bang.' He fired off the word through his

fingers: a pretend gun. Julia jumped at the sound. 'It's the only way to stay safe.' A heavy frown. 'We're in big danger.'

'Who from?' she asked, and was disappointed when he declined to answer, dropping his shooting hand into his lap.

Sounds of singing from a nearby room floated into their silence. Julia found herself trying to identify the tune, to unpick the lyrics. She could tell the boy was doing the same because he began to join in and do the actions.

'*Pen, Ysgwyddau, Coesau, Traed... Coesau, Traed,*' he sang, all at once happy and lively, finding the Welsh words to the well-known song, 'Heads, Shoulders, Knees and Toes', from Julia's own childhood.

She winked, wanting to let him know she was one of the good guys. When he smiled in return, she gulped it down before the moment was lost and he swung back to his aggressive self. Into the expectant pause that felt ripe with possibilities, Julia crossed out the word **Asperger's** and exchanged it for **Dabrowski Syndrome**. Braced it with a large question mark. Beneath this, another idea occurred. ***Intermittent Explosive Disorder***. She underlined it twice, then tapped the biro against her lower incisors and raked over what she knew of the boy's family background – along with the premature death of his mother, the history of his maternal grandparents: Polish refugees who arrived in Cardiff after the war. A paper read at university unfurled in her mind. Written by the American academic, Selma Fraiberg. *Ghosts in the Nursery*. She jotted this down too. Could the child's propensity for violence have been passed down to him through the generations, through the womb? Could the atrocities suffered by his maternal grandmother have somehow been remembered, learnt? Yes, she appreciated it was usually girls who were found to be affected by this phenomenon but even so, it was worth looking into.

'Are you feeling better now?' She saw the boy's colour had returned to normal.

He bestowed a contrite little nod. His capacity to twist from shocking outbursts to calm alarmed her. 'Do you want to tell me what it feels like when you get angry?'

He shook his head but because it was given with another small smile, Julia pushed him. 'Is that because you don't want to tell me, or because you don't know?' His cap of copper-coloured hair was as shiny as a conker under the strip lighting. 'How about you tell me what makes you angry? Start from there.'

'Why?' The word was muffled by his fingers.

'Because I'd like to know, if that's okay?'

No response. It worried her.

'I don't like it,' he began suddenly, then hesitated. 'I don't like it when people laugh at me.'

Progress at last. She clicked the nib of her pen in and out, in and out. Then stopped. She mustn't fidget, she must keep still, this one had enough nervous tics for the both of them.

'It's not fair.' His legs paddled the space between them. 'I want to be taken seriously.'

Wonder who taught him words like that? Julia's thoughts, as she got up and moved to the sofa. She patted the upholstery to invite him to join her, which, to her surprise, he did. His facility to discuss things typical seven-year-olds wouldn't have the vocabulary for interested her. He interested her. She could tell so much of him wanted to please, wanted to share, he was a walking contradiction – a real Jekyll and Hyde.

'Do you want to add anything to that?' She listened as he took a couple of tiny breaths.

'She did it.'

'She? Who's she?'

'My sister. Who d'you think?'

'Okay.'

'You say okay a lot.'

She noticed him looking sideways at her lap. 'Do I now?' She smiled.

'You smile a lot too. I like it. My teacher, Miss Feathers, she smiles a lot. I like Miss Feathers. I like school.'

'Why d'you think you like school so much?' That's better, a nice open question; she'd always tended to ask closed ones, regardless of the training courses and her reminders not to.

'I know where I am at school. There's rules to follow. I like rules.'

'Have you ever got into a fight at school?'

'No.'

'Only at home, then?' Another bad habit, leading the witness; she'd been doing the job too long.

Julia unbuttoned her cardigan and slipped it free of her shoulders.

'Why have you gone all red?'

She laughed. This kid didn't miss a trick. 'It's called a flush.' She flapped her notebook at her throat.

'I know what they are.' The voice was proud. 'Babcia gets them.'

'Is *Bab-sha* your grandma?' Julia picked up the foreign-sounding word and batted it back.

The boy nodded.

'D'you want to talk about her?'

'No.'

'Your sister, then? Did your sister laugh at you? Was that the problem?'

'Yes.' Unflinching, she could tell he believed himself justified.

'And that's why you did what you did to her, is it?' Gently, she couldn't come at this head-on.

'Yes.' He shifted in his seat and stared down at his shoes.

'Have you ever tried to hurt yourself?'

A nod.

Julia recalled something in his notes. 'How?'

'I tried to strangle myself. But it didn't work, did it?' He lifted his eyes to hers and she saw they were as clear and blue as a swimming pool. 'I'm still here.'

'Is that—' Julia cleared her throat; the poignancy of such a declaration from one so young momentarily floored her.

'Can I ask you something?' He had identified a gap in their conversation.

'Of course.'

'Please, can you tell me when we're all going to die? Because it would be really useful for me to know.'

'Why's that?' Julia, although faintly alarmed, did her best to maintain a neutral tone.

'Because I want to work it out on a calculator. I want to know how many days and nights I've got left.'

She gulped down her rising anxiety and considered how best to respond. 'It's, *erm...* Well, it's not something anyone can answer. You love facts, don't you?' Good – turn this child's worrying preoccupation with death into something positive.

'Very much.' He grinned and swung his legs again. Then, earnest and frowning. 'But this world's dangerous. People are out to trick you all the time. I told Yana, they're after your life.'

'Yana, is she your sister?'

The boy nodded. 'But she's a rotten scoundrel if you ask me.' His assurances fizzed around the room. 'Not that me and her are all that different. We're all walking in the footsteps of death. It's exhausting.' He produced a grown-up-sounding sigh, and Julia wondered, along with the quirky vocabulary, if he'd copied the mannerism from the adults in his life.

'Where do your ideas about this come from?'

'From the *Terrible Tudors* and the *Awful Egyptians*, I love those books. I know them by heart. I can quote you properly if you want?'

A squint at the clock told Julia that time was running out. 'When you and I meet next,' she assured him. 'For now, though, I'd like to go back to you telling me about Yana.'

'I'll tell you all about Yana, oh, yes.' He wobbled excitedly from side to side. 'She stabbed me. There.' He prodded the cut under the plaster on his neck.

'Ouch!' Julia, going along with it. 'And how did she do that?'

'With a knife.'

'Are you sure?'

'Course, I'm sure. I'm not stupid.'

'No, I know you're not stupid.'

'Don't you laugh at me.'

Julia felt the chill of his warning settle over her and hiccupped her response. 'I'm not laughing at you.' She penned... **laughed at = major trigger** ...on her notepad.

'You're always writing. What are you writing?'

'Things to help me understand you better.'

'It's my sister you should be talking to, not me. I'm always getting the blame for stuff I didn't do.'

'Do you want to tell me about that?'

'No.'

'Why not?'

'Because you won't believe me either.'

'Well, you have to admit, you do like telling stories,' she said, then instantly regretted it.

'Am I allowed to go home now? I want to go home.' His plea was the most childish he'd been.

How best to tell him? To tell this quite remarkable little boy his father couldn't cope with him and his outbursts anymore? That after the physical diagnosis Julia was about to make, he would undoubtedly be taken into institutionalised care and undergo a programme of cognitive behavioural therapy until it was deemed safe enough to release him back into society. This was a volatile situation, irrespective of the mitigating circumstances of losing his mother so young, and if she didn't act to stop something worse from happening, it would be her head on the block.

'That all depends on you. It depends on whether you can be honest with me about what happened with your sister.' She inhaled and rolled her pen between her fingers. 'Because we both know Yana is only a baby and can't hold a knife, never mind stab you with it.'

In her shared basement room, Angela Milligan tidied away her red hair in a plastic clasp and looked up at the only window: a slice of glass set at street level, where rain bounced against Cardiff's paving slabs. The sight of it depressed her, as did the idea of another shift starting at the Lloyd George Hotel in less than thirty minutes. She gathered her bag and zipped up her parka, letting out a sigh as she closed the door without waiting for her roommate's usual languid response to her goodbye.

Aside from Duncan, head down and busy at his desk behind the toughened glass, the hostel's foyer was deserted.

'Hi, Spike.' He flicked his dark flap of fringe out of his eyes and slid the screen across. Duncan always had time for her, it was a shame he had a girlfriend. 'How's tricks?'

'Oh, you know, *work*.' She pulled a face. About her nickname, mostly. A nickname, that because of her surname and her maternal grandfather's love of the legendary Spike Milligan, she'd been lumbered with since birth.

'I heard you're leaving us.'

Disbelieving the frown creasing Duncan's forehead, she

nodded her reply. 'My friend, Rhiannon... Her boss needs someone to cat-sit for a few months.'

'Whereabouts?'

'Roath.' She watched him chew the end of his biro, the blue ink staining his tongue.

'Smart part of town. When are you moving?'

'Today. After my shift.'

'Let us know if you need a hand.'

'Thanks, but I've not much stuff and Rhiannon and Geraint are helping me. Geraint's got a van. He's a plumber, he's got his own business.'

Angela waved goodbye to Duncan and stepped out into a muggy late-October morning that was as dark as dusk. Unfurling her umbrella as she walked, she dodged the cracks in the wet paving slabs... fearful of bears. This was a game she'd played since childhood, and it brought thoughts of home: before home became a Welsh backwater and her parents and brother, Robert, lived in a beautiful house in the Charlton Kings suburb of Cheltenham. Where instead of a world of shuffling, shifting green, that made her think the country was made of grass and leaves, there were wide, urban pavements, not unlike these, taking her to Brownies in the church hall. Regular as clockwork. Rain or shine. A jam tart in hand and instructions not to make crumbs. Even in the street? A memory of her mother's laugh to prove there must have been happy times before their world capsized.

Angela arrived at the red-brick rear of the hotel, a part of the building no paying guest ever saw, at a time when normal people were opening their eyes and thinking about breakfast. Once inside the staff entrance, she furled her umbrella and slid between the smeary vertical plastic strips, cringing when they dropped back against her coat. With a damp hand clamped over her nose, she pushed past a crowd of high steel trolleys stacked with dirty laundry and took the necessary steps down to the locker rooms, where she collected her knives in their canvas cradle and changed into her shapeless whites, chef's toque and safety shoes.

'Very fetching,' she kidded, catching her reflection in a mirror on her way out into the corridor that led her deep into the bowels of the hotel.

When she reached the kitchen, Angela swung open the door. The artificial glare engulfed her. As did the din. It was going to be hotter than ever in here today. The place was packed: a churn of harassed, perspiring faces under tall white hats through the steam, each sharing the etiolated look of creatures kept under stones. It could be any time of day or night in here or any time of year.

'Oh, you've decided to grace us with your presence, have you?' Sarcastic and surly, it was Tyrone, the section leader, who greeted her. The man whose job Angela hoped she was in line for when he left at the end of the month. 'Where the fuck've you been? We're right in the shit. Got three groups of fifty-odd booked for lunch and we're two men down.'

Angela, about to protest, to say she wasn't late, that she was never late, when Tyrone slapped a sweaty hand on her shoulder.

'I've done you a list.' He jabbed the point of his knife at a greasy sheet of paper covered in his scrawl. 'You've got five hours,' he growled, then left her to it.

A quick wash of her hands and she began carving into a huge pumpkin. A beautiful thing that made her think of orange sunsets, a colour not unlike her hair, with a private hoard of dark, slippery seeds she scooped out with her fingers.

'You're *Aboyer* today, 'n all,' Tyrone informed her when he sidled past sometime later.

'You are joking?' His expression told her he wasn't. 'I hate calling out the orders, can't someone else do it?'

'Just do as you're told, Spike.' She felt his dark-eyed contempt travel the length of her.

Angela pulled a face behind his back, then carried on working down the list. When she next looked up, she saw it had gone half twelve and left what remained of her jobs, to stand beside the hot service lamps. Where, for the next two hours, the waiting staff thrust torn-off chits at her to call through to the kitchen. On her feet since seven, she shifted around to ease the ache in her legs, while under her whites, her skin itched and beads of sweat rolled down between her shoulder blades.

Standing in full view of the kitchen barking out instructions, made her nervous. Not that there was room for timidity here. In a brigade of almost forty, where she was the only female, Angela needed to assert herself along with the best of them.

'You can finish up now, Spike,' Hakim, today's sous chef, called from his workbench.

Shifty-looking and skinny, he was at least friendlier than last night's sous chef. He was a bully who dug her in the ribs with a palette knife and shouted she'd be better off working in a McDonald's.

'Was that the last order?'

He confirmed it was.

'Hakim, have you got a minute?' She waited for him to put down his knife and join her before launching into the difficulties she had with juggling college work around the back-to-back shifts she was timetabled to do here.

'I s'ppose I could have a word with Chef when we do the rota.' He reached to turn off the hot lamps and she stared up at his misaligned nostrils. 'If the hotel's sponsoring you, we should make sure you get the same day off each week,' he continued in his desultory manner. 'I can't think it'd be... *Um—*' Spinning on his heels and straggling his indecision behind him, Angela could tell she'd lost him.

Then she saw who she had lost him to.

Toni Perry. The Tasmanian waitress the majority of the male staff at the Lloyd George were besotted with.

She tracked Hakim's leery-eyed interest as it followed her friend's progress from swing door to wash-up. It was hardly surprising. Toni, in her figure-hugging uniform of black pencil skirt and waistcoat, was bound to hold greater interest.

'Hi there, darlin', how's it going?' Dogged in his pursuit of the unattainable, Hakim whistled through his chapped lips. 'You're looking 'specially gorgeous today, if I may say?'

'No, you may not say.' Toni dismissed him with a filthy look and then beckoned Angela. 'Honestly, gal,' she hissed, close to her ear. 'I dunno how you stand it in here with these cocks.'

'They don't take much notice of me. Not like they notice you.'

Toni stepped back and gave Angela an exaggerated look up and down. 'Can't say I'm surprised in that get-up. Perhaps I should swap my uniform for a set of whites?'

They laughed.

'Been hell here today, hasn't it?' Angela wiped her hands down her front.

'Hotta than bloody Binalong Bay.'

'You still up for tomorrow?' Toni's perfume was sweet and refreshing; unlike Angela, she never stank of kitchens.

'I weren't sure you'd still have the weekend off.'

'They wouldn't dare, I've been owed it for months. So—' she wanted to firm up arrangements, 'you up for it?'

'Defo.' Toni swept a beringed hand through her blonde

bobbed hair. 'Mark's coming over tomorrow to clear out his stuff. No way I wanna be around for that.'

'Oh, so he's definitely moving out?'

The scarlet-glossed mouth twisted into a grimace.

'I'm sorry.'

'*Yeah?* Well, don't be.' Toni tossed back her head and Angela saw there were tears in her eyes. 'His flamin' look-out.' Her thumb buffed the substantial ring she wore on her right hand and the movement alerted Angela to the blue-green gemstone that was as large as a fish's eye. 'I'm a free agent now.' A forced laugh she could tell Toni didn't mean. 'Spain, here I come. I've told HR I'll work till mid-November, then I'm off.'

'That's the way.' Angela jollied her along, keeping to herself the reason she had for feeling bad about Toni's split with Mark.

'There's still time for you to come with me. I'm serious, there's nothing here you can't come back to.'

Angela didn't know what to say, she'd already given Toni a list of excuses; this was a conversation they'd had many times.

'Look—' she squeezed her friend's arm through its silky sleeve, 'I'll be finished here by three tomorrow. Why not come over around four? We could get a takeaway, or there's that pub at the end of the road. Rhiannon says it's good, it's up to you?'

'Awesome.'

'You can stay Saturday night too.'

'Might as well. I'm down for a late shift, Sunday. What's the house like?'

'Don't know, I haven't seen it yet. I only met Lin and Greg last week.'

'You're barmy, you are, Spike.'

Angela grinned. 'Whatever it's like, it's got to be better than that hostel.'

Toni twiddled the stud in her nose. 'Hey, think of the rent

you'll save. Unless... Jeepers, girly.' She frowned. 'Don't tell me they're charging you rent?'

'No rent. Isn't it brilliant? Brilliant of Rhiannon to sort it for me.'

'Least she could do after dumping you in it.'

'Oh, it's all right. She had her reasons.'

'Too soft by half, you are, Spike. Thought she was supposed to be your best friend? I wouldn't have let her get away with treating me like that. Anyway, why couldn't she do the cat-sitting?'

'Geraint's allergic to them.'

'And she has to be with him every second of the day and night.' Toni rolled her well-made-up eyes.

'Something like that. But it's worked out all right for me in the end.'

'Good on ya, mate.' Toni clapped her hands; the movement making her bangles jingle. 'And just think, you'll be able to pay that credit card of yours off and maybe save a bit for a deposit on your own place too.'

'That's the idea.'

'You got an address for me?'

'Sure have.' She rifled in her apron pocket. 'I wrote it down.'

Toni glanced at the scrap of paper Angela handed her. 'Coracle Road. What's the bus route?'

'Number seventy-five. Pick-up in Lloyd Street, just behind the hotel. It's only seven or eight stops to Albany Road. Then a short walk from there.'

'Easy.'

'See you tomorrow then.' Angela's exuberance inadvertently reminded Hakim she was there.

'Oi, Spike.' He turned on her, not half so nice since Toni's snub. 'You're not paid to stand around gossiping, get on with your work.'

Lunchtime service over, Angela finished the mayonnaise she'd been instructed to make and carried the mixing bowl over to the wash-up area at the rear of the kitchen. Set it down with its blade and sent the various utensils skidding across the slippery metal surface. Gathering them into a pile, careful not to cut herself, she failed to notice Toni sashaying in her direction. But hearing the usual orchestration of wolf whistles, she looked up in time to see her friend's blonde head disappear behind the splash screen. Odd. No one, let alone the restaurant staff, bothered with the crew who worked this section of the kitchen. Everybody – probably down to the unpleasantness of the job – gave the kitchen porters a wide berth. Angela didn't know one of them to speak to and doubted she would be able to pick any of them out in a line-up.

She thought about hanging around to find out what Toni was up to but, needing to leave on the dot today, she returned to her section to wipe down the surfaces and record the temperatures of the fridges. The angry shouts drifting over from the wash-up made it hard to concentrate. It wasn't that she was unaccustomed to the sound of raised voices in here; the tropical heat of this place meant the flash and flare of tempers were commonplace. What was unusual was her Tasmanian friend losing hers. Yes, Toni could be bossy and had a reputation for speaking her mind, but it meant she usually got her own way without raising her voice. The only person Angela had ever heard her shout at was her now ex-boyfriend, Mark.

Quite dramatically, Toni and the man she was arguing with, moved out from behind the stainless-steel partition and continued their disagreement under the full glare of the back-of-house staff. The kitchen porter: a tall, strapping man in his late twenties, stood with his arms crossed over his substantial torso.

He wore a floral bandanna knotted at the back of his shorn head and his sleeves rolled to the elbows showed off a hefty set of forearms scored with burns. This was someone who'd seen a battle or two, Angela supposed, jostling forward with the others for a better look.

The man was silent, staunchly so, and in her opinion all the more menacing. It was Toni who did the talking, well, shouting, not that she was making sense. It appeared by this point, whatever her quarrel had been with him, it had deteriorated into mere insult-slinging. Not that he seemed bothered, the man looked impervious, but Angela sensed the aggression rippling beneath his skin. His show of passivity wasn't fooling her – whoever he was, he was terrifying, even from this safe distance. Toni was impressive though, standing her ground and showing none of the fear Angela would have done to look up and into that stone-hard stare.

'Enough.' Hakim eventually marched towards them; a hand raised as if to stop traffic. 'Enough.' The word was as ineffectual as him and floated through the steam pumping out from the industrial-sized dishwashers.

'That's it, take his side.' Toni threw her arms in the air and Angela saw the delicate line of her cheekbones had flushed crimson. 'Boys sticking together. You're all the bloody same.'

'Come on, darlin', just calm down.'

'Calm down!' Toni scowled at Hakim, then thrust an accusing finger at the kitchen porter. 'I'm telling you, mate, you wanna sort him out, he's taking the piss. And I am not your *darling*, neither!'

Angela watched Hakim swallow. 'I don't think...' Whatever he'd been about to say, died in his mouth.

The kitchen porter remained silent, but Angela was on to him. She caught the look he gave Toni, and the blackness it communicated made her skin tighten beneath her whites. She swore, had no one else been around, the man would have throttled Toni with his bare hands, there and then.

'Right, if you won't sort him, then we'll see what HR has got to say, shall we?' Toni's parting shot, before storming out through the kitchen doors and into the corridor.

Hakim cleared his throat. 'Come on, you lot. Show's over. Back to work.' He clapped his hands as if rallying children. 'You too.' Angela heard him address the kitchen porter for the first time.

Not that the man moved. Motionless inside his royal-blue boiler suit, this one was spoiling for a fight. Angela knew it, and she suspected Hakim knew it also. It was why he didn't insist. It was pathetic. Hakim's supposed authority made no impression on this man who waited for everyone to return to their workstations before retying his bandanna over his head and shuffling back to his sink.

Angela was the only one still watching him and shivered despite the unpleasant heat of her working environment. She feared for her friend's safety when she saw what no one else could have seen – the hatred that darkened the kitchen porter's face as he made a quick, single-finger slashing motion across his throat in the direction Toni had gone.

THREE

Bang! I slam the car door as hard as I can. I don't usually get angry with the drugs I'm on, but after the day I've had – getting the sack – even they aren't strong enough to keep me calm. I think about how I could have happily throttled someone today as the juddering aftershock vibrates through me, splitting the silence of this quiet Victorian terrace where my grandparents live. I've not had the urge to kill for years, and I'm surprised by it.

Feeling cold, I pull on my beanie hat and sit with my knees rammed against the steering column. Because of my size, I could do with more legroom. My hands are wrapped around the steering wheel, red and raw and scarred from the horrible jobs I have to do. I reach over to flip open the glove box. Appropriately named, as this is where I keep the leather gloves I need to wear. Bad circulation is just one of the side effects of the meds I take. Pulling them on, they fit nice and snug against my skin. If it were up to me, I'd never take them off, but I can't wear them at work, I'd ruin the leather. I can't wear them when I go to see my grandparents either because of the grief Babcia gives me. She refuses to accept I suffer from cold extremities, in the same way she refuses to accept I've got an impulse-control disorder that without the cognitive behavioural therapy sessions and the medication to regulate and suppress my moods, I'd be prone to explosive episodes of unwarranted violence – like I nearly did today. Babcia's been this way since I was small and my troubles began. I can sort of understand it. Family is everything to her and she's riddled with enough remorse and disappointment, as the only child she could carry full term was my mother, and she died before she reached forty, so for her only grandson to be as screwed up as me, you can't blame her for burying her head in the sand.

My grandmother. Babcia. She's special, a really clever woman. I say this because she's about the only person who can rile me up nowadays – until today. Despite the cocktail of pills rattling around inside me, she still knows which buttons to press. But it's okay, with the correct dosage and the talk therapy sessions and consultations I must attend with my psychiatrist, Marvin Crow (part of the deal unless I want to wind up being sectioned again), I'm pretty much able to curb my aggression and only take it out on inanimate objects and not people anymore. Hence the slamming of the car door. Not that understanding myself helps me understand my grandfather's submissiveness as far as Babcia's concerned. Honestly, I don't know how he stands it. Nag, nag, nag. Morning, noon and night. But I suppose the man is as dumbed down as I am. Not that I'm suggesting he's ever popped more than an aspirin in his life, no, any spark he might have had was snuffed out in his childhood; a childhood only Babcia seems able to talk about. 'You've been married to her for nearly seventy years,' I like to remind him. 'Good God, man, you'd have got less for murder.'

It is with thoughts of murder that I look out through the windscreen at three people unloading a transit van – hazards blinking, illegally parked, Walters' Heating & Plumbing on its side – into the house next door to my grandparents. Two girls and a bloke around my age: mid-twenties, I'm guessing, although I need to remind myself, I'm a little older. I celebrated my twenty-eighth birthday last week. I say celebrated, that's a laugh, I've no one to celebrate with. I suppose people like me well enough, it's not that, it's just that despite my substantial physical presence, I'm easily dismissed… overlooked, for want of a better word. What I'm trying to say is that I'm not what you'd call memorable, I haven't exactly got a sparkling personality. The meds have seen to that too.

I watch the couple – I can tell they're a couple from the way they need to keep touching each other – and realise they are of little consequence. The bloke, tattooed to the neck, is whiskery and pinkish pale and the girl hanging off him looks like the high-maintenance type: all lipstick and nails and one of those year-round tans the colour of hangover piss. She's got a few tattoos herself, I notice, but I suppose most girls have. I can't say I'm a fan of tattoos, on men or women, and it's not just because I'm out of the loop, but more to do with a place in my family's not-so-distant past when a tattoo meant something altogether darker.

I shift my gaze to the other girl, as she's the one who interests me. With her generous figure and that headful of rich, red hair. I know why she's of interest. I'm pretty transparent once you get to know me. Redheads remind me of Mum. The colour of Mum's hair is about all I remember of her. The rest of what she was – her voice, her smell, her touch – is as elusive to me as the stars. It's a bit of a cliché, I know, but I've never come to terms with her death. Happening a few months before my seventh birthday, it was so traumatic, it triggered my troubles, Julia used to say. Well, this and the thing I did when I was eighteen, and coping – or not coping as it turned out – with the transition from child mental health care to adult services. An incident, because of my vicious and unprovoked attack on another man (I'm using their language here, not mine, so far as I was concerned the bastard had it coming), saw me swiftly sectioned until I'd been brought under control and made acceptable for the world they were keen to push me back into. Because I don't know if you're aware, but we grown-ups are supposed to be able to look after ourselves, even when most of us plainly can't.

I suppose I ought to be grateful for the tablets that make me safe to be around because if I'm frightened of anything, it's of being hospitalised again. Without the mood stabilisers and the psychiatric diagnosis, I'd have been facing a lengthy prison sentence for what I did ten years ago. Something, I've been informed since, that faceless bastard who provoked me, laughed at me that night in the pub, reckoned I should have had. That ten months incarcerated in a psychiatric ward, in his opinion, wasn't punishment enough for biting his ear off. But I don't want to talk about him, I don't even remember him, that night all those years ago is a blur. I want to talk about me, as in making me agreeable to society, I have become disagreeable to myself. The drugs, you see, as well as other undesirable side effects like restlessness and fatigue, agitation and a general lack of interest in sex, have blunted my senses and taken the fun part of me away.

I watch the redhead lean so far into the back of the van she almost disappears. For a moment all that's visible are the soles of her boots. When she re-emerges, it is with a large box and two bulging bin bags. Nothing of significance. There are no musical instruments, no artist's easel, no stargazing kit: the sort of stuff that makes people interesting. No, the only thing that's interesting to me about her, apart from the colour of her hair, is that she looks as washed out and as tired with life as I am. I see it in her face: a face that looks as starved of sunlight as mine. She drags an arm over her perspiring forehead and laughs at something the bloke says. But I can tell her smile is false, the same as her laugh, it doesn't reach her eyes. I recognise it because this is how I feel, living life on an enforced low burner, I've forgotten what it is to laugh and be happy too.

The girl swings her head in my direction. It's okay, she can't see me, the glare on the windscreen is too bright now the sun's come out. I don't know why, but I think I've seen her before. From work perhaps? But I'd have remembered that hair, so maybe not. But then again, I do work in a lot of places with a lot of people. Always the same short-term, low-paid, menial jobs, just in different catering joints around the city. This is especially unfair in my case, as I'm not good with disruptions to routine. Julia said it worked as another trigger to my aggressive outbursts and it was why she tried to manage things for me to keep disruptions to a minimum. But that was when I was a kid, life isn't so simple now.

I don't want you to think I care about this girl or anything. I can take or leave women in the same way they can take or leave me. If I'm honest, and I can be with you, I can take or leave people in general. As I've said, I'm not one for friends, I can't be bothered to feign the social graces. I make it my business to keep my head down at work and because I don't bother with anyone there, no one bothers with me. And anyway, the kinds of jobs I do means I never end up working with the same people two shifts running, so making friends is a waste of time. All in all, I prefer my own company. Safer not to let anyone too close. Whenever I have in the past, it's always ended badly. I've heard people calling me socially inept, it's a label a boss – an ex-boss, as of today – stuck on me. Not that this was his only label, he had another one too: *malingerer*. A word so foreign-sounding, I needed to look it up. Only to discover it wasn't a fair description. Not when it's the migraines (another side effect) that mean I can't be relied upon, and can't get better-paid work. It's the migraines that stop me from getting out of bed in the mornings.

Little Girl Blue.

I've named her. The unhappy-looking redhead who looks like she carries the weight of the world on her shoulders. I've named her after a favourite song. I start the engine and activate the wireless car stereo touchscreen I sourced on eBay for next to nothing. Scroll forward to my favourite Nina Simone track... 'Little Girl Blue'... and start humming the piano arrangement. It might be nice to see this redhead now and again; it might make my trips to this part of town more enjoyable. I think this, but not with any great enthusiasm; enthusiasm isn't something I can muster much of either.

I start the car and am about to ease out into the road when my phone bleeps from the pocket of my bomber jacket. I press my foot to the brake and turn the MP5 player down to read the text I've been expecting from the temping agency. One hand on the wheel, I use the other to pull my mobile free but because of the glove, I pull out the twenty-pound note Babcia gave me too. I watch it float to the passenger seat, then down into the footwell. 'It's all I can spare today,' she told me in the accent she's worked so hard to soften; because instead of thanking her, I asked if there was more. I always need more.

I hold my phone up to see if I'm right, to see if it is the message I've been waiting for. And bingo, it's a text from Blue Arrow. I feel my face contort and avoid my reflection in the driving mirror, I don't want to see my disappointment when I open it.

'What delights have you got for me now? Please let it be something better... Something I might enjoy for once.'

My voice sounds dull in the car's interior and, taking a second to counter it with the lullaby lull of Nina Simone singing to me about counting raindrops and a tender blue girl, I snap back my neck and bump my skull against the headrest. And breathe.

'Who am I kidding? It'll be just another shitty job, for sod all money.'

I say this when I'm ready to press the screen to activate the message and read:

> HURRAY! SHAME ABOUT THE LLOYD
> GEORGE BUT WE'VE FOUND YOU
> ANOTHER KITCHEN PORTER JOB. PASTA
> BELLISSIMO. CITY CENTRE. EVENINGS.
> START SAT. HC STILL WANT YOU TWO
> DAYS A WEEK, SO GOOD NEWS THERE.
> GIVE US A BELL TO CONFIRM. GAYNOR X

'Oh, the jolliness of it! Well, I've got to face facts.' I slump in the car seat, defeated, my kneecaps aching. 'It is all I'm fit for.'

FOUR

It was seven in the morning and Angela was back amid the hubbub and mordant heat of the hotel kitchen. Working on automatic pilot, she plated the usual medley of what constituted a cooked breakfast and lined them up under the white-hot lights ready for service. Behind her, José, the hotel's breakfast chef, was smashing eggs against the lip of a giant frying pan and aiming their empty carcasses into the bin. Angela had seen him do this before, it was a game he liked to play against himself, letting out a roar if he missed his target.

'The Scotch are here for the rugby. Town's full of 'em. Got that blue paint on their faces and wearing them skirt things.'

'Kilts. They're kilts.' She thought she might as well furnish him with the correct word.

'That's them.' He nodded.

'And, José?'

'Yeah?' He looked up from his egg-frying.

'They're not *Scotch*, you drink Scotch – they're Scots.'

'Stir that.' José had already lost interest. 'Then divvy them out.' He signalled to a huge vat of mushrooms and Angela did as she was told.

'Watch your back.' José again, swooping up behind her with the frying pan. She stood aside to watch him slide the eggs into position; their domes of yellow hardening under the row of searing service lights.

'Come on, you dozy bastards,' he yelled at the restaurant staff who had gathered to gossip by the swing doors. At the sound of his shout, they jumped to attention and whisked the plates away.

Breakfast went on forever. No sooner had these plates gone, they were repeating the cycle over again.

'Oi, Spike. Phone for you.' José waved her over. 'Do yourself a favour,' he scowled when he handed her the receiver, 'tell 'em to shove it. Personal calls ain't allowed in 'ere, you knows the rules.'

'*Mum?*' Angela's incredulity curled up through the smells of frying bacon like a question mark. 'Why're you ringing so early, what's up?' An anxious glance at the kitchen clock told her it was only eight fifteen.

'Why aren't you returning our calls, more like?' her mother bounced back. 'We thought you youngsters kept your mobiles glued to your hips. We've been worried sick here.'

I doubt that. Angela's thought as she cleared her throat. 'I'm not allowed my phone at work. I was going to call you after I'd finished today.'

'But we rang two days ago.'

'I'm sorry, Mum, I've been busy.'

'Yes, well, it wouldn't hurt you to check in with us now and again. You are our daughter, Angela. You're all we've got. I can't imagine Robert treating us like this. You never ring, you never come to see us... Honestly, we've forgotten what you look like.'

Angela wasn't stupid, she knew her parents' reason for

keeping tabs on her wasn't rooted in any kind of affection, it was about control. She had always been a dumping ground for their nasty feelings and there was no love for her even before her brother was born. But with six years between them, it was easy for her parents to label her as the jealous sister and to go about painting her in the worst possible light by inventing a badness that didn't exist. And then she went and gave them all the ammunition they needed, didn't she?

'Are you there? Did you hear what I said?'

'Yes, Mum.' Angela, identifying the hostility in her mother's tone, swallowed the pain she still felt about Robert. Her parents were right; he had been her baby brother and was, therefore, her responsibility. She had failed him in the worst way possible. 'I heard you.' She swallowed again. 'I can't talk now. I'm going to get into trouble. I'll call you later, okay?'

'Is that honestly all you've got to say?'

'I'm sorry, but I've got to go.' She had seen her po-faced colleagues filing into the kitchen in their immaculate whites. Then, to her horror, it was the Head Chef she was looking at, and worse still, he was looking at her. On the phone. Not doing the job he paid her for. Bugger it. 'I'll ring tomorrow, I've got the weekend off,' she said before hanging up.

Back under the blistering kitchen lights with breakfast finally over, Angela needed to make a start on the *mise en place* ahead of the lunchtime service. Preparation was everything in this job but dithering, her mind a whirl after the conversation with her mother, she couldn't decide what to do first.

'Oi, whatever your name is.' Breath, hot on her ear. Angela spun to receive it. Head Chef, ruddy jowls and barrel-chested, was standing beside her. 'A little birdy told me—' snide, mocking; deliberately loud for others to hear, 'that it's not good enough for you to learn the industry from them who've made their living from it? Oh, no, Little Miss Hoity-Toity here's gotta go to college.'

She focused on a vein that had popped up on his temple: an angry worm winding from hairline to eyebrow.

'What's up? Cat got your tongue?' Chef grabbed her arm and yanked her to one side.

Scottish or Irish? Angela couldn't be sure, but she knew he had a problem with women. Any women who joined his brigade rarely lasted the two-week induction, never mind sticking it out for a full sixteen months as she had done.

'Sorry, Chef.' Silently cursing Hakim, Angela didn't dare tell Chef she'd enrolled at college because she'd wanted more from life than sweating over a *bain-marie* and that a qualification in hotel management would give her choices. 'I should've come to you.' She looked down at her toffee-coloured safety shoes.

'What?' he roared and shook his head of lion-yellow hair.

'I should've come to you about the rota. Sorry, Chef.' And she made to return to her workstation, believing the reprimand to be over.

'Just now,' he started up again. 'What did you think you were doing?'

'Sorry? What was that, Chef?'

'On the phone. You know personal calls aren't allowed. How many more fuckin' times? Are you stupid?'

Around her, an outbreak of screechy giggles and snorting. But with her back straight, her stomach pulled in, she wasn't going to give the bully a reaction. Although close to it, she was determined not to cry and it took everything she had not to let the humiliation bubbling inside spill over. Experience taught her to wait, to bide her time, he would move on to someone else in his kitchen eventually. Angela wasn't the only one he picked on, there were plenty who fitted his favourite insult of 'Donkey' working this shift.

Chef's gaze continued to bore into her as the seconds flicked by. *Do your worst.* She churned the words around in her head. *You don't frighten me; I've had loads crueller than you in my life.* It worked. After a while, he walked away to ferret out his next victim. She sighed with relief and reached for a clean chopping board, positioned herself beside the double sink and drainer. The unpleasant encounter with Chef had flustered her almost as much as the exchange with her mother and, untying her bundle of knives, selecting something suitable for the job of shredding thirty Savoy cabbages, she began to portion and slice, her gaze wandering dangerously backwards and forwards to Chef's office, where he now sat with his select few compiling menus.

She felt the knife glide through something foreign and looked down to find blood. Crimson among the green leaves. Stunned at its brightness, she then felt a wave of pain and the next thing she was aware of, she was sitting in Chef's office, unable to work out what all the fuss was about. Then she looked up at her hand that was being held high above her head and realised someone had undone her necktie.

'Oh, there she is. So glad you could join us.' The sarcastic drawl of her superior rang in her ear. 'You silly tart, we haven't got time for your buggering about. Now,' Chef dropped his voice, reeled her in, 'how's about a wee drop of brandy, to make you feel better, lass?'

She nodded some kind of agreement and felt her body sag further into the chair.

'Right!' Chef pounced. 'I knew you were taking the piss. There's nothing wrong with you.' She responded to his bellowing by jolting upright in her seat. 'Get back out there and on with some fuckin' work. We've lunch to serve in less than an hour and we're already in the shit cos of you.'

Angela scrambled to her feet and managed to shift her wobbly self, quite convincingly, back to her workstation. Taking up the bloodied knife and board, she proceeded to rinse them under the hot tap. But the sight of her blood, congealing as it hit the white ceramic and swirling down the plughole, was too much. Her legs buckled beneath her and before she knew it, she was riding in the back of a taxi the hotel had paid for. Her damaged finger bound in bloodied gauze, on the way to Cardiff's University Hospital.

'You all right back there, luv?' The cabbie's concern found her through her waves of nausea and pain. Woozy and yawning, Angela couldn't reply. 'Filthy weather.' He sneered through his Roman nose.

He was right. Angela looked out of the window, saw the rain for the first time that day. She smiled and nodded politely as he rattled through his repertoire of small talk. He had all the alertness of a rodent and needed to sit low in the seat to reach the pedals. It meant he was forced to negotiate Cardiff's streets through the spokes of his steering wheel. He drove too fast. Flitting into empty spaces. Nudging other cars out of their lanes. Hopping the lights. But he was compelled to squeeze to a stop at a zebra crossing.

Shunted forward from her back seat vantage point, Angela recognised one of the pedestrians. It was the kitchen porter she saw Toni arguing with yesterday. Wearing the same flower-patterned bandanna, he sheltered under a large burgundy-and-white umbrella with a broad-backed woman old enough to be his grandmother. The pair strode out in front of the cab and passed close to the taxi along the pavement.

Then, for no apparent reason, the kitchen porter ducked down and peered inside the cab at Angela.

Their eyes locked.

Only for a split second but the shock of it hit her like a punch.

Heart racing, she sank back into the seat and realised she'd forgotten she was supposed to hold her cut and badly bound finger high above her head.

FIVE

I know her. She's that gobby waitress from the Lloyd George. What's she doing hanging around here in the dark and the pouring rain? Wet hair dripping, checking and rechecking her mobile, she looks totally pissed off.

'Eh, Toni?' I drop the window down and lean out through the downpour to shout.

I watch her confusion as she twists this way and that, unable to locate where my voice is coming from. A flash of the car headlamps helps her out and she nearly topples under the weight of her monster rucksack.

'You all right?' I ask as I unfold myself from the car.

'Oh, it's you.' She isn't as relieved to see me as I think she ought to be but she's never liked me much. And after that show she made of herself the other day, perhaps she's embarrassed. 'Is that your car?' She sways towards me, knees buckling, ready to drop.

'Yeah. Wanna lift somewhere?'

In the peachy blush of a street lamp, I see her mascara's run and her wet hair is plastered to her head. But she still looks pretty.

'Can you take me home?' The look is pitiful.

'Sure, I can.' I help unbuckle her rucksack and drag it off her shoulders. Her denim jacket is soaking. 'Where d'you need to go?' I drop the rucksack into the boot with a thump.

'Awesome. D'you know Danestown?' She blinks up at me through the hammering rain.

'Come on, get in.' I open the passenger door and chivvy her inside. 'Whereabouts in Danestown are you?'

'Linden Estate, off the *Lanrummy* Road.' She pronounces Llanrumney all wrong, but I don't correct her. No one likes a clever dick and I hate it when people do it to me.

'I sort of know it.' I yawn into my fist. 'But you can guide me, can't you?' I shut the door, stride around to the driver's side and get in.

'Mate, I'm soaking. Aren't I gonna ruin your seats?' She flicks wet hair off her forehead and rubs the legs of her jeans. The movement makes her bangles jingle. 'I don't think I've ever seen such a tidy car.'

'The car's not mine, it's my dad's. Better belt up,' I say, securing my seat belt and shaking the rainwater off my head. 'You're shivering, I'll whack the heating up.' And I do, to the max, seeing the windscreen has already steamed over.

'Flamin' Spike. Bailing on me.' Toni clears condensation from the passenger-side window and looks out on the sodden city streets. 'I've been waiting over three hours.'

'Spike? Is he your boyfriend?'

'Nah,' she laughs while I slide the Ford Focus out from between a row of parked cars, 'she's a chef. At the Lloyd George. You probably know her?'

'Doubt it. I always steer clear of chefs. They're not nice people and they treat us lot in wash-up like dirt.'

'They don't treat the restaurant staff much better. I only put up with any of it for the money.'

'What money? I can't believe your pay's any better than mine.'

'I s'ppose it's not. I get sod all per hour. It's the tips that keep me solvent.'

I nod, a little resentful. Us kitchen porters are the invisible people; we get bugger all by way of extras.

'Where were you going, anyway? You and this Spike? You've enough stuff in that rucksack for a month.'

She wriggles in her seat. 'Nowhere really. Spike's staying in a house along here, she invited me for the weekend.'

'Nice change for you. It's loads better round here than Danestown if you don't mind me saying. No wonder you're pissed off. You tried phoning?'

'Flamin' mobile keeps going through to voicemail. I've left messages and sent a text. Not much more I can do. Thank God for the pub at the end of the road. Not that it's much fun drinking with the flies.' She waggles a plum-coloured fingernail at the Pear Tree as we drive past its wide, square windows. 'Anyway, what were you doing? D'you live round here, or something?'

'Just visiting my grandparents.' It's difficult to hear her so I turn the heating down a notch.

'Cool. If I'd known, look, I could've called round for you.' I feel her turn her face to me through the dark, smell the booze on her breath and, from her vaguely slurry speech, I reckon she's downed a few. 'We could've shared a couple of cold ones.'

'Sorry, I don't do pubs.'

'What, never?'

I shake my head and pull up at a set of major traffic lights, listen to the rain pummelling the roof. Stationary, I watch people drift along pavements filmed in rain. See them dip in and out of the brightly lit shops. I follow the progress of a wire-haired terrier, watch it cock its leg against a litter bin.

'You're an odd bod, you are, mate. I can't work you out.' She shares her observation, not unkindly. I'm not surprised by it, it's not like I haven't been told I'm weird before. '*Brrr*, it's freezing. Gone really cold all of a sudden. The weather's mental in this country. It's a good job I'm off soon. I don't think I could stand another Welsh winter. Can ya put the heating up a bit more, mate?'

I turn the temperature dial to its highest setting again. 'Where are you off to?'

'Spain. Last leg of my travels. I've got a cousin in Madrid.'

'And then what?'

'Back home to med school in Hobart. Although,' she groans, 'because I've taken time out to travel, it'll probably mean Sydney for my final year.'

'So, what, you're gonna be a doctor?'

'*Gerroff*. Me? Let loose on the public. Nah, I'm gonna be a pathologist when I grow up.'

I pull away from the lights. Too sluggish for the car behind me, I'm rewarded with a long, hard blast of car horn.

'Blimey, mate, keep your bloody hair on.' Toni twists in her seat, squints through the rain-mottled rear windscreen. The movement releases a puff of her perfume. Nice, nothing too heavy. I breathe it in. 'People are so aggressive, aren't they?'

'I suppose? I don't notice if I'm honest.'

'No, I don't suppose you do. Nothing bothers you, does it?'

'Not anymore.'

'Sounds cryptic. Sounds like it might have done, once upon a time.'

I let the comment pass. Within minutes she's forgotten about it and is cupping her hands to the warm air belting out from the vent. It's then I notice a sizeable ring on her right hand. The nugget of gemstone catches the light from the dashboard and splinters the dark.

'Aw, that's betta. Shockin' night. Not that it's night, it's barely seven. Gets dark real early now, don't it?'

'Sure does.' I project my voice above the rhythmic thump, thump of wipers, the rattle of the fan heater. 'Clocks go back tomorrow night; it'll be even worse.'

'Yuk, I remember it from last year. *Brrr*, I'm still freezing… Couldn't have a lend of your gloves, could I, mate?' She rubs her hands together, assesses the length of her nails.

'Sorry, I need them. Bad circulation.'

'Oh, right.'

'You're hardly dressed for it. The weather, I mean.' The rain, continuing to fall, determined and vertical, bounces against the bonnet.

'Didn't reckon on me hanging around so long, did I?'

'Why didn't you just go home?' I don't know why I'm asking this, it's not like I'm interested.

'Couldn't.' She fiddles with the stud in her nose, then moves on to the ring. 'Mark was moving out today and I didn't wanna be there.'

'Who's Mark?'

'My ex. As of last week.' She digs through the damp pockets of her denim jacket for a tissue. 'Oh, hell.' She blows her nose. 'We nearly missed it. Hang a left at the junction, would you?'

I indicate. Listen to the tick, tick, ticking, as I wait for a gap in the traffic.

'You can go now,' she says to be helpful, and I swing the car out to join a steady stream of commuters.

Within a few miles the topography changes. Gone are the leafy streets of Roath with its smart terraced houses, art galleries, boutiques and coffee shops. They've been traded in for a series of boarded-up corner shops and cut-price furniture stores with graffiti-stippled sides. Rubbish in the gutters and condemned streets that open onto weed-filled waste grounds.

'Hell!' She picks up my tube of Parma Violets from the central console and shakes them under my nose. 'You don't seriously eat these horrors, do ya?'

'Yeah, I like them.'

'Yuk. Mate, you're more of a dag than I thought you were.' She laughs and puts my sweets back. 'Aw, hang on,' she jerks her head up, 'I'm not entirely sure, but I reckon it's a right at the next lights.' She wipes away fresh condensation and strains to see. 'Streets all look the same around here, 'specially in the dark. I get a bit confused. Nah, we're okay, I'm recognising it now... Yeah, hang a left, just past the school. My road's off there.'

I slow for a set of speed bumps and pass a sprawling secondary school. Its floodlit playing field dotted with youngsters in rugby shirts and muddy legs. I turn the heaters down and am grateful for the peace.

'It's real good of you to drive me home.' She drops the vanity mirror above her head and scrutinises her reflection. 'I didn't reckon on you speaking to me again.' She cleans her smudged mascara with her tissue. 'Not after the way I spoke to you.'

'Don't worry about it.'

'You're too nice for your own good. You should be well pissed off with me.'

'Why?'

'Because other people would be. I was horrible to you.'

'But I'm not like other people, you said so yourself. And besides, people are always pushing me around. I think it's what I'm here for.'

'Mate, that's not right. You've got a bit of menace about you, you wanna use it. I'm telling you, there's people who'd be dead frightened of you... You wouldn't even have to do much. Yeah, you wanna start standing up for yourself.'

'If you say so.' I yawn again.

'You wouldn't catch no one walking over me.'

'I can tell that.'

She chuckles. 'But yeah, apart from the menace.' I sense her studying my profile through the dark. 'You're not a bad-looking bloke... Well, you could be if you let your hair grow and trendied up your clothes.'

'Whatever,' I say, not believing her.

'Anyway, for what it's worth, I'm really sorry about having a go at you. I was well out of order. I didn't land you in it with management, did I?'

'I was already in trouble with them.'

'You haven't gone and lost your job?'

'No, I quit. I was sick of working there. I wanted a change,' I lie, I don't want her feeling worse than she already does. And anyway, most of what I say is true, I was sick of it.

'Even so, I shouldn't have gone blabbing to them, it weren't nothing to do with me... *Oh God,*' she shrieks and slams her hand against the dashboard. It makes me jump. 'Sorry, mate, I should've said, it's a left back there.' I look sideways, at a set of black iron railings encasing an expanse of parkland. 'Just past the swings. Oh God, I'm sorry. I'm really sorry.'

'Don't worry about it.' Talk about an overreaction. 'It's no big deal.'

'Mark does his nut whenever I give him dud directions.'

'Why? You'd hardly do it on purpose.' I indicate, pulling in front of a concrete council office with a plan of turning around. 'Look, no worries.' I mimic her accent to lighten the mood. 'I'll do a quick U-turn here.' And I do just that, smoothly and calmly, glad to feel her agitation lessen in the seat beside me.

'This'll do, I'm only over there.' She points to one of several squat blocks of flats beyond a strip of communal grass cluttered with silver birches and wheelie bins. 'You can park here. It's after six, no one's gonna bother you.'

I pull in behind a pair of industrial-sized skips piled with builders' rubble. The street lamp above us washes the car's interior in a pinky glow. I cut the engine and listen to it settle.

'They're upgrading this lot, apparently.' She seems keen to explain. 'It's got something to do with that dreadful Grenfell Tower fire in London. The authorities, they're clamping down on safety all of a sudden.'

I yawn into the back of my hand; I really am tired tonight.

She reads it as a sign to go and unclips her seat belt. 'At least the rain's stopped. Ta again, for the lift, mate.'

'Hang on, I'll give you a hand.' I remember the rucksack and haul myself out of the car, follow her to the boot. 'You can't lift that on your own; it weighs a ton.' I pull it free and glance up at a mellow moon that's silvering the edges of clouds. 'Let me carry it to the door for you.'

'You're all right, mate.' She is shivering, her teeth chattering. I'm tempted to put an arm around her but I don't. Girls can get funny about you touching them, it's best I keep my hands to myself.

'At least let me help you with it.'

'You're a real gent, d'ya know that?' She buttons her jacket and shakes out her wet hair. 'Go on then, I'm ready.'

When I've secured the rucksack across her shoulders, she reaches up and kisses my cheek. A fleeting contact. No more than two or three seconds, but it's enough to feel the softness of her lips. It's the kind of kiss Mum used to give me when I was little. It moves me.

'I'll wait h-here for you.' A blush travels up my neck. 'U-until you've gone inside... M-make sure you're safe.'

'Bye, then.' With a backhand flourish and hunched under the weight of her rucksack, she totters off into the shadows that drop between the street lights, then up the cracked stone steps to her block.

I notice the flats upstairs are in total darkness but the lower, curtainless floors are brightly lit and show off televisions large as cinema screens. A security light snaps on in the porch. It throws out a stark white beam that allows me to see her slip her key into the lock. But just as she's about to push open the main door, it swings back, and out steps a bloke with dark curly hair lugging a pair of holdalls as long as corpses.

I squeeze back behind the wheel of the car and drop the passenger-side window. The damp, dark breath of the October night invades the interior and disperses what remains of Toni's perfume. Could this be Mark? If it is, he's one handsome bastard. But he'd have to be, wouldn't he? To nab himself a girl like her. Then I remind myself – if this is the boyfriend, he's history.

I twist in my seat and crane my neck to see. Within seconds, Toni and the bloke I'm assuming is Mark, start tearing into each other: their angry shouts bouncing around the empty estate. I might be uncomfortable in my role as a voyeur but I'm not going anywhere, not until I've made sure she's all right. I peel off a Parma Violet. It's a tricky manoeuvre with my gloves on. I miss my mouth and the sweet drops into the footwell. I can't put the light on, they might see me, so I grope around in the dark until I find it. When I next look up, Toni is sobbing, her shoulders pumping up and down. Look at her, fighting to stay upright with that ridiculous load, she looks as vulnerable as a child. I'm thinking I ought to go and help her but stop myself, I really can't interfere. But why doesn't that Mark do something? The guy's big enough, the weight of that thing would be nothing to him.

Right, that's it, I can't just sit here watching her struggle. If he won't help, then I will. But there isn't time. The second I decide to open the car door, Mark lunges for her. Perhaps to steady her, perhaps to assist with the rucksack – it isn't clear. But what is clear, is the slap Toni gives him. Full in the face.

Everything stops. Stalemate. Until Mark zips his leather jacket to the chin, bends to retrieve the two holdalls at his ankles, springs down the steps and trots away. I watch him cross the strip of council-mown grass, see how his mouth is set in a thin, forbidding line. Cool inside his leathers, he looks the type to own a motorbike or play in a rock band. He's nothing like me, there's no way you'd ever describe me as cool. I'm a complete nonentity in comparison. I may have stood a chance before the tablets took hold and changed me when I had a better self-image and my hair was longer. I glance at my shaved head in the driving mirror and lift a hand to the new gingery bristles. I know it doesn't suit me like this, it's just easy for work. My father says when he's home between contracts, which thankfully isn't often, that I look like a clammy-knuckle bone. Which is fair enough, I do sweat a lot, it's another side effect of the meds.

Mark passes close enough to the car for one of his holdalls to scrape the bumper. He stops on the kerb and puts the bags down. Pats the pockets of his jeans and pulls out a bashed-up packet of fags. In the flash of the flame when he lights up, I see his face: clean-shaven, dark fringe and... *Ouch!* A nasty scratch running the length of his cheek.

I flinch.

Did Toni do that to him?

Seconds later, the smell of cigarette smoke. It drifts in through the open window as I watch him stride away, heading for the main road and the eternal traffic.

SIX

Late into the evening and Angela was still stuck in A&E. She stared at the clock above the coffee machine and worked out that she'd been there for over five hours. Her finger had been assessed but she was informed that she wasn't an emergency and must wait a while longer to be treated.

She looked around the waiting room with its rows of theatre-like seating. It was teeming with people: parents with children, elderly couples; the injured party among them hobbling or bleeding. As far as she could tell, she was the only one here on her own and although being on her own was something she was used to, she could have done with some company today. All of a sudden, a flurry of activity as a teenage boy with a bloodied face was rushed through on a stretcher. His mother, frantic in slippers and dressing gown and obviously caught on the hop, trotted alongside the paramedics. Seen immediately, he must have been what they call a genuine emergency and Angela hoped the boy would be all right.

Her mind, a dark-winged moth, flitted from thing to thing. It delivered an unwelcome memory of the pale-faced doctor who came to find her and her parents in the waiting room at

Gloucester Infirmary. She saw again how he pressed his soft hands together when he told them there was nothing he could do. She blinked the images away and focused on the large, muted TV screen. John Wayne and Gail Russell in black and white. The kind of 1940s film she would have watched with Robert, on wet Sunday afternoons. Until somebody changed the channel to BBC News and its breaking stories on a perpetual loop. Bored, her attention wandering again, she focused on a toddler playing with a set of chunky wooden farmyard animals. Angela didn't smile at him; she couldn't bring herself to. Thoughts of her brother and what happened to him were still too painful. Instead, she reached for one of the dog-eared magazines and turned the pages without taking anything in.

A staff nurse appeared from behind a murky synthetic partition. Brandishing a selection of mini weaponry in a kidney-shaped bowl, she looked officious in her latex gloves which, like the dish she clutched, were smeared with blood. She called out names in a voice as deep as a man. Everyone lifted their heads to listen. The name Angela Milligan was among them.

She was shown into a tiny side room that reeked of iodoform. Penetrating and distinctive, it shunted her back in time, and for a moment she was inside her mother's chemistry lab at Gloucester University. With its walls of glass cabinets and wet sinks, its fine views over the sun-dappled campus.

'Sit there, please.' Another nurse, stiff inside her uniform, directed Angela to a chair. 'And if you could just hold your arm up like that for me?'

Unable to look at her damaged forefinger, she stared past it and her hand, to the opposite wall. Saw an NHS poster advocating the need for childhood immunisations. The illustration was of a boy and girl running through a meadow of wild flowers. It triggered recollections of her and Robert playing in the soft summer lanes around Scobb's Grove. Of lengthy days spent catching toads and swimming with the Great Crested Grebes in Dowdeswell Reservoir. The same reservoir that went on to feature on the local news broadcasting her failure.

She screwed her eyes tight shut against the memories that were never far away.

'Sorry, if I'm hurting you. I'll be as gentle as I can.' The nurse's voice filtered through the layering of overplayed images of Robert thrashing around in the blue-dark depths... The spooky silence when he finally slipped below the water. 'It's a nasty cut but I don't think you need stitches.'

Angela nodded. It was all she could manage through her hot and painful tears. Tears that had nothing to do with her injury.

'There you go,' the soothing, lilting voice concluded. And when she, at last, opened her eyes, Angela saw her finger had been dressed and bound in a fresh, white bandage.

'Thank you.' She dropped her hand into her apron-clad lap.

'A pleasure, my love. Nasty cut. You're to take good care of it, okay? I'll give you some rubber finger cots so you can keep it clean at work.' The nurse turned away to rummage through a cabinet made up of tiny drawers. 'Here.' She handed Angela a bundle. 'Would you like me to pop one on for you now?'

Angela nodded again and wiped her tears with the clenched fist of her other hand.

'You're a chef, then?' The nurse gently positioned the protective rubber sheath.

She picked at a thread on her chequered trousers and nodded again.

'My son wants to be a chef.' A tight laugh. 'I'm trying to discourage him. I've said, it's not all glamorous like they make out on those telly programmes, it's a hard slog.' The nurse eyed her with a motherly concern.

'My parents went nuts when I said I was going to catering college. They think catering's for bums.'

'What do your parents do?'

'They're intellectuals.'

'Intellectuals, eh?' The nurse made it sound like some incurable disease.

'They were university lecturers before my brother—' she broke off.

'Before your brother?' The nurse looked over her shoulder.

'Oh, nothing.' Angela, unable to share the thing she could never forgive herself for. 'They're scientists. Very clever,' she said instead. 'I've never been good enough for them.'

'I'm sure that's not true.'

'I'm sure it is.' Blunt, Angela saw little point pretending.

'Why did you go into catering?'

'I needed something that would guarantee me a job. Something that provided accommodation, at least to start with. I needed to get away from home as soon as I could.' She stared at her jumbo bandaged finger and wondered how she was going to manage at work. 'What I really wanted to do...' She hesitated, reluctant to share her dreams.

'Go on.'

'I wanted to study art.' She waited for the ridicule she was used to. But when it didn't come, she added, 'I loved it at school, it was the one thing I was good at.' Embarrassed for sharing this with a stranger, she dropped her gaze to the floor.

'Do you do any art now?'

'I draw. I love drawing.'

'It's not too late, you're only young. How old are you?'

'Twenty-four. But—' Angela shrugged. 'There's no work in it unless you want to teach, and there's no way I could teach.'

'If you trained, you might be able to. Teaching's got to be a nicer profession than catering?'

'I'm not going to be stuck in the kitchen forever, I'm doing hotel management, day-release at Hafod College.'

'Good for you.' The nurse slid her eyes to the clock. 'Now then, my love, have you got someone who can drive you home?'

Angela shook her head.

'Someone at home you can call?'

Someone at home?

Then she remembered.

'Toni! Oh, God. I was supposed to be meeting Toni. It's been hours. How can I have forgotten? Where's my mobile?' She patted her apron pocket.

'Tony, is he your boyfriend?'

'No, Toni's a girl; she's my friend. I was supposed to meet her this afternoon. She's staying the weekend.'

'I'm sure if you ring her, she'll come and fetch you.'

'I can't, I don't know her number, it's on my phone. In the panic of it all, I've gone and left my bag at work. I haven't got my purse either. Oh, God, how am I going to get back into town?'

SEVEN

'Mark called me a murderer!' Toni shrieks when she sees me ambling towards her through the dark. 'Can you believe that? A murderer.'

'*Shh*, come on now. Let's get you inside, you're freezing.' And she is, I can hear her teeth chattering as I usher her into the lobby. A cold concrete cube that stinks of urine.

'How could I have had a kid with him? He's a bloody nightmare.' She wipes her nose on her hand. 'With his rules for this and rules for that.'

I find what I hope is a clean tissue in the pocket of my bomber jacket and give it to her.

'It's why I had to do it on the sly.' She blows her nose. 'He'd have skinned me alive if he'd known what I was gonna do.'

'Let me carry that.' I hoick the rucksack onto my shoulder.

'There's no way I could've had his kid, I'd have been tied to the bastard forever. But I'm telling you—' she jerks her head up, her face blotchy in the sickly half-light, 'when I find the shitbag who snitched on me, they're gonna be in for it. Big time.'

'Which flat are you?' I want to move things along; I just want to get home.

'Fourth floor.'

'Come on, you lead the way. I'll see you to your door.'

'Lift's buggered again.' She waves an arm over the Out of Order sign and heads for the stairwell. 'Sorry, but we're going to have to walk it.'

I follow her but I can't keep up; I'm out of puff before we even reach the first landing.

'Are you all right? You're breathing all funny.'

I wave her on. I haven't the lung capacity to answer.

'You're a real gent, d'you know that?' She pauses to wait for me further up.

'You did mention it,' I say, managing a smile when I eventually join her on the second landing.

'Good. Nice men need telling.' She leans into me and I think she is going to kiss my cheek again but she gives my arm a little squeeze instead. 'Cos, if you ask me, there's a shortage of decent blokes in this world.' She trots up to the next floor with ease and calls down, 'The ones I meet anyway.'

The climb is hard going. Sweat breaks out across my forehead and between my shoulder blades. It's nothing to do with the weight of the rucksack, I can easily carry it. As I've said, I'm a pretty big guy and can manage most things. Have to with the jobs I do. My problem is I'm out of condition. I can't remember the last time I did any serious exercise. It's another thing I blame on the meds, they make me tired; the kind of tired that can't be satiated by sleep. I used to go running not so long ago. I ran a marathon when I was seventeen. Raised a load of dosh for Julia's child and the adolescent mental health division. But since I was put under Marvin Crow's care and he put me on those drugs, it's about all I can do to get out of bed and into work most days. And some days not even that.

'You'll come in for a bit?' Toni says when we reach her floor. 'I could do with the company, if I'm honest, mate.'

I'm thinking ahead to my journey home, which is a fair spin

across the city and south to Fagins-on-Sea. But pitiful and teary, I can't refuse her.

'Good, man,' she says, reading my mind. 'Make yourself at home, go on. Stick some lights on.' She unlocks the door and hustles me inside her flat. 'I've just got to get outta these wet things. Won't be a jiffy.'

Alone in the stubby hallway, I drop the rucksack to the floor and inch forward into the living space to switch on the ceiling bulb. Too bright, I squint through the electric overkill, at the surprisingly spacious room. A room that's seen better days. But this isn't what bothers me as I scan the walls, the rag rug, the three-piece suite, the curtains, the lampshade dangling inches above my head. What bothers me is that everything is blue. And I hate blue. It reminds me of hospitals and worse, the psychiatric unit I was forced to spend the most awful ten months of my life in.

Out of breath after my climb, I'm hot and my face is tacky. I take my jacket off and drape it over the arm of a chair.

'Vile in here, ain't it?' Toni appears in the doorway.

She looks brighter, and she's swapped her wet clothes for polka dot pyjamas and a silk dressing gown with matching slippers. Has wrapped a towel, turban-style, about her head. When she's put the bag of toiletries she's carrying down on the glass-topped coffee table – a great ugly thing on a wrought-iron frame – she dips and darts around me, drawing curtains, plumping cushions, flicking off the overhead bulb in favour of a pair of blue tasselled lamps.

'The place came fully furnished, nothing to do with me.' She waves at the sofa, encouraging me to sit. 'Aw, mate. Would ya look at that.' She extends her right hand and I think she means for me to admire the ring, so I stoop to look. 'I've only gone and broken a nail.'

I remember the vivid scratch on her ex-boyfriend's face as she chews it off, lobs the expended nail into the tub of a pot plant. Green and luxuriant, it claims the far corner and is the only vibrant thing amidst the artificial blue.

'Go on, have a seat, mate,' she prompts and I sink into the neon-blue upholstery. 'Lemme get you a drink. What d'ya fancy?'

'Tea'd be nice.'

'A proper drink, I mean.' All smiles as she plays the expert hostess that she is. 'What'll it be? Red, white… Or there's a cold one. I'm sure Mark left a tinny in the fridge.'

'I don't drink,' I say, then, fearing this sounds rude, add, 'Well, the thing is, I can't drink, I'm not allowed.'

'*Duh*. You're driving, I forgot.' She slaps her forehead. 'But you can have a small one, right?'

I'm about to tell her it's got nothing to do with me driving, it's the pills I'm on. Pills I ought to be taking right now, especially as I forgot this morning's dose. But she's already tottering away, saying, 'I can't drink on my own.' And before I know it, she's returned with a bottle of red and a pair of tumblers stamped with a Warner Bros cartoon.

'It'll warm up in a bit. I've put the heating on.' It's a shock when she plonks down beside me on the sofa. 'Are you cold?' I see her looking at my gloves.

'No, I'm okay.'

'Take them off then.' She sets the wine and glasses down and tightens the belt of her dressing gown.

'Oh, no, I need these.' I make a show of tugging them higher up my wrists. 'My hands are always cold.'

'Aw, yeah, you said, didn't you? Trouble with your circulation. Sorry.' Another slap of her forehead. 'I'm such a drongo. Mark's always on at me for not listening.' She twiddles the striking blue-green ring. Something I notice she does whenever the ex gets a mention.

'Nice piece of jewellery.' I sneak a sidelong look at her. See the gold chain, thin as a thread, that follows the dip and rise of her collarbone. She suits her hair swept back off her face like that; it shows off her cheekbones. 'Looks like them pictures you see of Earth from space.'

'Blimey, mate. You're right. I've never thought of it like that before.' She spreads her fingers, stares at the gemstone. 'The sea is the blue and the land is the green. I like that.' She raises her gaze to mine and I feel myself flush.

'W-what?' I falter, acutely self-conscious. 'W-what sort of s-stone is it? It looks pricey.'

'It's a blend of azurite and malachite.' She takes her time over the words. 'But it's not that expensive.' She rests her wrist on the arm of the sofa, curls and uncurls her fingers: a cat testing its claws. 'Although I've been told the ring's a one-off.'

I wonder if it's an engagement ring? Babcia, being Polish, wears her wedding band on her right hand, maybe Tasmanians do the same.

'This is Yellow Tail Shiraz.' Toni lifts the wine bottle and presents me with the label. I feel like a customer in the Lloyd George's restaurant. 'It's about the best I can afford but at least it's Aussie.' When she unscrews the cap, she fills both tumblers, talking to me in her lovely, throaty voice. 'I can't be doing with them long-stemmed glasses. I hope you don't mind drinking outta these?' I usually hate the Aussie accent but I couldn't hate anything about Toni, she's way too lovely for that. 'Back home, if you can believe it, wine's cheaper than bottled water is here.'

'Suppose it must be, the amount that's produced.' I stare at the second glassful that is meant for me.

'Strewth, mate.' She must see me hesitate. 'It ain't poison.' And she bumps her body against mine: jokey, teasing; it releases a puff of perfume I remember from the car. Has she put more of it on for me since she came home? 'Go on, do you good.' I watch her gulp hers. 'Loosen you up a bit.'

I reach over my knees and pick up the tumbler. Take one sip, then another. Feel the warmth of it spread through me like sunshine. 'I like him.' I swivel the design on the glass to her.

'That's Taz. The Tasmanian Devil. Great, ain't he? Hey,' she swallows another mouthful, 'you can stay over if you like? The sofa's comfy.' She giggles and bumps up against me again. 'We could get totally legless together.' I surprise myself by contemplating her suggestion when her mobile bleeps. She picks it up and sneers at whatever the message is. '*Huh*, you reckon, do ya? I say you can shove it.' She throws her phone down on the coffee table with a clatter.

Then we hear banging noises from above.

'Uh-oh, here we go. The Monster's home.'

I envisage whoever it is lumbering around in the flat above, his knuckles colliding with the furniture.

'He reckons he's a chef.' She tilts her chin to the ceiling. 'Not that I've ever smelt his cooking.'

'Suppose he does enough of it at work.' I have another go at my wine. 'Probably lives off takeaways.'

'Hey, that's an idea, I could get us a takeaway?' She raises her eyebrows, looks at me all expectantly.

'Oh, no. I really should be getting back.'

'Aw, don't go. Not yet. You've only just got here.' When she pulls the edges of her mouth down like that, it makes my insides go all wobbly. 'I don't wanna be here on my own if Mark comes back.'

'What, tonight? After that performance?' I respond to her unease. 'But he's cleared his stuff out, you said.'

'He'll be back.' She pauses and I can almost see her filtering through her thoughts as she twists the ring behind her knuckle again. 'There's something he wants, something he won't let me keep once he realises.' She flings back her head and I see her eyelashes are wet. 'I slapped him. I cut his face.' She is sobbing now. 'I didn't mean to hurt him, honestly, I didn't.'

It distresses me when people cry, I never know what to do. I sit awkwardly beside her until eventually, her sobbing propels me to put an arm around her. I want to comfort her but it feels so clumsy and I know I'm blushing like an idiot again.

Another series of thumps from above. It's the excuse I need to pull my arm back.

'D'you know,' she sniffs and dries her face on the hem of her dressing gown, 'I've been living here for fifteen months and I've barely met any of my neighbours. I think I've only spoken to him upstairs once. Can't remember his name but the saddo reckons he's got a wife. Not that I've seen any evidence of her.'

'He's probably just saying that so you don't go getting ideas.' I smile a real smile for once and press a finger to it, disbelieving.

'Cheeky sod,' she splutters, but at least I've made her laugh.

More banging from above.

'It's a good job Mark ain't here.' She drinks her wine. 'He'd be doin' his nut. He was always going up there and telling him to keep the noise down. Which was a flamin' cheek when you think of the racket we used to make. *Arguing.*' She unwraps the towel and gives her head a vigorous rub. 'Don't you ever get fed up with the jobs you do?' She shakes her damp hair into place. Mark obviously forgotten.

'Could ask you the same. Waiting on tables isn't much fun. At least I don't have to deal with the customers.'

'You've gotta point there. Although, you've got a way better temperament than me when it comes to dealing with the public.' She pulls out a pack of face wipes from the bag of toiletries, removes what remains of her make-up. 'Nothing bothers you much, does it? God, I'd give anything to be like you. Mr Chilled.'

'You wouldn't want to be like me. Trust me.'

'Why not? You're a nice bloke, now I've got to know you a bit.' She's unscrewing a tub of moisturiser now, scooping some up on her fingers and rubbing it into her face and neck.

'That's just it. People don't get to know me, they're not interested. I just blend into the background.'

'I wouldn't say that. I reckon you stand out.'

I shrug. 'Whereas you – no one could ever accuse you of blending in.'

'That your way of telling me I'm mouthy?' She screws the lid back on the moisturiser and returns it to the bag.

'Well, you are a bit.' I let her believe this is what I mean when it wasn't, even though it's common knowledge she likes an argument. But to tell her how extraordinary she is, how unlike anyone else she is, is impossible. I'm way too shy for that.

'Maybe. But I've gotta say it if people piss me off.'

'People like me, you mean?'

'Nah, you're one of the good guys. I know that now. All that stuff I said, that was just me mouthing off cos I'd had a crappy day.'

'It's all right.'

'No, it isn't. I shouldn't have taken it out on you and I'm sorry.' She stares off into the room. 'It's funny. I used to think you were a bit... A bit of an—' She hesitates. 'Odd bod.' She puts a hand lightly on my arm, then pulls it back again. 'Thanks for being such a good mate and looking after me tonight. I think you're about the only friend I've got.'

I shift uneasily in my seat; I don't know what to do when she says nice things to me. 'I think you look loads prettier without your make-up.'

'*Gerroff.* I look terrible.' She squirms and goes all coy but I can tell she likes what I said. 'D'ya want me to open us another?' She waves a hand over the near-empty wine bottle.

'I think you've had enough.'

'Don't you start. That's another thing Mark was always on at me about. I'll fetch us another.' She slaps her thighs and gets to her feet. 'How's about we liven things up a bit? Put some music on? Something nice and loud to drown The Monster out.'

'Go on then.'

'What kinda music d'you like?'

'Jazz, blues... classical.'

'Doubt you're gonna like my stuff then.' She shares what's left in the bottle.

'It's not "Waltzing Matilda", is it?'

'Very funny.' She laughs and gives me a pretend cuff around the ear, then picks up her mobile and does a funny walk over to the wireless docking station, where she scrolls through her playlist.

I laugh too. And because it's real – I am actually laughing for real – I want to share with her what a great time I'm having. Tell her I can't remember the last time I laughed. But I don't, Toni thinks I'm weird enough as it is. I sip my wine and feel the alcohol skid into my veins, down to my groin and my budding erection. Which is a surprise, as this is another part of me that's been dead for years too.

I don't recognise the music but I like it and, before I realise, I'm tapping my foot. Toni is shimmying towards me and her dressing gown has come undone. When she leans forward to pull me towards her, I see she has a tiny butterfly tattoo between her breasts.

'I love this song.' She is holding my hands and rocking around on the rag rug. She looks giddy and gorgeous and ignorant of the effect she is having on me. 'Dance,' she coos. 'Be a sport.'

'I can't. I can't dance.' I propel my voice above the music. If I stand up, she'll see what she's done to me. 'I've never danced before.' I rub a nervous hand over my bristly head.

'First time for everything.'

'I can't. I've gotta take a pee.'

I want her more than I have wanted any woman in a very long time. But I've got to get away from her. Confused by my arousal, I don't know what to do – what does she want me to do? I look at her dancing, smiling, giving me the come-on. I know what she wants, she wants me.

'First on the left.' She wiggles a finger in the direction I need to go. I can tell she's teasing, that she's playing with me. But I like it. I like her.

Upright, on wobbly legs, the alcohol I'm not used to has gone to my head and I stagger along the hall to the bathroom. Tug on the light pull which is a blue ceramic fish. I weigh it in my hand. I like this kind of detail and smile as I duck inside, my head narrowly missing the lintel. I carry my smile to the mirror above the basin and talk to myself.

'You've only gone and got yourself a stiffy.' I whisper my disbelief and see my smile widen. I push the heel of my hand to my groin, still disbelieving. 'She likes you; she really likes you.' I tilt my head to check my nostrils, breathe into my hand and test my breath. 'She said you weren't bad-looking, didn't she?' I step back to assess my reflection. 'Yeah, you've gotta go for it, boy.'

Fizzing with excitement, I need a moment to steady myself and look around. See a box of Tampax by the loo, bottles of shampoo on the rim of the bath. Shelves of exfoliators, body lotions, bubble bath, waxing kits. The paraphernalia and mystery of women has always fascinated me, and I let myself imagine what it might be like to see her things arranged on the shelves in my bathroom.

'When's the last time you had a chance with a girl?' I return to my reflection. 'Never mind a girl like her... Just don't fuck this up.'

A warning shot to myself before I switch off the light and stride back to the living room, certain I'm going to get what I want.

The heavy rock music has been swapped for something soft and romantic. Toni, cavorting abandoned, has collapsed on the sofa. Her pretty slippered feet propped on the coffee table. When she notices me, she pats the space beside her and I can see she hasn't bothered to do up her dressing gown. I take it as a sign and move into the room to sit beside her. Gripping my knees, unsure what to do next, I notice she's lit a little row of candles. The sulphur smell of an expended match fills the room.

'I've opened us another.' Close, her breath on my ear, she hands me my glass. 'Don't go, stay with me,' she murmurs through the smooth incidental music. 'It's dead comfy.' She pats the sofa again to demonstrate. 'I've got a spare duvet and pillows; you won't be cold.'

Without taking my eyes off her, I bring the glass of wine to my lips and swallow mouthful after slow, sweet mouthful. I know what I'm going to do, I'm going to kiss her. Properly. On the mouth. Looking at her, at the way she's being, I can tell she wants me to.

I take a deep breath and press myself against her. Using my weight to push her back into the sofa, I hold her there, then moisten my lips to make them ready for hers.

EIGHT

Angela alighted the bus outside Cardiff Castle. It was dark now and looking up, she saw its floodlit, pristine walls and red dragon flags flapping proudly against their poles. The nurse gave her the money to travel back into town and, remembering her grandfather saying how angels always turned up exactly when you needed them, she decided the nurse was an angel.

She hurried along Duke Street, through the abuse of car horns and burn of diesel and took the next right into the illuminated pedestrianised area with its late-night Christmas shopping hours already underway. Angela loved this city. Loved the mix of nationalities contained within its attractive Morgan Quarter and Victorian arcades. The unexpected green of churchyard gardens and St David's shopping centre. Not that she had the confidence or the time to be part of the scene. Any notions about joining Weight Watchers or art classes, activities promoted on the insides of bus shelters or in the flyers she takes then throws away, never evolved beyond ideas. Accompanied by the sound of her safety shoes against the wet pavement, she left St Mary's Street behind and turned down towards the Millennium Stadium, glancing over her shoulder at the River

Taff: oil-black and greasy under the rippling reflection of a thousand city lights. A few further paces and she caught sight of herself in a closed-up shop window. *Can that really be me?* She quizzed it, disbelieving the person mirrored back to her. When did she evolve into this? She stared at the shapeless form clad in sexless chef whites. Abandoning her reflection, she walked right up to the front of the Lloyd George Hotel and gazed into its ochre-lit interior. Imagined what a guest might feel when they arrived at this plush, five-star establishment. She squinted up through the needles of drizzle and weighed up whether to go in through the front but stopped herself in time. Too risky in her chef uniform. Back-of-house staff caught in the guest quarters was an instantly sackable offence.

The wet-bricked alleyway that led to the rear of the hotel was dark and slippery. Fearful of falling, she couldn't rush but neither could she dawdle. Doing her best to form purposeful strides in case eyes were watching from the dark, she repeatedly checked behind her for the trouble she expected to be there. Then the staff entrance was at last in sight and, once in through the plastic screen, she was hit by the diabolical stench of the bins. A smell she carried with her down into the deserted changing rooms, where she snapped off the wristband with its key on it, opened her locker and grabbed her bag. After a quick change into the clothes she'd worn into work that morning, careful not to bang her finger, she dropped her dirty whites into the laundry bin on the way out.

The electronic sign said the bus to Roath wasn't due for another ten minutes and she sat down to wait with other passengers, taking the last available pop-up seat beneath the domed plastic screen. Glad to get out of the rain, she yawned and saw the woman seated next to her give a shy sideways smile at her strapped-up finger.

'I cut it at work. I've been at the hospital all day.' Angela smiled back and lifted her bag onto her lap, taking care to keep her finger out of harm's way. She pulled out her mobile to call Toni. Saw there were four missed calls and a voicemail from her, along with a single text message:

WHERE R U?

GETTING DROWNED. MEET @ 4 U SAID

BEEN WAITING 3 HRS. GOING TO THE PUB

SOME MATE U R

With a sudden agitation bubbling behind her ribs, Angela tapped her screen and scrolled through to Toni's number. She pressed the green icon and listened to it ring out against her ear.

Reluctant to leave a message, she hung up, then rang three, four times more. Only on the fifth attempt, with her bus home at last moving into view, did she let it go through to voicemail and attempt to explain where she had been until now.

NINE

'*Hey*! What are you doing? Getting all fresh with me.' Toni bats me away and scrabbles to her feet. Wine slops over my hand. 'We were getting on great, what d'you wanna go spoiling it for?' Upright and screeching, she scrubs at her mouth like my kiss was the most disgusting thing ever.

'I thought it's what you wanted.'

'Get real. Last thing I want is a new man in me life.' Mad-eyed, she flaps her arms around like some demented bird.

I'm on my feet too, moving towards her, determined to finish what she started. It's the strongest urge I can ever remember and it frightens me because I don't think I can stop myself.

'Hey! I said, didn't I? I just wanna be friends.' She slaps me away.

'But you said you liked me.'

'Yeah, but it don't mean I want ya to jump me bones.'

I don't understand what's going on. Why is she being like this? She's the one who started it. I didn't ask to sit beside her, to drink her wine, to dance with her and share her troubles. She foisted all that on me.

'This is what you wanted. You wanted me. What was all that flirting about?'

Her mobile buzzes. But I'm listening to a different kind of buzzing. Inside my head. It's the sound I used to hear in the bad old days. The one that worked as a precursor to my violent flare-ups before Marvin put me on the drugs.

Toni lunges for her phone but in her desperation to distance herself from me, she topples backwards. And I watch as if in slow motion, the heel of her slipper snagging against the blue rag rug. Her arms flail instinctively to try and break her fall. But she falls anyway and the back of her skull strikes the sharp-edged coffee table with a sickening crack.

'*Shit*! No... No!'

A yawning, choking calm settles in the room.

The seconds pass.

Toni is lying face-up on the rug. Her top lip is taut across her teeth. The tiny diamond in one nostril glints like a faraway star.

I kneel beside her head. How pale and still she is. She isn't breathing. Then I see the blood.

'What the fuck have I done?'

I say this over and over. My voice a rasping whisper as I am willing and pleading for what's been done to be undone. But with each passing minute, a new reality crowds in from the blue-papered walls.

I've killed her.

Sweat breaks out across my back. Across my forehead. Sweat runs down into my eye. It stings. I wonder, blinking it away, about giving her mouth-to-mouth. I might if I knew what I was doing. Then a voice from somewhere inside me tells me not to touch the body. To stay away from it.

I get up off the floor. Head spinning, heart thumping. I think about calling for help. Calling for an ambulance. The police. I get as far as pulling my mobile out from my jeans pocket. Then hesitate. What's wrong with me? Just ring them. This was an accident; I've not done anything wrong. Then I listen to me telling them what happened. See them reading the situation. How it will look through their eyes: a man and a woman alone in her flat. Drinking, dancing, flirting. The man tries it on, gets the big brush-off and then there's some kind of altercation that ends with the woman dying from a blow to the head.

She fell, I tell you. She fell.

Really?

I can read their scepticism from here. They'll never believe I was innocent. Not someone with my violent history. My mental health record. The fact some bloke is walking around out there with his left ear missing. I wouldn't stand a chance. Sex. Violence. A beautiful woman using me as a shoulder to cry on. I was taking advantage. That's what they'd say. No one will believe me. And this time they will lock me up for good.

I feel suddenly weak. As if my body has been drained of blood. I take a few steps backwards, feel my calves press up against the sofa but I don't sit down. I've got to try and think my way out of this but the room, with its smothering blueness, seems to close in on me. I honestly don't know what to do.

Then it dawns on me with vivid clarity.

I need to get out of here.

Now.

I grab my jacket. Stuff my arms into the sleeves and jingle the pockets to check the car keys are there before blowing out the candles. Glad for my gloves, there'll be no dabs. Good, I think, and transfer the wine from one tumbler into the other, slide the one I drank from into my jacket pocket.

'You're going to be grateful you did this later,' I murmur as I leave the flat.

The Danestown estate is deserted and I'm grateful for a reprieve from the rain. My pulse jumps about in my wrists as I hurry through the eerie, silent world that only exists in the hours before the sun comes up. The sharp smell of night stings my nostrils and I see a ginger cat slink out from between the bins and cross my path. Lucky, or unlucky? Or does this only apply to black cats? My thoughts tripping over themselves as I follow it at a slow jog down the slight incline in the direction of the car. I shouldn't drive, I've had too much to drink but it's riskier to hang about here.

A scan around for CCTV cameras. Why I'm bothering, I don't know? There's nothing I can do about it if I've been caught on one. It worries me, I know these kinds of places are monitored round the clock.

Heart pounding, my mind a whirl, I get behind the wheel and start the engine, fastening my seat belt as I accelerate away. A few anxious seconds at the junction, indicator ticking through the dark. I drum my fingers on the dashboard and wait for a space in the traffic before swinging out into the main road to head back the way I came. I pick out certain landmarks: an Esso garage, a Spar... The school with its acres of playing fields. All deserted now and swathed in blackness. I pull up beside a white VW Caddy at the first set of lights. Stationary, I imagine the passenger is looking at me.

Can he tell what I've done? Can he see from my face the dreadful thing I've left behind?

Fresh sweat breaks out over my forehead. I dab it away with a gloved fist and chance a sideways glance at the bloke in a baseball cap. Realise he isn't looking at me at all, he's laughing at something his driving companion is telling him. His mouth an opening and closing wide black hole. The lights change to green and we're on the move again. I'm safe. No one knows that the woman I've spent the best evening with in years, now lies dead on her living-room floor.

My pulse slows to normal and, changing up through the gears, building to forty where the speed signs allow, I tell myself to breathe, to relax. I don't know what it is but I feel different all of a sudden. Perhaps the difference is that I'm *feeling*. Pushing beyond the shock, there is something close to exhilaration. Wow, what is this? It's weird but I like it. I prop my wrists on the steering wheel, flex my gloved fingers and adjust my body in the driving seat. I want to sit upright and stretch my spine. Lighter, that's it. It's like I've emerged from the horror of what's just happened, to find a world brimming with possibilities. Strange as this may sound, the heaviness I've been dragging around for as long as I can remember, has rolled off me like a stone.

I pull up at a set of road works and sniff the acrid burn of tar. Beyond the windscreen, deciduous trees shake out what remains of their yellow leaves. They spiral down like gold sovereigns through the gloom. I wonder when I stopped noticing stuff like that?

'This is pointless,' I shout and slap the wheel. Enjoying myself. I always did like a good shout, although, I'm supposed to pretend I don't. 'No bugger's working; there won't be anyone here until morning.'

I smile into the optimism that fizzes in my chest and stare at the red-eyed light, willing it to turn green. When it does, I take it as a sign – a sign of things to come – and drive on.

'I'm invincible.' I share my thoughts with the dark of the car's interior and slow for the torrential rain that has begun again.

Beyond the car, everything looks brighter, cleaner. The city's night-time suburbs, metrically cut by the repetitious swing of the windscreen wipers, seem to glisten with possibilities. Watching the rain bounce against the gleaming tarmac, I find myself yearning for the long, light days of spring. When blossom, pink as confetti, drips from the now leafless cherry trees along this stretch. This is strange for me, I don't ever remember thinking ahead or looking forward to anything, never mind springtime and blossom.

Sudden spray, from a low-loader passing on the opposite side, hisses against the windscreen. Then, when the rain eases to a drizzle, I cut the wipers and swap their squeaking for the spooky stillness of the virtually traffic-free streets. At last, I sigh, picking up speed, the tail-lights ahead of me thinning out until a handsome fox saunters into the road. I skid to a stop just in time. A car toots its horn from behind. I twist in my seat and stick two fingers up at whoever it is.

'I'm waiting for the fox. There's been enough killing tonight,' I shout – it doesn't matter, the arsehole can't hear me – I like it, it feels good to assert myself for a change.

The driver overtakes, impatient, tooting again. I tailgate him. Flashing my full beam. Aggressive and bullying, I don't know what's got into me. It's like the rush of adrenaline has turned me upside down. I'd never usually react this way but I like it: driving on his red tail-lights, taking risks like never before. It gives me a thrill. I know if he decides to stop suddenly, I've had it, but for once I don't care. Whoever it is in front, accelerates faster and faster. Excitement surges through me and I press my foot to the floor to keep up. I inhale: deep and indulgent; enjoying the quivering in my chest, low down in my stomach. Whatever's going on, it's like I've been reborn, it's the only way to describe it. Really, it's like I've been rejuvenated and the fog that's been dulling the spark I used to have, is finally clearing.

What am I doing?

I come to my senses and realise in the nick of time that I can't go around acting the goat, I've got to keep my head down. A foot on the brake and I slow to thirty, grudgingly letting the tosser in front get away. I tell myself this is good, it's sensible, I can't risk getting caught for speeding, let alone drink-driving. Or worse. Because supposing they trace my movements tonight, link them back to Toni and find her body? I can't let that happen, not now, I've too much to lose now. I'm on the cusp of something better, I know it.

Sudden flashing blue lights. I glance into my driving mirror but can't work out where they're coming from. Then I see it. The cop car gaining on me through the dark.

My balls shrivel up into my body.

I'm done for.

Panic flares behind my ribcage, I press a hand to it. The euphoria I was feeling has been replaced by a sickening sense of dread.

How could I be so bloody stupid? Driving like a madman, letting some ignorant fucker get the better of me. It wasn't worth it.

This is the end. It's not fair. My life is going to be over, just when I thought I was getting it back. But it's too late for self-recriminations. The patrol car: silent and deadly, swoops up behind me. No two-tone siren, just its spinning LED light. The icy-blue filling the Ford's interior and throwing me into terrible confusion.

TEN

Angela slept with an arm flung out to the side. The room was chilly, the radiators cold. The instructions Lin and Greg left her was only about the cats and said nothing about how to work the central heating.

Her lips moved. What was she saying?

'Robbie. Robbie. Robbie.'

She was dreaming of her brother pedalling his bike around Dowdeswell Reservoir. The bounce of summer sunshine in his hair.

Angela opened her eyes onto the ceiling and followed a crack from coving to light fitting. She didn't immediately register where she was. Sounds of the city filtered through to her, throwing her back to the house of her early childhood and the room where she would lie awake listening to the reassuring shuffle of branch-line trains. A house with a tidy garden and a woodshed filled with her father's tools, where Robert kept his bike. A house with central heating and neighbourhood barbeques. Until torn apart by the death of their only son, her parents lost their jobs and were forced to downsize to a crumbling-walled cottage in the wilds of rural Wales.

Her dream had taken her back to the summer of her sixteenth year, where her ten-year-old brother had appeared as alive and real as the blustery autumn day leaching in through a gap in the curtains. It was a dream she'd had many times and she supposed it was her mind's way of processing a trauma in her past she probably wouldn't ever recover from. She dozed for the next hour. Only when an arrow light of sunshine burst and faded against the wall did she sit up, pulling the duvet over her as if someone had entered the room unexpectedly. And in a way they had. Although, no one that could tell tales. A black cat with marzipan-yellow eyes jumped on the bed and prowled the mattress, startling her. There was something creepy about him. *Bimbo.* Lin and Greg's note had furnished her with his name.

'No bimbo, though, are you, boy?'

The cat ignored her. But unbeknown to Angela, the creature had been sussing her out from the floor all night.

'You're such a pretty boy. D'you want to come and say hello?'

She tapped the duvet to beckon him closer, careful not to knock her damaged finger. But Bimbo didn't budge. Then she made an involuntary noise and he fled from the room as if he'd been shot.

'Scatty Catty,' she renamed him, listening to the thump, thump, thump, as he ascended the stairs.

Sudden hail clattered against the window. It was accompanied by a cold draught of air which alerted her to a sizeable gap in its frame. It prompted her to push back the bedcovers and get up. On her way to the bathroom, she poked her head inside the spare room she had prettified in readiness for Toni's stay.

Where was she? Why wasn't she answering her phone?

Her friend's stubborn silence was worrying. Had something

happened to her? She didn't know why, but the memory of Toni arguing with that kitchen porter sent a chill through her as she closed the door.

The bathroom was mostly a huge cast iron tub on shiny, black claws. No shower. Instead, a pot of ivy hung from a hook, its tendrils long and dry-looking. It didn't matter, she'd been using the showers at work and could carry on doing so. But she had time for a bath today and it would be easier to keep her bandage dry. She fancied lying chin-deep in bubbles, it would warm her up. But turning the tap, she reminded herself that like the cold radiators, there was no hot water, she hadn't worked out how to operate the boiler either. She couldn't be bothered to go upstairs to the kitchen and boil a kettle, it wasn't as if she was going anywhere today, so she brushed her teeth and lathered her flannel. Gave herself a quick once-over, followed by a rapid towelling, before trotting back across the chilly landing to the master bedroom to dress. A slow business on account of her finger, she deliberately chose a pair of skinny jeans – the ones just tight enough to work as a reminder not to overeat – and her favourite fleece: dark green with GAP stitched in bold white letters across its front. The better of her charity shop buys.

Instantly warmer, she tied her copious hair in a sloppy ponytail. Let the wispy bits trail down her neck. She pressed the tip of her nose to the cold windowpane, her breath misting the glass as she looked out at the identical terraced houses on the other side of the street: tall, elegant, Victorian brick dwellings topped with sky-grazing chimneys. She watched families pushing buggies along the pavement blown with leaves. Wrapped in scarves and linking arms, they looked as if they were making the most of a Saturday. It had her wondering where Lin and Greg might be and her imagination dropped the couple sitting amid the bustle of tourists and artists at an outdoor café in Montmartre. Elbows propped on a chequered tablecloth, the sun warming their backs. Rhiannon said they were starting in Europe and they intended to head east into Asia after a week or two. So, Paris was possible. It was where Angela would go if she was brave enough. Earn her keep from making portraits of holidaymakers, living the dream life in a rooftop garret with views of the Sacré-Coeur. Not that she'd experienced Paris, it was a place learnt about from books, but she had plans to go one day. *Think big. Dream big.* A favourite mantra of Toni's and, from the adventures she claimed to have had, Angela agreed it sounded a good one. She was right to turn down Toni's offer of travelling with her to Spain, wasn't she? She wished she could be carefree but she wasn't like Rhiannon and Toni, with a loving family who would bail her out if she took a wrong turn. Angela was on her own.

Her finger was throbbing and, abandoning the view, she dug through her wash-ups for painkillers. Swallowed them down with a mouthful of water kept by the bed. Then she looked at the bed. A large brass affair with a vermillion-red eiderdown and lacy pillowcases. It was quite the most romantic thing she'd ever seen. Tidying the covers with her good hand, her thoughts curved to Rhiannon, as she was someone who loved to surround herself with glamorous things. It hurt to think Rhiannon didn't tell her to her face that she was moving in with Geraint. That she let her wake up to find boxes and bin liners clogging the hall of the place they'd rented since leaving college, Geraint's van parked outside. It was sly the way she did it. Angela, like the parent of a drug addict, or the neighbour of a serial killer, was the last to know and it left her feeling stupid, insignificant.

Bed made, she grabbed her sketchpad and pencil case and rechecked her mobile, hoping for a message from Toni.

Nothing.

'Answer me, why can't you?'

She tucked her phone in the pouch of her fleece and slipped her socked feet inside the sheepskin boots she'd been given last Christmas. Heading upstairs, trailing her dream, she sensed the ghostly presence of generations past as she patted the peeling wallpaper. Imagining the souls of the dead pressed between the decades-old layers of colours and patterns, she shivered under her clothes. This was a draughty place, where hinges squeaked and the exposed floorboards were pockmarked by hammers. The heavy curtains and tassel-edged rugs scattered throughout offered little insulation. It was a topsy-turvy kind of house, with the kitchen at the top and the bedrooms below. Climbing the narrow stairwell, she paused to look out of low landing windows that gave onto a tumble of roofs, that wasn't a tumble at all. Every roof related to a precise space and the tilt of the land if you looked at it properly. Angela was good at looking, it was something her art teacher at school taught her to do.

'Bimbo!'

She almost tripped over the cat who was now pretending to be the tread of a stair. Bimbo mewled at her.

'You after breakfast too, little fella?'

She sidestepped him, onto the landing, only to jump again at the ventriloquist's dummy on a chair on the turn of the stairs. The thing was grotesquely human, with its wild staring eyes and red-painted mouth. Ideally, she would have liked to hide it away for the duration of her stay but was strangely afraid to touch it.

The kitchen was chilly and last night's dirty dishes were still in the sink. She stood on the threshold and inhaled its fusty smell, decided it had the same neglected feel as the rest of the house. The outdated décor of the place came as a shock, as the Bowens' top-notch beauty salon in Cardiff Bay, kitted out in primary colours and finished in chrome, was ultra-modern by comparison.

The cats wore collars with bells and, hearing a tinkle at her feet, she looked down to where Bangles, a silver tabby, was circling her ankles. Galvanised into action, she put down her pad and pencils and consulted the list on the fridge, still unsure what amounts to feed. When she had, she placed the cat bowls slightly apart on the floor tiles and listened to the little snuffling sounds they made as they ate.

'Nice, is it?' Talking to them as if they could understand, she laughed at herself. But when they'd finished and turned their furry jowls to her before tiptoeing out through the cat flap, she could half-believe they did.

She and Robert had a cat. Round as a peach with a furry nap. They never did decide on a name and he was known affectionately as Cat until he got sliced in half by a car on the busy road outside their Charlton Kings home. An image of her father, sobbing behind his spectacles as he shovelled him up on a spade and buried him in the garden. She thinks it was a Saturday, not unlike this one, with hail showers then bursts of sun, but she couldn't be sure. The only thing she was sure about, was the beating her parents gave her when it was discovered she had been the one to let the cat out.

Angela boiled the kettle, used some of the water to wash up last night's dinner things. She then rinsed out a cloth and made a half-hearted attempt at wiping down the surfaces. Scooping up a collection of dead flies, a leftover from summer, with the sides of her hands. The entire house could probably do with a clean but she wasn't going to be the one to do it. An image of her mother: house-proud, waspish, the chic swish of her dark bobbed hair. A woman who was easy in T-shirt and jeans. A woman who was frightened to be still. A woman who was nothing like Angela.

The steel-framed windows opened onto a third-floor roof garden trimmed in fairy lights and mottled river stones that had probably been acquired from a garden centre. Looking beyond the cactus-cluttered sills, she could appreciate properly, now she was seeing it in daylight, just how high up she was. She pushed her gaze over the huddle of roofs and chimneys and beyond, to the great, grey smudge that, on a clearer day, would be the geometric rise and fall of the city.

Angela abandoned the view and made a mug of tea and two rounds of toast. Ate sitting down at a square table scarred with knives, looking around at the cobwebby corners, the cracked wall tiles. Licking butter from her fingers, she rinsed her plate and left it to dry, went over to the boiler and prised open the metal door. She stared at its complicated innards, the buttons and dials she didn't understand. Afraid to touch anything, she dashed off a text to Rhiannon, asking if Geraint would come over and take a look. There was still no news from Toni.

She took her tea, along with her pad and pencils, down to the living room below. A large space confused by mirrors; it filled most of the second floor and the sight of her reflection multiplying off into infinity made her feel acutely alone. There was an upright piano and, mindful of her bandaged finger, she lifted the lid. Its sound was impaired and the keys chipped like a rat had gnawed the ivory. Cold enough to see her breath, she girdled the room, aimlessly dragging her fingers over the tatty spines of paperbacks. Found both a stuffed crow perched on a wooden plinth nailed to the wall, its beak varnished an artificial yellow, and a giant rubber plant with large, dusty leaves. Testing the soil and finding it dry, she emptied what remained of her tepid black tea into the plant pot. The only framed photographs were of the cats.

She plumped down on a hulking leather couch; its sides shredded by cat claws. Tilted her head to the cornice, where a damp patch had stained the ceiling brown. It looked like the liver spots on her grandfather's hands and thoughts of family reminded her of her promise to ring home. Not that she could bring herself to make the call. She had a college assignment to finish too, but she didn't have the impetus to do that either. Instead, she opened her sketchpad in her lap and flicked to a clean page, careful not to bump her finger. The paper was postcard size. It was the kind of drawing she wanted to do. It would be like spying through a keyhole. Pencil in hand, she looked about for something suitable. There was plenty to choose from, the watery light filtering through the high glazed windows magnified the room's contents and its flaws. Shabby chic, she supposed those trendy homeware shops called it, but she didn't care what it was, she was just grateful to be here.

She outlined a wooden fruit bowl heaped with apples. Her eye was out. She didn't draw enough. You had to draw every day to keep your eye in. And your hand. And all the other things you needed to draw from life. It frustrated her, she used to be good. Better to do a drawing than not do one, she persevered, wanting to produce something, it didn't matter if it wasn't perfect. She drifted away, as drawing allowed her to do, only the chill forced her to stop now and again to rub her legs through her jeans. The day was already darkening beyond the windows and, with it, a fleeting thought about lighting the fire. But she wouldn't, she knew the basket of logs wouldn't last long, same with the stack of wood piled up on the ground floor. She would wait until winter had well and truly blown in before lighting it.

The house was quiet enough to hear the ticking of the carriage clock on the mantelpiece. A lonely sound that had her contemplating the weekend she was unsure how to fill. The plans she had made were for her and Toni. Thinking of her strangely silent friend, she rechecked her mobile. Again, nothing. Toni hadn't replied to a single one of her messages. It was odd. Yes, she knew Toni could be tricky but she wasn't unreasonable, and ignoring her because she cut her finger and needed to go to A&E, *was* unreasonable.

She tried Toni's number again. Listened to its unanswered ring oscillate through the emptiness. When the mechanical voice, at last, invited her to leave a message, she did:

'I know you're cross with me but honestly, it wasn't my fault...'

With a hand clamped to her forehead, she rushed through her explanation yet again.

'...I left my mobile at work in the panic of it all, it wasn't deliberate.' A sigh. 'Just send me a text, yeah? Let me know you're all right. I've been worrying about you since I saw you arguing with that kitchen porter. Look, if you want, you could still come over, I'm off tomorrow too, remember. Let me know either way, *okay?*'

She ended the call and sat staring into space. An uneasy feeling had lodged in her stomach, and she set her drawing to one side, no longer able to concentrate. Should she go to Toni's flat? The idea fizzled out before it properly formed when she thought of the journey. Too late in the day to head off now, the numerous buses she'd need to catch to travel to that side of town would take an age. She would go first thing tomorrow if there was still no word, it would give her something to do and set her mind at rest. Needing the distraction, she rose from the couch to rifle a box of DVDs. Nothing suited her mood, so she put the television on. Aimlessly flicked through the channels with Bangles purring like a pigeon on her lap. She found a documentary about climate change. Polar ice caps melting, penguins shuffling across the frozen continent where ice met the sea in a sub-zero wind. She stroked Bangles with a steady determination. Watched white-grey hairs fall onto her jeans and float to the floor. The programme depressed her more than sitting alone in the quiet, so she switched the television off, tipped the cat out of her lap and got up to wander over to the cocktail cabinet, where she spied a bottle of vodka lurking at the back. Bad news, drinking alone; she hadn't succumbed to this kind of succour since the lower sixth at her new Welsh school and struggling to cope in a world without her brother.

Toni's message from the previous evening came to mind. Poor Toni, it can't have been much fun drinking alone in the pub, no wonder she was annoyed with her. But Angela couldn't keep pestering, she had to back off and give her friend some space; there was no reason to think Toni hadn't got home safely or that she wasn't okay. She knew why she tended to fuss and fret when there was no need. It stemmed from her failure to rescue her brother from drowning in Dowdeswell Reservoir. And an irrational fear of something like it happening again on her watch made her overcompensate for the people she cared about. Fear had heightened a deep sense of responsibility in her that she doubted she possessed before the horror of that summer.

Angela consulted her watch. It had gone five. It was fine, she wasn't going to make a habit of this. She might still be sad about her brother but she was no longer suicidal. She poured a generous measure of vodka and took the glass up to the kitchen where she added orange juice, fresh from the fridge. She drank it standing by the sink, her eyes following a flock of unknown birds journeying over the rooftops. The clocks go back tonight, her thoughts as she sipped and swallowed, watching the sun going down red beyond the city. This time tomorrow it would be dark and, with a sudden desire to make the most of what was left of the daylight, she carried her drink to the door and flung her head to the wide, Welsh sky. The cold wind against her skin felt almost human and she listened to it nudge through the pots of bamboo that flanked the door.

Shivering, she was about to close up, when a flicker on her periphery made her look out over the roof garden again. To the old woman who lived next door. A chilli-red cardigan buttoned over her broad shoulders, her skirt billowing in the wind. Watching with interest, Angela saw the gentleness with which she tended her herbs, her hutches of little brown rabbits. Noticed, with a jolt – when the woman rolled up her sleeves – a row of faded grey-green numbers on her left forearm.

ELEVEN

The rapid staccato of next door's knitting machine that woke me over an hour ago, continues to clatter on. Usually, the seagulls provide the alarm call but I suppose Mrs Thomas must have Christmas deadlines for her to be up this early on a Sunday. As a kid, I used to think the sound was her and Mr Thomas snoring. That their headboard was just the other side of my bedroom wall. But I was wrong. A nice-looking woman in her prime was Mrs Thomas. As a teenager, I used to look down on her sunbathing in her bikini from my bedroom window. Watch the slow turn of the sun transform her pale winter body into a rich, polished mahogany.

I'm in no rush to rise and greet the day. I called Gaynor at Blue Arrow and cried off work again, came back to bed with a mug of tea. I blamed it on a migraine. I know all there is to know about migraines, so I sounded convincing. Pretending to mix up my words, which is what happens. Saying things like: 'I'm confused, too confused to drive, too confused to be left in charge of a cleaning trolley or a polishing machine.' Then embellishing my lie with details about vomiting through the night and how I'm floating between imagination and reality. All true, when I'm having one. I told her I wouldn't be up for going in tomorrow either, just to sound authentic.

When I do get up, I go to the bathroom to confront myself in the mirror. My face is creased by the pillow and I dislike what I see. I swivel this way and that, hoping for a glimpse of the person I used to be. I usually avoid mirrors, I'm reluctant to see what others see, but I force myself to look today, expecting some visible change after the awful thing I've done. Because the episode with Toni has changed me. How could it not?

So, what happens now the greatest crime has been committed? Because there's no going back and it's only a matter of time before Toni's body is found. And then what? An image of her lying stiffly, buckled at an impossible angle, eyes popping as if surprised by death. I judder into it and rub a hand over my bristly head, over my chin. Aware of the shake in my hand when I reach for my razor and shaving foam. Then I stop, decide: No, I'll let my hair grow. Julia used to say I had lovely hair and Toni said it would suit me longer. And supposing someone did see me Friday night? Supposing I was caught on CCTV? Let them go hunting for a clean-shaven, bald bloke.

Talking about a close shave... The cops that pulled me over? It was only to tell me one of the car's tail-lights was out. God knows how I wasn't done for speeding, or at the very least breathalysed – it was a good job I had the sense to pop one of my Parma Violets in, it threw them off the scent. I've taken it as another sign that Mum's looking after me. She does this, from beyond the grave – it's what she is doing now. Because everything's for a reason. It may not always be clear, like the reason for Friday night isn't clear, not yet. I've always believed that everything I do and everything that's done to me, however bad, is Mum's doing – she is my guiding force. And if I heed the direction she pushes me in, I'll be rewarded one day. It's my philosophy for life. A life, because of the drugs I take and the way things have turned out, I haven't always valued; in the same way I haven't always valued the lives of others. I know this must make me sound unfeeling but I can't lie, I can't say that life has mattered much. I think I belong to the dead, I'm of their lineage after all. For as long as I can remember, so much of me has wanted to be with them, preferring their company. I've more affiliation with ghosts.

Will I now be living with Toni's ghost in the same way I do with Mum's? The ghost I see sitting on the bottom stair here at home. The one I tell no one about, for fear of ridicule. It's my secret and I know I'm privileged. Although, sightings of Mum are usually a precursor to a migraine; a shimmering on the left side of my vision. Those severe bouts of vomiting, blindness and despair, when I will weep and beg for her to make it stop. Migraines, along with the memory of Mum, rule my life. When I'm not in pain, I live with the ghost of it, much as I do with her. I think about the lost hours when all I can do is go to bed. It's why I could talk convincingly to Gaynor.

It's a good job I'm trusted by the people I am going to need to lie to. That I've banked a solid ten years' worth of good behaviour with my psychiatrist too because, along with the employment agency, I'm about to cash it in. Not that I think I'm going to need to fend the fuckers off for long, the image I have of Toni's dead body is already blurring at the edges like an old photograph. I'm sure, in a few days, I'll have shaken it off completely. But not the violence. It was the violence that excited me. Awful to admit and I know it will alarm you, but the excitement when she fell and cracked her head open on that coffee table – lit me up inside. I haven't quite got the vocabulary; all I can say is that it sparked something in my brain once the initial shock subsided. I've never experienced a kick like it, not since I stabbed my sister with a fork when I was a kid, or when I attacked that geezer in the pub when I was eighteen. Triggers, Julia used to call them. I think Toni's death is another trigger, and because of it, I could be dangerous.

I brush my teeth and run the shower, adjusting the temperature dial until it's almost too hot to hold my hand beneath the spray. I lather up my sponge, wash my neck and torso, down my thighs, the near-scorching water cascading over my head. Finished, I switch off the shower and get out, towel myself dry. The mirror above the basin has steamed over but rather than wiping it and risking smears, I prise open the small sash window of frosted glass, feel a cold tongue of wind lick my damp nakedness. When the condensation clears, I look at myself again. I am different. The excitement of Friday night has done something, I can see it in my eyes. I gulp back sudden anxiety. If it's this obvious to me, is it going to be obvious to others?

I pick a pimple on my forehead. Evidence of my bad diet and lack of fresh air. I notice a tiny fleck of something on the mirror and rub it clean with the towel. Spend the next few minutes adjusting it so it hangs straight and square again. I can't stand disorder of any kind. It's why I don't cook, choosing to exist on a diet of microwave meals and fast food. I know it's bad but I refuse to spend all day scrubbing pans and come home to more. I grab a portion of my midriff, squeeze it between forefinger and thumb. I'm going to have to do something about this. Perhaps I'll have a walk later; after the sleep I had, the most refreshing I can remember, I've bags of energy today. I'll nip over to Dino's, grab a bite to eat, then have a yomp along the seafront. Nice day for it, I lift the blind to check what the weather is doing, then shut the window.

I amble back to my bedroom to dress in a carefully ironed shirt I take from my wardrobe and the jeans I wore yesterday. I'm grateful my father is off the scene after what happened with Toni. I couldn't cope with his interference; I need time and space to sort my head out. Jacob Mackenzie, Mac for short – the unwieldy image I carry of him bounces into view and I try to boot it away but fail. Last I heard he was working the oil rigs in Aberdeen and it suits me fine. This house of his is the only place I can be myself. Only here am I safe from prying eyes and the eternal questions of: 'How are you?' 'Are you taking your meds?' 'Have you had any angry episodes you want to talk about?' You wouldn't believe the scrutiny I get from psychologists, psychiatrists and the clinical team who run the group psychotherapy sessions I'm forced to attend each month.

As well as work, I've cried off my group session too. How could I go to that tomorrow and pretend everything's normal? The cunning bastards would've seen straight through me. It took all my trickery avoiding Marvin on the phone, leaving my excuse with the woman on reception for her to pass on. You'd know what I mean about Marvin if you met him. He's a ninja in the world of psychiatry and has this uncanny knack of digging down to the guilty core of me to wheedle out the truth. No, I'm not robust enough to fend any of that lot off yet, for now, I just want to be left alone. You wouldn't believe the way they pick away at you, I've had it all my life, there is little of the real me left.

I pull on a sweater, then my gloves and return to the bathroom. I open the cabinet and fumble for my bottle of serotonin reuptake inhibitors, or, as I like to call them, the little yellow fuckers. Because they are fuckers, they've been fucking me up for years, blunting the spark and enthusiasm I once had for living. They weren't ever going to cure me and don't fully eliminate the chronic disorder I'm supposed to suffer from. All they do is lessen the intensity of my hallucinations and delusions, mute my aggressive tendencies and volatility. In essence, they stop me from feeling. I'm not stupid, I've always understood how they reduce me, but terrified of being carted off to the loony bin again keeps me swallowing them. But it's always a battle. A fight between the man I want to be and the man they want me to be, to keep you lot safe.

I tip the prescribed dose into my palm and stare at them. Take them or not? I missed a whole day Friday and again yesterday. I've never done that before; I've never so much as missed a single dose when I think about it. I wonder if this could have something to do with the great night's sleep I had and why I'm feeling energised this morning? Would the effects of missing them show this soon? It is possible.

I return the tablets to the bottle, twist the lid back on. I want to see how I go. Risky? Marvin would say so. But I've had enough of starting and ending my days with pills gulped from my palm. Waking queasy and removed, requiring another load to feel better again. I think of Friday night with Toni. How close I came to kissing her, touching her, maybe more, if she hadn't freaked out. Even to feel like doing it with a woman is amazing because as I said at the time, nothing down there has worked since I've been under Marvin Crow's jurisdiction.

So, what do I want? To be stuck living this nothing life – the life I've been living since I was shoved into adult psychiatric care? Or, do I stop taking the antipsychotic drugs and the stuff in the other bottles too? The pretty pink ones. The tempting little green ones. I lift them from the shelf, rattle them against my ear as if goading them into persuading me to swallow them.

But, of course, they don't.

<h1 style="text-align:center">TWELVE</h1>

Back in the hot and noisy kitchen after her weekend off, heat prickled the back of Angela's neck, down between her shoulder blades. The paracetamol she took before starting her shift had barely taken the edge off her period pains. Uncomfortable in her chef whites, she loosened her apron and cast around for someone to lift the heavy pan of pilau rice from the oven. Fearful of reprisals, she never usually asked for help from her male colleagues but she was desperate today. The handicap of her bandaged finger aside, sometimes the sheer physical strength this job required was beyond her.

As tired as if she'd completed a double shift even though it was only ten in the morning, she yawned and slid a giant frying pan onto the flames, poured in oil and proceeded to slice in mushrooms. The hot fat stinging her wrists. She slept badly again last night. Waking intermittently to listen to the strange noises of her temporary home. Whenever she did drift off, it was only to slip back into the same dream about Robert. A dream that exhausted her, so that when the alarm went off, she knew she would be straggling it behind her all day.

Angela returned from the stores wheeling a trolley piled with bread, to discover Tyrone had finished slicing the smoked salmon. Obviously not to be trusted with sharp knives and expensive produce, she set about topping up the garnish trays. A job, considering her elephant finger, she managed well. This was one of the few tasks Angela enjoyed. The intricate slicing of tomato skins to produce an unbroken piece to coil into roses and the incisions into the rinds of lemons to make little baskets. It appealed to her artistic nature. *Pretty.* She smiled, holding one up to admire before setting it down on the tray.

Enjoying herself too much, she was only dimly aware of the usual chorus of, 'Yes, Chef. No problem, Chef,' as her superior patrolled her periphery. Everyone wanted to be on the right side of Chef.

'I've told you before, get a fuckin' move on.' His voice gave her a start. 'What is it with you? Are you deaf as well as stupid?'

'No, Chef. I'm going as fast as I can.' She surprised herself by retaliating. 'But I'm finding it a bit of a struggle with this.' And she shot out her bound-up forefinger.

Pleased she'd stumped him, she listened to him grunt then give an awkward cough. 'Yes, well, just get on with it, will you? Chop-chop.'

When Chef left for the day, she heaved a sigh of relief. Now she could focus on what was really bothering her: Toni's persistent silence. She wished she could have talked things through with Rhiannon over the weekend. It was why, after traipsing across town to Toni's flat yesterday, only for her to ignore the doorbell, she took a bus to Llandaff. Yes, she wanted a nose at their house but she also wanted to talk. Not that she did. She got as far as the end of their street, then bottled it. It was stupid, supposing they'd seen her? Even imagining this scenario made her squirm. She knew enough of life to never show you needed people. If you let them know your feelings, they only stamped all over them. If Rhiannon and Geraint wanted her to see their new place, they would invite her over, simple as.

'Hey, you lot, listen up.'

Angela raised her eyes and saw the restaurant manager pacing the service area.

'Have any of you lot seen Toni around the last couple of days?'

Unruffled, in a smart black suit, he projected his voice into the steam.

Toni? Did he say Toni? Angela tried to catch someone's eye, unsure if she'd heard correctly.

'Toni Perry. Anyone seen her?' Mr Suit again. 'Tasmanian. Works in the restaurant.'

Angela put down her paring knife and rushed forward. 'Was Toni supposed to be working today?' She pushed past Hakim who was guarding the hot lights.

A tight nod from Mr Suit. 'She was down for a late yesterday too, but she didn't show for that either.'

'I know 'er.' Hakim licked his lips with interest. 'Tasty bit of stuff, 'er.'

'Is she a friend of yours?' Mr Suit thrust his question past Hakim to Angela.

'Yes. She was supposed to come to me for the weekend but I did this.' She showed him her bandaged finger. 'By the time I got home from A&E, she'd gone. I've been trying to get hold of her but she's not answering her phone.'

'Not like her, is it?' Hakim, determined to join in with their conversation.

'No, she's never let me down before.'

'First time for everything.'

The restaurant manager gave Hakim a dark look, then

addressed Angela again: 'You say you've been trying to contact her?'

'That's right, since Friday night.'

'And you've heard nothing?'

'Look, Dom.' Hakim jostled between them. 'She's probably just fucked off travelling, ain't she?'

'Maybe.' Mr Suit twisted the point of a corkscrew against his palm. 'She did say she had plans to head off mid-November.'

'There you go then.' Hakim rubbed his bony hands together. The rasp of dry skin set Angela on edge. 'She's just fucked off early, that's all this is. I wouldn't worry about it, man. If you ask me, you can't rely on any fucker nowadays. We've got a job holding on to anyone in 'ere.'

'Yes, but it's a shame. She's my best waitress, the punters love her. I suppose she could've just forgotten to say she was leaving.' The restaurant manager tucked the corkscrew away in his jacket pocket. 'Well, what can you do?' He had snapped back to the job in hand, the whereabouts of Toni Perry forgotten. 'You got that order for five-o-four? I need it to go.'

'Oi, Tyrone,' Hakim shouted over to Angela's section leader. 'Whoever's on room service, tell 'em to get a shift on with that toasted cheese and ham, will ya?'

The restaurant manager retreated through the swing doors, back to his domain. Watching him go, Angela was left with the same knotty feeling in her stomach. Then something occurred to her.

'Who's that guy working the pot wash? The one built like a brick shit-house.' She used the language she knew Hakim could understand.

'No idea.'

'Yes, you do, Toni was arguing with him the other day. You had to go and break it up, don't you remember?'

'Got the hots for 'im, have you?'

'*No.*' A frustrated sigh. 'I just want to ask if he's seen her.'

'Why would he have seen 'er?'

'Because she was arguing with him.'

'*Huh*, that one was always gobbing off at someone.'

Undeterred, Angela followed him to the hot-mouthed salamander, watched as he turned down the flames. 'But you know who he is, right?'

'No idea, darlin', like I was saying to Dom, they come and go in here so quick, all of 'em foreign, all on zero-hours... Them's in the pot wash are worst of all. Don't last five minutes. None of 'em you'd recognise from one shift to the next.' A jerky laugh. 'Hardly surprising, is it? Who the hell else'd do a shite job like that? Nah, nuffin to do with me, darlin'.'

When Hakim sloped off, Angela rushed over to the wash-up area. Saw the slippery wet hands moving below the splash shield: hands that appeared quite detached from the anonymous bodies they belonged to.

'Where's your mate today?' She thrust her question into the boiling steam and clatter of crockery. 'He's really tall... Big.' She spread her arms wide to demonstrate. 'Wears one of those bandannas.'

'Not my mate. Only saw 'im one time. He left.' One of the kitchen porters eventually answered. She watched aghast, as he picked up a chicken thigh from a plate that had been returned from the restaurant and pushed it between his teeth.

'Oh, he's gone for the day, has he? D'you happen to know when he's next in?'

The man chewed on the drumstick and swallowed his mouthful before answering. 'No. You not listen.' He licked grease from his lips and reached for a pint glass of water, drank down half.

Angela watched the bob of his Adam's apple and waited for him to finish whatever he was going to say.

'That man you look for, he left hotel.'

'Yes, I know, you said. But when's he next in?'

'You not listen. He gone. *Gone.*' The man's tongue moved between the gaps in his teeth. 'He trouble... Big trouble. Summit wrong up here.' He jabbed a finger at his head.

THIRTEEN

The view from my bedroom window is of fields. Acres and acres under a pewter sky. They extend down as far as the cliffs out at Lavernock Point before dropping away into the sea. Networked with rivers and ditches where I'd go rabbiting as a boy, it's been this way for centuries. But I overheard Whatshisname in the shop saying things are all set to change. Soon it will be bulldozers and JCBs breaking the horizon and then a new housing estate with gravelled driveways and underfloor heating. I can imagine the types who will move in. Those who've probably already put their names down for the local schools in readiness for when their sprogs are born. Professional couples who have separate bank accounts and split everything from utility bills to the annual Tuscan holiday down the middle. Modern couples who run their marriages like small businesses, of which they own an equal share.

I wish I could find someone to share my life with and live like a grown-up. I'd love to be king of my castle. Shame I screwed things up with Toni, I was definitely in there. I have to be honest though, I didn't like the idea she could go through with having an abortion. If I'd been her boyfriend and she did that to me, I'd have been pretty pissed off too. If I did ever meet a special someone, I wouldn't want it to be like the couples I've been imagining. For a start, no woman of mine would go out to work, she'd stay at home and bring up our kids. I'd be the one bringing home the bacon. I don't care if this makes me sound old-fashioned, there's no way I could tolerate any woman of mine mixing with others... other men. If I ever get lucky, I'd make sure to keep her close; to keep her all for myself.

I can hear you mocking. *Me?* With my poorly paid jobs, my lack of security. Yeah, okay, but let me tell you something, it isn't as much of a pipedream as you think. For one, my grandparents are old, they're bound to pop their clogs soon, and I know they've no intention of leaving anything to my father, he's nothing to do with them, all he did was marry their daughter. With no other family, apart from my sister, Yana – who lives half a world away and hasn't bothered with them for years – their house in Roath is worth a packet and, along with whatever they've got stashed away after running that shop of theirs, I shouldn't have to wait too long to get my hands on what's mine.

My mobile summons me from its charger in the hall. It may sound as sunny as a canary but I know a ringing telephone seldom brings good news. I don't rush downstairs to answer it; I know who it is. It'll be Gaynor from the agency, checking to see if I'm going to be well enough to go to work tomorrow. She's been texting me all morning but I still haven't replied. The caller isn't Gaynor, it's my psychiatrist, Marvin. I stare at the screen, wait for it to go through to voicemail. I'm still not ready to speak to him and anyway, I'm not in the mood. And what is my mood? I'm not sure, I just know I'm sick of having to explain myself. To Marvin, to anyone. All he wants to do is rake over my childhood and the things that make me what I am. If I thought he was truly interested, I'd tell him what's wrong with me but he's not, so I don't. As far as Marvin's concerned, as long as I'm taking my meds and behaving myself, he couldn't give a damn. He doesn't care that the drugs he prescribes deplete me, that I can't enjoy anything in the same way anymore. These people working in the mental health service pretend they're my friends and say they're on my side but the truth is, no one's on my side. All they want to do is tick boxes and file me away. No, Marvin can wait, I'm sick of being pushed around. Toni said it, didn't she? Well, I'm going to listen to her. This time I'm going to sort things out myself. In my own way. On my own.

I want to tell you a bit about Marvin, starting with his name. It's something I asked him about once because it isn't a name that suits him. Say Marvin to someone, anyone, and they'd think: spirited, vigorous, a certain American pizzazz. But trust me, the name Marvin doesn't fit with his home counties accent or his private education and lace-up brogues. Or, come to think of it, his mouthful of crooked teeth. It turns out he was only named Marvin because he was conceived, then born, near an American airbase. I can't remember where in the UK he said this was but I remember joking with him about there being something his mother wasn't telling him. And that went down like a lead balloon, I can tell you. Marvin Crow doesn't do jokes; he doesn't do humour or irony either. He is Mr Literal. If I was to assess him the way he constantly assesses me – and I know a bit about these things – I'd guess he was somewhere on the autistic spectrum himself. Anyway, that's why his parents slapped the name Marvin on him. And I thought I had a shit start. Poor bastard.

The screen flashes its missed call notification. I try but I can't ignore it for long. Curiosity gets the better of me and I follow the automated voice along the corridor of maze-like instructions and find Marvin's voice at the end of it.

'I need you to ring me as soon as you get this,' is how it starts: all officious and peeved; it makes me bristle. 'Why didn't you call and speak to me? You shouldn't leave messages with Denise.' He drones on and on, I'm only half listening. 'You know the rules: if you can't make your session, then you must speak directly to me…' My mind wanders off, but not before identifying the edge in his voice. I blame the dog that's yapping in the background. The dog that attends every one of my sessions. Snoring and farting from his great fat cushion under Marvin's desk. He claims it's a Jack Russell and because I'm not much cop with dog breeds, I have to take him at his word. I know I might have said I wanted a puppy instead of a sister when I was a kid but that was just a phase I was going through. Now I've grown up, I don't get the craze for dog ownership, or ownership of any animal, come to that, and I certainly can't see why you'd want to share your home with it. The hairs for one. No, thank you very much. It can't be hygienic. Someone posted a cartoon on Twitter about people sleeping with their dogs on their bed. It was supposed to be funny but it horrified me. It can't be true, can it? God, am I the only person in the world who thinks that's disgusting?

I asked Marvin once – pinching my nose against the ripe, green fog being pumped over to me from the dog's side of the room – whether the NHS knew he brought the thing into work with him? His face was a picture. Honestly, you'd have thought I'd heckled his kids in a nativity play. Not that Marvin Crow is the type to have kids, if you catch my drift. 'Yes, I've cleared it with HQ,' he said, all curt and hurt in that camp way he does. 'Badger's a rescue. He's got separation issues. He can't be left on his own.'

'Haven't we all,' was my response and I remember enjoying myself at his expense. Marvin may be clever but he has to be the easiest person to wind up. And this dog of his, with its separation issues and bad arse, is just the kind of creature he would adopt. All needy and dependent. Marvin's the sort of person who needs to be needed. He thinks I need him but I don't.

'...I've got to talk to you, about this and, and, erm... I've some other news. It would be better for you to hear it from me first.' I tune into Marvin's voice again, that, raised to a shout to compete with the barking Badger, is difficult to ignore. 'Will you just shut up.' I assume the instruction was to his dog and not to some unassuming person who'd just wandered into his office. 'Just call me, okay? I need to make sure you're all right. And we need to reschedule you into another CBT session… Badger, will you stop it… *Erm*, I thought you could join Jay's group, he's got a free slot, fortnight on Monday… For heaven's sake, Badger… *Shh*, boy. *Shh*.'

I chuckle at his ineffectiveness so far as the dog's concerned because there aren't many who can run rings round Marvin. It's why I daren't speak to him yet, not until I've sorted my head out and got my story straight. As highly trained as he is, in examining, assessing and analysing, he'd be onto me in a heartbeat.

'Look—' It's difficult to decipher who Marvin is addressing, 'Just ring and reschedule that appointment, will you? Soon as. Don't make me have to chase you.'

When Marvin finishes speaking, I delete his message immediately. I always do this; I hate stuff clogging up my inbox. I then do the sensible thing and dash off a text to say I'm happy to join Jay's group and that I haven't time to speak to him today but I'll ring as soon as I have. I blame it on the pressures of work and, even though I'm not due back until tomorrow, I am on my way out. I've booked the car into the garage for its annual service and MOT. I thought I might as well, it's due soon and I was already taking it to have its rear light fixed.

FOURTEEN

'Mind if I take my break now?' Angela asked Tyrone but, without waiting for a reply, she scooted out into the corridor. Despite her need for a top-up of painkillers and some breakfast in the staff canteen, her need for answers about Toni and the missing kitchen porter was greater. She took the service lift up to the fifth floor, certain Anne-Marie would help her get to the bottom of it.

The detour to Human Resources ate into more than a quarter of her break time so, after knocking, it was without waiting to be invited, that she rushed inside the office that oozed lethargy with its muted wallpaper and lavender air freshener. Anne-Marie was on the phone and the conversation sounded way too leisurely. *Come on, hurry up.* Angela wrung her hands and jiggled from foot to foot as if in need of the lavatory. When the handset was eventually returned to its cradle, Anne-Marie motioned her to a couch then disappeared into another room and closed the door. She picked at a spray of tomato pips on her apron, eyes on the clock. She counted a full three minutes before her friend reappeared.

'What's up? You look washed out.' Anne-Marie peered at her through her spectacles.

'Period pains.' She dragged her mouth south.

'You taken anything? I've got paracetamol.' Mid-reach for her handbag, Angela stopped her.

'It's all right, I've got some. I'm here about Toni. To ask if you've heard anything from her?'

Anne-Marie looked blank.

'Toni Perry? She works in the restaurant.'

'Oh, yes. Tasmanian. Pretty girl. Heard from her, what d'you mean?'

'She's missed two shifts and she's not answering her mobile.'

'O-kay.' A quick frown. 'And Dominic sent you, did he?'

'No. He was asking if anyone's seen her, but he didn't seem concerned when no one had.'

'And you are?'

'Yes, I am. She was supposed to come to me on Friday. She was staying the weekend.'

'You had a weekend off?' Anne-Marie looked surprised.

'I know, a bloody miracle. But there was no Toni.' Angela held up her bandaged finger.

'Ouch! When did you do that?'

'Friday morning. I had to go to the hospital and I'd left my mobile in my locker...'

'So you couldn't let Toni know where you were,' Anne-Marie finished.

'I got in touch soon as I could but she's been ignoring me ever since. I even called round to her flat yesterday. I don't know if she was there or not, she didn't answer the bell.'

'*Oops.* She is pissed off with you.'

'Being pissed off with me is one thing but not turning up for work? She'd never do that; she needs the cash.'

'Wasn't she set to go off travelling again soon?'

Angela nodded. 'But she wouldn't just go. She'd have said goodbye and let you guys know first.'

The two young women fell into a reflective silence.

'I don't know if it's important,' Angela hesitated, 'but the last time I saw her, she was giving this kitchen porter a right rollicking... hell of a scene. *Well,*' she rolled her eyes, 'it was Toni who was making the scene.'

'Dear me, why was that?'

'No idea, but she was dead angry. With Hakim too. Going on about the kitchen porter taking the piss and threatening to go to HR to report him.'

'D'you know who this kitchen porter is?' Anne-Marie fiddled with the gold medallion around her neck.

A shake of her head. 'Never clapped eyes on him before. But he was pretty menacing. And not just because of his size, because he's big. But he's, oh, I don't know... weirdly quiet, in a dangerous sort of way.'

'What? Like all broody and mysterious? *Mm,* I like blokes like that.'

'Huh, you wouldn't like him, trust me. He put the shits up me.' Angela shivered.

'And you say Toni came to see us in HR?'

'It's what she said before she stormed off. Didn't you see her?'

'When was this?'

'Thursday afternoon.'

'Can't have. I had a dental appointment.'

'All right, well, maybe you could find out what it was about?'

'I haven't got access to that kind of info, Spike.'

'But you could ask Jasmine.'

'Why?'

'Because it's a bit of a coincidence. The two of them arguing and the next thing Toni disappears without a word, and then he disappears too.'

'He disappears?' Anne-Marie frowned again.

'Yes, and I went and asked them working the pot wash if they knew anything.'

'*And?*'

'Didn't get much. Didn't even get his name. The bloke I spoke to just said he was trouble and that he wasn't working at the hotel anymore. Not that he seemed to know why.' Angela paused, a thought occurring. 'But you'd know – HR would know, wouldn't you?'

'Know what?'

'His name for starters and why he's not working here anymore. You do all the hiring and firing.'

'Not me.'

'No, all right, not you, but HR does... Jasmine does. And you work for Jasmine.'

'I only do the admin, Spike.' Anne-Marie went to sit behind her desk. 'But leave it with me, I'll have a word, ask her to look into it.'

'And you'll let me know if you hear anything?' Angela was hopeful.

'Course, I will. But try not to worry, I'm sure Toni's fine.'

Her shift over, Angela was on her way to meet Rhiannon.

WE R GOING OUT.

The text: assertive, demanding; was delivered along with news that Geraint would come and look at the boiler as soon as he could.

ME AND GIRLS FROM THE SALON. U GOTTA
COME. NOT SEEN U IN AGES. GOT BIG
NEWS.

There wasn't time to nip back to Roath to change and it made Angela feel sorry for herself when she imagined the others with their high hemlines and lipstick. So, she did all she could, she unclipped her hair and brushed it out, fanning it over her shoulders, down her back. Who else had hair like her? She admired its glassy sheen, its red and orange tones, grateful she'd washed it before heading to work that morning. What they'd give to have hair like hers. Close to the mirror, dissolving into her image, Angela failed to notice Anne-Marie standing by the hand dryers.

'Going anywhere nice?' Her friend's County Sligo accent slid between Angela's vanity.

'I was only...' her excuses dying in her mouth... Admiring herself, loving herself. What was she doing? 'Sorry,' she said and blushed.

'What for?' The question seemed genuine but Angela didn't trust it.

'For being...' She shrugged, there was nothing to say; she'd been caught out and now she was ashamed.

'Don't be daft. You've beautiful hair. And if you've got it, flaunt it.' Anne-Marie raked her inky fingers through her dull, tan curls. 'God knows, I would.'

'I'm meeting up with Rhiannon and some of her mates tonight. She's got news she wants to share.'

'Well, have fun.' Anne-Marie stood aside to let her pass.

'I'll try.' She raised a sheepish hand and left the building, clean forgetting to ask if HR had any news on Toni's whereabouts.

Daylight had been exchanged for a textured orange miasma, as street lamps quivered against the encroachment of night. The wind had dropped and a cold, syrupy fog now shrouded the city. It blanketed the buildings and the rain-blackened boughs of trees like a living, breathing thing. To Angela, this time of year meant rarely seeing the sky. It was invariably dark when she journeyed into work and dark when she resurfaced from the underground kitchen. She hurried along, zipping her parka to the throat and pulling up her hood. She felt the treacherous slide of pavement beneath her plastic soles as ambiguous shapes loomed and faded around her. She was in unfamiliar territory and it made her nervous. Meeting Rhiannon in Cardiff Bay meant a different route and the disjointed rise and fall of voices merging with the blare of horns and growl of traffic in this part of town alarmed her.

When she eventually joined a queue at a bus stop, part of her wished she was just heading home. Keen as she was to be catching up with her best friend, she was too exhausted for socialising. Her period pains may have eased but her finger ached as much as her joints after being on her feet all day. The city's damp had seeped through the seams of her cheap shoes and, stamping her feet to get warm, she looked up at the electronic screen and saw the bus she needed was seven minutes away. Deciding to telephone her parents to kill time, her father answered on the third ring.

'Hello, Dad.' Angela infused her voice with a chirpiness she didn't feel. 'How's things?'

'Hello.' His lacklustre reply. She heard the disappointment in his voice: the disappointment she wasn't Robert, could never be Robert. It was the same whenever he picked up the phone. 'I'll just fetch your mother.'

'No, wait—' She would have liked to talk to him but he'd already gone.

'Angela.' Her mother's vinegary greeting. 'You said you'd ring on Saturday.'

'I was working.' The lie hardened in her mouth.

'But you had the weekend off?'

'I had to work in the end.' Angela lied for a second time. Her mother had always claimed she was sly and secretive, she might as well live up to the part.

'What kind of establishment gives you time off, then takes it away again? Honestly, Angela, isn't it about time you got yourself a proper job?'

'It is a proper job.'

'What was that? Don't mumble, girl. Oh, never mind about that, your father and I want to know when you're coming home?'

'I'm not. I've got too much on.'

'Well, that's charming.'

'I can't help if I'm busy.'

'Then why bother calling?'

Angela couldn't answer. Why had she called, why did she ever call? Hoping things had changed and her parents had decided they loved her after all?

'Where's your compassion? Especially now you're not coming home for Christmas.' The moaning was unrelenting. 'You know we're stuck out here. We don't see anyone from one week to the next.'

This was what she wanted, wasn't it? For them to miss her, to notice the space she'd left behind in the way they noticed the space Robert had left behind.

'It would help your father if he could see you.' Her mother sliced between the hurt. 'He's not been good these past few months.'

Angela read between the lines: *Not been good* meant *He's been hitting the bottle again.* Because her father, a man who always liked a drink, took to the booze with a fervour she'd never seen him apply to anything after Robert died.

'You're all we've got.' Her mother continued to hack away with the family knife. 'It's not unreasonable to want to see our daughter now and again.'

'I'm sorry, Mum.' Angela couldn't stop the tears. 'But I can't do this now.' They were pretending, the pair of them. They still hadn't forgiven her for what happened to her brother. And why should they? She couldn't forgive herself.

Her mother was onto her. 'What've you got to snivel about? Pull yourself together, you silly girl, you don't have the...'

The bus had arrived. Its turquoise sides sent up a spray of rainwater and a flurry of leaves as it pulled into the kerb. Whatever had remained of her mother's irritation, Angela refused to listen to it and hung up. She dropped her mobile into her coat pocket and felt around for her purse in the ever-growing throat of her bag. Everything was a struggle with her oversized, bandaged finger. It was there, she persisted, shuffling blindly through the other items spinning around in its depths. Finding it, at last, she boarded the bus.

'Cardiff Bay. Contactless, please.' She placed her debit card on the card reader, waited for it to flash green.

'Take your ticket,' the driver reminded her.

Angela saw the lower deck was full, so she clambered up the metal stairwell hoping for a seat at the top. She'd always liked riding the top of buses, seeing the world from up high always made journeys more pleasurable. Not that there would be much of a view tonight, the world beyond the condensation-dripping windows melted into opaque obscurity.

She saw the top of his crown first. Bony and knuckle-hard.

Then his broad, sloping shoulders and the substantial body they were attached to. A body that looked too big for the seat.

Bloody hell, it's him.

The sight of the kitchen porter made her heart beat faster and, sweeping past, breathing back his oddly floral smell, the buckles of her bag slid over the nylon-shiny sleeve of his jacket. She made a beeline for a seat at the rear and sat beside an old man in a brown raincoat. Amidst wet umbrellas and the smell of damp shoe leather, she kept the kitchen porter she'd seen Toni arguing with, in her eyeline. It was a quarter to six already and her stomach growled from beneath her layers like an angry bear. She wished she'd eaten the biscuits she'd been offered with her mug of tea at break time. Along with the state of her finances, her body shape was another full-time preoccupation. Something that wasn't helped by the bombardment of posters depicting impossibly sleek female models on the sides of passing buses and department store windows.

Angela kept one eye on the kitchen porter and, careful not to bang her finger, dug out her mobile to scroll through the sunny lives of others. Usually, she steered clear of social media sites, the perception that everyone else was leading such glamorous, successful lives, only made her feel worse about her own. But she'd left her novel at home, so it would have to do. The bus, wheezing and juddering like an old age pensioner, emptied and refilled itself with each stop. Unfamiliar with this route, she had no idea how long the journey took, or if she needed to change buses. She looked around for someone to ask. But who? It wasn't safe to talk to strangers.

Bored with her Instagram feed she stared at the back of the kitchen porter's neck and shuddered. Whoever he was, something was frightening about him, she decided it the moment she clocked the look he gave Toni. She hoped she was wrong about him but the longer time went on with no news from her friend, the deeper her suspicion of him.

When he lunged forward in his seat to press a finger to the bell, she snapped out of her deliberations and returned her mobile to her pocket. Felt the grind of the engine vibrate through the floor as the bus slowed to a stop. When he tugged on a beanie hat and got to his feet, Angela rose from her seat too. Curiosity, like a fish hook through her gut. *Follow him. Follow him.* And without fully realising why, she found herself out on an unknown street in an unfamiliar part of town. A voice in her head telling her to see where he went... Find out where he lived, that it might prove useful.

Over six feet tall, the man looked heavier and more dangerous now he was upright and it was a relief to see she wasn't alone. That others were spilling off the bus too. Except these others were taking too long. The kitchen porter had lumbered off by the time they'd opened their umbrellas, tied scarves and put on gloves in preparation for their walks home. And Angela, reluctant to lose him, broke away from the crowd to go after him.

The cold gnawed through her clothes. It really was a filthy night. Without fully knowing why, she followed him around one corner, then another, fearful her clattering heels against the pavement would alert him to her but he didn't once turn around. Breathing hard, she shadowed him over a deserted road at a zebra crossing, the thick fog silting her lungs. Off around another corner, close enough to see the white puff of his breath, she trailed him down dark, cobbled passageways and along eerily deserted residential streets lined with parked cars.

On high alert, she squinted through the cloying gloom. Visibility was poor, the only illumination was from the sickly blush of street lamps and his big, dark shape was reduced to a smudge in the murkiness. What the hell did she think she was doing? This was madness. Out on her own after dark, following an unknown man in this strange part of town. She should have stayed on the bus and met up with Rhiannon as planned. Or better still, gone home. *What was driving her?* The idea Toni was in trouble and this man had something to do with it, she answered herself.

The dystopian setting unnerved Angela. As she walked, she scanned the abandoned streets yawning off into obscurity, the rows of dark-fronted houses with their curtains closed to the world. She had no idea where she was but she could tell the sea was out there somewhere, she could sense the steady pulse of the tide. A lone herring gull floated overhead. Ghost-like, she listened to the heavy flap of wings as it rode the equally heavy air. A shiver of unease rippled through her. It seemed as if she and this kitchen porter were the only two people in the world. There was something sharp in her shoe and, stopping to shake it free, she inadvertently knocked her damaged finger. She gasped in pain and needed a minute to recover. When at last she looked up, she couldn't see him.

Where has he gone? Where has he gone?

Angela's mobile beeped into the muffled dampness. Rhiannon's name flashed up on the screen. 'Not now,' she told it and, panicking it could give her away, she switched her phone off.

There.

A bulky silhouette lit by the headlamps of a passing taxi. It had to be him; it was the only other human shape around.

When he turned in her direction, her brain shrank in fear. For one heart-stopping moment, she feared he might be onto her but he ducked down and disappeared into a shadowy shop doorway. The sign above it, a cold eye, beckoning from the gloom. Relieved, she trotted over, leant against the wet brick exterior to wait for him to re-emerge. Alone in the dripping shadows, she listened to herself breathing and pinched her cheeks that were numbed by the cold. She repeatedly checked her watch. Seven thirty. She couldn't believe how late it was. *Hurry up*, she willed what she supposed to be his shape through the mottled glass of the shop door.

Angela stamped her feet and thumped her arms against her sides to warm up. The frantic barking of a dog echoed around her, and a car slithered past. The hiss of tyres on wet asphalt. She monitored the progress of a young mother pushing a buggy along the pavement. Hunched against the cold, the woman eyed her warily before dipping inside the shop to the accompanying tinkle of the bell. Seconds later, another tinkle and the kitchen porter shambled back outside. A carrier bag swinging against his thigh.

Off again. The floral soapy smell she first identified on the bus drifted towards her in his wake. He couldn't be going much further; they must have walked miles. A van skimmed past. The bounce of headlamps briefly lit the way ahead. Then all went quiet and still again: a forgotten land of fog. The perspective lengthened to the entire street, as he led her on past endless doorways shrouded in mist. Close up, some houses were shabby and weathered with flaking paintwork. Broken down heaps of metal that had once been cars, squeezed into rectangles of scanty grass that grew between bay windows and kerb. Other houses looked well maintained, with white-glossed window frames and stained-glass-panelled front doors she imagined opening onto plush hallways.

Where did he live, then? He appeared to be heading for the house at the end of the terrace. The one with a street lamp squatting out front. Its tangerine heart blinking off-on, off-on. Pulse steady. A bin, blown sideways by the wind, its stinking contents spilt on the pavement. Angela watched him step around it, seemingly oblivious, before pushing through a garden gate and moving up the path. She hid in the dimness on the opposite side, watched him take a key from his jacket pocket, slide it into the lock and disappear inside. Only when she saw a light go on in the hall, then a ground-floor room, did she risk crossing the road to peer inside.

She watched him moving around its lighted innards then looked for the house number on the brick façade and hunted the low garden wall for the street name. Finding both, she pulled an old receipt and a pen from her bag and, careful not to knock her finger again, scribbled them down. Now all she had to do was find her way home. But with no idea where she was and no one to ask, she flung a final, desperate look at the house and saw, to her dismay, what she believed to be a blonde-haired woman standing with her back to the downstairs window.

'Toni?' she yelped, her hand flying to her mouth. 'Is that you?'

FIFTEEN

The car is at the garage, so I had to catch the bus home from town tonight. What a drag that was. I hate public transport. Not only does it cost a packet, you've got to share the little space you have with other people. And I'm not good at sharing space. I'm not good with people. Full stop.

It's a foul night and I'm feeling the cold more than ever. I pull my beanie hat down over my ears, zip my bomber jacket to the chin, then tug the elasticated cuffs down to meet my gloves but they soon rise up again. This is the kind of dampness that finds its way into your bones. What I need is a decent overcoat but I can't afford one; my wages barely cover my weekly food bill and petrol, there's nothing left for luxuries. I'm not a fan of the winter dark and with a sea fog thick enough to draw your name in, night has dropped down over the neighbourhood earlier than ever.

I've got that uneasy feeling again. Like I'm being followed. I spin round, whipping off my earphones and severing the melancholy soulfulness of Nina Simone. But no one's there, the street is empty, there's barely a car. I've been having this creeping sense I'm being watched for a while now. It could just be my paranoia – the guilt I have about not going to the cops about Toni is weighing heavy on me. Not heavy enough to act on it but weighing on me all the same. My problem is that I think everyone knows what I've done and that it's only a matter of time before they find her body and link her death to me.

The street where I grew up runs parallel to the shore and everywhere is the sense of the sea. I sniff its briny breath through the dark, feel the bracing thrust of the tide. Something I know from experience can come in quicker than galloping horses. It's strange, I've never known this part of town to be this deserted. I'd been expecting fireworks in the back gardens along here; they usually always kick off a week before bonfire night. But nothing is going on, everywhere is spooky and still. It must be the weather that's keeping people inside, it's cold enough to freeze your balls out here.

I lengthen my strides in an attempt to warm up. I have to say I'm finding the exercise enjoyable. It's great to stretch my legs and do something that gets my heart pumping for a change. The jobs I do are physical but this is different – this is doing me good. It's got me thinking, even when I get the car back, I might leave it at home and do this more often. I'm tempted to break into a run but don't, I'm not fit enough yet and I wouldn't last long, not with air quality as poor as this. But if I build up to it, get some regular walking in first, I don't see why I couldn't take up running again.

It's not my imagination, I've definitely had more energy the past few days. I put it down to being off the meds because I've been sleeping better too. If only I could stay off them permanently by keeping Marvin at bay, I love feeling like this. I love *feeling*. Why do the likes of him get to tell me what to do? It's not fair. Isn't it about time I had my life back? But I'm living some crazy fantasy if I think I can fend him off forever. The man's like a dog with a bone, he won't let up until he's got me in front of him to assess and monitor, ticked his bloody boxes so he can file me away. If I could only explain my state of mind to him, say that since missing Friday's dose and deliberately going without it over the weekend and again today, the future is somewhere I can actually imagine being part of.

But who am I kidding? He'd break my balls if he got wind of any of this. Scared that without what he calls the balancing effect of mood regulators and antipsychotic pills, I'll slip back into my volatile and dangerous self.

I cross the road, the measly items purchased from the corner shop, swinging in the carrier bag. I pass alongside the cemetery where Mum's buried, glance through the wrought-iron railings into the darkened land of the dead. I know the exact feel of that headstone. Cold and firm. The letters in the inscription. Just your full name, the name you were called before you were married: Kristina Wytrazek. The date you were born, the date you died underneath. Nothing more. No reflection on your life. No clues. Not even your married name. There was a rosebush once but it's died since. All the listing tombstones in this cemetery used to belong to St Mary's Church until the place burnt down, killing the vicar of the parish and four of his God-botherers. I stopped going to church and Sunday school when Mum died. I didn't see the point. She was the centre of my world and no God was going to replace her.

I look up in time to see next door's tabby cat tear along the wall, tail quivering in the street light. Now there's a creature with hang-ups, just like I've got hang-ups; I've seen them taking shape behind its jade-green eyes. It's Mrs Thomas's cat. Nothing to do with her husband. How do I know this? I've heard him shouting at it, rounding on it in the garden, making it hiss and spit. Careful, always out of earshot of Mrs Thomas. Like all evildoers, Mr Thomas takes great care to hide his private face from the public world. Except Mr Thomas goes one better because even his wife doesn't know what he's capable of. It's an interesting concept, don't you think? To have the brains to hide your true self from your nearest and dearest. It's what I'm going to have to do if I'm to keep Marvin off my back. Not that Marvin could be called my nearest and dearest, but even so. I'm going to have to be as cunning as hell with him, I'm going to have to pretend I'm still as compliant and obliging as the drugs made sure I was.

Our house – my father's house – is an end of terrace encased in a high privet hedge. Beyond its south-facing wall is a lane that's busy with horses and farm machinery in the day but quiet at night. My parents bought it just after they got married almost thirty years ago. I learnt to walk in that house. Bumping into things I'd stared into shape from my cradle. Not that I can remember that, but I do have an early memory of the pub car park out the back: the tarmacked rectangle that belongs to the Cat and Fiddle, where I learnt to ride my bike.

I can see Mum now, walking backwards and me shouting, crying, for her not to let go of me. Not understanding this was what she needed to do. Farther and farther she goes. As the sun's yellow eye peered down, lighting up her hair like a flame. I see her lift a shielding arm to her brow, blinking, her face half-hidden by shadow. Then I am pedalling. My cries of, 'Help me. Help me,' exchanged for, 'Look, I'm doing it!' And Mum claps her hands and moves towards me again, laughing.

Babcia's always telling me to be careful of my memories. Says we can all be fooled by photographs and that our memory is unreliable. I don't understand what she means, all I know is the only time I've ever been truly happy was for the first six and a half years of my life.

Key at the ready, I negotiate the wobble of path that's only just about identifiable through the grass and flowers that have gone to seed. I've never bothered much with the garden, keeping the inside tidy is all I'm interested in. The garden can do as it likes. We blitzed it once, the old man and me, when he was home between contracts. Set about it with spades and shears, but it soon grew back and took hold again. You can't keep out the wild, nature always wins – it's like trying to hold back the tide. I eye the straggly loganberry bushes the garden produces with suspicion. Notice the miserable handful of raspberry-coloured fruit no one bothered to harvest have rotted into mildewed clusters.

I let myself inside the house as usual. Dump my shopping on the draining board and turn on the light to find a sheepskin jacket hanging over the back of a kitchen chair.

I know this jacket.

I know what it means and my heart sinks.

I stare at it. Imagine the body inside it. Empty clothes have always troubled me. I touch it, feel its weight, which is considerable. Wearing it must be like lugging a whole sheep around.

It shouldn't be here, coats don't live here, they belong on the pegs in the hall. I move to lift it and the chair topples backwards. Its crash summons my unwanted house guest from the downstairs toilet.

Muscular and threatening-looking, my father fills the doorway offering no explanation. He is big, but I'm bigger. Dressed in shirt and jeans, I can see he's let his hair grow.

What does he look like?

He looks like a girl, his blond curls are like Robert Plant's in his heyday, except he's not half as pretty. Part of me wants to laugh but laughing is the last thing I feel like. And anyway, I think, remembering in time – I'd better not show him I can laugh again.

SIXTEEN

Down in the hotel locker rooms, her long shift finally over, Angela changed out of her grubby whites and tied her hair off her face. It seemed that her job amounted to standing up for a living, for she stood long after her feet throbbed and her calves ached, and the ache was still there the next morning when the standing began all over again. No one should have to stand hour after hour in intense heat, breathing fuggy air for eight, nine-hour stretches. It was why, when her shifts ended, she dashed out of the building as soon as she could, to gulp down the air. Albeit air polluted in other ways, it was still fresher than the kitchen.

She stared at her reflection in the mirror above the hand basins and, thinking a little make-up might improve her pallor, applied some blusher. Sucking in her cheekbones and sweeping the soft-bristled brush up and over them the way Toni showed her.

Toni.

Angela pressed a hand to her stomach, to the knot of apprehension she was carrying around. She'd been in danger of letting her imagination run away with her when she saw that blond-haired person in the window of the kitchen porter's home. At once convinced it was Toni until she saw that it was a man. Not that the realisation stopped her from churning the scenario in her mind all night. It was why she'd decided – because Toni still wasn't answering her phone and had failed to show up for work a third day running – to visit her flat again after work today. It might have been that she was too ill to answer the intercom on Sunday, was still too ill to answer her phone. Perhaps she'd already left for Spain. How did Angela know? Anything could have happened. She didn't care if Toni told her off for fussing. For her own sanity, she needed to make sure her friend was all right.

It was a surprise to come up to street level and find it dark. Not that Cardiff's streets were ever truly dark, the artificial blush that sheathed the city saw to that. It was after responding to yet another text from Rhiannon, who was still angry with her for standing her up last night, she zipped her parka against the cold and set off along St Mary's Street at a brisk pace for a bus to take her to Danestown.

'Hey, Spike!'

Angela spun on her heels.

'Jeez, you walk quick.' Anne-Marie, gasping for breath. 'I had to run to catch up with you.'

'Sorry, I was miles away.'

'Have you...' Her friend's hesitation was muffled by a yellow scarf. 'Have you heard the news?'

'No, what news?'

'Right, okay.' Anne-Marie linked an arm through hers. 'You got time for a drink? There's something I need to tell you.'

Angela darted her a look of concern. 'Is it about Toni? Have you heard from her? Is she okay?'

'Let's find a pub first.'

'Why? What did she say?' Angela held Anne-Marie's gaze. 'Can't you just tell me?'

'I'd rather we had a drink in front of us.'

Frowning in puzzlement, she allowed herself to be steered towards the shops and bars.

'Has Toni contacted the hotel to say she's in Spain? Did she give you a message to pass on to me? It's a shame if she's gone without bothering to say goodbye...' Angela mumbled, more to herself. 'I don't care, as long as she's safe.'

'Come on, let's get out of the cold.' Anne-Marie pushed through a set of dark oak doors, and Angela followed her into the busy bar. 'You sit there.' She allowed herself to be shepherded to a table in a relatively quiet bay window. 'What would you like? I'll get a round in.' Anne-Marie removed her coat and unwrapped her scarf, dropping both into a leather bucket chair.

'I don't know... A vodka and tonic?' Stumped, she held her hands up in front of her face. Her big, bandaged finger looked almost comical.

'I'll get you a Guinness.'

Angela plonked down on a chair without taking her parka off. She didn't intend to stay long. She watched Anne-Marie's tall figure and head of hair that was as curly as the coat of her grandfather's Bedlington terrier, disappear into the crowd of drinkers. Looking around at the leather-clad bar and pendant lighting, she saw the place was strung with plastic skulls and spiders' webs for Halloween. She tilted her head and tracked their journey from beam to beam, above the chatter of those who'd dropped by for a swift pint before the commute home.

Angela liked pubs. Liked people-watching. Especially these

self-assured office types. They were a different species from the people she worked with at the hotel. This lot had sharp suits and hair that was as shiny as their buffed leather uppers. They had briefcases poised at their ankles like faithful dogs. They had money. She fished from the conversations she was close enough to join in with, had anyone noticed her, but reluctant to catch anyone's eye, she dropped her gaze to the tabletop and twiddled an earring, small as a freckle, under her hair.

'Lord, it's busy for a Tuesday.' Anne-Marie was back from the bar with two pints of her country's famous dark stout. Set them down on the table with a gratifying clunk.

'Thanks. I've never tried this before.' Angela eyed the Guinness with suspicion. 'Right, well, I've got a drink in front of me now, so can you please tell me what you've got to say?'

'O'Neill's.' Anne-Marie swallowed a mouthful, then smacked her lips together. 'It's about the only place in town you can get this.'

'*Anne-Marie?*'

'Yes?'

'Tell me what's going on. What did Toni say?' Angela stared at the gold disc her friend always wore around her neck.

'I will. Just have a couple of swigs of that first.'

SEVENTEEN

I'm on my way to catch the bus to work but I'm hungry, it's been hours since I last ate. Dino's Diner is open. I tap the pockets of my jeans, fish out a couple of tenners and a handful of change and decide I've enough. Grateful to leave the snoopy bastards who are no doubt watching me from behind their nets on ground-floor windows, I push open the café door and am greeted by a warm blast of fried food. The people huddled at tables automatically lift then drop their heads. I recognise a few of them, not that anyone acknowledges me. Elbows glued to the wipe-clean tablecloths, they quickly return to their meals and their conversations about me because I'm sure that everyone knows the unforgivable thing I've done. Perspiration breaks out along my top lip. I am dabbing it with my guilty fist when Dino slides out from behind his counter, wearing his greased-back hair and beady stare. His pen and pad at the ready.

'Give us a sec.' I opt for one of the relatively private booths.

I know what I'm having, Dino knows it too; I have the same each time I come in here. But this is a game I like to play, pretending to study the laminated menu with its photos of food and everything with chips. The pictures show exactly what you get. No one could get arsy about trade descriptions here. One day I'll surprise him, I think, as I wipe away condensation and stare out through the window at the disappearing world. But not tonight.

I may not be in any great hurry to get to work but I sure am hungry, so the game doesn't last long. A nod to Dino and he moseys over to take my order for burger and chips. Why not? After the hike I've just had, I reckon I deserve it. Waiting for my meal to arrive, I check my phone and see I've another text from Marvin. I've been dodging his messages all day and doubt I'm going to be able to fend him off much longer.

When my burger and chips arrive, I remove my gloves to eat and tuck my phone, along with all thoughts of Marvin, away. But lifting the first forkful of chips to my mouth the café door opens and lets in a chilly gust that settles around my ankles. It's Rita Morgan from three doors down. A single mum to a nine-year-old boy I can't remember the name of. But I can remember her getting pregnant, the mystery of who the father was, or where he was, has been rattling around the neighbourhood ever since. Poor Rita. It's not fair for women to be left to bring up children on their own. The only man to visit her at home nowadays is the guy who reads the electricity meter, and even he doesn't need to go inside. There was a dog once, her only company, apart from the boy. Bastard thing used to bark all night; it kept half the street awake. It kept me awake. Until I went and silenced it.

Rita and her kid sit in their anoraks at a table near the counter. She passes him a menu and points at what she wants him to have. Dino is silent, his oil-dark hair shiny under the fluorescent light.

'But I don't want a milkshake. I hate milkshake.' The boy's grizzling generates a swell of amusement from Dino's customers. 'I want a knickerbocker glory. You said I could have one. Why can't I have one?'

Rita's embarrassment spreads from ear to ear as she plucks her purse from her cracked plastic handbag.

'I don't think we've got enough, *cariad*,' I hear her whisper as her fingers, raw from household chores, scratch around inside her purse for coins. 'Please don't make a fuss.'

'But you promised, Mammy. You promised.' His whiny demands bounce around the unventilated space. 'I want one. I want one.'

I watch Dino. He's staring at Rita from his clean-shaven deadpan face. Let her go eat somewhere else – I read his thoughts – this woman who dresses like a jumble sale, she'll get no charity here. What does Dino care for her brat with his demands for this, that and the other? Her fault for getting up the duff with no man around. I interpret everything I need from his expression and it makes me hate him more than I already do.

'I'll have a knickerbocker glory, please.' Rita empties her purse onto the table, counts out the last of her change.

'Righty-o.' Dino nods and closes his palm over the money.

I return to my tea, now and again reaching for the gluey-topped ketchup container that's shaped like a tomato. See, out of the corner of my eye, the tall, fluted goblet of whipped cream, ice cream and fruit that's delivered to Rita's table. A thing so large and sickly-looking, it's a sure bet the kid will leave half of it.

I don't remember being given such indulgences when I was a child. As far as my memory serves me, I wasn't given much of anything after Mum died. I had to construct myself from whatever was to hand and make myself into a person that fitted the space my family, or what remained of my family, made for me. As a boy, I was done to, explained to... lied to, and I've been trying to fit in ever since.

Burger and chips finished, I'm up on my feet. Gloves in pocket, jacket zipped to the chin, I go to the counter to pay. I look at Rita who sits dumbly while her child digs a long-handled spoon delightedly in and out of his treat.

'I'll have one of them milky coffee things.' I'm unskilled in the language of coffee – coffee isn't something I drink, I can't bear it, not even the smell of it.

'A *latte*, you mean?' Dino furnishes me with the word with a defensive air. Straight as a soldier in his uniform of black shirt and trousers, it's a good job he's barricaded by tiers of confectionery and his ancient till, or I might be tempted to punch him. 'Regular or large?'

I glance at the chalkboard above the barista machine and do the sums.

'Large. And put it in one of them glass mug things. Oh, and a KitKat.' That noise in my head is back again, it's because I've stopped the pills. It used to work as a warning, it's doing the same now. But despite this, part of me welcomes it back like an old friend.

Dino nods and takes my money. He gives me twenty-pence change, which I drop into a pot on the counter that's raising money for a children's hospice.

I carry the coffee and chocolate bar to Rita's table, chin on neck, determined not to spill a drop.

'There,' I say, stooping low to the table. I'm pretty sure she likes coffee and that I've seen her drinking it in here. 'This is for you, Rita.' And without waiting for her response, I start shouting at the kid: 'As for you, do you have any idea how lucky you are to have a mother? A mother who puts you above herself, above everything?' So angry, I don't give the brat the chance to answer. 'I lost my mum when I was younger than you.' The kid stares up at me, astonished, his open mouth full of ice cream is churning like a washing machine. 'I miss her every single day.' I don't know what's got into me, I can't remember the last time I challenged anyone, let alone a stroppy little kid. 'What I'd give to have her back, just for one hour.' The buzzing intensifies and I look down at Rita's hand on mine. Feel her squeeze of sympathy and gratitude. 'Your mum's a good woman. The best.'

I want to say: *look at her, look at her greasy hair, her red-rimmed eyes, that tatty beige anorak she's never seen out of.*

'If I ever hear you speaking to her like that again, then you'll have me to answer to, d'you hear?'

Rita pulls back her hand and, feeling other eyes on me, I scurry to the door. Desperate to get out of there. But my getaway is blocked by my neighbour, Mrs Thomas – or Mrs Knitting, as I call her – who is on her way in from outside.

'Hello.' She greets me with a smile.

Lost for words, I stare at her homespun jumper. Think how I might not know this woman's first name but I sure know every inch of her body, watching her, when she thinks no one can see, from my bedroom window.

'Haven't seen you in ages.' All chirpy and bright-eyed she continues with her smile. 'What've you been up to?'

'What d'you mean, *up to*?' This must be a trick question, like at school, when a teacher knew what you'd done and had already decided on your punishment but asked you anyway, knowing you'd lie. 'I haven't been *up to* anything. I don't get *up to* things.'

'All right, boy, calm down.' My rising anxiety is reflected in her surprise. 'I was just wondering how you were, that's all.'

'How I am is none of your bloody business.' I struggle to think past the buzzing that's started up again. I must steel myself against it. If I do anything to show I'm dangerous, I'll be carted off to the psychiatric ward again.

'Oh, dear. There's no need to be rude. It's not like you. Are you feeling okay?'

I push past her, onto the street, and I nearly trip over a rough sleeper wrapped in a filthy grey blanket. His legs hog the pavement as he lolls in the doorway. The man mumbles something I can't hear but I see his outstretched palm and, making sure I hold on to my last fiver, drop my loose change into it, then stumble away. Carrying the sorry stink of him in my nostrils on my bus ride to work.

EIGHTEEN

Angela tried her Guinness and found it tasted surprisingly good. When she saw Anne-Marie take a long, deep drink of hers, she copied her.

'It's about Toni.' Anne-Marie put down her glass and sighed.

'You've heard from her? Oh, that's brilliant, I'm so relieved.' She slumped in her chair. 'I've been imagining all sorts. I'm such a worrier. Toni's always on at me to loosen up—'

'No. *Stop!*' Anne-Marie placed a restraining hand on her arm. Angela felt the ominous weight of it through her sleeve. 'I'm sorry, Spike, but there's no easy way to say this.'

'What?' Identifying the catch in her friend's voice, she jerked upright. 'You're scaring me.'

'It's bad news, Spike.' Anne-Marie pulled back her hand.

'*Bad news?* What d'you mean?'

Anne-Marie threw her gaze to the ceiling and Angela saw there were tears behind her spectacles. 'The police... They, *erm*... They found Toni's body at her flat this afternoon.'

'H-her *body*?' Angela spluttered in disbelief. 'H-her... her b-body's been found at her flat?'

Anne-Marie replied with a slow, rhythmic nod.

'But what the hell does that mean? I don't understand.' A frantic shake of her head. 'Are y-you… Are you saying Toni's dead?' Eyes pulled wide; fearful of the answer.

'I'm so sorry, Spike.'

'B-but.' Angela couldn't speak, the words wouldn't come.

'It's a terrible shock. I can't believe it myself.'

'B-but how? How can she be?' Angela found her voice again. 'She was fine when I saw her last.'

'The police are saying she was murdered.'

'*Murdered?*' She clamped a hand to her mouth and pushed the horror of what she'd been told through her fingers. 'I don't understand. How? Are they saying how?'

'They're not saying anything much.'

'But w-w-who… who in the world would want to hurt Toni?' Angela burst into tears. 'Murdered? This is crazy.' She hiccupped through her sobs. 'I can't believe it. I can't believe what you're telling me.'

'They've taken her boyfriend in for questioning.' Anne-Marie, sombre, drank from her pint. Her hand was shaking.

'Mark? Whatever for?' Angela blew her nose with a tissue she found up her sleeve.

'They must think he's got something to do with it.'

'That he killed Toni?' She yelped her surprise.

'Maybe.'

'This has got nothing to do with Mark.' She flopped back into the curved embrace of the bucket chair and pressed a hand to her cartwheeling insides. 'He'd never hurt Toni; he thought the world of her.' A flash of the kitchen porter: his size, his malevolence, his dead-eyed stare. 'They're questioning the wrong man.'

Anne-Marie didn't ask her to elaborate and they sat in brooding silence. The distress and grief for Toni trapped in their throats as Cardiff's boisterous nightlife, oblivious to their misery, churned around them.

'I can't believe it.' Angela, the one to break it, had started crying again. 'Toni can't be dead. She can't be.'

'You poor thing, it's a dreadful shock. Bad enough for me and I didn't know her all that well.'

'I can't understand it, it doesn't make any sense. I'm sorry, Anne-Marie, but I can't just sit here.' Angela leapt to her feet and flapped her arms around. 'What are the police doing? I mean, why aren't they saying how it happened?' She was thinking about the kitchen porter again. 'I've got to do something.'

'Take it easy, Spike.' Anne-Marie reached out to comfort her, but Angela batted her away. Agitated and panicky, she didn't want to be consoled, she wanted action.

'But I can't take it easy. How can I take it easy?'

'Because you can't do anything. Come on, sit down.' Anne-Marie guided her back to her chair.

'If only I hadn't cut my finger. If I'd got home on time.' Angela returned to her seat and began to sob again. 'This is my fault.'

'Come on, you can't go blaming yourself.'

'But if she'd been staying with me as planned, this wouldn't have happened.'

'Please don't say that, none of this is your doing. Get some of that down you.' She pointed to Angela's glass. 'Honestly, it'll make you feel better. Oh, dear, you do look a bit grey; d'you want something stronger? A brandy, maybe?' Anne-Marie, poised to return to the bar.

'No, I'm all right. Don't leave me.' Angela squeezed her soggy tissue into a ball. 'I'll have this.' She reached for her drink, swallowed a mouthful, then another. Felt the alcohol calm her a little. 'It's funny.' She sniffed. 'When I first met Toni, I didn't like her much.' A hollow laugh as she wiped away fresh tears. 'I suppose we got friendly after Rhiannon and Geraint hooked up together.'

'You did, you seemed pretty close.'

'She was good for me, so chilled about stuff, nothing bothered her.' Angela, devastated to be discussing Toni in the past tense.

'That's the Aussies for you.'

'She was so looking forward to going to Spain and making a fresh start. Mark moving out hit her hard.'

'Hang on – are you saying they'd split up?'

Angela nodded and dabbed her nose with her wet tissue.

'I didn't know that.'

'It's why I invited her for the weekend, to cheer her up. *And* I felt guilty.'

'What for?'

Angela took another mouthful of Guinness, weighed up whether or not to say. 'Because it was me who told Mark about Toni having an abortion.' Her insides went cold. 'I know I shouldn't have, not when Toni swore me to secrecy.'

Anne-Marie's eyebrows shot up; this nugget obviously news to her. 'So why did you?'

She wiped away another tear. 'Because I like Mark. I felt sorry for him.' She shrugged.

'But why would you care so much? It was none of your business.'

'I hated it that Toni was lying to him. It was his baby too, wasn't it?'

'Sounds like it's a bit more than that.' A wry look. 'Go on, admit it, you've always had a bit of a soft spot for him.'

'No, I haven't.' A guilty glance at the floor. 'He's just a nice guy, that's all.'

'Oh, come off it. I've seen how you are with him.'

'I don't fancy him, *okay?*'

Anne-Marie raised her hand and flagged her surrender. 'Is that why they split, d'you think?'

'Yes.'

'No wonder you feel so bad about it.'

They fell into another lengthy silence and used it to work through their pints.

'Her poor family. Has anyone told them?' Angela was remembering the fondness with which Toni spoke of her folks in Tasmania.

'Jasmine gave her details to the police. They said they'd get in touch with them.'

'This is all so awful. *Awful.*' A fresh wave of grief crashed over her. 'Oh, God, I think I'm going to be sick.'

'D'you smoke?' Anne-Marie, alarmed.

'No, I don't.'

'Shame. Now would've been a good time. Nicotine helps with shock. Try taking some deep breaths. That's it, nice and slow... Feeling better now?'

'A little.' Angela swallowed, pressed her fingers to her temple. 'Thanks.'

'That's okay.'

'Do you remember me telling you about Toni arguing with that kitchen porter?'

Anne-Marie nodded.

'D'you think you'd be able to verify the address I got for him?'

'How come you've got that?'

'I followed him home last night.'

'I thought you said you were meeting Rhiannon.'

'I was, but then I saw him on the bus.' She rubbed an agitated hand across her face. 'And when he got off, I followed him.'

'Are you mad? I thought you said he was dangerous.'

'I still think he's dangerous.'

'So why follow him?'

'I don't know really. I just did.'

'You worry me, you do.' Anne-Marie gave her a funny look.

Angela ignored it. 'Can you verify his address and get his name for me?'

'That kind of stuff's data protected, I can't just hand out people's details, Spike. It's against the law. I could lose my job.'

'I'm only asking you to verify it, give me his name.'

'I've said I can't, it's confidential information. What d'you want it for, anyway?'

'I'm going to pass it on to the police.'

'The police!' Anne-Marie teased out a curl and wound it around a finger. 'I'm not sure that's a good idea.'

'Why not? I saw the way he looked at Toni, remember? He dragged a finger across his throat, for God's sake. He's evil, trust me. He meant her harm; I know he did. And now—' She couldn't bring herself to say Toni was dead... *murdered*. 'Now, I'm convinced he's got something to do with it.'

'And you want to say this to the police?'

'Unless you've any suggestions?'

'Only one.' A ghost of a smile. 'Why don't we go and get something to eat?'

'Oh, no, I couldn't. Not with what's happened to Toni. I've got to report this man, I've got to do something.' Angela pushed away what was left of her pint. 'And to be honest, I still feel a bit sick.'

'Come on, this is a hell of a lot to take in, you're not thinking straight. You'll feel better if you eat something, and then, before you go doing anything rash, perhaps sleep on it first, eh?'

NINETEEN

It was awful coming back to work after calling in sick the last three days. They gave me a right grilling when I dropped my timesheet in. Wanting to know how I was and frowning when I told them how bad I've been. I laid it on thick about my migraine, making more of the sob story I gave Gaynor over the phone. Not that their frowns meant they were sympathetic, they told me what a nuisance it's been. Going on about the extra strain my absence caused and how I must work two double shifts, back-to-back, to compensate the others who needed to cover me.

I didn't argue – arguing isn't what I'm supposed to do. I want them to think I'm the same compliant me, don't I? I just nodded my agreement and went to fetch my cleaning trolley. The one I kid myself no one else has been tampering with while I've been away. I can't help it, I'm a bit obsessive about these things, it's one of my failures and, devoting a section of time to restocking and refolding the array of hand towels, soaps and cleaning materials I need to do my rounds, I did give myself a talking to. I told myself not to care so much. But I'll never change, this is who I am.

I go for my break and check my phone for messages. I've another from Marvin. This time it's written in block capitals. I gawp at the screen, then send a text to explain that I'm at work and can't talk, which is true, but say I'll telephone soon as I'm done, which probably isn't true, but hope it's enough to get him off my back for the next day or two. When I've sent it, I tuck my mobile away in my jacket that hangs from a nail inside the cleaning cupboard. All I've got for my break is a boring egg and cress sandwich bought with my last fiver on my way in. Usually, I'd get something hot from here, staff get subsidised meals. But missing three days' work, days I don't get paid, I haven't the funds.

I eat my sandwich standing up and wait for the kettle to boil. I keep my mug, something I'm responsible for washing out, in a drawer on my cleaning trolley. The staffroom is dismal and I usually steer clear of it. The filthy floor, filthy tabletop, the food-splashed walls and sink unit, are enough to bring me out in hives. I keep my rubber gloves on when I'm in here, my leather ones are safely stowed in my jacket pocket.

Chewing and swallowing, the bread is like cotton wool and sticks to the roof of my mouth. I'm not all that hungry but it's been a while since my burger and chips at Dino's, so I force it down. My feet are killing me and I'd give anything to sit, but the plastic chairs aren't much cleaner than the floor with their discs of flattened-down chewing gum and fag burns, dating back to when staff were allowed to smoke in here.

I look out of the only window. A thin rectangle that would be above the height of your average person. Not that there's much to see, the back alley it looks on is dark now the sun's gone down. The kettle fills the room with steam and I make my tea, stirring in milk once I've sniffed it to check it hasn't gone off. There's an abandoned copy of the *Western Mail* on the table and I scan the headlines for any news on Toni Perry. They must have found her by now. There's nothing on the front, so I leaf through the pages.

What's this? I know that face.

No way. Julia can't have died.

But there it is. In black and white. Slotted in before the classified ads and the property section. Julia Opie's obituary. A pioneer of child psychology, whose bestselling book *The Fragile Mind* was revolutionary in the 1990s.

I read the condensed history of her life, her career highlights. Written by some unknown journalist who probably never met her. They should have talked to me, I was the one who knew her, I was under her care all through my childhood. Why hasn't anyone asked me to contribute to this? It isn't fair. Tears wet my cheeks. Disbelieving them, I lift a hand to my face, feel the wet slide under my rubber-clad fingers. It's strange, the only time in my life I ever remember crying was when Mum died.

It says here that Julia battled with cancer for two years... *two whole years*... I had no idea, why didn't anyone tell me? Poor Julia. I could have gone to see her, I'd have found a way, even though it's against the rules. More tears come. Then, reading on, I gasp. This can't be right? It says her funeral was Saturday. I see the date. What, *last* Saturday?

'You're not telling me I've missed it?'

'Missed what?' A middle-aged woman I don't like breezes into the staffroom.

I turn away; I don't want the nosy cow to see I'm upset. Because I am upset. This is Marvin's fault; he should've been the one to tell me. The bastard's always been jealous of my connection with Julia; he's never been able to reach me like she did. Marvin goes on about building relationships, but he isn't my friend. Not like Julia was. Julia helped me control my behaviour by getting me to talk about my feelings and thoughts. And I could tell her anything. Nothing shocked her. She actually cared about what happened to me. It's why she never prescribed tablets and found other ways to calm me down. And it worked. For years. It worked until the powers that be ripped me away from her after my eighteenth birthday. I'm not being melodramatic here; this is what it felt like – it was like losing Mum all over again. Julia was the most amazing listener; she always had time for me, never judging or criticising. I probably could've told her what happened with Toni, and she'd have understood my reasons for not going to the cops.

'Are you crying?' The woman pushes past in her sloppy shoes.

'Mind your own business.' The buzzing starts.

'*Ooh*. Don't wanna talk, I take it?' She turns the tap, refills the kettle, then stretches up into the cupboard.

'No, I don't.' The noise gets louder and I must distance myself from her before I do something rash. It's like I've got a voice in my head, telling me to do stuff, telling me to damage. And it would be easy to give in to it, to gratify it. But I can't. I really can't. Not if I want to keep my freedom.

'I don't bite,' she jeers through uneven teeth. Then I see her expression harden and she slams a jar of Nescafé down on the counter. 'For fuck's sake, what bastard used the last of this?'

'Don't look at me.'

'I am looking at you.' Her eyes are small and sour, dug out of her puffy face with black eyeliner.

'Nothing to do with me, I can't stand the stuff.'

'So you say.' Hands on hips, all indignant and righteous – I've got a strong urge to smack her one.

'Just shove off, will you?'

'No, I won't. There's money been going missing from 'ere too since you started.'

'Are you saying I've been stealing?' I can hardly hear myself above the whirring between my ears. *Give in to it, or don't give in to it*? I wrestle with myself. I know the drugs would stop it but I don't want to go back on them.

'Seems so, don't it?'

I leave the tea I've barely touched to squeeze out my mop in the bucket. Tip the murky, grey water down the sink.

'Oi!' She tries to elbow between me and the drainer but I'm more than twice her size and besides, I'm done with being pushed around. Toni said I've got a bit of menace to me; I think it's about time I started using it. 'You're not supposed to do that, it's not hygienic. We wash our dishes in there.'

'*Not hygienic*? Have you seen the state of this place?'

'You're trouble, you are. You're bloody unhinged. I'm gonna report you to management.'

'Knock yourself out.' I refill my bucket from the hot tap. The sight of the fresh, soapy water satisfies me. 'I couldn't give a shit.'

'You will. There's people who've lost their jobs for less.'

'Look—' I bend close to her face, enjoying the way she cowers. 'You don't like me… I don't like you. Let's agree to give one another a wide berth, *yeah*?' I look down on the top of her head. She needs her roots doing, the manky cow. 'And I dunno about you, but I've work to get on with.'

I lift my bucket from the sink and retrieve my mop. I leave my tea behind, deciding it will lessen the impact if I hang around to finish it.

The place is in the process of being closed up for the night and I wheel my cleaning trolley out into the black shadows, aware of the echoing emptiness spreading around me. I won't be long; this is the last leg. I've only the dining area and entrance area to mop and then I can clear off home. The idea lifts me a little until I remember the trouble that's waiting for me there.

TWENTY

'I think I fancy an Italian, how about you?' Anne-Marie led the way when they left the pub.

'Sorry, what was that?' Out in the street, the air was obdurately cold and Angela could scarcely feel her face. 'Oh, you choose, I don't mind.'

Still reeling from the shocking news about Toni, she was remembering the hate on that kitchen porter's face as she looked up at the moon. It had risen clear and high above the city and the streets sparkled under the first frost of the season.

'There's a nice place down the Morgan Arcade. D'you want to try it?'

'If you like.'

Accompanied by the sharp clicking sounds of Anne-Marie's heels, they tracked across the near-deserted pedestrianised area. Angela, worrying about affording a meal out, reminded herself she wasn't paying rent at the moment and it would be okay just this once.

She loved this part of Cardiff and thought the elegant Victorian grandeur of the Morgan Arcade especially beautiful.

With tables spilling out from the cocktail bars and brasseries, the independent boutiques, art galleries, bridal shops and top-notch men's outfitters set out beneath the filigreed ironwork and glass-panelled roof, was like walking into another world.

'This place looks the biz.' Anne-Marie stopped outside a pastel-fronted restaurant to read the menu. 'What d'you reckon?'

Angela couldn't speak. Suddenly overwhelmed by her sadness about Toni, she tilted her head to the hand-painted sign swinging above and swallowed her tears.

'It's mostly pizzas...' Anne-Marie chattered on. 'But they've pasta dishes too.'

She must have made a noise in the back of her throat, loud enough for Anne-Marie to hear.

'Aw, don't be sad.' A consoling arm was looped around her. 'Toni wouldn't want you to be upset.'

How do we know? Angela resisted the urge to bat the platitude away and forced a smile instead. Anne-Marie was only being kind, saying what everyone said when someone you cared about died; people did the same with Robert. But she couldn't help being sad, it was right to feel this low. How could it be that her beautiful, feisty friend was dead? She didn't, couldn't, totally accept it. Not when she could still hear her voice, her throaty laugh. How could someone as vibrant as Toni Perry be gone?

'Come on, Spike. Even if you only have some bread and a glass of wine.'

Angela nodded and they pushed inside the restaurant. Swapped the raw autumn night for warm garlicky smells of the Mediterranean and a cosy table tucked away at the rear.

'How's your finger?' Anne-Marie noticed Angela was struggling to unzip her parka and got up to help. 'Must be hellishly difficult at work.'

A waiter whipped their coats away.

'It is a bit. Chef had a go at me for being slow, so I stuck it up in his face.'

'Shame it wasn't your middle finger that you cut.' A caustic chuckle. 'He's such a bully boy, that man. I'm scared of him, if I'm truthful.'

'So am I, but don't go telling him.' Angela looked at her finger and saw the rubber cot had split. She peeled it off and set about replacing it with a new one from her bag. 'These help me to keep it clean.' She rolled the condom-like sheath into place.

'You're good at that.' Anne-Marie giggled. 'When are you having it off?'

'*Having it off?*' Her turn to snigger. 'You're beyond, you are.'

'I meant the bandage. God, you've got a filthy mind.'

'In a week or so,' she said, rolling her sleeves back to the elbows.

'Ouch! They look nasty.' Anne-Marie had seen the burns on the tender insides of Angela's arms.

'Hazards of the job.' She tugged her sleeves down again.

The waiter, back at their table, handed them each a menu, then leant forward to light a stubby candle. Angela looked to see how far it threw its light. Not far. The space beyond their table, although busy with other diners, dissolved into obscurity.

'I'll give you ladies a minute, *yes?*'

'Please,' they chorused, exchanging looks.

'Nice in here.'

'If you like eating in the dark.'

'I do. It's romantic.'

'Shame we haven't got a sweetheart between us to share it with.'

'I've sort of met someone.' Angela unravelled the white linen napkin and spread it over her lap.

'*Ooh*, you're a dark horse.' The gold earrings that matched

Anne-Marie's medallion, winked in the candlelight. 'Go on, spill.'

She wriggled around in her seat and regretted saying anything. 'There isn't much to tell.'

'How come?'

'Because I haven't actually *met* him, I've just seen him around college a few times.'

Anne-Marie, head down, was scanning the wine list. 'Is he on your course?'

'No. I'm not sure what he does there.'

'What's he like?'

'Shy.'

They both laughed a little at this.

'Do you prefer this Mr College Man to Mark, then?'

'I'm going to ignore that you said that.'

Anne-Marie winked at her. 'Well, if that's the case, it's going to be up to you.'

'What is?'

'You're the one who's going to have to make a move on him.'

'I can't do that. I wouldn't know how.' Secretly thinking that perhaps she could.

'You'll think of something.' Anne-Marie looked up. 'The wine's a bit pricey, shall we just get a bottle of house red?'

'Cheaper than buying it by the glassful.'

'Are you going to order something to eat?'

'I suppose I should. I am feeling a bit shaky. But a pizza?' Angela pushed a thumb between her and the waistband of her skirt. 'I should just have a salad.'

'God, no.' Anne-Marie blinked from behind her spectacles. 'You and your dieting, you're daft you are.'

'It's all right for you.'

'*Huh*, I'd give anything to have your figure.'

'Don't be silly.' Tucking a strand of hair behind her ear, she was suddenly shy.

'I'm serious. Anyway, sod the diet tonight, you need some stodge. It'll make you feel better.'

'All right, I'll have pizza.'

'Good girl.' Crunching sounds as Anne-Marie worked her way through a breadstick. 'Anyway, you said Rhiannon had some news. Did she tell you what it was?'

Angela shook her head. 'Not sure she will now. She still hasn't forgiven me for letting her down last night.'

Their meals arrived within minutes and, despite the brutal news of Toni's death hovering between them, Angela found she was enjoying herself and this made her feel guilty.

'I can't stop thinking about Toni.'

'Me neither. It was a horrible shock. I was dreading telling you.' Anne-Marie picked out a shrivelled disc of pepperoni and ate it with her fingers.

'It feels bad having fun without her.'

'Yes, it's grim. But nice for us to have time to talk for a change.'

'You're right, it's always a rush at work. One eye on the clock.'

'How's work going?' Anne-Marie's expressive face looked rosy in the flickering flame. 'Aside from Bully Boy.'

Loosened by the wine, Angela shared the problems that came with being the only female in a brigade of men. 'You have to be so much better than them, just to be equal.' A lengthy sigh. 'And I get frustrated when I can't lift things. I know it's something to admit and I hate myself for it, but I just don't have the strength the men have got.'

'And what about your course?'

'Good. Except they use it as another stick to beat me with.' Angela gave up on her cutlery too and ate with her fingers.

'Bullying's always been rife in the food and beverage department. I've read some appalling stories. Complaints on forms that never go further than the filing cabinet in Jasmine's office.'

'But that's not right. Can't management do something about it?'

'They reckon they are but it seems it's a culture that's proving impossible to stamp out.'

'But that's not good enough.'

'I agree, it's shameful. I admire you, Spike, there's no way I could do your job. Even in my pathetic dealings with that lot, I can see how awful they are. You've done well sticking it out for as long as you have.'

'God knows how. Every day I think about quitting.'

'I've got to ask – do you really want Tyrone's job when he leaves?'

'I need the money a promotion would give me. I can't survive on a commis chef's salary, and overtime's killing me.'

'I've got an interesting proposition for you.'

'Yeah?' She ate the last triangle of pizza, then licked her fingers.

'How's about putting in for a departmental transfer? I know they're always on the lookout for well-presented people to work in reservations and sales.'

'And I'm a well-presented person?'

'Yes, you *eejit*. You'd be perfect. And the hours, yeah, okay, they're kind of similar to what you're doing now but the environment's loads nicer. And you get a smart uniform. No more ugly whites.'

'And the salary?'

'At least three to four grand more than you're already on.'

'Sounds amazing.' A glug of wine. 'Is there anything I can do to get the ball rolling?'

'Leave it with me. I'll sort you an interview with the front-of-house manager, soon as he's back off holiday.'

'This is brilliant.' She grabbed Anne-Marie's hand and was in the middle of thanking her when her mobile rang between them.

Careful of her bandaged finger, she dug it free and stared at the screen, then returned it to her bag.

'Who was that?' Anne-Marie enquired through her chewing.

'My mother.'

'Aren't you going to answer it?'

Angela pulled a face and finished her wine, then topped up both their glasses.

'You don't get on with your parents, do you? Tell me to keep my beak out, but can I ask why?'

'They blame me for what happened to Robert.' She saw little point in going around the houses.

'Oh, Spike. Surely not?'

'Yep.' Afraid of tears, Angela jutted out her chin. 'And if I was them, I'd probably blame me too.' Her gaze wandered to the last tables of diners who were finishing up and paying for their meals.

'But he fell in, didn't he? He drowned. It was a dreadful accident. There was nothing you could've done.'

'I suppose.' Automatic, while secretly thinking, *of course there was something I could've done – I could have saved him. He was my baby brother. He was my responsibility. I let him down.*

Angela sees herself as she was on the day of Robert's funeral. Befuddled by grief and needing to be buttoned into her black coat. The feel of that unidentified hand that, curled into the small of her back, manoeuvred her from house to crematorium and afterwards, to a small function room at the rear of Cheltenham's Queens Hotel. For there was food after the cremation. To prove to the ones left behind they were still alive. She remembered the ham. Scored through with diagonal lines and glistening with honey.

The clatter of cutlery on crockery. The waiter sliced between her memories and cleared their empty plates.

'Can I tempt you ladies to the dessert menu?'

They shook their heads.

'Best not, it's getting late. Could we just have the bill, please?'

The waiter dipped away.

'I suppose we should get off home, we've both got work tomorrow.' Anne-Marie groaned and scraped back her chair. 'Won't be a jiffy, just need the loo.'

The bill arrived within seconds and, opening her purse to count out her share, which wasn't half as much as she feared, Angela was alerted to sudden slopping sounds coming from behind her. She swivelled in her seat to find a man mopping the terrazzo-tiled floor. His colossal shadow was thrown high against the far wall. With a hand pressed to her hammering heart, she watched him stoop to smother the last remaining candle: a dark-winged moth, drawn to the flame. It cast the space he worked in into near darkness. He was as formidable as he was compelling and, mouth agape, she sat watching him manoeuvre his mop between the tables and chairs, his great, sloping shoulders hunched to avoid hitting his head on the beams.

Whoever this man was, he fitted her criteria for a murderer exactly.

When Anne-Marie reappeared, collecting the bill and saucer of money and adding her own, Angela turned to her and shuddered.

'What's the matter with you? You look like you've seen a ghost.'

'He's here.' She jabbed her bandaged finger into the darkened rear of the dining area.

'Who is?'

'That kitchen porter. He's working here.'

Anne-Marie shoved her glasses up onto the bridge of her nose. 'Are you sure?'

'Definitely.'

'Well, he's not here now.'

Angela, on her feet, went in search of him. 'Look, he's left his mop and bucket behind.'

'Yeah, okay, but it doesn't mean it was him.'

'It was. No doubt about it.'

'We've both had a bit to drink and you're probably still in shock about Toni. I know I am, and I've had longer to get my head around it than you.'

'I'm not imagining things, I'm telling you, he was here. Seconds before you got back from the toilets. I was watching him.'

'Tell you what, if you go and settle up, you can ask the cashier who he is.'

'What did the woman say?' Anne-Marie asked when Angela joined her out in the covered arcade.

'Not much. All she was sure of was that he'd gone home for the night, she didn't know him to speak to.'

'Let it go, Spike. *Please?* I'm worried about you. You're shaken up about Toni, I'm the same. It's the worst thing, but you've got to leave it to the police. If this kitchen porter did have anything to do with it, they'll get to the bottom of it, won't they?'

'Not if no one tells them about his connection with Toni,' Angela mumbled under her breath. Having seen him again, the frightening effect he had on her made her decide to go to the police as soon as she could. If he was responsible for killing Toni, what's to stop him from killing someone else?

TWENTY-ONE

I have only known two houses in my life. The one I must share with my father when he's home, the other where my grandparents live. And I'm on my way to my grandparents' now. But with the car still at the garage, it's the bus again. It dumps me at the bottom of Coracle Road and it's a fair hike before I reach number eighty-six. Babcia's age. Her age today. I've bought her some red roses and a box of macarons from Marks and Sparks.

Weaving past couples with shopping bags, some bloke in a pinstripe suit and shiny shoes, the near-bare branches of trees rooted in the pavement sing with Cardiff's starlings. A sound like urgent conversation that reminds me of the mental health team I was handed over to after Mum died. The sad thing is, I'm as ill-equipped now as I was then, to understand what they say about me, and it gets me thinking how much of the world and its curious workings have been pieced together from things half heard. No wonder I'm fucked up.

Here it is, the little gate that squeaks when I push it open. Setting my nerves on edge before I even step over the threshold. The front door is bruise-coloured and its rusted knocker, hanging by a single nail, bleeds each time it rains. I have a key. Necessary, because neither of my grandparents will answer the door. Whenever someone comes to the house, Babcia hides on the stairs and hisses: 'You get it.' I've no idea what she does when I'm not here.

I ferret out a tube of Parma Violets from my jacket pocket. Pop one in my mouth as I unlock the door and step into the dark, tiled passageway. I am greeted, as always, by the house's musty breath and breathe my floral one into it as I negotiate the stairs. It is rare for Babcia to leave the house nowadays. If she does, it's only as far as the cash dispenser and Tesco Express at the bottom of the road. Officially, this is because of her bad hips but I know what cripples her is a deep-seated suspicion of strangers. That the further she journeys into the future, the further she withdraws into her past when a distrust of others saved her life. On the rare occasion she does venture out, I wonder if I shouldn't check her for a knife hidden in the folds of her clothes. Something she says she needed to do as a youngster.

I climb to the top of the house without needing to stop halfway to catch my breath like I usually would. I crunch down on the last of my sweet and lean into the open-plan living space; see its white-tiled kitchen. The only sound is the murmuring voice from the little transistor radio on the windowsill. At the table, motionless and upright on his wooden chair, is Grandpa. Immaculate as ever in his fawn cardigan with leather buttons, his blue shirt tucked into trousers pulled up to his chest. There are armchairs, but he prefers to sit here; seemingly staring out through his lacklustre eyes and the nets that are parted to let just enough of the soft, Welsh light spill in.

'Hello,' I say, emerging on the top landing into the warm sweet smells of baking. And something else, something that throws me back to childhood Sundays when Mum was alive. 'Hi, Grandpa.' I squeeze his shoulder.

He lifts his clean-shaven jaw and smiles benignly.

'Everything all right?' I look down at the designer watch on his wrist and lick my teeth, enjoying the long-lasting aftertaste of my

Parma Violet. What he needs a watch for, I don't know. He doesn't need to know the time; he doesn't go anywhere. The watch is as puzzling as his running shoes and the stick he props against the table. It's a smart piece of kit and I'm sure it would fetch a few quid. 'Where's Babcia?'

There isn't time for him to answer. When I turn, she is there. As solid as one of her upholstered armchairs and tied into an apron on which she long ago embroidered a large purple flower. Bigger than anything in nature, its luxuriant petals spread out over her comfortable middle. She taps it, the pads of her fingers working along its stitches, no doubt journeying her back to some unexpected place. Somewhere that unsettles her. She frowns.

'Happy birthday.' I bend to give her the obligatory kiss she tilts her head for. My lips bumping against her powdered cheek.

'Oh,' she grimaces and pulls away, 'you've been eating those horrid sweets again.'

'Here you go.' I ignore the comment and hand over the roses and macarons.

Her demeanour changes and she beams up at me. 'You are a naughty boy.' She presses the petals against her nose, sniffs the perfume that isn't there. Then scrutinises the rainbow-coloured macarons through their transparent lid. 'You shouldn't waste your money...' Her objection fizzles out. 'I've made cakes, and there's roast chicken for tea.'

That's what the smell is. 'Great. I'm starving.'

Her smile slips. 'Don't exaggerate, how can you be starving? Look at you, the likes of you have never known starving.'

I stare down at her tight, brown curls she swears she doesn't dye. This may only be a thing the rest of us say but it has a sinister subtext in this house. Babcia, although round as an apple since my childhood, claims she hasn't always been fat. And I have to believe her. I've seen the photographs of those places, the people imprisoned within barbed wire.

Roast chicken is a big deal in this house. Today it is to celebrate her surviving all these years, despite what the Nazis had planned for her. I offered to take them both out tonight, told them about the nice little Italian I'm working in. Family run, I said, thinking she'd like that, because to Babcia, as with Italians, family is everything. But no, the suggestion was ruled out with protests at the extravagance, and excuses about the food being too rich for Grandpa. Not that he breathed a word.

'Sit, boy. Sit.' She motions me to the sofa before waddling off to find a vase for the flowers. 'And take those blessed gloves off.'

I do as I'm told. About the gloves and sitting down. Conscious my big body fills the sofa, I always feel too large for this house, like a bear at a picnic. Babcia rarely sits. I think she's afraid to be still. Afraid to drop her guard in case the monster she still calls Hitler, comes and takes her away again.

'Dad's come home.'

Babcia, standing at the sink arranging her roses, throws me a look that says it all. She knows me and my father don't get on. That we've never seen eye to eye. On anything. According to her, it's because we're too alike. A theory she doggedly sticks to, as the idea I could resemble anyone from her side of the family, namely, her beloved dead daughter, my precious mother, is too much to bear.

I eat the little Polish cakes that are hot from the oven. Mechanically chewing and swallowing, I look beyond Grandpa's shape, out through the gap in the nets at Cardiff's skyline jutting like teeth. He spends all day every day sitting there, secure in the knowledge the nets prevent unwanted eyes. But who could look in? We're too high up for passers-by. You never know – the answer I was given when I dared to ask that question.

Grandpa's hair is as white as snow and thick enough to see the grooves his comb leaves behind. His musician's hands are spread out over the tabletop, the fingers, buckled by arthritis, moving to a rhythm he plays in his head. I look sideways at his cello gathering dust against the wall. A permanent fixture that, like him, doesn't go anywhere nowadays either.

'Oskar, sweetheart.' Babcia is whispering close to his ear. 'Try one of these, love. You like these.' She sets a pretty side plate down between his splayed hands.

He doesn't speak. Instead, he reaches out to give her an affectionate squeeze around the waist. He has tears in his eyes even though he isn't crying. Something deeper than words is communicated between these two.

I remember Grandpa used to be taller, thinner. The memory is corroborated by the photographs in their alloy frames on the dust-free shelves. But since they sold their shop, Buttons 'n Bows, by far the smartest haberdashers in Roath – not that they sold bows, far too frivolous, the buttons were silly enough – he has sat there. Still as a post. Staring at nothing. Saying nothing. They were always roping me into working in the shop, weekends, school holidays when I wasn't in care being psychologically stabilised. Not because they liked having me around but because they could get away with paying me bugger all. It was my job to match up the buttons. To sew them onto little strips of card. I can't stand to look at a button now. It's zips, zips, zips for me. And it's why I'm not being mercenary when I say that whatever I've got coming to me is only what I'm owed.

'Penny for them?' Babcia is top-and-tailing beans. Her hands, mapped with rope-like veins.

I like watching her. Her automatic movements are comforting. The steady transference of bean from paper bag to the chipped enamel colander. The room fills with their raw, green smell and the only sounds are the ticking of the stove and the continuous hum of the radio. The occasional cough from Grandpa to show us he's still alive.

'I saw that girl moving in next door.' This is the first opportunity I've had to ask about the redhead unloading the van.

'Did you?' The look is of surprise.

'She's got hair like Mum's.'

Babcia stops what she's doing to stare at me. Her face framing a question she doesn't ask.

'The Bowens haven't moved. What's she doing there?'

'She must be cat-sitting.' Babcia adjusts herself in her chair.

'I thought they got you to look after them when they went away?' I know all about the Bowens' cats: a pair of mangy moggies they coo over because they haven't any children.

'They've gone away for longer this time. I suppose they didn't want the house left empty.'

'All right for some.'

'It's to patch up their marriage, Lin said.'

'She looked nice.'

'Who?'

'The girl.'

Babcia resumes her top-and-tailing.

'Have you met her?'

'Since when did you get interested in girls again?'

'I'm not interested. I'm just curious.'

'It's the same thing in my book.' She gives me one of her long, steady looks.

'D'you want a hand with those?' I point to the colander.

'No thank you, dear.' She smiles and I know it's because she doesn't trust me with knives. 'Now, about this girl.' I listen as she dispenses one of her protracted sighs. Familiar to me, I've been copying them since I was small. 'Curiosity will only land you in trouble. You know what happened the last time you got mixed up with a girl. As much as I'd like you to meet someone.' She pauses and I can tell she is measuring out how best to say what she wants to say. 'If you ask me, I think you've got enough on your plate just looking after yourself.'

I must smile because she asks me what I'm smiling about like it's some kind of rarity. Which it is.

'Nothing.' I give her what I hope is my enigmatic look and lick my sticky fingers.

'Are you some kind of imbecile?' She pushes the plate of cakes towards me, egging me on.

I take another and watch the longing held in her expression as I peel off the corrugated sides of its paper cup and bite the cake in half. Poor Babcia. With her diabetes and her old heart... A ticking bomb. I give her another smile, compensatory this time, for the fact I am more like her than she will admit.

'I thought that girl from next door looked really sad.'

'Course she's sad. We're all sad. Now—' A slap of her nylon-clad thighs, the beans finished. 'How's about a nice cup of tea?' Babcia doesn't wait for a reply, she trundles off to fill the kettle. Sets it to boil on the gas stove they've had since they were first married.

I watch her fill the pot and squeeze the goodness from the teabags. Nothing is wasted in this house and everything is appreciated. Babcia is particular about her tea. I sometimes think the making of it is more significant than drinking it. Which we do, as always, out of a set of dainty cups, accompanied by matching saucers. Despite the handles being too small for my fingers and too delicate for her swollen arthritic joints, we persist with it for the sake of some unspoken protocol. Because she believes this is how every British person takes their tea. Civilised and out of the best china.

'Milk?' The question is automatic, she knows how I like it.

I watch her pour in a tongue of milk from a fat-lipped jug and I plump for another cake. The inside is as yellow as the butterfly Grandpa taught me the name of as a child; a butterfly from the banks of the Vistula in his native Gdańsk. The name was forgotten years ago but not the colour. I'm undeniably one for colours. I used to dream of being a designer when I was small. 'There's no money in that, lad. Be practical. You've got to get yourself a proper trade.' Well, I've got no trade, I say to those doubters now, all I do is mop floors and scrub pans and I'm always desperate for money.

We sit beside the cold hearth. Babcia on her hard, wooden chair, me on the sofa. With the sun still hanging golden above the horizon, I know, without needing to ask, that she thinks it would be wasteful to light the fire just yet. The door to the rooftop garden is open and I watch plump cream clouds sliding over the city. Grandpa gives every impression he's watching them too, but I know he isn't. You could forget he was here if it wasn't for the occasional wet cough into a balled-up tissue. Abandoning what remains of the disappearing view, my gaze travels the room. Over the petal-pink walls to the pale carpet. Up and over the spines of heavy furniture with their embroidered antimacassars.

'How's work?' Babcia quizzes and, focusing on her face, I see her lipstick has bled into the wrinkles around her mouth. It makes her look vaguely ghoulish.

She isn't going to be happy when I tell her I lost my job at the Lloyd George, so I take my time, building up to it slowly. Not that I'm fooling her.

'You're not at that posh hotel anymore, are you?'

The question makes me flinch. She's always on at me about my poor work ethic, which is a cheek, I'd like to see anyone else get out of bed to do the jobs I do. Unlike my grandparents – who are eternally grateful for the chances the UK gave them – I don't think I've anything to be grateful for. Babcia's so grateful, she's still trying to soften her accent and be more British. Whatever that means. I suppose it must stem from always feeling like a foreigner, living on foreign soil. Because of the racial abuse they suffered when they first arrived from Poland, the racial abuse they may still get, for all I know, they needed to learn to adapt, to blend in, to prove their worth to the country that saved them. 'We are guests here,' she will say from time to time. 'We worked hard and paid our taxes because it was our way of saying thank you.'

'Miedźy, tell me.' Babcia's voice fishes me from my contemplations.

Miedży is the name Mum gave me and the only person who still uses it is Babcia. But she's got nicknames for everyone, it's a Polish thing. I want to tell her not to use it, to use my proper name, but I don't.

'You know how bad I suffer from migraines. I suppose I called in sick once too often.'

She throws her hands in the air. Exasperated. '*Migraines.*' The word is coated with enough bitterness for me to taste.

I can tell she wants to say that I'm weak and pathetic and that compared to her and Grandpa, I haven't the first idea what suffering is.

'You want to man up,' is what she says instead. 'Isn't that what you youngsters say?'

'But I can't help it.' My protestations sound feeble. 'When I get one of those headaches, I can't do anything. I can't even get out of bed. It's them tablets I'm on.'

'*Those* tablets,' she corrects me, sharply from her chair. 'No wonder you can't get proper well-paid work, your English is appalling.'

'It's not my fault.'

'*No*? Whose fault is it then?' She knits her brows together. 'The British government provided you with twelve years of free education, you're the one who squandered it. If you'd worked harder at school, you wouldn't need to do the crummy jobs you do now. Perhaps, if you'd kept up with your Welsh, you were good at Welsh at school… You were good at lots of things at school…' She runs out of steam.

Thanks to the Nazis, my grandparents' education was patchy; it's why education is another big deal in this house. Babcia, learning to read before being carted off to Auschwitz, was able to teach the younger children there and never misses an opportunity to correct my grammar.

'I could see about evening classes?'

'And how are evening classes going to help you with your headaches?' She returns a clear, appraising gaze.

'You make it sound like I do it on purpose. I can't help that I get them.'

'Yes, yes,' she dismisses me. 'I know all that. Your generation has excuses for everything.'

'It's not like I'm not working. I told you about the Italian restaurant.'

'But you liked it at the hotel. You had regular hours, nice staff meals.'

'I get subsidised meals at the restaurant.'

'But, mopping floors for a living? I really thought you'd do more with your life.'

'Trust me, it's all I'm fit for.'

'I don't agree. You're a very capable young man. You were a real asset to us in the shop.'

I search her face for the irony that isn't there. 'It's all Blue Arrow can get me. My references aren't good enough.'

'Would you like me to have a word with them for you?'

'Bloody hell, *Babcia*, I'm not five.'

'No.' She nods in agreement.

'It's okay, the shifts are regular enough.'

'Yes, but they can let you go at the drop of a hat on those zero-hour contracts, it's not like it was at the Lloyd George.'

'It was still only working the wash-up. The way you're going on, anyone'd think I was running the joint.'

'But it was washing up in a five-star establishment no one in this family could afford to stay in. In a kitchen that has two Michelin stars. You were an idiot to lose it.'

'Why are you always having a go at me? You're never satisfied. I'm just a big fat disappointment to you, aren't I?' The buzzing begins: warning me I'm about to lose my temper. I try not to let it take hold but it's difficult, it's becoming more difficult with each passing day. It's a battle not to show how dangerous I am. It would be so easy to give in to it.

She shifts uneasily in her chair. Fidgets with the hem of her apron. 'Of course not.' I watch the dark of her eyes work the room, land on the back of Grandpa's head. 'It's just that you were such a clever little boy. You could have done anything, been anyone.'

'You reckon, do you? With the start I had?' I clench my jaw to hold my anger in.

'My dear boy, if you think you've had a terrible time, a terrible childhood, then you should've had mine and Grandpa's.'

'Yeah, I forgot. The two of you've got the monopoly on hell, haven't you?'

'Actually, yes, we have.' Stiff from her chair. 'We've been there.'

'I can't stand this.' I shift my feet but I don't get up. 'Either you get off my case, or I'm gonna stop coming round.' I say what I want to say but I don't lose my temper – I make a point of keeping my voice slow and measured, to sound like I've always sounded. I can't have her guessing what I've done.

'Then where would you get that bit of extra cash I give you, eh? You only visit us when you want money.'

'And you could give me a lot more than you do, and all.'

'Oskar!' She gets up to stand beside Grandpa, wanting his support. 'Are you going to let him speak to me like that?'

He doesn't move. He keeps on facing ahead.

'I want an apology from you this minute!' She snaps the back door shut.

'Why should I? You're always having a go at me.' The droning sound gets louder, it's fogging all reason and I know I'm in grave danger of losing it with her.

'I think you ought to have a bit of respect, young man.' She speaks in a voice I've always imagined she used when she was teaching English to her African students. 'Do I need to telephone your father? Tell him to take you in hand?'

'For crying out loud, woman – I'm twenty-eight years old!'

She makes me want to thump the wall, throw a chair. Do some real physical damage. But I can't, I must be careful; I must learn to curb these urges myself without the help of my drugs. I've got to keep my head down and stay under the radar, my liberty depends on it. If I'm found out and they lock me up again, Toni's death will have been for nothing. The sacrifice she made for me so I could find myself again, would be wasted. But when that buzzing starts it's a strain to hold the anger in. But if I don't, I'm going to be in serious trouble.

Babcia, her arms held out to me. 'Don't let's argue, not on my birthday.'

I can't remember the last time someone hugged me. But I don't want it, not from her, and shrink into the sofa.

'Is this all you've got to get you through the winter?' Her voice is gentle as she pinches the shiny material of my jacket between finger and thumb. 'It is, isn't it? Let me go and find Grandpa's old overcoat, he doesn't need it anymore.' I see her measure me with her tailor's eye. 'It'll fit you pretty well.'

She disappears downstairs and, listening to her moving around in the room below, the noise in my head subsides a little. I go to the kitchen with the empty tea things and pot rattling on the tray. Spy Babcia's stout, leather handbag on the sideboard. I'm desperate for money, I've hardly anything to last until payday and, from our exchange just now, I doubt she'll be handing out extras today.

I dump the tea tray on the draining board and open the handbag to find her purse. Dextrous without my gloves, I flick the press stud, undo the zip and expose a line of crisp-looking notes. After a quick check on Grandpa – not that he ever sees anything – it's with a sharp intake of breath that I slide out a pair of twenties in one easy movement and return the purse.

But only by the skin of my teeth.

Babcia is back. Slightly out of puff from her short climb. She's clutching a plush, dark-indigo coat to her bosom. I close my palm over the money and whip my hand behind me, push it inside the back pocket of my jeans. I sigh through the crazy fluttering in my chest, I can't believe she hasn't noticed and the kick this gives me is amazing. I might be developing a taste for getting away with stuff.

'Try it on.' Babcia passes me the coat. 'Slip your jacket off first.'

I do as I'm told and push my arms against the red silk lining, down into the sleeves. The overcoat smells musty, like it's been kept in a cupboard that hasn't been opened for a long time. I twist to check my reflection in the full-length hall mirror and like what I see.

'Have you lost weight?' She stretches up on tiptoes, irons the cashmere with the flat of her hand. 'You look as though you have. It's a nice fit across your shoulders. It wasn't cheap, it's a proper Crombie.' Her voice is proud as she inspects the elbows and cuffs. 'Very little wear too, which is surprising because your grandpa had a lot of use out of it… Didn't you, Oskar?' He doesn't hear, or if he does, he chooses not to answer. 'He was easily as broad-chested as you but maybe not as tall. And you are tall. You get that from your father.' She circles me like a shark. 'I could see about letting it down an inch… There's plenty of hem.'

'Stop fussing. It's fine.'

'I don't know…' She taps her fingers against her lips.

I button up the front. I know I said I didn't like buttons but I'll make an exception for this; I look good in this. And Babcia's right, I have lost weight, I've noticed the waistband is slacker on my jeans.

'Oh, you do look handsome.' There are tears in her eyes and I don't know why, but it makes me hate her more. 'You need a poppy. Haven't you bought one? Naughty boy. Here, have mine.' She unpins it from her jacket and sets about fixing it to the coat's lapel.

'I'll do it. You'll damage the material.' I push her away, then jerk my head to something on the radio.

I cross the room to turn the volume up.

'…*Police called to a property in the Danestown area of Cardiff yesterday afternoon and found the body of a twenty-four-year-old Tasmanian medical student, Toni Perry... They are treating the death as suspicious... A man is helping the police with their enquiries...'*

I wait for the report to finish, then turn the volume down again.

'Dear me, you are agitated today. Whatever's wrong?'

'You're what's wrong with me.'

I can tell she's shocked by my outburst but I can't help it, I'm up for a fight. I can usually cope with Babcia and her nagging but not after hearing that. And certainly not without the numbing effects of my meds. I'm going to lose my temper and grit my teeth, try to rein it in but it's a battle.

They've found her. This is it; this is the end of me. What did the report say? Something about a man helping with their enquiries? What the fuck does that mean? Does it mean they've got a witness... that someone saw me?

My insides flip over. I feel like throwing up.

Babcia is watching me.

'Dear me, are you all right? You've gone a very strange colour.'

Thankfully, she doesn't tally my reaction to the news bulletin. But even so, I've got to get out of here, I need some peace to sort my head out.

'I'd better shoot.'

'You're going?' She follows me to the landing.

'Yeah, I've gotta go to work.'

'Tonight? I thought you were off tonight.'

'Change of plan. I had a message when you were fetching the coat...' I trail my lie down the stairs and slip out into the street under a weird, yellow sky.

TWENTY-TWO

Out in the watery afternoon light, Angela's gaze travelled the wide façades of office blocks. Old or new, they gave little away as to what went on inside. Knotting her scarf and zipping her parka, she took a sharp right onto Castle Street and bumped up against heavy traffic sounds and the spill of sightseers as brightly clad as the peacocks parading the motte-and-bailey beyond the rise of castle walls. She googled the whereabouts of Cardiff Central Police Station and, discovering it was only a ten-minute stroll from where the bus dropped her, decided the walk would give her the opportunity to clear her head and get her story straight.

Taking another right down into a cobbled side street squashed between the high wet sides of buildings, she needed to sidestep a sudden spray of steaming urine. The homeless man responsible gawped lopsidedly from his cardboard bedroom in the doorway of a disused shop. Homeless people made her nervous with their visceral demands for help she couldn't afford to give, so she shifted her attention to a gang of Cardiff's pigeons. Watched them swoop down on the overhanging roofs and dump their load, streaking the already ravaged brickwork with grey.

The wide stone steps of the police station were cornered by soaring Corinthian columns set high above the traffic. Intimidating, they threatened to crumble her resolve and doubts flooded in. Could she go through with this? What did she have to say to them anyway? On the verge of turning back, she took a deep breath and climbed the steps, pushed through the huge set of storm doors and into a tiled vestibule. Noisy under her heels, it announced her arrival before she was ready.

Angela told the desk sergeant's pencil-holding hand, twitching in readiness for crime, that she had information about Toni Perry they may be interested in.

'Take a seat, Miss.' The man stared at her bandaged finger.

Too nervous to sit, she ignored the row of plastic chairs set out against the far wall and wandered over the squeaky floor. It couldn't be a less welcoming space. The peeling paintwork, the psychedelic posters of: 'Open your Eyes to Abuse' and 'Lives not Knives'.

The clock hanging above the vending machine was ten minutes slow and Angela watched its arms tick across its face until the door behind the reception desk swung wide and she transferred her attention to a uniformed officer who guided her into a nearby interview room.

'If you'd just wait here, someone will be along shortly.'

This time she did sit and, rubbing her aching knees, she looked around the sparsely furnished room. Finally, the door opened and she rose to greet a small, black-haired man in dark jeans and polo neck.

'Miss Milligan.' He read off his notepad. 'I'm DS Varrius.' His hand felt small and dry when she took it in hers.

She sat back down and waited for him to speak. But he didn't and, afraid of the awkward silence, she kicked off proceedings by launching into her reasons why she thought the kitchen porter was involved in her friend's murder. It was like wading through mud and she was as inept at reading the situation as she was at reading Varrius who, although taking copious notes, had a disconcerting habit of throwing his gaze heavenward. She stopped talking when she ran out of things to say and listened as her voice was replaced by an eerie stillness.

'Just to clarify things, Miss...' He hesitated, and she watched him flick back through his notebook to find her name again. 'Miss Milligan... Could you please confirm when you last heard from Miss Perry?'

'Last Friday.' Angela scrolled through her text messages. 'Six forty-five. She rang me a couple of times, left a voicemail then sent me a text.'

'May I read it?'

She handed him the phone and stared at the epicanthic folds above his eyes.

'And you say you were late meeting her because of your hospital wait?' A glance at her trussed-up finger, as he returned her phone.

'That's right.'

'You say you also called round to her flat on Sunday. What time was this?'

'About eleven, I think. I rang the bell for ages, but she didn't answer.'

Varrius made a small noise, then scraped back his chair and stood up. 'Well, thank you for coming to see us.'

'Don't you want the name of the restaurant where this kitchen porter's working in now?' Worried Varrius was about to walk off, she needed to stop him. 'I've written it down for you.' She lifted her bag into her lap and rummaged for the information she'd brought with her. 'His home address is on there as well. HR at the hotel will be able to verify it. They'll be able to give you his name too, if you ask them.'

'Okay. We'll look into it, thanks.' He scanned the sheet of paper she gave him. 'If you'd just like to follow me, I'll show you out.'

Angela left the police station, unsure if anything she told the detective was of interest.

With the hood of her parka pulled up and the sharp autumn air in her throat, she strode along the pavement. She needed to get a move on, her shift started soon. A little bruised by her meeting with DS Varrius, she failed to notice the sea of Remembrance Day poppies fanning out from Cardiff Castle like a big red skirt. She yawned into her hand; she was already exhausted. The upsetting news about Toni combined with a few too many out with Anne-Marie meant she'd been tossing and turning for most of the night. She let her tongue travel up to the raging ulcer on her gum, felt the eye-watering sting yield to something that hovered between sweetness and decay. Then her phone purred deep inside her bag and, using her good hand, she pulled it free.

'Mark!' she squealed with delight when his name flagged up on the screen. 'Oh, God, Mark. I'm so sorry about Toni.' She rushed through her condolences, denying him the opportunity to speak. 'It's all so horrible what's happened to her. I still can't believe it.'

'Not half as sorry as me.' He gulped through his tears.

'Are you all right? I mean, I heard you were helping the—' She stepped aside to allow an elderly woman tugging a tartan rollator bag to pass. She still couldn't believe that Mark had actually phoned her, had thought of her. It gave her a glimmer of hope, that maybe, just maybe, he liked her as much as she liked him.

'I've been trying to get hold of you. They won't let me use the phone in this place. I'm desperate, Spike. I'm fucking desperate.'

'What's happening, Mark? What place, where are you?' she responded to the panic in his voice.

'I'm at the police station. They're gonna charge me.'

She gasped. 'With what?'

'Murder.'

The word spun in the chilly air.

'But you were just helping them with their enquiries, they can't think you had anything to do with it, surely?' *No wonder DS Varrius wasn't interested in what I had to say – they've already made their minds up.*

'They do. I'm totally fucked. They found me DNA under her fingernails.'

'Your DNA?'

'I explained about her slapping me. I showed them the cut on me face. But I think it just made things worse. They're saying she hit me in self-defence.'

'She cut your face? When did this happen?' Angela, listening to him sobbing, fought back tears of her own.

'Friday night. She turned up at the flat just as I was moving the last of me stuff out. We had this massive row. The worst ever. I said some real nasty things to her, Spike.'

'Because of the abortion? Oh, Mark, I've been feeling so guilty about that. I should never have told you; it was none of my business.' She echoed Anne-Marie's complaint as the wind blew her hair in her face. 'If I hadn't stuck my nose in, the two of you might still be together.'

'It wasn't only that.' He was crying so hard, she struggled to hear all he was saying. 'There was loads wrong with us. Getting rid of me kid without telling me was the final straw. Thing is,' she listened as he cleared a way through his tears, 'people saw us fighting that night, outside the flat. Witnesses. Police say neighbours have made statements saying they'd heard us arguing loads over the past few months.' He took a breath. 'I could've told them that. It's all we've been doing, for fuck's sake. But, Spike,' he was crying again, 'I didn't kill her. I swear.'

'I know you didn't. You couldn't hurt Toni; you couldn't hurt anyone.' Her thoughts twisted to the kitchen porter again and the same uneasy chill settled inside her.

'Then you're the only one who believes me. None of me mates will even speak to me. Not me brother, or me sister. They all think I'm guilty.'

'Oh, Mark, this is awful... *awful*. What about your parents, aren't they on your side?'

'Me parents are dead.'

'I'm sorry, I didn't know.' Angela felt as wretched as he sounded. 'You didn't kill Toni, what's the matter with them? They can't treat you like this.'

'Will you come and see me?'

A pause, unsure if she had heard him correctly. '*Me?* You want me to come and see you?'

'Please, Spike. I ain't got no one else.'

'Well, y-yes. If that's what you want,' she spluttered, hardly daring to admit that the idea he needed her thrilled her despite the awfulness of the situation.

'They're gonna send me to some remand centre near Bristol. I'm hardly gonna get bail, am I?' he croaked. 'I'm really frightened they're gonna lock me up for the rest of me life, Spike.'

'Oh, Mark, you poor thing.' Angela's tongue crept up to worry her ulcer again. The pain of it made her wince. 'Can you let me know where you're going to be?'

'I'll text you,' he sobbed. 'You will come, though, won't you? Say you'll come?'

'Yes, I will.'

She listened to the muffled voices in the background. 'Oh, I've gotta go. Me time's up. You will come, though, won't you? Promise me you'll come...'

'I will, yes,' she stressed, keen to assure him; unaware the line had already gone dead.

TWENTY-THREE

The homeless man reaches out to me like a child. The sight of his pleading eyes grasps the core of me, uncurls my spinal cord. Too close, I smell the sourness from his filthy grey blanket. I don't know why but hot painful tears come; I find I'm crying far too easily these days but suppose they are for dear, dead Julia. For Toni. Mum. For this poor dispossessed soul. For the wrongs I have done.

'Spare some change, man?'

He shakes his empty paper cup. The urgency of it makes me jump and, wiping away tears, I look past his shape to his meagre world of carrier bags. He responds by leaning further out into the street, his fingers a mere hand-span from my ankles. I hunt what I can see of his face in the amber street light, wanting the human being beneath the knitted hat. I think I might find him, and when I do, I try to hold him there, but he slips away again.

'Anything. I'll take anything, man,' he croaks in an accent I can't place.

I rub a hand over my bristly head and the designer stubble I'm cultivating; there's something oddly familiar about this man but I can't for the life of me think where I know him from.

'*Anything*?' he repeats, sensing me waver, which I do. But only because I've got sod all myself. I want to explain: don't be fooled by the cashmere overcoat, I haven't bought it, I was given it; there's no way I could afford luxuries like this. Then I remind myself, if it weren't for my father letting me live in his house, this would be me. Was me, for a short, terrifying time: sofa-surfing, sleeping rough. I wriggle the last few coins from my pocket and drop them in his cup.

'Ta, man.' He gives me the hard, flat blue of his eye: a startling gem shining amid the grime.

I shove my gloved hands deep into the pockets of Grandpa's old Crombie, hunch my shoulders and turn away. With long, purposeful strides, eager to distance myself from whoever this is, I remember why he looks familiar: this is the same rough sleeper I nearly tripped over the other night coming out of Dino's.

Are you following me?

I slow to toss my silent question over my shoulder. Then chide my ridiculousness. Whatever I think this is, it's only my guilty conscience playing tricks; no one is after me, no one knows what I've done. If they'd linked me to Toni Perry's death, they'd have come for me by now. And anyway, why would the likes of that poor bastard give a damn about me? He's enough of his own problems to wrestle with. No, he's chosen this part of town to set up camp because this is where he feels safe, nothing more. Nothing for me to fret about.

Dumping my uneasiness about the homeless man, I pick up the pace and stride through the night-time neighbourhood where I grew up. Back straight and feeling more confident than ever, I'm enjoying the exercise. The webbing of interlocking streets that are made up of red-brick terraced houses have their curtains drawn across their bay windows, so barely a sliver of light escapes. The car is still in the garage, undergoing work to get it through its MOT. I've been told it won't be ready to collect until later in the week and I'm worried about the cost because I can't afford it. I'm hoping it will be a bill my father will pick up without me needing to ask.

When I think of my father, I slow down and drag my feet. I'm in no hurry to return to the tip the house has become since he came home. It drives me up the wall the way he squanders his time. He must have eyes, he must see the work that needs doing around the place: the missing roof tiles, the wobbly guttering, the tip of a garden front and back. But he can barely be bothered to crawl out of bed most mornings and only pulls on a pair of trousers if he's going down the Cat and Fiddle. Which he does, if one of his knobhead mates calls round, doing the beer-swilling hand gestures to tempt him out. Not that he needs much tempting, beer is about the only thing that motivates my old man; it's been this way since Mum died.

Home at last. I take a fortifying breath and slide my key into the lock. When I step into the kitchen, I am hit by a wall of heat. He's gone and turned the radiators up to max and the first thing I do is reset the thermostat to normal; it's way too warm for me. It's not my imagination, despite the sudden dip in temperatures, my circulation is something else that's been improving. I'm telling you, since I stopped taking the tablets, it's been improvements all round.

I shrug out of the overcoat and look at the detritus. I could weep at the sight of the overflowing swing bin, the blackened frying pan with its half-inch of hardened lard from the breakfast my father cooked himself hours before. The greasy fingerprints on the fridge door he hasn't bothered to close properly. I cleaned that yesterday. It's not fair. Why did the bastard have to turn up now? Just when I was starting to find myself again. He'll be onto me as soon as he sees me, with his questions, his *How are things? How are you? What've you been up to?* I may have placated Marvin for the time being but I'm going to have to work hard to fend my father off now we're living under the same roof.

I grit my teeth and inch into the living room. Breathe the stale, airless squalor, the stink of his cigarettes. The curtains are still drawn from the night before and the carpet is swamped with his expended beer cans and unwashed crockery. And every imaginable bulb is on.

Burning electricity. Wasting money. It's like Blackpool bloody illuminations in here.

'Who the hell does he think pays the bills?' I mutter through the buzzing that's beginning in earnest and I go about turning off the lights. Then I remind myself – he does. In the same way he'll settle the bill at the garage, so I can have the car. To my shame, my father pays for everything.

I know it's a waste of time cleaning while he's here but I can't leave it like this, it looks like there's been a break-in. I toy with the idea of ringing the cops and pretending we've had burglars, just to put the shits up him. Then I remind myself about Toni and decide this wouldn't be a good idea. I peg the Crombie up in the hall and realise I've left my bomber jacket in Roath. No matter. I'll want it again when the weather warms up but I don't need it now.

'Dad, are you there?' I quiz the shadows up the stairs.

Nothing.

Then I remember there's a match on and he's probably down the pub. Boozing. I'm glad he's out of the way, it'll give me the chance to sort things. Gloves on or off? I take them off, tuck them into the back pocket of my jeans and circle the room. Collecting his dirty plates, his empty beer cans, his overflowing ashtray. This is like being at work, cleaning up other people's mess, and the buzzing builds in my head as I unwind the cable and plug in the vacuum. The thing weighs a ton and hauling it around is heavy work. Anger spurts inside me and I smack the powerhead against anything that gets in my way. It feels good to let off steam and, taking a breather, I wipe the back of my arm over my sweaty brow and grin at the emergence of this brand-new, expressive me. But I'm glad I'm at home. At home, alone. Whenever I'm in public and this happens, it's like I've got these two voices in my brain: one telling me to *do it, do it,* give in to the fury and damage, harm… The other, the voice of self-preservation and reason, telling me that if I did *do it,* I'd be in serious shit.

Rage ebbing, I return the vacuum to the cupboard and brace myself for the mess in the kitchen. But before I can get there, the back door wheezes open… and with it, two voices: my father's diluted Sutherland burr and someone else, their accent Welsh and more like mine.

A woman.

Quick.

I dart to the hall and hear my father talking: low and rumbling, slurring his words, I can tell he's downed a few. I inch towards the fluted glass of the dividing door where I stand and listen.

'…I'm only telling you how he seemed to me…' The woman's talking now, but she's got her back to me and I can't see who it is.

'Aye, but you probably just caught him unawares.' My father coughs his smoker's cough.

'He was hostile, Mac…' I lose whatever else she says.

'He's fine… you just don't know how to read him.'

'…Didn't look fine to me… he was really aggressive.'

'Trust me, I live with him, he's all right. He's the same as always.'

Yeah, Dad, that's the way. Thrilled with my cunning because I'm obviously behaving just as he expects me to.

'I thought you said he was being weird about the state of the house? Going about checking everything before he leaves for work?'

'Aye, he's always been a bit OCD. Nothing new there. I'm not the tidiest of people, and turning up after months away, it's bound to take some adjusting.'

'Are you sure, Mac? Don't you think it would be safer if he was in care?'

This chills me to the bone. Whoever this is, she wants to have me locked up.

'His psychiatrist's on top of it, he's a real professional. There's no way he could pull the wool over his eyes.'

I could laugh at this. No, not Marvin, but I've pulled the wool over yours, haven't I, Dad?

'If you say so.'

Yeah, he does, so keep your nib out, you interfering cow. The cheek of it, the cheek of her – I want to barge in there and shut her mouth. But I can't, they'll know I've been listening if I do that, and experience tells me you always learn more about what people are really thinking if you listen in on them.

'Thing is though, Mac…' The woman is whispering, I can barely hear her. 'You're not always around to keep an eye on him, are you?'

'But I'm home for the foreseeable.'

My heart sinks when I hear this. I just want rid of him. I want things to go back to normal – I want this place to myself.

'It means we'll have plenty of time together.'

I squint at their shapes through the bumpy glass. Yuk! I think I'm going to be sick… They're only kissing.

'Just promise me you'll talk to him,' the woman says when she pulls away from my father.

I hate her. I hate her voice: all measured and reasonable. I shift my weight to the other leg and squeeze my eyes into slits to peer through the fluted glass at their warped forms.

Who is she?

'D'you wanna drink?'

The woman chuckles. 'Best not, we can't have him catching us together.'

'Don't worry, he's not due home for ages.'

'Not your son, you twit.' Another chuckle. 'My Frank.'

'Oh, aye. Another time then?'

I lean around the door in time to see her shrug out of my father's sheepskin jacket and hand it back to him as he shows her out. The jumper she's wearing gives her away. It's one of her knitted creations, a lime-green thing no one else would be seen dead in.

What a cow. What a meddling cow. I glare at the back of her head and will my hatred for her into her brain.

You tricked me, I thought you were one of the good guys. How dare you talk about me like that, like I'm some... some... oh, I don't know. Some problem to be dealt with and locked away.

But I'm going to get her back. I'm not sure how, but I'll think of something. Just you watch this space.

TWENTY-FOUR

Break time and Angela collided with Anne-Marie at the entrance of the staff canteen.

'You all right, Spike? You look done-in.'

'Rough day. But it's nearly over.' A weak smile.

'You're still really upset about Toni, aren't you?'

Angela bunched her lips together and nodded that she was.

'Come on, d'you want a chat? Are you on your way in or out?'

'In.'

'That's good, so am I.' Anne-Marie put an affectionate arm around her and guided her to the nearest free table. 'Give us a tick. I'll go grab something to drink.'

True to her word, Anne-Marie was back within seconds and set two paper cups of brown sludge down on the table. 'It's supposed to be coffee.' She sat opposite Angela, frowning as she rubbed a biro mark off her wrist with a wet finger. 'Looks more like something dredged up from the Taff.'

'I'm glad I bumped into you; I wanted to let you know that I went to the police yesterday to tell them where that kitchen porter's working so they can question him about Toni.'

'Okay. But on what grounds? Just because you don't like the look of him?' Anne-Marie sniffed; she was mocking her. 'You don't know the first thing about him. You don't even know his name.'

'And whose fault's that?'

'What d'you mean?' Anne-Marie looked affronted.

'You could've helped. You could've got me his name. But it seems it's more important not to go breaching some stupid data protection law than to help catch a murderer.'

'A murderer! For God's sake, Spike, have you heard yourself? I can understand you being upset about Toni, we all are, but you can't go around accusing innocent people.'

'You don't know he's innocent.'

'And *you* don't know he's guilty. Anyway, I heard they've got their man.'

'Mark? They're wrong. He didn't kill Toni.' Angela took a sip of coffee. It tasted foul, so she put it down again. 'I know it looks bad, them finding his DNA under her fingernails, but he's got a perfectly valid explanation about that. Honestly, Anne-Marie, I don't know why, but they're using Mark as some kind of scapegoat. Can't you see it?'

'No, I can't.' Her friend removed her glasses and buffed them on the hem of her jacket. 'Anyway, did the police say you were helpful?'

Angela ignored the patronising tone. 'Yes, they were very grateful.'

'Good.' The glasses were repositioned. 'Well, you've done your bit now.'

'Unless you've any information? You did say you'd ask Jasmine to look into what Toni's complaint about him was, and why he left the hotel.'

'All I know is this bloke you're so obsessed with was given the push.'

'*Sacked?* D'you know why?'

'Chef said he was unreliable. He kept calling in sick, apparently.'

'And does this *he* have a name? An address?'

'So you can go running back to the police with it?' Anne-Marie made a show of stirring a spoonful of sugar into her coffee, then dropped the spoon on the table with an irritated clatter.

'It would be better coming from HR, from Jasmine.'

'But you don't need his address, you said you got it when you followed him home the other night.'

'Maybe. But supposing he doesn't actually live there.' Angela tried the coffee again, hoping it had improved. 'He might've been visiting a friend, or something.'

'I don't know why it's so difficult for you to accept it, but they aren't looking for any other suspects, are they? And I don't know what you expect me to do about it.'

'You could get HR to give the police this kitchen porter's name and confirm his contact details. It might help Mark.'

'Why would anyone want to help him?'

'Because he's done nothing wrong.'

'You don't know that.'

'I do, he told me.'

'When?'

'He phoned me.'

'Explains how you knew that detail about his DNA.' Anne-Marie splayed her hands on the tabletop and stared at them. 'I can see why you like him, this Mark. He's a good-looking guy. But being good-looking doesn't mean he isn't capable of killing. Don't you think you're being naïve? I'm telling you, Spike,' she dropped her hands into her lap, 'you've got to get this kitchen porter out of your mind and let the police do their job. You could end up in trouble yourself if you don't watch it.'

'I saw what I saw. I didn't make it up.' Angela was firm.

'Maybe, but it's not some crime drama off the telly. Some things really are that simple. Sometimes it is the most obvious person who's done it. And that's that.'

Angela declined to answer.

'I don't mean to be so... *so*, oh, I don't know. All I'm trying to say is, they wouldn't have arrested him if they didn't think he'd done it.'

'They've done more than arrest him.' Eyes downcast. 'Mark said they're going to charge him.'

'There you go then. They wouldn't be doing that if they didn't have solid proof.'

'But he didn't do it. He's innocent. And before you ask me – *No*, I don't fancy him, if that's what you're about to accuse me of again.'

'Are you sure about that?' Anne-Marie quizzed over the top of her spectacles. 'Because you're going to an awful lot of trouble on his behalf.'

'I'm helping him because he doesn't have anyone else. I'm all he's got.' Angela scratched the side of her nose. 'Don't look at me like that. He told me he hasn't any family and that his mates have all turned their backs on him.'

'And you're coming to his rescue, are you?'

'I want to help him, yes. What's wrong with that?'

'Nothing.' A small smile.

'Look,' Angela pushed on, 'I thought that scary bloke from wash-up had done something to Toni ages before they took Mark in, don't forget.'

'Okay. Let's say you do get the police to listen and they end up dropping the charges and Mark is released, then what? He's going to be so grateful he'll just fall into your arms? The coast is clear now, I suppose. What with Toni being out of the way.'

'Bloody hell! That's a disgusting thing to say.' Angela was

appalled. But perhaps what appalled her more was that deep down in her heart she knew Anne-Marie was right. She did have an ulterior motive to one day have Mark for herself. To have him grateful to her. Indebted to her. And even though she hated to admit it, this was the drive behind her quest to clear Mark's name and prove the kitchen porter was the one who murdered Toni.

TWENTY-FIVE

I have come home to find my father marooned in a sea of his curls. Perched on a stool in the middle of the kitchen floor, a towel draped over his shoulders, he's balancing the washing-up bowl aboard his large knees. Mrs Knitting's here too. Snipping, snipping. It seems that as well as weaving pullovers she can cut hair. Her perfume fills the room, it competes with the reek of my father's tobacco. They are laughing; laughing like it's the middle of something and I've arrived too late to join in. The situation, their easiness with one another, embarrasses me. It's too intimate. I don't know why, it just is.

'Hello, lad.' My father's wearing a new jumper. An early Christmas present? I can tell it's one of Knitting's creations and want to snigger at the polka dots and green triangular trees but don't, I stand here dumbly. I've got to remember to pretend I'm the same as I always was. 'How did your therapy session go?'

I shrug. I'm buggered if I'm discussing anything in front of her.

'And the motor's running okay after its service?'

I jingle the car keys in my pocket. This is my answer, even though I know he expects a thank-you for paying to keep his ancient car on the road.

'You are gonna clean up this mess, I hope?' is what I say

instead. Making sure to sound as unemotional as I did when I was on the tablets.

I spot the half-empty bottle of whisky next to his recipe books on the work surface and it annoys me to see they've been drinking. But worse than this, along with what I know to be the last surviving Rhayader crystal glass out of a set he and Mum received on their wedding day, to my horror there's another glass – the tumbler I took from Toni's flat.

'Aye, we will.' He drops his chin on his chest and gives Knitting a look. I can tell it's a struggle for him not to say more. 'Sue will be needing to give you a trim, before long. I didn't think you liked having hair on your head. Or your face, for that matter. What you got growing there – designer stubble?'

I shrug again.

'You run out of razors, or something?'

'No, I just fancied a change.' I lift a hand to my lengthening hair, then down over my bristly chin.

'You wouldn't mind sorting him out, would you, Sue?'

'No, ta. I've had enough of looking like a pickled onion.'

'Ha!' My father's laugh is too loud. I suspect he's trying too hard on account of Knitting. 'D'you hear that, Sue? The boy's got a wee sense of humour after all.'

Sue?

I stare at them. I don't like them being so friendly. I still can't get the image of them snogging out of my head.

I'm a hefty bloke but usually to stand beside my father is to stand in the shade. Mrs Knitting is certainly in the shade. Not that she's little by anyone's standards. She's rather tall for a woman, but compared to my father – a man who is as wide as a wardrobe – she looks small. As a kid, I used to want to open the buttons of my father's shirt and peer inside him to see what he was made of. I'm pleased to say I grew out of that.

'Been cultivating a sense of humour while I've been away, have you?' Why he wants to make conversation with me, I don't know. Perhaps it's to show Knitting that things between us are fine, which they're not. 'Growing it like you're growing your hair?'

He thinks he's being funny and I turn away without replying. I want to check on the state of the rest of the house. He's got a cheek, it's bad enough I have to share my space with him, I'm not putting up with her too.

I tiptoe over my father's redundant yellow curls and lean into the living room. I'm relieved to see things are better than I anticipated, that some attempt has been made to tidy up and I suppose it's for Knitting's benefit. Not that my father's idea of cleaning is anything more than a frenzied minute, the place still needs expert attention from me. I move away from the dividing door, slowly, knowing I must keep what I know – and Knitting is bound to discover soon – to myself. Thinking about what I've done to get her back for the things she said about me the other night, is like holding a glass that's too full. I daren't move fast, fearful of spills, I manoeuvre around the room inch by inch. Testing plugs are switched off, adjusting the tasselled fringes of the rug so they lie in evenly spaced lines against the carpet.

Satisfied with things down here, I head upstairs to my room and slump on the bed. I reach across to the bedside table for the photograph of Mum. The edges are blurry, echoing the indistinct memory I have of her and the way I used to feel before I stopped taking my drugs. Ghostly. Someone has left the photograph in direct sunlight and the left side of her body has been lost forever. I press it against my chest. Wanting her gaze to look inside me and read my thoughts. For her to tell me I'm doing the right thing by not handing myself in. For her to steer me through my torments and doubts. To guide me in what I am projecting to the world and to help me stay out of trouble and hide the truth. Because I'm frightened my private self may be seeping out into my public self without me realising, and if I'm to stand any chance of maintaining my liberty, I must keep these sides separate.

I get up and peel off my work clothes, put on an old rugby shirt of my father's along with a pair of jogging pants. I stare at myself in the mirror that hangs on the back of the door. I'm getting to like the way I look and wonder about going shopping for some new gear. I bought a shirt the other day but I could do with more things. But where am I going to get the money from? I could try Babcia's purse again, I think, going next door to the bathroom to drop my dirty clothes into the laundry basket. While I'm in here, I remember to empty some of the tablets I'm supposed to be taking down the toilet. I'm clever, I wrap them in loo paper and flush them away, just in case my father's checking up on me.

Downstairs, the kitchen door bangs shut and then the sound of heavy boots on the stairs.

'I know you're up here. D'you wanna show yourself? I think you and me need to have a little chat.'

'Your *girlfriend* gone, has she?' I emerge from the bathroom and get my question in first. My voice is nice and calm, I'm careful to keep up the act.

'Don't be ridiculous, lad.' He reaches the landing and dismisses me with a flick of his heavy hand. 'She's not my girlfriend.'

'You looked pretty cosy to me.'

He pulls his silly jumper off over his newly cut hair. Then removes his shirt. Tosses them both in the general direction of the laundry basket. He misses, and they slide to the floor. He doesn't pick them up, he leaves them there. It speaks volumes. Despite his girth and the fact he's pushing sixty, he's decently muscled. I stare at his big bare body and think about pressing him on Knitting.

'Why are you trailing around after me? Got a guilty conscience?'

Guilty conscience? What does he know? I follow him to his bedroom and wait for him to dress in a fresh set of clothes.

'You coming down?' He tucks his unironed shirt into his trousers. 'I'm cooking tonight.'

'*Sue* not joining us?'

'No, Mrs Thomas had to get back to feed her cat.' The look he gives me is one I recognise. And going by what I heard him and Knitting talking about the other night, I know what's coming. 'I'm making spaghetti carbonara for tea.' He sings his invitation to tempt me, knowing full well how much I love it.

'All right.' I agree, but only because I'm hungry.

'Come on, then.' He jogs away down the stairs. 'You can help if you want.'

I follow him, join him in the kitchen, watch him tie an apron around his middle. He cites me as the reason he never found himself a long-term girlfriend, someone who wanted to set up home with him when he was still young enough. And I have to agree. Who'd have wanted to take me on? Nobody ought to be expected to put up with a skinny, sulky boy with an adult's reasoning; a boy who went on to be a teenager who was just as sulky and spoiling for a fight. I do have an element of self-awareness. Secretly, though, his inability to find anyone pleased me, I didn't want another mother to replace the one I lost.

'Beer?' He opens the fridge and gets himself one.

I shake my head and am surprised by his question. He knows I'm not allowed alcohol and it gets me wondering if he's twigged; if this is his way of testing me.

'Right then.' He rubs his large hands together, then leans inside the fridge again, this time to retrieve a posh pack of bacon and a block of cheese. 'D'you wanna tell me why Marvin's been ringing the house for you?'

'Marvin?' I talk to his wide back. 'He's been ringing the house?'

'Is there a sodding echo in here?' He rotates to face me. 'Could it be that you've not been answering your mobile, by any chance?' He lifts a pan from its hook above the stove, then turns the hob and lights the flame. 'What's going on?' His throaty demand.

'Nothing.' I keep my voice down, even though it's near impossible to think past the buzzing that's started again. 'Marvin's just fussing. He's always on at me and I haven't always got time to talk to him when I'm at work.' I've got to try hard to pretend I don't feel much, to pretend I'm still functioning on a low burner. It's a strain but if he smells a rat, I'm done for. 'But I always text him back.'

It feels like my head is going to explode. It takes everything I've got not to scream at him and smack the wall but I don't, I push past him into the hall instead. Lift Grandpa's old Crombie from its peg.

'Oi, don't run off.' He lifts the pan off the heat and rushes out to me. 'Come on, talk. Something's up. You've got to admit you've been acting weird since I came home.'

'Are you surprised? Look at the state of the place. It's not fair, you know I can't cope with disruptions to my routine.' I tell him this quietly, calmly. It's brilliant, I'm brilliant. He isn't the least suspicious.

'But this is my house. My home.' He talks with his hands.

'Huh, you treat it more like a hotel. Bringing your women back.'

'Women?' He cracks his knuckles in the way a fighter might. 'What women?'

'Don't give me that bollocks. I know something's going on between you and Knitting... I mean, Mrs Thomas. Christ, Dad, she's married. We live next door to her husband.' I say it how it is but I'm keeping up the act. Clever, eh?

'I don't have to justify myself to you.' I can tell he's on the verge of losing it too, it crawls up his neck in angry red blotches. He lifts a meaty arm and swings it wide. I duck out of the way, thinking he's going to hit me. *Just try it*. I eye him, the whirring rising to a deafening crescendo. I steel myself against it, there's no way I can give in to it. 'What I do is my business.'

'And what I do is mine.' I exhale. 'I'm not a kid no more, Dad.'

'Aye, I know that, lad.' He softens and I can tell he's working out another way to say what he wants to say. 'Come on, let's go and have a sit in here for a minute.' He takes a step or two towards the living room but I stay where I am. 'Babcia says you've been a bit aggressive with her recently. She's worried about you, worried you're not taking your tabs.'

'Talking about me behind my back again?'

'It's only because we care.'

'You don't care, you're never here.' *Steady*, I remind myself, don't get carried away.

'That's not fair.'

'I'll tell you what's not fair. *You*. You and her. On my case all the time.' I button the overcoat and pat the pockets for my gloves. 'If Marvin doesn't consider me to be a risk, and he doesn't, why can't you just leave me alone? It's not your job to monitor me. Turn the spotlight on someone else, why can't you?'

I think of Mark Fairfax and how much of a spotlight he must be under. Hearing the news earlier that he's been charged with Toni's murder, it looks like I'm going to be lucky enough to get off scot-free. I know I'm bad to want him to cop for the lot but deep down inside I think: good, it evens things up a bit. Who cares if Toni's death had nothing to do with him, if the cops have him in their sights, they won't come looking for me. And let's face it, it's only me I'm concerned about. From what I saw of that Mark, he can take care of himself. It would kill me if I was sent to prison, or worse, locked away in some mental hospital again.

'Where d'you get the money for a coat like that?' My father grabs the hem, inspects the stitching, the silk lining. 'Please tell me you're not up to your old tricks again?'

'Are you saying I nicked it?' All big and dark inside the Crombie, I feel I could take on the world. *Careful, don't confront him, don't raise your voice – you're not supposed to get angry, remember.* I turn away and pull on my gloves.

I must communicate something without realising it, because he withdraws a little, stands with his spine pressed to the kitchen door-jamb.

'Well, did you?' His look is hard.

'I'm going out.'

'But I'm cooking your favourite.'

I whiff his tobacco breath. 'You have it.'

I've got to go before I do something I regret... Before I give myself away.

TWENTY-SIX

Geraint was waiting for Angela on the front step of number eighty-four, Coracle Road. His white transit van parked up on the kerb. It irritated her to see him. She'd specifically said to come at half past four and he was early. On the go since five that morning, what she wanted, home after a lengthy stint in the kitchen, was to change into something comfy and sit down with a cup of tea. But there was no chance of that now.

'Hello.' She injected her voice with a cheeriness she didn't feel. 'Thanks for finding the time to come over.'

The wind whipped her hair across her face as she dug through her bag for the key. Geraint, silent beside her, as she unlocked the door and they both stepped inside.

He set about the boiler's controls as soon as they reached the kitchen.

'You have read these, I take it?'

'Yes.' She peered at the manufacturer's instructions. 'But they don't make sense.'

'They're pretty straightforward.'

'To you, maybe. But you're in the business.'

Geraint grunted his answer and Angela, giving up on him,

backed away to fill the kettle from the tap. She selected a pair of mugs and dropped a teabag into each. Then took the opportunity to study him while waiting for the water to boil. He was the spit of that Ed Sheeran. Even down to the rolled-back sleeves of his lumberjack shirt, showing off his armfuls of tattoos. Not that the similarity did him any favours in Angela's eyes; she didn't get the craze for the singer.

'It's really good of you to come and help me out.' She wanted to be polite, he was doing her a favour.

'S'right.' He blinked through his pure-white eyelashes. 'Can't have you freezing to death, can we?'

She ignored the vaguely sinister comment. 'Well, thanks for sorting it.'

'I haven't yet.'

'But you will.'

'Nice you have such faith in my abilities.' He didn't smile.

Angela made him tea and was passing it over when Bangles jumped up onto the work surface to sit beside Geraint. The cat proceeded to clean himself, licking a paw and then wiping the paw around the back of his ear. Once, then twice more. Leisurely, all the while eyeing their unsolicited house guest.

Geraint sneezed and clapped at the cat to shoo him away. But he didn't budge. *You can't tell a cat what to do,* Angela thought with a smile, liking the way Geraint's irritation – a cerise sunset – bled up and over his neck and face. Clever Bangles who, understanding this man's dislike of him perfectly, sauntered over to rub his stripy head against his arm.

'I hate cats.' Geraint sneezed again.

'Oh, yes, I remember Rhiannon saying you were allergic to them.'

'Yeah, I am.' He flapped his freckled hand. 'Just get the thing away from me, will you?'

Bangles – tail high, the bell on his collar jingling and jolly – dispensed a disdainful look that made her giggle.

Geraint sneezed again.

'All right.' Angela to the rescue, she lifted the cat down and encouraged him out through the cat flap.

'Rhiannon's well pissed off with you.' The whites of Geraint's eyebrows bobbing like rabbits' tails.

'Is she?'

'Well, yeah.' He fed her a look she couldn't be bothered to decode.

'I said I was sorry.'

'She's still pissed off. She's been a good friend to you, she deserves better.'

Angela stared at him in astonishment. This was between her and Rhiannon, it had nothing to do with him. Frightened by what she might say, she turned away. Her gaze travelled out through the window to the jagged skyline.

She couldn't blame Rhiannon. Standing her up was bad enough, but standing her up to go traipsing off after some strange bloke, was obviously unforgivable. What had she been thinking that night? Not much as things turned out. It's as she tried to explain to Rhiannon, wanting her to understand, there was this unforeseen force driving her on. Yes, she'd known it was dangerous but she just hadn't been able to stop herself. It was partly why she went to the police, the aggro it had caused getting that kitchen porter's address would have been for nothing otherwise.

'Did you get the invite to our engagement party?'

She spun back to Geraint. 'I did, thanks ever so much. Many congratulations to both of you.' She hated how the salutations stuck in her throat, she wanted to be happy for them, but they hadn't exactly been very nice to her.

'Cheers.' He dismissed her in his usual way.

'D'you mind if I leave you to it for a minute?'

Deciding the chilly remains of the day were preferable to his coldness, she stepped outside and closed the door. Sky gazing was one of Angela's favourite things and she got a good view of it from up here. It was all the company she needed. She wiped rainwater off the bench and sat down to watch the sun, a ball of orange, slip below the horizon. She was glad she'd kept her parka on and pulled the hood up for the extra warmth. Determined not to go inside until Geraint had finished, she sat on, drinking her tea and marvelling at the formations of clouds that floated over the metropolis below.

A light came on in the house next door and she saw, through the parting in the nets, an old man seated at a wooden table. The motionless white-haired figure was familiar, she'd seen him sitting there before. She thought he looked sad and so raised a tentative hand in solidarity. Felt vaguely embarrassed when it wasn't reciprocated. The door then creaked open, and a stout, elderly woman Angela also recognised, emerged in her floral apron and slippers.

'Hello.' She waved to her.

The woman nodded as she busied herself among her potted marjoram and mint. Her hutches of little brown rabbits. Angela remembered the woman's tattooed arm and wondered if she was like her mother: afraid to be still, afraid to have time to think.

'Aren't you cold?' The woman grimaced as she straightened her spine.

'A little. But it's so lovely to breathe fresh air. I've been stuck inside all day.'

Another nod.

'I love your garden. Have you lived here long?' Angela got up and wandered to the low wall that divided the two roof gardens.

'Since nineteen forty-eight.'

'Wow. That's nice. Nice to be so settled, I mean. I've never been settled.' She scrabbled around for something more significant to say. 'I'm only here until the spring. I'm cat-sitting for Lin and Greg.'

'We thought you were.'

She wondered who the *we* might be, then supposed it was the man sitting at the window. 'Don't the cats bother your rabbits?'

'If they weren't in cages, perhaps.'

'What happens to them come the winter?'

'To my herbs or my rabbits?'

'Both, I suppose.'

'It's perfectly sheltered against our back wall. I manage to keep my herbs going all year round.' Angela looked at the purple-headed sage, rosemary and lavender, their ceramic tubs carefully, rigidly placed. 'I'll cover them over if the weather turns bad. Not that Wales ever gets that bad. It's far milder than Poland. You'll never know cold unless you've survived a winter there.'

Angela eyed the dry-stalked thyme, the sweet-scented bay. She'd already guessed the origins of the woman's accent. Although, not overly pronounced, working alongside so many at the hotel who were from that part of the world meant she was familiar with it.

'D'you know much about herbs?'

'Some.' Already identifying the marjoram, she was imagining its peppery taste as the cold moved in beneath her clothes. 'I'm a chef.'

'Ah, that explains your early mornings and late nights.'

'Oh, dear.' Suddenly concerned. 'I don't disturb you, do I?'

'Not at all. I've always been an early riser. Where is it that you work?'

'At the Lloyd George Hotel.'

'I've heard of it. Very posh.' The woman closed her mouth abruptly and Angela suspected she had more to say, but for some reason changed her mind.

Over their backs, the city was disappearing into the blue shine of evening. It would be dark soon; the city would only be identifiable by its lights.

'I'd better get this lot in.' The woman scurried sideways to her washing line and Angela watched her struggling in the wind. The huge white sheets snapped back against her face.

'Let me help.' She hopped over the wall into the woman's garden and, without a word, each holding opposite corners of the sheets to fold them, they moved backwards and forwards as if in a dance.

'I'm Spike, by the way... Oh, no, I meant Angela. My name's Angela.'

'*Spike?*'

'It's my nickname.'

'Why?'

'Because my surname's Milligan.'

The old woman paused mid-fold and frowned, not understanding.

'Like the famous Spike Milligan?'

'Oh, I see. My Oskar loved him. He'd been through the war too. Different circumstances, of course, but he understood.'

A nod, awkward, unsure what she should say.

'So, An-gel-a... I prefer Angela. Such a pretty name.' They both reached up to unpeg the last sheet, then folded it together – Angela, careful not to bang her bandaged finger, liked how the woman delivered her name: carefully, as if it were a precious package. 'Although, I'm certainly one for nicknames. I give everyone nicknames.' The woman let go of a surprisingly girly giggle, the prune-dark of her eyes twinkling and mischievous. Angela warmed to her even more.

'And what's your name?'

'Me? I'm Zofia.' The Z, delivered with an exaggerated flourish, before bending to retrieve the laundry basket.

'Let me carry that for you,' Angela offered, springing forward.

'Dear me, young lady. I may be old but I'm not completely decrepit.'

'I know that.' She laughed. 'But at least make the most of me as I'm here.'

Angela followed Zofia to her kitchen door and deposited the laundry basket on the threshold.

'You'll stay for a little while?' Zofia placed a hand on Angela's arm. 'Try one of my little cakes. *Yes?*'

'Thank you but I'd better get back.' Sniffing the warm, comforting smells of whatever had been baking, she wished she could stay. 'Geraint's here, he's fixing the boiler.'

'Geraint?'

'He's my friend's boyfriend. *Oops*, no, that's wrong, he's her fiancé.' Angela picked over the word and found herself surprised by it.

'Another time?'

'Yes, another time.' She pushed her gaze past Zofia's bolstered bosom to a jacket that had been draped over a wooden chair. A jacket made of a shiny material she thought she recognised. 'I'd like that,' she said with a shiver of concern.

TWENTY-SEVEN

Herring gulls wheel and screech under a black bank of storm clouds. They echo my mood. A mood I carry into the corner shop where I look for a snack to eat on my way to work. It's not like I don't have the readies for once. I raided Babcia's purse again yesterday.

I walk down the only aisle and discount the fresh fruit and veg, it's carbs I want and I'm plumping for the last potato and beef pasty when a commotion starts up behind me. I turn to see a mother smacking her little boy. The woman has a large, bitter mouth and I hate her on sight. As a kid, I'd look up at my father's smacking hand, then into his face, push my silent questions into his eyes: *Why do you tell me off for doing childish things? Why did you bother having me if you can swing from cajoling to fury in the blink of an eye?*

I hate the mother with her vicious, slapping hand. I want to shout and stop her. Tell her I'd love to have children if I ever got lucky and met the right girl. I thought I found her once, and for a gilded moment, she thought she could be pregnant. We were told by the powers that be, we'd have been just another notch on the bedpost of social scroungers. A statistic demonised by the government. So, perhaps it was for the best that the shadow of possibility wasn't dragged into the light and can remain, as Babcia says, in the land of chances missed.

'How's your Zenith?' The man in front of me asks Whatshisname who is manning the till.

'She's exceedingly well, thank you.' He dons the same syrupy, lovesick look I've seen him give whenever his wife is mentioned. 'Her ballet company's touring Lithuania at the moment but she's told me she'll be home in time for Christmas.'

'Do pass on my best,' the man says, before exiting the shop with his purchases.

'I will. See you again, Arthur.' Whatshisname's smile slides when he sees I'm next in the queue. 'Is that all?' His sour enquiry, avoiding eye contact.

I don't answer. I stare beyond him at a wall of photographs of his habitually absent wife, captured mid-*grand jeté* and *arabesque* on a spotlit stage. I glimpsed the lovely Zenith Rees once, extricating her gazelle-like self from the passenger seat of Whatshisname's Saab on a rare visit home. Great legs, was how I described her to my father, who was keen for specifics. You could tell she was somebody, with her luscious head of hair. She looked like that Kate Middleton.

'Do you want a bag?' The pasty, the Mars bar, the two tubes of Parma Violets... Even the can of Sprite is picked up and scrutinised. 'It'll be an extra five pence.'

I nod and watch him stuff my things inside the thinnest plastic sheath and brace myself for his usual quip. Because this one never misses an opportunity to have a jab at me. And sure enough, as if on cue:

'You could cut bread with those.'

'You what?' I glare at him.

'Your jeans. Dear me, no one irons creases in their jeans.' He laughs at his joke and his eyes are as hard as the boiled sweets in the jars behind his counter.

'Oh, yeah, very funny,' I bite back for once and I can tell it surprises him. 'Cos the likes of you are all high-end fashion in your worn-out shop coat. D'you wanna know what people round here call you?' I am shouting now. I want other shoppers to hear, I want an audience. 'Mr Oxfam.'

A titter from somewhere deep inside his shop.

'Keep your hair on. You never usually mind sharing a joke.'

'Well, I do today. And while we're at it, maybe you'll be able to clear something up for me?' Whatshisname shifts uneasily from foot to foot. He's obviously frightened of me and it spurs me on. 'What's a bloke like you doing with those photos of a ballerina? Cos there's no way you're married to someone as glamorous as her.'

'You leave my Zenith out of this.'

'I bet she makes the most of it when she's away from you. I sure as hell would.'

'That'll be four pounds seventy-five.' His palm opens like a clam for my money. Then, with the ping of the till, he counts out my change onto the counter, like I'm not good enough to make physical contact with.

'Oi! I gave you a twenty. Where's my change?' The buzzing starts. It's dangerous when I'm in public.

'I've given it to you if you care to count it. And for your information, you gave me a ten.'

'I gave you a twenty, you thieving git.'

'I think you'll find—'

'You've been diddling me for years. You're a rotten crook. Now give me back my money.' As I've said, I can contain myself well enough if people don't piss me off, but this one is pissing me off big time. This din inside my head… It's people who do it. Stupid people, like this one, stirring me up.

'Okay, lad. No need to get worked up.' All smiles.

'Don't you bloody lad me.' I lean over the counter. Close enough to his weaselly face to smell his peppermint breath. A red mist floats in front of my eyes and the droning is booming. I'm a hair's breadth from decking him. I don't know how, but I pull myself back just in time, smack my palms against the counter: 'I've caught you out,' I shout and watch him shrink away. He looks terrified. I like it.

Whatshisname does as he's told and I hope I don't let my astonishment show. I take the tenner he owes me, along with the rest of the change and put it in my pocket.

'Dear me.' It's the woman who was bullying her kid. 'There's no need to be so aggressive.'

'What did you say?' I twist to confront her and see her child. His cheeks red and blotchy from crying. My anger sprouts a fresh set of wings, it muddles my brain – fighting these urges is becoming increasingly difficult.

Timid now, the woman clears her throat. 'I said that there's no need to be so aggressive.'

'Isn't there?' I grab my carrier bag, then bend at the waist to address the boy. 'I saw what she did to you, mate,' I whisper. 'But don't worry, you'll be able to get your own back one day. Really make her eyes water.'

I give the boy a generous wink before striding out into the street, carrier bag swinging.

Excited by my performance, I rip open the wrapper and bite the pasty in half. That bloke in there's always walked over me, thinking he can get one over on me. But not anymore. My thoughts, as I chew and swallow. I'm done with being pushed around.

TWENTY-EIGHT

Angela, home after a long, hot shift in the hotel kitchen, opened the door that led out to the roof garden and discovered a plate of little cakes had been left for her on the step. Carrying them inside, she peeled back the cellophane to look at them. The cakes smelt sweet, they smelt of love, and the kindness this demonstrated brought a rush of unexpected tears. Transferring them to a Tupperware box, she rinsed and dried the plate and carried it out into the fading afternoon.

'My dear, there's no need to thank me.' Zofia stood in the doorway of her kitchen in a short-sleeved dress the colour of an April hedgerow. 'Come in.' The look was warm, inviting and, returning the plate, Angela stepped inside. 'This is Oskar. My husband.' Zofia put the plate in the sink and gestured to the old man who sat up at the table.

'Very pleased to meet you, Oskar,' she said and blushed without knowing why.

His rheumy eyes seemed to stare without quite seeing her.

Then they drooped suddenly, the eyelids closing fast over his eyes.

'Do go through, dear.' Zofia fiddled with the amber pendant around her neck, her gold rings flashing. 'I'll put the kettle on. You'll have tea, I'm sure.'

Angela moved into the large living space that adjoined the kitchen. Painted a pastel pink, apart from an oval mirror on a chain and a collection of little wicker baskets, the walls were bare. She identified the smell of ironing. The hiss and scorch of steam. And sure enough, an ironing board in the corner was piled with what she supposed to be the sheets she helped Zofia gather in the other evening.

A cello leant against a heavy, wooden sideboard. Sheet music on a stand. She sidled over to its gloriously curved figure and dropped a hand on the slope of its shoulder, feeling its womanly shape.

'Oskar hadn't wanted to play at first.' Her find hadn't gone unnoticed. 'But when people got to hear he'd been a musician in the camp, they persuaded him to pick it up again. They even clubbed together for a cello – that cello. He used to play in a band. Weddings, parties, bar mitzvahs. The British Legion on Saturday nights. You see that watch.' Zofia, excessively proud, pointed to the classy timepiece adorning Oskar's wrist. 'That's a Daniel Wellington. It cost a small fortune. The band bought it for him when he retired.'

'My dad used to play the cello. It's my favourite instrument.' Angela surprised herself by mentioning this aspect of her father. Especially as he sold his cello before moving to Wales, claiming he was too grief-stricken to play after Robert died.

Behind her, Zofia opened a drawer and chose a cloth that, like the antimacassars on the backs of the furniture, looked as if it had been embroidered by hand. She placed it on a tray and laid out a matching set of cups and saucers.

'Do you still play, Oskar?'

The man didn't move. Staring ahead, out through the crisp white nets, Angela assumed he hadn't heard. Not that there was any need to ask, she could tell the cello hadn't been touched for some time: it attracted dust like the mountains surrounding her parents' cottage attracted clouds.

'Not anymore,' Zofia answered for him, and there was a sudden sadness behind her eyes. 'He kept it up for as long as he could. But he's quite blind now.'

'Oh, I'm sorry, I didn't know.' Choked with a sudden emotion, she turned away and noticed a vase of roses; their petals dropping like tears on the windowsill. 'Pretty colour,' she said quickly, to compensate for putting her foot in it.

'They were from my grandson.' A frown. 'For my birthday.'

'Oh, happy birthday.'

'*Uch.*' A soft laugh. 'I've started counting backwards.'

The kettle whistled between them as it came to the boil. Within minutes, Zofia had made the tea. The amber pendant around her neck swinging when she bent forward to place the tray on the table.

'Apologies for my appearance.' Another flash of her rings as she raised a hand to the headful of curlers under a triangle of scarf. Angela wasn't looking at her hair, she was more interested in her choice of lurid blue eyeshadow, her drawn-on eyebrows, the faint moustache. 'Shampoo and set. I do it myself when I can be bothered. Now, would you like a slice of pie with your tea? Apple and blackcurrant. Sadly, not fruit from our garden. Not any longer.' The look was wistful. 'Home-made pie is such a treat, don't you think?'

'I'd better not.' She tapped the waistband of her jeans.

'Don't be silly, child. You're perfect as you are. You'll have some with Oskar.'

Angela stood back as the fridge was opened and a golden-topped pie was retrieved from under a plate.

'Oh, my. Would you look at that? My blessed grandson's been at it.' Zofia cut a line across the spoilt part, then a wedge for Angela was slid onto a plate. 'Cream?' There wasn't time to answer, it was already being poured, thick and yellow, from a jug inside the fridge door. 'You go and sit down through there and enjoy it.'

Angela sat on the sofa with her plate of pie. The crust had been patterned with pastry leaves and she picked out a chunk of apple, ate it with her fingers. It was sweet and sharp all at once. She was hungrier than she realised but she wouldn't rush it like she would if she was eating alone. Hating to be thought of as greedy, she took her time, savouring every spoonful.

Zofia put a slice down in front of her husband, his nose twitching like the rabbits in their wire hutches below the window. The way she guided Oskar's hand to the plate, her hand balancing over his until his fingers took hold of the spoon and lifted a piece of pie to his mouth – Angela doubted she'd ever witnessed such tenderness.

'This is delicious.' The inside of the crust was white and gluey. Thinned at the top so the red of the berries showed through. She spooned up a pool of cream. Sugar gritting her tongue.

'Praise indeed, from a professional such as you.'

'Pastry's always been my downfall. You have the touch, though. You can't learn stuff like that, you've either got it or you haven't. Bit like being able to draw, I suppose. Because you can't really teach people to do that either.'

'I'm useless at drawing.'

'I love it.'

'How wonderful.' Zofia twinkled. 'Are you any good?'

'My art teacher said I had potential.'

'Can I see some of your work?'

'I'll bring my sketchbook with me next time if you like? I mean, if I'm invited again.' A self-conscious giggle.

'You're welcome here anytime, my dear. You remind me so much of my Kristina, seeing you lifts my heart. Now—' Zofia pulled up a wooden chair and sat down. 'How d'you take your tea?'

With the short sandy texture of pastry in her mouth, Angela didn't like to ask who Kristina was. Instead, she looked beyond Oskar's head, out through the half-netted window to the lowering sun bleeding red over the city. 'Aren't you having any?' She watched Zofia stir a sweetener into her tea.

'Best not. My doctor says I'm to avoid sugary things. Which is hard, because I love sugary things.' A mischievous smile that crinkled the corners of her eyes.

'Me too.' Angela licked her lips and accepted the delicate cup and saucer Zofia offered her.

'What happened to your finger?'

'I cut it at work.'

'My grandson's forever cutting himself. It's the ghastly jobs he does. Is your finger still sore?'

'No, it's loads better. I'm not sure I need the bandage anymore but I'm afraid to look at it.'

'D'you want me to see to it for you?'

'Would you? I'd be ever so grateful.'

'I'll do it after our tea.'

Angela didn't want to ask how old Zofia was when she told her it had been her birthday. Eighty... eighty-five maybe, she guessed, counting up the years since the end of the war. Her grandfather was only seventy-four but he looked years older than Zofia with his old man's eyes, filmed and inward-looking. Zofia had the eyes of a child.

Time passed. Broken only by the faint crackle of news bulletins from the radio and the hum of household appliances.

'You have a lovely home.'

'Thank you, dear.'

'I love next door too. It's amazing having gardens at the top, with the views and everything. I doubt I'm ever going to be able to afford my own place. Not a place like this, anyway.'

'I do feel sorry for you youngsters. Not that we own this house, we live here at the mercy of our landlord. We haven't much of anything, truth be told. We managed to put a bit by for our retirement but we aren't rich by anyone's standards. I wish we had bought this place when we had the chance but Oskar wouldn't hear of it. He said we were guests in this country and guests had no right owning property.'

'I suppose this area of Cardiff's very expensive.'

'*Ooh*, way beyond us, especially now. I feel bad about it because we haven't much to leave our grandchildren. I've never talked about it with my grandson but I've a feeling he thinks we own this property... That he's a fortune coming to him when we go. What a disappointment that's going to be.' She watched Zofia smooth her skirt over her arthritic knees and likened the skin on her hands to the skin on a roast chicken. 'But things aren't important, are they? Life's what matters. I know you feel the same.' Angela felt the intensity of the woman's gaze, it was as if she could see right down inside her. 'You've suffered too. It's written all over you.'

Unsure what to say, Angela swallowed her mouthful and looked away. Her eyes settled on a framed photograph on the sideboard. Black and white, it showed a smooth-faced couple sharing faraway looks and halfway smiles.

'Who are they?'

'My parents. Ruth and Mayer.'

'Your mother's very beautiful.'

'Inside and out.' Zofia dabbed away a sudden tear. 'The Nazis murdered them.'

Again, at a loss to know what to say. The cold, bald fact took her breath away.

'I was forced to leave my parents behind in the ghetto. I never saw either of them again.'

She listened to the slow, sombre quality of the woman's voice.

'D'you know, I can remember what I was doing when they came to take me... I was having a music lesson.' Zofia paused; the strong emotions were obviously making it difficult to speak. 'I was deported to Auschwitz with my brother.'

'Dear me, that's terrible.' Angela gently put down her empty plate. 'What happened to your brother?'

'He died there.'

Shocked at this, she covered her mouth with a hand. Angela knew all about what it was like to lose a brother, but not in such brutal circumstances. 'I'm so sorry, that's horrible.'

'*Bah*, they didn't think twice. Those monsters murdered babies and children. Indiscriminate, they were. My brother was nothing to them. Less than nothing.'

The minutes ticked by in silence: Zofia's dark history settling over them like a shroud.

'How do you think you survived?'

'Just luckier, that's all.'

They drank their tea; silent, save for the chinking of china and sipping sounds.

'Oskar refuses to speak of it. Survivor silence, they call it.' Zofia put down her cup and saucer and talked about her husband as if he wasn't there. 'It's how he deals with it. I think he wanted to be invisible and to be disbelieved because then he could try and make his memories vanish. It isn't a method that's worked for me. I need to purge it by talking... telling.' A shrug. 'I need to speak of what we went through, to share my nightmares and be understood.' As she talked, she squeezed the slackened skin of her forearm. Working, between finger and thumb, the blue-grey tattoo that seared her into history. 'I can barely trust what I witnessed with my own eyes, so I know how hard it is for others to believe. Better not to know.' A dry chuckle. 'Mankind cannot bear too much reality, don't you find?' That look again: unwavering and firm; it was difficult to escape it. Angela nodded; it was all she could do.

'No one listened to us when we went home,' Zofia continued. 'They didn't want to hear our stories. Deaf to us, they were. Our experiences were censored but as I say, I wanted to talk about what I'd seen and undergone, but I couldn't find anyone to listen. My words couldn't reach them. What I had to tell was beyond the realm of their understanding.'

'I suppose it was.' Angela took a breath. 'It must have been tough leaving Poland and starting over in another country. I don't think I could do it.'

'It wasn't so hard.' A purse of the lips, the ruby-red of her lipstick barely there. 'Poland sold us out. The only person in this family who nurtures romantic notions about the place is my grandson. But I tell him, we tried, we gave it three years, but in the end, we left our homeland and built a life for ourselves here in the UK. This country saved our lives and for that, I shall be eternally grateful.' Zofia's knees creaked when she rose from her chair to cross the room to stand beside Oskar. 'We waited until we were sixteen, and could marry. We were orphans together in that place.' She squeezed her husband's shoulder. 'We had no one but each other.'

Angela studied Oskar. Saw how his expression was both stern and sad. But for Zofia, at her touch, a sudden smile cracked his face wide open. A silent, gentle, demonstration of joy.

'Oskar's ambivalent towards our heritage, and you can understand why – it had once been punishable by death.' Zofia had returned to her chair. 'There was nothing to be done, we had to denounce our Polishness in the same way we did our Jewishness. And anyway, we needed to fit in.' A humourless laugh. 'The last thing either of us wanted was to stand out.'

'You poor things. I don't know what to say.'

'Ah, you sweet child. Take no notice of me and my ramblings. I'm just an old woman whose past is catching up with her.' Zofia held her gaze with the same unblinking steadiness. 'There's nothing life can throw at me; I've lived through the worst. It's why you can tell me anything, I'm unshockable.'

Another of Zofia's sudden smiles had Angela wondering if she could confide in her but as much as she would have liked to talk about Robert, after hearing of such suffering, she feared it would sound paltry.

'Go on,' Zofia encouraged, sensing her dither.

'I've been feeling pretty low. A friend of mine, Toni... Toni Perry. She was, *erm*... She was murdered.' Angela dispensed the word she could hardly bear to say. 'I can't believe she's gone.'

'Was that the girl I heard about on the news? Nasty business. I'm so sorry to hear she was your friend. We wondered why you looked sad.' That *we* again. Who did she mean? Was she talking about her and Oskar? But how was that possible? Oskar couldn't see her.

'It's been horrible, and worse now they've charged her ex-boyfriend because they've got the wrong person. Not that I can make anyone listen. I've been to the police; I've tried telling them.'

'Telling them what?'

'It doesn't matter. Everyone thinks I'm barmy, I don't want you thinking that too.'

'I won't do that, dear.'

'No, it's okay. I'd rather not trouble you with it all.'

'Well, if you don't want to talk about that, how about you tell me about your boyfriend... Or maybe you have a girlfriend. Love's love, however it finds you.'

Angela laughed.

'Why do you laugh? A pretty girl like you must have a special someone.'

'I don't. It's difficult to meet people.' She focused on the woman's gold wedding band. 'What with my college work and the shifts I do. But I...'

'Yes?' Velvet-eyed, Zofia had again sensed her reticence.

'There is someone I sort of like. We haven't spoken or anything, I've just been noticing him around college. I'm doing a management course, day-release.'

'Good for you. *And?* Who's this fellow you've got your eye on?'

Angela blushed.

'This is the twenty-first century. Women's lib, and all that. You can do what you want nowadays. You've got to talk to him, how else is he going to know what he's missing out on.'

'My friend, Anne-Marie, said the same.'

'I like the sound of Anne-Marie. You should listen to her.' Zofia twisted her wedding ring around behind the prominent bulge of her knuckle. 'I was the one who started things with Oskar, if I'd left things up to him, well—' She winked. 'You think he's quiet now. Always the strong, silent type my Oskar.' Angela saw the way she looked over at him, her eyes brimming with love.

'I've been invited to an engagement party at this swanky place in Cardiff Bay. It's a plus one.'

'There you go then. Perfect opportunity to ask this mystery man to accompany you.'

'D'you think? I'm not sure I'd have the nerve.'

'When is it?'

'Week Friday.'

'Then you've no time to lose.' Zofia looked excited. 'Have you something to wear?'

Angela pulled a face. 'That's the problem, and I can't afford to go splashing out on something new.'

'Perhaps, I can help you out in that department.'

'You could?'

'Yes, I think I may have just the thing. But we'll quickly sort your finger first, yes?'

That look Zofia gave her, it was as if she'd met her expectations exactly and again, Angela suspected this woman knew more about her than she first thought.

TWENTY-NINE

My father is sprawled on the sofa watching the rugby. I contemplate him from the hallway: tracing the bulge of his nose, the thick body beneath his jeans and shirt. The flesh swag of his chin. Listening to him belch, I think of what an unyielding presence he's been in my life and with no hope of him clearing off any time soon, the idea of days and days like this, yawning off into infinity, depresses me. I'm going to go off my head if I'm stuck in this hell with him for much longer.

I've got to take charge.

I've got to *do* something.

I peg the Crombie up in the hall then go straight up to my room to surf the net for ways to kill someone and get away with it. You wouldn't believe the amount of stuff that's available. There are even videos on YouTube giving step-by-step guides. Go on, check it out. I know there'll be lots of you who'll find it disturbing, but not me – it excites me.

Patricide.

Now, that's a nice new word. I love the sound of it. But is it possible? I search more sites, wanting to work out various options but it's difficult to concentrate, nothing is sinking in. The rugby must've hotted up because he's turned the volume to max and the roar of the crowd sounds as if it's coming through the floorboards. The buzzing starts again and, along with this, a tightening in my chest that makes it hard to breathe.

'Selfish bastard,' I shout and smack my desk with an angry fist. Deliberately loud. Half of me wants him to hear, wants him to come storming upstairs so I can have it out with him.

'How am I supposed to live here? With you?' I slam the desk again. Feel it wobble. My head's going to explode. I've got to get out. Go somewhere, anywhere… I'll drive anywhere.

I give myself a quick once-over in the mirror on the back of my door.

'Fuck him,' I tell my reflection and run a hand over my hair, which has really started to grow. It suits me longer; I'm looking more like my old self these days.

The racket from downstairs is worse. It competes with the noise that's getting louder in my head. I've got to avoid aggravation if I'm to stand a chance of holding it together. But how? When my father aggravates me more than anyone or anything and I have to share my private space with him.

I close the lid of my laptop and scoop up my mobile, along with the pile of change from the bedside table. I go downstairs and peer in on my father again. See the way he lurches from sofa to fridge and back to sofa again, clutching yet another cold tin of lager. A sudden, dangerous fury spurts inside me. Fuck, I hate him. I slouch away, the disgust I have for him tastes sour in my mouth.

I'm about to leave, but something stops me. I'm kidding myself if I think I can go out and leave the house in this state – it's a bombsite.

'Can't you clean up after yourself?' I say, barging in on him.

Marooned on the sofa, surrounded by empty lager cans and redundant crisp packets, he doesn't even look up. My hatred for him bubbles in my chest.

'It's like living with a teenager. It's not fair, you're behaving like a jerk.' I fuss around him, gathering his empties, tidying cushions. 'I can't cope with you and your mess... I really can't.' I smack his ashtray down. Spilling fag butts on the floor. It's not the only thing spilling over – my private self is spilling out too. The side of me I'm supposed to hide from him. 'It's not fair.'

'*It's not fair.*' He reckons he's imitating me. 'That's been your catchphrase since forever. When are you gonna grow up: life's not fair, don't you get it yet?'

He doesn't shift his eyes from the screen and, watching him exhale a lungful of cigarette smoke; nonchalant, casual, it takes everything I've got not to punch his lights out.

'I'm on holiday, laddie.' He screws out his cigarette and I see how yellow his fingers are from all his years of smoking. 'Give me a sodding break.'

'I'll give you a sodding break – I'll break your bloody neck,' I hiss and snatch up the ashtray to go and empty it.

'Leave it, will you?' He smacks my hand down. 'You're like an old woman about the place.'

I've always detested the smell of fags and living with him constantly puffing away, it turns my stomach. Look at the state of him. I'd love to tell him straight. Say how it's a good job Mum isn't around to see the person he's become.

I stare at him. Anger rising to a fever pitch. Not that he notices, he's too drunk. The circumstances that now and again force him and me to cohabit don't draw us closer, all it does is magnify our differences and our mutual dislike. It's a waste of time trying to communicate with him, I've never been able to. But this time, for some reason, things are worse than ever between us. I'm sure we never used to be as bad as this, that we used to be happy just ignoring one another. It's him, it is, he's the one who's changed. Nothing to do with me. And anyway, things between me and him have gone way beyond words – what's required now is action. I've got to get rid of him. It's the only way I'll have any peace.

And I'm going to do it.

Right now.

While his attention's focused on the game and the fact it's Wales 33, Ireland 3, with only fifteen minutes to go, this is my chance and I'm going to take it.

I move into the kitchen, stand at the sink and gulp down my rage. How to do it? How to stop this torment? I dart a look at my father's prized eight-piece knife set. Grab the largest knife and feel the weight of it in my hand. Appraise the length of the stainless-steel blade and decide it's more than adequate to do the job.

The phone chirps from the hall.

I jump at the sound. Listen to it ring and ring.

'Are you gonna get that?' my father bellows from the living room.

'No. It'll be for you.'

'It had betta be,' he growls and I wait for him to drag himself off the couch and stagger to answer it.

Pleased to see he's well-oiled enough not to notice me coming for him. I step quietly up behind him, just as he's lifting the receiver to his ear.

'Hello?' He rubs his eyes and yawns. 'Aye... Aye.'

I stare at his great, fat back, measuring where his vital organs are. My heart is racing, the buzzing in my head, thunderous.

Do it. Do it.

Stab him there? Or there? I can't screw this up. I've got to get it right. I raise the knife to head height... This is going to be as easy as slicing through butter.

'Marvin. For you.' My father swings around to face me. 'And you betta bloody talk to him, or I will,' he threatens through lowered pink eyelids.

I whip the knife behind me and slide the blade down inside the back of my jeans. It's a miracle he doesn't see it.

Why the fuck did I hesitate? I've gone and missed my chance.

I lift the receiver from his hand and take a few deep breaths.

Force myself to be calm. I can do this. Nice and gently... nice and gently. Marvin's a clever bastard but I'm cleverer.

'Hello, Marvin.' The droning ebbs and my mind clears as I watch my father shamble back to the living room, to what remains of the rugby game. 'Yes, shame I missed our session. Yeah, I know I haven't been in touch. I'm very sorry if I worried you.'

I'm pleased with my slyness and cunning – I'm surprisingly good at this acting lark.

'No, I haven't been well. I had another one of my migraines. Yeah, it's o-kay. I'm all right now. Jay's group? Yeah, it was good. Oh, no problem... Fix another time to come and see you? Tomorrow? Fine by me.'

Marvin doesn't suspect a thing. Why would he? I sound as compliant and laid-back as always. I punch the air. Thrilled with my deviousness. I can't tell you how brilliant it is to be getting one over on him.

'Yeah, I'm still here...'

THIRTY

The orange glow from street lamps that spilt in through the single sash window was abruptly exchanged for an electric bulb so bright it made Angela's eyes sting.

A creak when the big, curved doors of a wardrobe were opened. 'This used to be my daughter's room before she left home to get married,' Zofia said, rifling its contents.

'Your daughter – Kristina?' Angela tipped out the name she hoped she'd remembered correctly.

'That's right. My Kristina.'

Angela looked around at the highly patterned wallpaper, the bank of soft toys on the bed. A framed embroidery of brown rabbits playing in the snow was mounted above it.

'Is this your daughter?' She pointed to a framed photograph positioned beside an old Singer sewing machine on the workbench.

A rattle of coat hangers and Zofia twisted to see. 'That's her. Now you know why you remind me of her, she had beautiful red hair too... Like sunsets over the Vistula river back home.' Her expression dreamy-looking. 'It's hard to believe she's been gone more than twenty years. It's why I haven't changed it much in here, even though it's now my sewing room. I didn't want to lose her totally.' Angela supposed she was talking about the soft toys, the posters of ABBA and David Cassidy. Another of Red Rum on the back of the door. 'Horse mad, she was.' Zofia saw her looking. 'I've no idea where she got that from, no one in our family ever got near a horse.'

'Did she have an accident?' Angela had always been afraid of horses. Her fear of falling off and breaking bones, or worse, meant she'd never sat in a saddle.

'If meeting and marrying that husband of hers was an accident.'

Angela dropped her gaze to the scrubbed-to-white workbench, her fingers stroking the knots of wood that were as shiny as glass. She picked up a tube of Parma Violets.

'*Uch*. My grandson eats those. Disgusting things.' Zofia returned to the wardrobe and guided out various items, only to push them back inside again. 'He's never been right, my grandson. It's because he lost his mother so young, before he was properly formed.'

'But you lost your mother when you were young.'

'I know but he's different to the rest of us. He's never been able to accept it. He grieves for her still. But I suppose we all continue to grieve, don't we.' It wasn't a question and Angela didn't answer it. 'The trauma didn't stop with me and Oskar, you see. I think we somehow passed it on to our daughter. Yes, I think Kristina inherited our guilt and shame. And then our grandchildren too... That's my theory.' The tone was pensive. 'But then happiness in childhood isn't necessarily a good thing. Too happy and you'll learn nothing. A bad childhood can often be the making of you. You've got to survive the bumps. That's half the problem with this country, the world – it's run by middle-class white men, who've never felt a bump in the road. You have to have felt to have any understanding.'

As she listened to Zofia, Angela stared at the dark, black shadow cast by the tailor's dummy over the carpet. Then she inspected her finger. Thanks to Zofia, the bandage had gone and all that remained of her injury was a sticking plaster.

'Is this your grandson?' She picked up another framed photograph and studied the three faces that had been captured in a sun-filled park: the pretty redhead she now identified as Zofia's daughter had a baby girl in her arms and a young boy pressed against her thigh.

'That's him.' Zofia, head deep in the wardrobe again, had removed something black and flowing. She swished it around for a second or two, then changed her mind.

'Does he live in Cardiff?'

'Yes, he's not so far away.'

'And your granddaughter, where's she?'

'Yana?' Zofia stopped what she was doing and stared off into the middle distance. 'She lives in Israel.'

'That's a long way to go. What made her move there?'

'Her brother.' Zofia pulled a face. 'Yana's, well... she's rather scared of him.'

'Dear me, what d'you mean?'

'Something happened between them years ago. When they were children. It's a shame, Yana's such a lovely girl, I miss her terribly.'

'Does she ever visit?'

A shake of the head. 'Not for years. Busy with her own family.'

'Do you have any pictures of your grandchildren as grown-ups?' She had scanned the room and found nothing.

'D'you know, I don't think we do. I suppose the photographs stopped when their mother died.'

'That's sad.'

'Oh, you look so like my Kristina.' It was obvious Zofia

didn't want to talk about her grandchildren, and Angela didn't press her. 'I thought it the moment I saw you. The resemblance is uncanny.' She reached over and lifted the photograph from Angela's fingers, stroked her dead daughter's face through the glass. 'Such a pretty girl, such a pretty smile. And her laugh...' She sighed as if she was listening to it again.

Zofia set the photograph down and returned to the wardrobe. Slid out a dress in emerald-green and made it pirouette on its hanger. 'This is your colour.' The satiny material was pressed up against Angela's body. 'Near perfect, I think.' Fingers pressing here and there. 'Try it on for me, would you?'

Angela removed her sheepskin boots and slipped out of her jeans and top. Stood in the centre of the room self-conscious and squirming in her underwear.

'No need to be shy.' Zofia helped her with it. Holding her hair out of the way and zipping up the back. '*There.*' An appreciative gasp. 'Look, come and see how beautiful you are.' And Angela let herself be guided to the mirror.

The material felt cool against her body and she stood before her reflection, amazed by what she saw. Off the shoulder and to the knee, even she could see the vibrant green complimented her hair and the luminous quality of her skin. Flared at the waist, it was finished off with a perfect row of pearly buttons that meandered down the front.

'Do you like it?'

'Very much. It's beautiful.'

'Then you must have it.'

'But I couldn't possibly—'

'I insist.' Zofia circled her, gathering the satin in at the waist, tailoring it to Angela's figure. 'A little too big here, I think, but not a problem. Oh, my, you do look lovely. I remember when I used to fit into this. I wasn't always fat, you know.' The confession was almost an apology. 'I was slim like you are once.

But I suppose it's because we were starving as children. It's made me afraid of being hungry, I can never turn down a second helping.' A burst of laughter.

'I'm hardly slim.' Angela assessed what she considered to be her thick waistline and heavy thighs.

'Oh, darling girl, you're gorgeous.' There were tears in Zofia's eyes. 'And you must make the most of it. It's fleeting. One day you'll wake up old like me. That's why you must be happy. Are you happy?'

'I'm all right.' Angela, afraid she might cry too, bit on her bottom lip.

'*All right?* Dear me, that's no good. These should be the best years of your life.' Zofia, her mouth full of pins. 'It's that job you do. There's no time for fun.'

'I'm not going to be doing it for much longer. My friend, Anne-Marie—' She waited for Zofia to slide in another pin. 'She's hopefully sorting me a job interview for front of house.'

'I bet they'll snap you up. Shame my grandson couldn't get himself a job like that, but I suppose...' Her voice tapered off. 'Stand still for me, just let me get this section right.'

'You really know what you're doing.' Angela watched Zofia working quickly and deftly, tucking and adjusting, so the dress fitted her exactly. 'How come you're so good?'

'Like many of us Jewish migrants, we worked in the *shmatta*.' Angela frowned, not understanding. 'The rag trade,' Zofia explained. 'We used to have a haberdashery here in Roath, with a little sideline in repairs and alterations. It was exhausting but we were – *are*,' Zofia corrected herself, 'a great team. It provided a decent living. I'm profoundly grateful for the life I've had. My only regret is not having more children. I wanted to fill this house with children.'

'But you said you have grandchildren, who will go on and have children – none of them would've been born without you.'

'What a dear girl you are.' Zofia placed a hand on Angela's. Her cold fingertips made her look down at it: old, vein-embossed; what tales it could tell. 'You're right to remind me. Hitler didn't win, did he?'

This was said without bitterness or disillusionment and Angela thought it demonstrated the quiet, unanswerable quality of this woman's endurance.

'I also used to teach English to foreign students. Ugandan and Kenyan youngsters mostly – children of Asian descent who'd been expelled from Uganda by Idi Amin.' Zofia sucked back her breath. 'They'd lived through unspeakable horrors. But you're probably too young to remember what that monster did to his people.'

'I think I must be.' Embarrassed by her ignorance. 'Your English is impeccable.'

'Both of us refused to speak Polish when we came here. Oskar's always struggled with English but he still refuses to utter a word of his mother tongue. *There* – how does that feel?' Zofia had secured the final pin.

Angela checked herself out in the mirror. 'You're a genius, this dress is amazing. Thank you so much.' She kissed Zofia's cheek, breathed in her sweet lavender smell.

'You are such a dear, you try so hard to please, don't you?'

'Do I? I'm sorry.' At this small show of kindness, Angela burst into tears.

'Aw, now then. There, there, child.' Zofia opened her arms, and she let herself be cuddled in a way her mother had never done. It made her cry harder. Her tears wetting the shoulder of Zofia's dress. 'You're such a dear soul.' It felt lovely to have her back rubbed, to feel the warmth of another body against hers. 'I could tell at once, what a special one you were.'

'Thank you.' Angela pulled away and dabbed her eyes with her wrist.

A clap of hands and Zofia, tunnelling inside the wardrobe, retrieved a pair of green satin shoes. 'Try these on for size.'

'The colour's perfect.' She peeled off her socks and pushed her bare feet inside. The slingbacks, with their dainty kitten heels, felt a little on the small side but so pretty, she could put up with the discomfort. 'I love them.'

'They're yours.'

'You're so kind.' Feeling herself welling up again, she twisted her face to the wall.

'You know you can talk to me, don't you? About anything.' Zofia made her offer again, and with such sincerity, Angela believed she could.

'I'm sorry for getting upset like that. I don't know what came over me. Nothing I've experienced is as bad as the things you've lived through.' She gulped down the emotion, ashamed for giving in to it.

'I'm sure it would help if you talked about it.'

'I suppose,' she sniffed, 'it's that I've just never fitted in anywhere. I've always been out of step with everyone else.' *That's it*, she told herself, *you skirt around things, no need to go mentioning Robert.* 'And I'd give anything to fit in.' Angela wriggled out of the dress, careful not to prick herself on the pins and put on her jeans, fleece, socks and boots.

'*Ahh*, the black sheep of the family, eh? I guessed as much. Well, let me tell you something – you may want to fit in now, but one day you'll be grateful you weren't like all the others. That you weren't ordinary.'

'But I am ordinary. My parents say I'm ordinary, worse than ordinary.' Angela draped the dress over Zofia's arm.

'I don't like the sound of your parents. Do you have much to do with them?'

'Not really.'

'Good. They don't deserve you.'

The front door slammed shut. Forceful. Windows rattled in their frames. The sound severed their conversation.

'That'll be my grandson. He said he might call over.'

'Has he got his own key?' The idea of this appalled her. Angela was someone who valued her privacy above all things and suspected Zofia was the same.

Another nod. 'Oskar gave him one. The boy lets himself in whenever he likes.'

'Goodness.' Angela pulled a face. 'I'd better get going, it's getting late.' Sensing something tightening in Zofia's expression, she decided it would be best to leave them to it.

'Pop over tomorrow, I'll have finished altering the dress by then.'

Angela planted another kiss on the woman's cheek, then nipped up the stairs. She trotted past Oskar who didn't look as if he had moved and, with a quick 'Goodbye,' she was out the door and hopping over the low dividing wall.

THIRTY-ONE

My father is tugging on his sheepskin jacket and giving me a look that says: are you still here? He's heading out for the evening. Some bash down at the rugby club that I'm not invited to.

There's a film I want to watch coming on after the news, and I go and put my pyjamas on, fetch the packet of Jaffa Cakes I bought on my way home from work. I hide them in the tumble dryer we never use, along with the other things I buy that are just for me. My father will eat them otherwise, he's greedier than I am. I'm sure he knows I do this but he never lets on. It's been the way of things between him and me. It was the way of things for me growing up – everyone knowing things but pretending they didn't. And tonight, these Jaffa Cakes are an extra-special treat. Since my new clean lifestyle, I haven't eaten anything sugary for over a week.

My father leaves, at last, banging the kitchen door behind him. The house settles around me and feels like mine again. I can relax for the first time in weeks. I circle the room, turning out all the lights and sit in the dark. The glow of the television is just enough to go by. *Insomnia*. Al Pacino, wide-eyed and wired in a place that never gets dark.

It's nudging midnight when my father comes home. He staggers in and opens the fridge, its sickly yellow light on his face. He pulls out a can of lager, cracks it open and drinks most of it down. Belches without apology.

'You still up?' He sways into the living room, puts his can down on the table, then shakes off his jacket and drops it to the floor.

'No. This is a hologram.'

'*Sarky*.' He doesn't laugh. 'You're usually in bed by ten.'

'Not sleepy.'

He gives me an odd look like he's working something out. Folds his arms over his chest.

'Saw Rita Morgan down the club.' He says this like I'm interested, which I'm not. Does he think I like her or something? 'Smooching with some bloke, she was. Hands all over her. The stupid girl will get herself knocked up again if she don't look out.' And he laughs, hearty and loud; like he's laughing down a well.

'And I suppose you were *smooching* with her next door, were you? I heard the two of you giggling outside just now.'

'I had to walk her home, it's only gentlemanly.'

'Yeah? I wonder if her husband thinks that.'

He sits down and smacks out a fag from a bashed-up packet he finds in his shirt pocket. Lights it. My father doesn't wear socks, even in the winter and, when he sits, his trousers rise up to show his hairy ankles.

'Thought I'd chop some wood tomorrow.' His unexpected announcement, before draining what's left in his can. 'Wanna give me a hand?' He sucks on the end of his fag.

I nod, refusing to make eye contact. I lean sideways and look past him to the flickering television screen.

'What are you watching?'

I can tell he wants to be friends and this is his way of doing it, by making pointless conversation. But I'm not interested, it's gone way beyond that for me.

'I was watching a film. It's finished now.'

He nods, his mind turning to his next question. 'How's work going? That agency found you anything decent yet?'

'They say they're gonna fix me up with a night porter's job soon.'

'Better than scrubbing pans. Although, it's tough working nights.' He sounds as if he knows what he's talking about. 'But at least it's clean work, and you'll have your days to yourself.'

'Yeah, if you keep the noise down and I can get some kip.'

I'm thinking of the axe. The sharp blade. The force when it comes down. Splintering the logs every time.

Something that would be lethal in the wrong hands.

I look at his hands, the way he holds his cigarette tucked back in his fist, smoke leaking between his fingers. I'm thinking of the axe again. How we used to get a rhythm going and wondering if we can find that rhythm again. It was my job to place the wood on the block and his to wield the axe. He used to say we were like two parts of the same machine; such was our trust in each other.

Stupid fool. He doesn't realise that to trust absolutely is dangerous. That it could cost him his life. Perhaps I could be in charge of the axe for a change tomorrow? A chink of light illuminates a way out of this deadlock and the idea of bringing the axe down on his head cheers me a little.

'Want a tea?' I get up to hide my face. I can't risk him cottoning on to the new plan I'm hatching.

'Nah. Get us another lager.'

I pretend I haven't heard and make him tea. I know it's petty, but these small acts of defiance are what sustain me. When I return with two mugs, I see my father looking at the pair of framed photographs of me and Yana that live above the hearth.

'You shot up like a rhubarb stalk.' His eyes are full of tears and a fresh hatred bursts inside me. 'Funny, but you used to have such dreams about what you were going to do with your life. You were really bright as a kid.'

'I still am bright.'

I don't know what else to say. My father's right, I used to have dreams but I can't remember what they were anymore.

'D'you remember how good you were at running? You ran for your school.'

'I ran for Julia too.'

'Aye, you did.' His face lights up. 'Raised a fair bit of dosh, far as I remember.'

'Julia's dead. She had cancer.' I feel the sting of this news afresh but it's worth it to see the horror that floods his face.

'Oh, God. That's awful. She was such a lovely woman.' He looks sad and this makes me happy. 'Are you going to the funeral?'

'I've missed it. It's been and gone.'

'How come no one told you?'

'It's what Marvin was ringing about the other day. Why he was ringing the house? He didn't want to tell me in a text.'

'Oh, that explains things. You should've said.' He looks relieved. I shrug.

'I'm sorry, lad, I know how much you liked her.'

'Yeah, well, that's Marvin for you. He knew she was ill but he didn't bother to tell me. He doesn't give a shit about me, he never has.'

'Don't be daft, course he does.'

'No, he doesn't. Not like Julia did.' I stand my ground. 'Couple of days ago, I go all the way over there to have a full session with him but he could only spare me ten minutes. All he's interested in is covering his arse.'

'They do their best, lad. Be reasonable. You know they're stretched to breaking down there.'

'*Mac! Mac!*'

A frantic rattling and banging on the back door. Mrs Knitting – I recognise her irritating whine. Dressed in some needle-defying creation of bobbles and loops, she's lit up by the light in the porch. Her mouth a distorted black hole against the glass panel.

My father leaps to his feet. I don't think I've ever seen him move so fast.

'Sue? Is that you? What the hell's the matter?' He unlocks and opens the kitchen door.

'It's... it's... Oh, Mac.' Her face is wet with tears and her mascara's run in dirty black rivers down her face. She throws herself into my father's arms and bawls her head off. 'It's Frank. I know it's Frank.' She hiccups through her sobs. 'He's always hated him. He's done it this time... he's... he's. Oh, Mac.'

'For God's sake, what's happened?' My father presses her against him and strokes her hair. 'What's Frank done?'

'He's killed my Tigger.'

I turn away and leave them to it. My job here is done. I climb the stairs, go into my room, smiling at my badness as I undress for bed. It wasn't Frank who dealt with Tigger, it was me. Punishment for sticking her beak in where it isn't wanted. I told you I'd think of something, didn't I? And that cat's last breath at least silenced the humming in my head. For the time being anyway.

THIRTY-TWO

Angela was on her way to Rhiannon and Geraint's party and had taken a slight detour via the city centre to source an engagement present. Not that she had the first idea of what to buy. If she had been to their house, it would have given her ideas, but they still hadn't invited her. She wondered about calling Rhiannon to ask if there was something she wanted but didn't. They may have been on speaking terms again but Angela noticed a distinct frostiness the last time they spoke on the phone.

Safely zipped away under her parka, the emerald-green satin of Zofia's dress felt luxurious against her skin and, coupled with her hair arranged in an untidy heap in a way she hoped she suited, Angela felt quite buoyant when she alighted the bus. But now, out under a lowering sky and the afternoon dropping away into its early dusk, the surge of optimism had dissipated. Angela wasn't sure she wanted to go to this party anymore and thought, had Zofia not made such an effort with the dress, she would have made some excuse and cried off. Perhaps if she'd had someone to go with – she kept a lookout for that guy at college yesterday, not that she would have had the nerve to ask him –

but even then, she doubted it would have made a difference. She was coming to believe, now Rhiannon had moved on a stage in her life, that they had nothing in common anymore, if they ever did.

Angela glanced up at a row of plane trees shaking out the last of their golden plate-sized leaves over the stream of shoppers who jostled past with carrier bags and set out across the pedestrianised area. The slingbacks were already pinching her toes and giving her trouble. But worth it – look at them. And she did. She couldn't help but appreciate them in every reflective surface and wished that guy she had her eye on at college could see her – or even better if Mark could see her. Poor Mark. What must it be like for him locked up in that place? Hadn't the guy suffered enough?

Angela moseyed along the avenues of Christmas stalls and pop-up cafés, flaunting everything from tree decorations to mulled wine, the cascading white waterfalls of beaded lights above her head. Denying herself both breakfast and lunch, to ensure she fitted into the dress, her stomach grumbled when the mouth-watering smells of frying onions found her. Any other day, she would have bought one of the hotdogs she could see others enjoying. Slathered it in ketchup and ate it while walking along the street. Something she would never have been permitted to do in her mother's company.

When she found a stall selling everything from handmade beanbags to embroidered throws, she tried to forget her need for food and stopped for a nose around. The plump velvet cushions were beautiful and after doing a rapid calculation she decided she could afford three. Then, mid-reach for her purse, she stopped. She couldn't buy these; she didn't know their colour scheme. And frustrated to have finally opted for something, only to have to abandon it, she put her purse away and tried to summon the enthusiasm to continue her search.

She dipped in and out of the swish department stores. Their gleaming futuristic spaces were full of elevators carrying scores of shoppers up and down the various floors. They seemed to offer the most choice but, in the end, she left each of them empty-handed and found the chain stores, much like the arcades with their abundant shops, offered no solutions either. By now, her feet were killing her but she didn't slacken the pace and, turning back the way she'd come, she stumbled on a small homeware shop that looked promising. It had bay windows crammed with everything from designer jewellery to garden ornaments and she ventured inside to wander the razzle-dazzle of lavender bags, crystal glasses, pashminas, silk delphiniums, gold sandals and carved sheep. Time was running out, so she selected a quirky teapot and, listening to cheering and shouting going on in the street as she paid, she waited for it to be gift-wrapped.

With her back to the door, she trawled through a rack of greetings cards that had been further reduced in the sales. She'd already posted a card but there might be something she could fix to the present.

Out of nowhere, a man appeared. Large and forceful, he barged past her and out of the shop. Outraged by his discourteousness, she turned her annoyance to his big, broad back and sniffed the kitchen foody smell that radiated from his clothes. And something else. The oddly floral smell she identified that time on the bus.

She gawped at him, doubting what her eyes were telling her. It was that kitchen porter Toni was arguing with.

Follow him.

The decision was instantaneous. It snapped at her heels like a rabid dog and she charged to the door.

'Excuse me.'

About to push out into the street, the shop assistant was at her shoulder, pressing Rhiannon and Geraint's gift – now beautifully bound in gold wrapping – into her hands.

'Oh, yes.' She took it, barely registering, her mind sprinting away. And without saying thank you, she exited the shop to find the daylight had vanished. Sucked away into the dark sky.

Out on the pavement, twisting this way and that, the claustrophobic swell of shoppers pressed against her, hemming her in.

There.

Beyond the netting of fairy lights smothering a clump of night-blackened trees. Head and shoulders above the crowd. Without thinking too much about it, she set off after him, cursing her encumbrances: the impractical shoes, the unwieldy present under her arm, the bag slung over her shoulder that kept sliding down. Up ahead, a brass band started up. Strident and brash, it plugged her senses like cotton wool and she couldn't think straight. Zigzagging through a sea of bobble hats and scarves, struggling to keep pace, she whisked down deserted side streets, listened to the dangerous clatter of her heels reverberating against brick-walled alleyways until he eventually led her into a lonely cobbled courtyard lit by yellowy lamps, its flashy beds of hothouse flowers glowing in the uncertain light.

When he stopped, it forced her to do the same. Their breath was suspended in the raw dank air and a hideous silence descended. He swapped the Primark bag he was carrying to his other hand and, seeing his giant shadow thrown against the wall, she began to panic. The vacant expression on his textured face was terrifying and seeing the whites of his eyes from under his beanie hat, she gasped as if splashed in the face with icy water. He looked strong beneath his overcoat and the sense of danger tightened its grip. There was something nastier about him this time, it wasn't her imagination, he looked different. As if something had happened to change him and he no longer had anything to lose.

She spun on her heels. The only way out was back the way she'd come but she couldn't be sure where the exit was. Everything looked the same in the gloom. She hunted around for help. Anything. But to her dismay, there wasn't one lighted window she could shout up to. She froze. The courtyard had shrunk into some kind of hell and she was trapped in it. The man rubbed a heavy hand over his chin and his stone-hard stare made it difficult to breathe. It was colder than the stare he'd given Toni the last time Angela saw her.

She couldn't move. Nothing worked. Her body was rigid and numb with shock. No wonder Toni hadn't stood a chance – look at him, look at those arms. Did she seriously think he was going to let her go? Her heart thrashed like a netted bird and her pulse, dangerously fast, banged in her ears, at the base of her throat. The bastard had led her here deliberately. He must have twigged that she was following him.

What the hell was she thinking? She must have been mad to risk this after the last time.

This man was dangerous.

He killed Toni.

And now he was going to kill her.

What did she think it would achieve by following this man? It wasn't as if she was prepared to challenge him... Accuse him. This was crazy, not even the cops were interested in him. So why was she?

Then, as abruptly as he stopped, the man was on the move again. But instead of walking away like anyone else would've done, Angela, bizarrely, took off after him again. Convincing herself she hadn't been in danger; he hadn't really seen her. That she must see this through, it could prove vital. There had to be a reason why she'd seen him tonight. She wasn't being stupid and irresponsible; she was doing this for Toni.

For Mark.

A flash of his handsome face, his gorgeous smile, and with it, the soaring sensation in her stomach whenever he chose to turn his attention to her. The feelings she had for him were strong, she admitted this, and the idea he was going to be locked up for the rest of his life for something he didn't do was what propelled her to follow this man however perilous. Mark's freedom depended on her. It was down to Angela, she was his last hope – unless she could find a way to prove the kitchen porter was Toni's killer, Mark would be lost to her forever. And she didn't think she could live with that.

Within minutes, the man she was following re-emerged into the main pedestrianised area. Angela, calmer now there were people around, stayed as close to him as she dared. Jogging one second, forced to an agitated standstill the next. When the way ahead became blocked, she let out a faint howl, fearing all was lost and he'd got away. Then, pinpointing him again, she ignored the pain of the straps on her shoes that were carving holes in her heels and scurried after him. Even when something gave way under her and she wobbled, nearly falling, she still didn't stop. She ran as far as the castle, only to watch him slip aboard a bus that was already too far away for her to catch.

Mouth agape, she stood panting in the gutter, as the bus accelerated into the traffic. Only then did she notice it had started to rain, and the hair she'd taken such care to pin into a tousled pile had slipped free of its moorings. Hot and sweaty, she pressed an exasperated hand to her slippery brow. She couldn't believe it. All that effort for nothing.

She heaved out a defeated sigh and, turning, began to hobble back the way she'd come. Realising the present had ripped free of its pretty gold wrapping and the heel of her left shoe was hanging by a thread, and to go to the party looking like this was impossible.

THIRTY-THREE

The television is on when I come down in the morning. From the kitchen, I hear the familiar jingle that leads up to BBC *Breakfast News*, as I pour milk over my cereal and carefully sliced banana. My new healthy breakfast, for the new healthy me. Feeling pleased with myself, I carry my bowl and mug of tea into the living room and sit on the sofa to catch the headlines before leaving for work.

When the programme shifts to the Welsh newsroom, an unexpected image of Toni Perry fills the screen. The shock of seeing her makes me slop milk down the front of my new sweater. I reach for the remote to turn the volume up. '...*The man the police have charged with her murder has been named as Mark Fairfax...*' Then it's a photograph of the ex-boyfriend I'm looking at.

'Nasty business.' My father's sudden appearance gives me a start. 'That girl's body being found like that.' He exhales fag smoke in two grey tusks and turns the TV volume higher.

'I suppose,' I say, trying to sound normal.

'You knew her, didn't you?' Hovering, smouldering fag in hand, dropping ash on the carpet.

'*Knew her*? No, I didn't.'

He drops the remote. I can't leave it like that, so I lean over my cereal bowl and line it up neatly beside the DVD and Sky controls. Not satisfied until they are straight and measure a double thumb's width from the table edge. My father sees what I'm doing and tuts.

'Aye, you did.'

He's still talking about Toni and I don't respond. Spooning in my breakfast, I look sideways as he stubs out his cigarette. Grinding the spent butt fiercely into the ashtray that will be my job to empty.

'She was a waitress at that hotel where you work. What's it called again?' He clicks his fingers, unable to bring it to mind. 'That posh place... Come on, lad, help me out.'

'The Lloyd George,' I say, but it's all he's getting.

'Aye, that's it. It's why you're so interested.'

I ignore him and don't bother telling him I don't work at that hotel anymore.

'Come on, you can tell me.' The bastard isn't giving up. 'She gave you that funny glass, didn't she?'

'What?' I jerk my head, nearly choking on a slice of banana.

'That tumbler. I found it in the kitchen. I recognise the cartoon. It's the Taz Devil, innit? And this waitress girl was Tasmanian, wasn't she?'

'Yeah? So what if she was?' *Shut up, shut up*, I scream my silent scream, wishing I'd had the sense to sling the glass before old Hawkeye had the chance to find it.

'Come on, don't be shy. A pretty girl like that? You're not telling me you didn't fancy her.'

'I'd seen her around.' I am forced to concede this much. 'But I didn't know her.' I stretch over my knees and push him aside so I can see the screen.

'She why you've been buying new clothes? It's not like you to care what you look like, and that sweater's new. Where d'you get the money to go shopping for clothes?'

'It was cheap enough, I got it from Primark.'

'Nice. Might go and have a snoop in there myself.' He reaches out to touch my shoulder but I flick him away. 'This Toni girl, she why you're on a diet too?' He chuckles and peers into my breakfast bowl. 'That's fruit, ain't it? Since when d'you eat fruit?'

'I'm just giving the fry-ups a miss for a while.'

'Oh, aye.' He rubs a hand over his whiskery face, then leans down, close to mine. 'Wee bit outta your league, was she, son?'

'Just leave me alone.' The buzzing begins again. Dangerous, overwhelming, it takes everything I've got not to show how riled I am.

'*Ooh*, touched a nerve have I, laddie?'

I blank him, focus on the television. What I want to say is: Why's it inconceivable for a girl like Toni Perry to be interested in me? If it's only about looks, then how come a bloke like you ever got a chance with Mum? Talk about punching above your weight. But I don't. It's too risky. I might let something slip. But it's a strain to keep up the act, I'm frightened I'm going to burst at the seams, trying to hold it all in. Like I almost did the other night, I think, remembering the feel of that knife in my hand.

The news report goes live to Cardiff Central Police Station and Detective Sergeant Varrius tells us that Mark Fairfax, charged with Toni Perry's murder, had a motive. Varrius is a small-boned, black-haired man who talks with his hands. He looks too washed out to be up to much, which pleases me. 'The evidence is pretty conclusive,' then Varrius's watery gaze slides to the camera. 'We've a positive DNA match and Mr Fairfax and the murder victim were seen arguing outside their flat the night she died. Neighbours have provided statements saying they'd often been heard fighting... that their relationship had deteriorated during recent weeks. We are not looking for any other suspects... The case is expected to go to trial in the New Year.'

'They've got their man, then?' My father smiles his self-satisfied smile.

'Seems that way.' Mind churning, I'm not listening... *DNA... seen arguing...* Thank fuck I listened to that voice in my head. My mother's voice, I know that now. Telling me not to touch the body.

'Why have you gone a funny colour? Are you all right?'

I've got to get away from him. It would be so easy to knock him to the ground, finish him for good. But then what? The voice of reason finds me through the fog. I'm grateful to it, I must listen to it. If I go gratifying myself by resorting to violence, then I'll lose my liberty and how is that fair, when I'm managing myself well and beginning to enjoy life again?

'Oi, don't storm off.' My father lumbers after me into the kitchen. 'I asked if you were all right?'

I dump my cereal bowl in the sink. Usually, I wouldn't be able to leave the house without washing it up. But not today. 'I'm gonna be late for work.'

'God, you're acting weird.' He is watching me from the doorway. 'Was Babcia right? Have you been mucking around with your meds?'

'No way. You know I wouldn't do that.' I manage to put on my calm voice. Not quite the one I need to use with Marvin, but not far off.

'And you've been going to your therapy sessions?'

'You know I have,' I say, biting my lip to stop the anger from spewing out.

'Good. That's good. Because it'll come down hard on you if you don't.'

'I'm okay.'

'You betta be.'

'God, Dad, just back off, yeah? Marvin's cool with me, so what's your problem?'

'Because I know you better and you look a bit frazzled to me.' He drops his voice an octave and thinks he's reeling me in. 'I hope to God there's not more to this than you're letting on?'

The words shimmer and, like a double-edged knife, cut me wherever they touch.

THIRTY-FOUR

'Hello, would it be possible to speak to DS Varrius, please?' Angela, sneaking out before the end of a lecture, found herself a quiet corner in the college canteen to make her phone call.

'Who is this?'

'Angela Milligan.' She pulled off a boot and peeled her sock down over her heel to reposition the plaster.

'I'll see if he's available.'

The hold music was 'Greensleeves' and it reminded her of the ice-cream vans of her childhood. The vehicles that trawled the streets of Cheltenham scouting for kids.

'DC Thompson,' the gruff voice introduced itself.

'Oh, hello.' She jumped at the sound of it. 'Would it be possible to speak to DS Varrius, please?'

'He's not here.'

'Oh, well, the thing is, I do need to speak to him as a matter of urgency.'

'What about?'

'I'd really rather talk to him.'

'DS Varrius does have a rather busy schedule. Can I take your name?'

'Angela Milligan.'

'And your reason for calling?'

'It's about Toni Perry.'

'I'm aware of that case. And?'

'*Erm*, well...' Stumped by the officer's rudeness, Angela grappled with how best to say what she wanted to say. 'I just wanted to ask if he'd had any joy with the address I gave him?'

'Address?'

'For the man we talked about when I came to see him.' Angela was struggling, DC Thompson had caught her on the back foot.

'I am sorry but you've completely lost me. Who are you talking about?'

'The kitchen porter. From the Lloyd George Hotel. The one I think is involved in—' She needed to pause and clear her throat. 'In the murder of my friend, Toni Perry. I gave DS Varrius his address, so he could interview him.' The seconds passed without a response. '*Hello?* Are you still there?'

'I'm still here, but I don't know what you mean: *had any joy?*' Thompson spoke slowly, as if she was some kind of idiot.

'What I mean... What I meant. Well—' She broke off, then started again. 'What I wanted to know, was if it had been helpful with his enquiries?'

'Enquiries?'

'Into solving what happened to Toni Perry.' God, this was like pulling teeth. 'Because, I'm telling you, that kitchen porter was involved. I know it.'

'You know it, do you?' The tone was sarcastic.

'Yes, I do.' She was firm in her response. 'And you need to question him.'

'Oh, we do, do we? And what makes you—'

'Look,' Angela said, cutting him off. She knew it was impolite to interrupt but she didn't care, she had to make this man understand. 'I don't know how he did it, I don't know how he got inside her flat, he just did, okay? And I'm afraid you're going to send an innocent—'

'Can I have the name of this man you're talking about?' It was his turn to interrupt her.

'His name? I'm sorry, don't know his name.'

'Ah, right, you haven't got a name? So, let me get this straight, you came to see DS Varrius to report a man you don't even know the name of?' She could tell Thompson was mocking her. 'Sorry, and you're ringing up, why, again?'

'To ask if the address was of any help. To ask if you've interviewed him yet?'

'Interviewed a man you don't even know the name of?'

'Yes. I thought... I was just trying to be helpful.' She screwed up her face; this was excruciating. 'And I just wanted to let him know I've seen him again.'

'Right, well, please be assured that we take any information we are given seriously and will be pursuing this. Thank you for taking the time to telephone.'

DC Thompson ended the call and Angela was left feeling like an idiot. Yes, okay, she didn't know the kitchen porter's name but he didn't need to be so rude. HR would hand over his name if the police bothered to ask for it. She returned her phone to her bag and with Thompson's sarcasm ringing in her ear, she navigated the near-deserted canteen. There was more than ten minutes to go before her one-to-one session with her tutor, and she decided to chill for a minute and get a coffee.

The heels of her boots pitter-patter against the linoleum floor. The sound brought unwanted attention from the few who'd snuck in before the lunchtime rush. Vaguely aware of eyes, accusing orbs in the stillness, she ignored them and loosened the belt on her skirt and pushed her wayward hair off her face.

When she finally reached the glass-topped counter, she grasped the chrome surround with both hands as if victorious in a swimming gala. Only to come face to face with another challenge: the vending machine. Black and ominous, its squatting façade was a writhing flash of orange lights. All she wanted was a coffee, but what to have? The choice was infinite. Fiddling with the hem of her scarf, she scanned the deserted service area for a member of staff. All she saw was a teenager who, moulded to the till, wore an expression that shouted: *Don't even think about asking me.*

She opted for a cappuccino and jabbed what she thought were the corresponding buttons. Ignoring the teetering stacks of polystyrene beakers, she slotted a china cup on the sticky-looking grille and pressed MEDIUM. This triggered a sudden discharge of scalding froth that, showing no sign of stopping, had her grabbing another cup to catch the overspill.

'Five pounds thirty-five.' The teenager extended a marshmallow-plump hand.

Angela, scanning the laminated board above their heads, did a rapid calculation. 'Surely that can't be right?'

'Two coffees.' The pink palm bounced up and down: juggling an imaginary ball.

'Oh, I see what's happened.' Angela, waving a hand over the tray. 'Sorry, look, this is a medium. I made a mistake; I should have got myself a bigger cup.'

'Don't have no big cups.'

Angela exhaled. 'I just wanted a medium cappuccino. I pressed cappuccino, then medium. The cup was too small, so I filled up a second one.'

'Mr-Cha-k-ma.' Miss Pink Palms sings, *X Factor*-loud in the virtual emptiness. 'Mr-Cha-k-ma. We got-ta prob-lem.'

'Excuse me, there's no problem. I just... Oh, forget it, I haven't got time for this.'

'Yes, Scarlett, what's the matter?' A small Asian man in a brown nylon suit bobbed out from behind the mirror-smooth screen.

'There's nothing the matter.' Angela opened her purse and pinched out the coins. 'You can keep the change.'

Without looking where she was going, she swung around and bumped her tray against something solid that stood directly behind her. The cups tipped sideways and hot coffee slopped over her hand, over the floor... Over the feet of the person she had collided with.

'Oh, hell. I'm so sorry.'

'No harm done.' He grabbed a serviette and bent to mop the toes of his grubby trainers.

'I'm such an idiot. Are you sure you're okay?' Angela poured her anxiety over the hefty set of shoulders.

'Don't worry. I'm fine.'

When he stood up, she realised who it was.

It was him.

Angela couldn't believe it.

'You didn't burn yourself, did you?'

She watched him reach for another serviette from the metal holder, his expression bursting with a tender concern as he patted her hand dry.

'No.' She gawped up at him, still gripping the tray. 'I'm fine. I'm sure I'm fine.'

'Good. That's good.' A shy glance that made her insides wobble. 'Are you going to get another?' He squeezed the sodden serviettes into a ball.

He was tall. Way taller than she'd realised. Admiring him from afar, this was the first time she'd stood next to him and she barely came up to his shoulder. She continued to look up into his face, searching his expression for the lost look she first identified in him all those weeks ago. And thinking she found it, was flooded with a desire to have him hold her, to sweep her up in his arms and carry her away to a better place, a better life. The intensity of feeling was instant and so overwhelming, she almost forgot to breathe.

'Hello?' His voice filtered through to her.

'Sorry, did you say something?' She gave him what she hoped was her best smile.

'I'm Leon.'

He shot out a hand. Such an old-fashioned gesture. She liked it and held on to it for far longer than necessary and when, at last, he pulled away, she hoped he hadn't noticed. A blush travelled up her neck. She slapped a hand over it and felt the heat through her fingers.

'I've seen you around here before, haven't I?' She thought how much better looking he was up close, too. Better looking, dare she say, than Mark.

'I doubt it. I only started last week. Accountancy. Well, my ATT level two, to be precise. Up to now, I've been studying from home but it's more complicated than I first thought.'

'Oh, right. I must be confusing you with someone else. H-how are...' She coughed a nervous cough. His eyes were beautiful, like a pair of deep, blue pools. 'How are you finding it?'

He gave an exaggerated eye-roll. 'Mind-bendingly boring. But I've got to stick at it.'

'Oi, d'you mind, mate?' Someone who wanted to pay for their lunch was at the till. 'You in the queue?'

'No. You go ahead.' Angela stepped aside and felt her blush intensify.

Leon followed her and they stood side by silent side, next to the trays of cutlery, the sachets of sauces. Listened to the thrum of voices as the canteen filled up around them.

'I need to pay for this.' He showed her the can of Diet Coke he'd been holding. 'You sure I can't get you another coffee?'

'That's sweet of you but don't worry, I haven't really got time now.'

'That's a shame. When will you have time, then? D'you want to give me your number? Maybe we could meet up and do it then.' Leon took out his mobile and she saw his expression ripening into expectation.

She reeled it off. Watched him save it into his contacts.

'Don't you want my name?' She laughed when she realised she hadn't given it to him.

'Oh, yeah.' He grinned. 'I don't know it, do I?'

'It's Angela.'

'An-gel-a. Angela. Yeah, nice name.'

'Thanks.' She smiled back, loving the way he made it sound.

What remained of Angela's afternoon classes were lost on her. She doodled the time away in a kind of half-dream. She couldn't believe her luck. Bumping into Leon like that, what are the chances? When she smiled, she pressed her fingers to it. He'd asked for her number, hadn't he? He'd actually asked for her number. She wanted to stand up and shout it out. You only asked for someone's number if you wanted to see them again, right? It must mean he liked her. She should be concentrating; she was going to have to write an essay on worker and employee rights this week but the drone of the lecturer's voice had her mind wandering again. Back to Leon, with his big soft smile, his heart-stopping eyes. She was grinning widely now and didn't care who saw. As right down inside, in the most intimate part of her, keeping time with her heartbeat, Leon had already taken root.

The lecture dwindled to a close and she got up to file out with the others. But when her mobile beeped from inside her bag she stepped aside. Expecting another dressing-down from Rhiannon, she nearly didn't bother activating her inbox but lucky she did.

> ROATH PARK. THURSDAY 2PM. SAY YOU'LL COME. LOVE LEON XX

It was a message she needed to read several times before she let herself believe it.

THIRTY-FIVE

I come home after another horrible day at work and the kitchen is a tip. The old man's dumped my walking boots – the ones he's commandeered since he's been back – by the fridge. They are filthy and the bin is full to bursting. The lazy bastard's even left the recycling for me to sort ready for tomorrow's collection.

'How many more bloody times?'

I fire my complaint at the lights I can see burning in the living room and carry the boots that will need a damn good cleaning before I can wear them again, out into the porch. Then I wet the floor cloth I keep under the sink and get down on my hands and knees, still in the Crombie, to clean the muddy smears off the floor. The effort makes the blood rush to my head and with it, the warning sound starts up again. It makes perspiration break out over my top lip and across my back.

'Is it really too much to ask? Am I being that unreasonable?'

Up on my feet, I hurl the cloth at the sink.

I've had enough.

I'm going to finish him.

Tonight.

No more Mr Nice Guy, I can't take this anymore.

I grab a knife from the wooden block on the work surface. It's the same long blade I chose for the job the last time and, looking at it, I know I won't fuck it up again. This time I'm going to do it. How do I know? Because I've been living with this pressure cooker inside my head since he came home and something's got to give.

My pulse bounces wildly in my wrists but my hands are surprisingly steady. I like the cold feel of steel and tilt the blade backwards and forwards, delighting at how it snares the light. The feeling of power it gives me just holding it is amazing. I've never felt so in control, so sure of what I'm about to do.

I test the sharpness of the blade against my thumb. It will do the job for sure. I smile, through the intensifying buzz in my brain. Think: I am changed now. Toni's death changed me. There's no going back from that. All of us can change. How many times have I been told that in those group psychotherapy sessions? Too often. But for the first time in my life, I know it's true. Of course, it usually means change for the better and that rule may well apply to some but not to me. I've emerged from my chrysalis as a fully-fledged killer. Accidental, or otherwise, a killer is what I am. Because once you've done it: once you've looked the darkness in the eye; the second time is easy. Or so they say. And I've been feeling great about things, and if it weren't for this one fly – this one giant, stinking fly in the ointment – I would have a chance at living a full and happy life.

I'm telling you, the bastard has had this coming for weeks, it's not like I haven't given him enough warnings. Show it your fist, show it who's boss, that will bring it into line. A favourite saying of Mac's and one I intend to turn on him, right now.

Fired up like never before, it's without thinking much beyond what needs to be done, that I follow the trail of mess, the knife held stiffly behind my back, ready to strike. I can smell the disgusting reek of his cigarettes from here, and see the flickering television screen, the lamps blazing beyond the fluted glass separating kitchen from living room. I'm not thinking much beyond killing him. All I want is for this torment to be over. For this racket in my head to stop.

'Dad, are you there?' I call ahead of myself, although God knows why. It's stupid to warn him.

With a cold, hard determination, I swing open the door and feel a numbness spreading through me. Not numb like when I was on the drugs. This is different. This is deadly.

THIRTY-SIX

'Hey, Spike.'

Angela, in her whites and taking a break from the kitchen, was queuing for her evening meal in the staff canteen. It surprised her to see Anne-Marie.

'Hi, you don't usually work this late. What's up?'

'Had to take minutes for Jasmine. There was a meeting with housekeeping, they can only do late. It went on and on. Anyway, I'm glad I bumped into you.'

'You are?'

'Yes, I've found something out.'

'Go on?'

'Shall we find a table first?' Anne-Marie smiled. 'You look great, by the way.'

'Do I? In this get-up?' Angela looked down on herself, then followed on behind with her tray of tea and toast.

'I'm serious. That lot over there have noticed you, anyway.'

The place was packed out. Despite the lateness of the hour, there were hardly any free tables. Angela could see who *that lot* meant when they circled the room looking for somewhere to park themselves. The increase in numbers was mostly due to a large group of contractors brought in to refurbish the hotel's upper floors.

'You can join us if you like.' One of them – small, well-muscled, covered in tattoos – beckoned them over.

'See what I mean?' Anne-Marie gave her a jokey shove.

'There's a table. Quick, before someone else nabs it.'

They sat down. Slotted their trays between the spills of previous diners.

'Come on then.' Angela looked up from the buttering of her first round of toast. 'What've you got to tell me?'

'Never mind about that, I want to know about you. I've never seen you look happier.'

Angela bit off a corner of toast and chewed it slowly.

'Come on, spill.'

She laughed at her friend's impatience. 'Guess.'

Anne-Marie sipped her tea and the steam fogging her glasses made her look vaguely comical. 'Hell, I don't know. You, you... Oh, I give up.'

'You remember I told you about that bloke I liked.'

'Mr College, yeah?'

'We got chatting the other day.'

'You did?'

'Yep.'

'And?'

'He asked me for my number.'

'No way.'

Angela giggled. 'And then he sent me a text to ask if I wanted to meet with him on Thursday.'

'Tomorrow! Bloody hell, Spike, you're a fast worker.' Anne-Marie looked pleased. 'How d'you do it? Did you ask him?'

'No, it was sort of a happy accident. I tipped coffee on him.'

'Love it.' A clap of her hands. 'You better let me know how it goes.'

'Course I will.' She finished off her first slice of toast and buttered the second. 'Anyway, what did you have to tell me?'

'Oh, yes, I nearly forgot. It's about that kitchen porter bloke.'

Angela gulped. She had hoped Anne-Marie's news was about the front-of-house interview.

'You know he lost his job because he was calling in sick when he was really working elsewhere? Well, it turns out, Toni was the one who shopped him to HR.'

'Toni? How the hell would she know he'd cried off work? Why would she even care?'

'I thought that. Anyway, that's why he got the sack, but Toni had some issue with him before this, apparently. Accused him of nicking from her locker, or something.'

'Really? Toni never mentioned any of this to me.' Angela put down her knife and licked butter off her fingers.

'She was out to get him big time going by the number of complaints she made against him.'

'I had no idea. That must've been what their argument was about.'

'Maybe.' Anne-Marie pulled a face. 'But then Toni ended up finding what she thought he'd nicked.'

'That's embarrassing.'

'I know. But imagine how pissed off he must've been with her.'

Angela stared at her toast, unsure if she wanted it. 'How come you found all this out? Last time we spoke you were pissed off with me for still going on about it.'

'I just happened to come across it the other day when I was doing some filing. Philip must've dealt with it.'

'Who's Philip?'

'One of the temps.'

'Well, you know what this means, don't you?'

Anne-Marie shook her head.

'It means that man had a motive. Motive to kill Toni.'

'Oh, come on. You can't be serious?'

'I am. Totally serious. This is the link – can't you see it? HR have got to tell the police. They won't listen to me but they'll listen to them. God, this is brilliant, I can't wait to tell Mark.'

'Hang on,' Anne-Marie reached across the table and squeezed Angela's hand, 'I didn't tell you this so you could go off on your crusade again.'

'But you *have* to. You have to get Jasmine to tell them. This is crucial. This is evidence.'

'Spike, for God's sake, listen to yourself. Why d'you have to make a drama out of everything?' Angela felt the pressure when Anne-Marie removed her hand: the warmth was replaced with a cold feeling that settled inside her. 'There's no evidence. Not against this kitchen porter. If there was, the police would've found it by now.'

She watched Anne-Marie lean back in her chair and lift up her tight curls in both hands, holding them there on the top of her head. The skin on her neck vulnerable, milky-blue. Then she let her hair fall again.

'They aren't idiots, Spike, they know what they're doing. They're saying no one broke into the flat, which means she must've known her killer. And she knew her killer because it was Mark. They've got their man, how many more times? I know you don't want to think that Mark could be capable of something this terrible, but he did it. He killed Toni. You're just going to have to accept it.'

'How long have you known about Toni shopping that kitchen porter?'

'A couple of days.'

'And HR can't see this is valuable information?'

Anne-Marie shrugged and drained what was left of her tea. 'It's not up to me, is it?'

'I keep seeing him around.'

'Who?'

'That kitchen porter.'

'Weird.'

'He's the one who's weird.'

'Being weird doesn't mean you're capable of murder.'

'Why did you bother telling me any of this, if you didn't want me to do anything?'

Another shrug.

'Mark didn't kill Toni. For God's sake, Anne-Marie, the police are making a massive mistake. I know it. I can feel it.'

'You can feel it?'

She could tell Anne-Marie was mocking her; that it was a struggle for her to keep a straight face. '*Yes*. And if HR doesn't hand over this crucial information, then I will.'

'You're going to the police again?'

'Yes, I am.'

'Huh, they'll laugh you out of the place.'

'I don't get you at all. Why won't you even consider this bloke could be involved? D'you know him, or something? I mean, you've accused me of fancying Mark, do you fancy this kitchen porter? Is that it?'

'Don't be ridiculous. I don't even know who he is. I don't even know what he looks like.'

'Then why does it feel like you're protecting him?'

'I'm not protecting him, you *eejit* – I'm protecting you. You've got to leave this alone.'

'And if I don't?'

'Then I'm not sure I can be friends with you anymore.'

THIRTY-SEVEN

I storm into the living room. The carving knife held at a right angle to my body. I'm ready for him. Whatever he comes at me with, there's no way he's getting away this time.

I dart a look around the room. The television's on, the sound turned right down, barely there. There's a dip in the sofa from where he's been sitting, and I tilt my head to the ceiling, crane to listen for any sign of him moving around in the rooms above. For the flushing of the toilet. His tread on the stairs.

I wait.

Tuck myself in behind the fluted glass of the dividing door. Knife at the ready.

Then I see it.

A small white envelope propped on the mantelpiece next to the photos of me and Yana in our school uniforms. I cross the room to retrieve it. Noiselessly, an eye on the door, on the stairs. The handle of the knife still pressed against my body, the blade sticking out into the room. Head whirring, I rip the envelope open and pull out a note in my father's neat engineer hand. His handwriting is the only neat thing about him.

I can't believe it. I have to read the note again and again. And still, I don't believe it. It can't be true.

I glance at the stack of logs by the fire. Imagine the ones in the woodshed. My father would have done this, thinking of me. He must have spent the day chopping them.

I still don't trust what it says in his note. I need to check upstairs first. Which I do, clutching the note with its envelope, along with the knife.

I throw open the bathroom door. Nothing. Do the same with the spare room. Nothing. I go inside my father's room and sit on the bed, still holding the knife. I don't like coming in here. This is the room where Mum died and to return to the memory is like picking a scab, making it bleed, making it hurt, but I can't stop myself from doing it…

I'd been kept home from school that day without explanation. Aunty Morgan – Rita's mum, from three doors down, who wasn't an aunty at all, just another example of the lies grown-ups tell – had been summoned to sit with me and my baby sister. She was reading me a story. *Chicken Licken*. My favourite. But she was spoiling it. Reading too quickly, snapping the pages over, now and again throwing her head to the ceiling and the muffled sounds from the room upstairs. This room, where Mum lay dying. Not that I knew this yet.

Aunty Morgan's voice: monotonous, drifting; irritated me. Her breath smelt stale from the syrup-thick Polish coffee Babcia had made, which sat half-finished and cooling at her ankles. I wanted to pinch her, tell her she must do the different voices and point out who was who from the full-page illustrations the way Mum did. But she kept bursting into tears and dabbing her nose on a tissue fished from her sleeve. It was called: 'Not giving it your full attention', it was something I'd have been told off for. And it made me cross.

A thud had come from above. Aunty Morgan jerked at the sound and the storybook slid from her lap to the floor. It knocked the cup from its saucer and she leant down to mop it from the carpet with her already soggy tissue. That won't do it, I had eyed her coldly and a smile crept over my mouth when I thought how annoyed Babcia was going to be: Babcia who squanders nothing and hates any kind of wastefulness in others. It served the silly woman right for not concentrating, but it gave me the opportunity I'd been waiting for. I ran upstairs and found my father, seated in the shadows on the landing, crying. A chilling, terrible sound. But with an arm flung over his eyes, it meant I could inch past him unseen and slip inside my parents' bedroom.

It was dark, the air close. The smell wasn't one I recognised and, mixed through with the sweetness of air freshener, not one I liked. I identified Mum through the murkiness. Saw her red hair had been scraped back in a band and her face was oily with sweat.

'Mummy!' I threw wide my arms and rushed towards the bed. 'Mummy.'

But the colourless lips of the woman who was propped on a mountain of pillows stopped me in my tracks. As did the bright eyes swimming in their sockets. Instinct told me there was something dreadfully wrong, that all those trips to the hospital that I'd been told would make Mum better, were lies.

I tracked her shape beneath the weight of the kingfisher-blue counterpane we'd bought on our only visit to Gdańsk. Watched the rise and fall of her ribcage as she breathed. Just. A sidelong glance at this same bedside table to count up the squat brown bottles of antiemetics, steroids, a sticky-sided bottle of Oramorph with spoon. A box of Kleenex, a glass of lemon squash with its curious pink straw. I realised later, years later, these were accoutrements of the dying; things to make the last stages of Mum's life more comfortable.

The rustle of bed-sheets had been accompanied by a faint sigh from the mattress, as she shifted her non-existent weight. Cloud-soft, the covers released a puff of chemicals, and a feeble voice floated through the gloom.

'I'm nearly there.' Her words were punctuated with snatches of air. 'You must promise me you're going to be brave, my little one.' A hand, bruised by the IV needles from recent chemotherapy, patted the bedcovers, wanting me to move closer. 'Let's say our goodbyes quietly. No fuss, eh? There's a good boy.'

I didn't move. Couldn't move. The curtains fluttered at the open window and a chill breeze travelled the room. And something in the unravelling seconds told me I would remember this moment forever. It was, I thought, a foretaste of what my life would be; this dying time, the gloomy light, Mum's shape cut from the shadows.

Then the door swung open behind me.

'Oh, come now.' It was the doctor, smiling his treacherous smile. 'This is no place for little boys.'

'But I want my mummy,' I pleaded. 'I want a cuddle.'

'I know you do, but mummy needs her rest.' The doctor's chipped blue gaze held no pity and a restraining hand was laid on my narrow shoulders. 'She's going to be fine. Just fine.'

Liar.

My glowered accusation before exchanging a silent look of goodbye with Mum and, ducking under the doctor's arm, I pitched from the room.

It's hard to believe it now but it took Babcia and Grandpa five whole days to tell me. My father was nowhere, he'd taken himself off to lick his wounds, Grandpa said. This too was an indication of things to come.

'Your mummy died.' They were unanimous. The grief for their only child gurgling in their throats.

'I know,' I replied and eyed them coolly, enjoying the way they swapped nervous glances.

That was the moment I knew the whole world was blighted and all grown-ups were liars. Because they lied to me all the time. Saying things like they had eyes in the back of their heads when they had no such thing. No, they weren't to be trusted and I've never forgiven them, any of them. For Mum's death. For deceiving me.

I reread the note I'm still holding like I'm still holding the knife. It tells me my father's gone. Gone to Germany. That the money was too good to pass up. It says he'll be back in February and he'll ring when he's settled to give me his address.

February? That's months away. This is brilliant. This is the best news I've had in ages.

The buzzing subsides and I get to my feet. Drowsy, wobbly, I lean against the wall until I can trust my legs to hold me upright. I'm so tired, I reckon I could sleep for a week. I look down at my hand, my knife-holding hand, and feel my pulse slow. It's like I've run the longest race, and now the race is over. The inner struggle to appear normal and of a sound and balanced mind has worn me out. At least I don't need to pretend at home anymore. Now he's gone, I can be my new self within these four walls. And what is my new self? That's something I'm still working out. It's probably why I'm exhausted. It takes a lot of energy to keep my thoughts intact. To stop my private self from seeping out and betraying me.

Calmer now, and thinking more rationally, perhaps what I'm feeling is relief. I don't suppose I really wanted my father dead, but when that noise starts, I can't think straight, I lose all sense of reason. And anyway, what would I have done with his body? There wouldn't be anyone else who could take the rap for me this time, not like they've taken it for Toni. I'd have been the number one suspect.

I go downstairs. Return the knife to the block with the others. I've got that edgy sense I'm being watched again, but I'm pretty sure no one is out there. I fight the urge to close the kitchen blinds. Let the night look in if it wants to, there's nothing more to see here.

<h1 style="text-align:center">THIRTY-EIGHT</h1>

Angela couldn't see the lake but, following the narrow tarmac path down one slope, then another, dodging the duck and goose muck, the recent puddles, she saw it flash through the thin line of trees. She reached the water, found the bench she had agreed to meet him on, and sat down to wait.

She hoped the sketchbook she'd brought with her would work in the same way as bringing a dog. People, and there were a few about, would think you're legit. They would smile and keep on walking, knowing you didn't want to be bothered. This was what people did in parks – they exercised their dogs, or they came with their pencils to draw.

She opened her sketchbook and worked. Realising, after about half an hour and without needing to think too much about it, that she'd stopped expecting Leon to come. Above her, a plane unzipped the perilous blue sky. It seemed to dodge the gold-rimmed clouds in a way the sun couldn't quite manage. Watching its progress, she worked through a list of countries it might be destined for and a sudden gust of wind blew her hair around her face. She pushed it away and moved a little, settled herself and turned the sketchbook around, squeezing her eyes into slits to filter out the glare off the water.

The lake brought a memory of the silver-skinned reservoir set within its cushion of neatly striped yellow and dark-green conifers. The fence-posts, with their lonely strands of wire, marked out the bridleways and cycle paths. Then came an unwanted image of her brother when he dipped below the lip of the water. His upturned face, as round and pale as the moon, floating away from her, always just out of reach. Until it was eventually swallowed up by the ink-black depths.

On the opposite bank, a huge disturbance. Using her hand as a visor, she squinted through the sunshine as something big and bulky stretched itself up from the water beside a darkened clump of willows. A swan. It hauled itself into the air, gaining height, slowly, slowly, until it had climbed into the sky. She ducked instinctively under it, looking up at its white undercarriage passing low overhead.

'Magnificent creatures.' Leon, emerging from the shadows.

'Amazing.' She pretended not to be surprised by him.

'You can see how they got the idea for aeroplanes.'

Angela ripped off the sheet of spoiled paper and scrunched it into a ball. She was about to drop it into the litter bin beside the bench when Leon reached out with a gloved hand to take it.

'Don't look. It's no good.'

She watched him smooth it flat.

'I have to disagree. You are good. Very good.' She felt the bench shift slightly when he sat down beside her. 'Would you draw me?'

'*Draw you?*' She cleared her throat. 'Well, yes, if you want.'

A small nod from him and she flipped to a new page and began to draw quickly. Leon's face was tense and focused. This must be how he looked when he was working. An accountant's face. Adding and tallying, working things out in a leather-bound ledger. She didn't quite touch him but an inch closer and her fingers would have brushed his cheek. Drawing him allowed her to study him. She was supposed to look; it was what drawing from life was all about. But as the afternoon closed down around them, what she wanted to do was put down her pencil and cup his face in her hands and hold him there forever. She measured him with her eyes. The width of his thighs, his chest, and she liked how much bigger than her he was. This was a man who would take care of her in a different way from how she would take care of him.

'Can I see it yet?' Leon broke the spell and, shifting a little, he crossed his legs.

'Oh, I don't know. I'm no good anymore. You have to draw every day. Every single day, if you're going to keep your eye in.'

'Your *what* in?'

'Your eye in.' She giggled. 'You've got to teach yourself to look. It's all in the looking.'

'I used to like drawing when I was a kid. But then I suppose all kids like to draw.'

'I'll just—' Her words evaporated as she blocked in a shadow beneath his chin, that instantly changed his image. Made her feel half-pleased with it. 'There, that's better. Although...' More frantic shading, she knew she was rushing but she had to show him something.

'Doesn't it frustrate you, if you don't get it perfect?'

'Oh, no.' She sucked on her lip, frowning in concentration. 'Better to do a bad drawing, than nothing. I'll be able to do a better one tomorrow.'

'I'd get frustrated, I hate it when things don't go how I like them.'

'There, that's the way I see you.' And she turned the pad around for him to see.

A bubbling embarrassment as she watched him. His

expression gave nothing away. Until a sudden smile. His eyes, which to her looked blue as the sky, going into their creases. She knew she'd impressed him.

'Can I keep it?'

'No. I'll do you a better one. Another time.'

'Oh, so we're going to see each other again, are we? You've decided.'

She closed the pages of her sketchbook and felt herself blush as she returned it to her bag. Leon leant sideways and bumped against her. Jokey. Teasing. Giving her that smile again. They walked around the lake. Breathed back its slightly stagnant breath.

'The swans are beautiful, aren't they?' Angela counted up seven. 'Very calming.'

'Except when you think what's going on beneath the surface.'

She nodded. 'Rather like holding a mirror up on real life.'

The lowering sun was warm at their backs and, side by side, conscious of his size, his height, she felt feminine and delicate – things she wanted to feel but never did. Needing to take two steps to one of his strides, she bobbed along beside him, her bag bouncing against her back. At some point, he produced a container of something that looked like yellow teeth from a pocket in his coat.

'It's sweetcorn.' He'd seen her looking. 'I won't lecture you on the dos and don'ts with waterfowl, but bread's quite the worst thing you can feed them.' She watched him throw it down for the ducks and swans that crowded the path. Saw him toss a handful over to the crows that had landed on the nearby strip of grass, saying, 'They can't help that they're crows.'

They walked, so close, they could have been handcuffed. After quickly confirming what each of them did – Angela, embarrassed about being a commis chef, made out she worked in hotel management to impress him – their talk was mostly of inconsequential things: the weather, the beauty of the park that was dressed in its autumn colours. How good it was they both happened to be free that afternoon. It was as if he already knew all he needed to know about her and she liked it. It was easy, he was easy, so much of him reminded her of Robert and she couldn't remember a time when she'd enjoyed someone's company as much.

They followed their lengthening shadows, long and thin, and always a few steps ahead. Then she realised he must have sensed the cold creeping under his clothes in the same way she did because he said, 'Want to go and get that coffee I promised you?'

He'd stopped and was looking directly at her. His hands thrust deep inside his coat pockets gave her the impression he couldn't trust himself not to touch her. And she would have liked him to touch her. For him to gather her in his arms and keep her safe.

'I'd like that. But I think I'd prefer a proper drink. Maybe something to eat?'

'Good. I'm glad you don't have to rush off.' He held her gaze and moistened his lips with the tip of his tongue. 'I wouldn't be ready to say goodbye to you yet.'

They headed in the direction of the park gates. His walk was easy, the dying sunlight picking out tones in his short hair she hadn't noticed before. Up ahead, on a bench beneath the majestic sweep of a weeping willow, a row of four Japanese tourists sat eating shop-bought sandwiches, a tartan blanket spread over their knees. Angela thought how nice they looked, enjoying the brisk autumn day. Leon chuckled when he saw what she was looking at.

'Makes a change from them taking selfies.' And he brushed under the low branch of a tree, held it up, waiting for her.

They walked past a homeless man, his head and shoulders wrapped in a soiled grey blanket. His face hidden. He sat propped against the side of a bus shelter, his back to the queue of people who were doing their best to ignore him. Angela suspected this was because they were a little afraid of him, in the same way she too was afraid of him.

But Leon was different. He wasn't afraid. He strolled boldly up to him and looked into the man's face for the longest time. Then, exchanging some words of sympathy she was too far away to hear, he dug through the pocket of his jeans and produced a handful of change which he dropped into the man's empty cup.

Cardiff was heaving.

'We should've gone out of town.'

This was the fourth time they'd cruised this block, looking for somewhere to park.

'Oh, aren't you totally marvellous,' Leon crooned when a grey-haired woman reversed her red Toyota out of a space.

'Do we need a ticket?'

'No, it's after six. We should be okay along here.'

The pub's exterior was festooned with sparkly lights and there were a few sets of tables and chairs set out front for the smokers. They ducked inside and swapped the dark street for an equally dark interior swarming with people, and picked what seemed to be the last available table in a far corner.

Leon took off his coat and gloves, then helped with hers.

'Nice coat.' She watched as he folded it neatly over the side of a chair.

Leon, back from the bar with their drinks and a couple of menus, slid onto the seat beside her. 'I hope the vodka doesn't give you a headache.'

'I'm hoping it'll get rid of it.' Acutely aware of his body pressed close to hers. 'All that squinting into the sun, it isn't good. Is that all you're having?' She pointed to his glass of cola.

'I'm driving, remember.'

She leant back and felt the vodka track through her. Felt the press of his thigh against her own under the table. The more she drank, the less self-conscious she felt about the short skirt Toni once persuaded her to buy. She was glad she'd worn it, looking around at what other women were wearing, she was pleased she'd opted for her leopard-print top too. It seemed it was all the rage.

One vodka was followed by another. Insisting she paid for the next round, Angela forced a twenty-pound note into Leon's reluctant hand. She looked at his hands and he must have seen her looking because he reached for hers and soothed it between his own. She could feel the rough calluses on his palms as he sighed close to her ear. Then he turned his head and they kissed. His mouth was soft and unexpected to begin with. Then becoming increasingly urgent, his tongue pushing between her lips, searching out hers, his stubble rasping against her skin.

Angela gasped when at last he pulled away and, pressing her fingers to where his lips had touched, she felt the pressure of his kiss long afterwards. She heard his laugh filtering through to her as if in a dream. A loving laugh. An *I like you* laugh. Then he put his arm around her and scooped her against him. She could feel the vibration of his laugh quiver through him while his hand – mesmeric, rhythmic – caressed the length of her hair, root to tip, root to tip.

'Hello, hello, hello.'

A man's voice from somewhere behind them. They jerked apart. Angela opened and closed her mouth, she couldn't speak, the words wouldn't come.

'Dear me, Spike, are you all right? You've gone white as a sheet.'

'*Geraint.*' She swallowed her shock. 'What the hell are you doing here?'

'That's charming.' He ducked down and planted a beery kiss on her cheek. Angela flinched, he never bothered with her normally. 'Aren't you going to introduce me to your friend?' She saw the way he eyed Leon in a thoroughly masculine way and didn't like it.

'Geraint, this is Leon. Leon, this is Geraint.' Her voice was mechanical.

'Hi.' Geraint nodded.

'Is Rhiannon with you?' Angela asked.

'Yeah, she's here.' He swigged from his pint and Angela followed his gaze to the bar. Thought she could see the back of Rhiannon's blonde head. 'But she ain't interested in talking to you.'

'Why?'

'*Huh!* Are you having a laugh? After you let her down like that. *Again.*'

'But I explained what happened. I told her I couldn't help it.'

'Save it, Spike. She ain't interested.'

'Oh, come on, this is daft.' Angela, loosened by alcohol, felt she could take on the world. 'Let me speak to her. I know I can make things right.'

She jumped down from the seat only to feel Geraint place a restraining hand on her shoulder.

'I said, *leave it.*'

'Please, Geraint. At least tell her I'm here. Try and get her to come over.'

'I can't, we're with people. And anyway, like I said, you've blown it, mate.'

'But you haven't even asked her.' Returning to her seat she was aware of Leon shifting awkwardly beside her. 'Can't you just ask her?'

'No can do, I'm afraid.'

When Geraint moved away, Angela and Leon's eyes met in joint bemusement.

'Who the hell was that?'

'My friend's fiancé.'

Leon pulled a face. 'Poor friend.'

'He is a bit of a dick. I don't know what she sees in him.'

'Why does he call you Spike?'

'Because of my surname. Milligan.'

'Ah, right.' He nodded but she wasn't sure he'd understood. 'What did you do to upset this Rhiannon friend of yours then?' Leon was now studying the menu.

'I let her down.'

'How d'you mean?'

'I missed their engagement party.' She couldn't tell Leon why she missed it. When she revisited the events that prevented her from going, it sounded ridiculous. 'I didn't mean to; I was all set to go. I'd gone into town to buy them a present but before I knew it—' She closed her mouth; she didn't want to say any more.

'Don't worry about him. This friend of yours will be all right. Give her time to cool down, then try talking to her again.'

'D'you think?'

'Sure. If she's a friend worth having. Now,' Leon flapped the menu in her face, 'I reckon you need to eat something; we don't want you conking out.'

'I won't be a minute.' Angela excused herself from the table after she and Leon had finished their meal. She pushed open the door to the Ladies' and found Rhiannon at the wash basins touching up her lipstick.

Angela waited for her to speak but seeing how she refused to even meet her gaze, it was going to be up to her to break the stalemate.

'I'm sorry—'

'Save it, Spike,' Rhiannon said, cutting her off. 'I don't wanna hear it.'

'But, I'm sorry. Honestly, Rhia, I'm really, really sorry.'

She watched Rhiannon blot her mouth on a square of toilet tissue. When she turned to her, the expression was blank and cold. It wasn't one she'd seen Rhiannon give anyone before.

'I'll tell you what your problem is, shall I? You're jealous of me, you always were.' With a haughty tip of her chin, she communicated without needing to spell it out, that Angela was not to interrupt. 'You hate seeing me happy. You can't stand it that I've found someone. I don't know how I could've been friends with you for so long, you've shown a real side of yourself lately that I don't like. I'm sorry, Spike, but I want you to leave us alone. If you can't be happy for me, if you can't be a friend...'

Rhiannon seemed to have run out of accusations to sling at her and Angela extended what she hoped was a consoling hand. Only to have it swatted away with a perfectly manicured hand.

'Get off me.' Rhiannon's eyes, popping with indignation. 'You not turning up to our engagement party was the last straw, Spike. I mean it this time. You've let me down too often. You can't even give me a proper excuse, can you?' A quiver from the microblade eyebrows. 'Because you chasing around town after some bloke you think the law should be interested in, isn't an excuse. I'm sorry Toni died, of course I am, it was horrible, but you're obsessed with it. Obsessed with whoever this bloke is.

Why can't you leave it alone? After all we talked about the other week, you went off after him again. Christ, Spike, it's – it's stalking, that is. You do know that, don't you?' A wag of a long synthetic nail. 'This bloke, this poor bastard you've got some stupid fixation on, he's got nothing to do with anything, can't you see it? Toni was killed in her flat, the news said. So, if this kitchen porter did it, how come he got in, *eh*? Answer me that.'

'I, *erm...*' Angela bunched her eyes shut, felt the room spin.

'See—' Rhiannon, borderline gleeful. 'You hadn't thought of that, had you? I'll tell you who did it, it's that ex of hers. He was the one in the flat. See how stupid you're being? How stupid all this is? You're hounding an innocent man.' She paused for breath, then carried on, her face flushed. 'And anyway, what the fuck did you think it was going to achieve? Did you think you could confront him? Honest to God, you've totally lost the plot.' An exasperated sigh. 'I don't want you contacting me again, d'you hear? And don't come spying on us neither.' Angela made a small noise of protestation. She wanted to say it wasn't how it looked, that she'd intended on ringing the bell but was worried she wouldn't be welcome. 'We saw you, so don't bother denying it.' Rhiannon glared at her. 'What were you thinking? Coming to our street, standing there for half the bloody afternoon. *Staring*.' She twirled a finger at her temple. 'God, you can be so bloody weird sometimes.'

Rhiannon squirted scent on her wrists, under her hair. Then, after a final glance in the mirror, she buckled her bag and pushed out into the pub. The tail of her salon-straightened hair whisking behind her. A burst of laughter, then the door swung shut; the laughter ending in a wheeze. And sagging, defeated, against the toilet wall, Angela sniffed the slightly nauseous reek of perfume and burst into tears.

THIRTY-NINE

It's nice to be back in the car. In its city smell of used-up air. I start the engine, turn my music on and reverse out of the parking space. I've got that feeling I'm being watched again. I keep on, driving faster than I should, not looking back. The night is thinning to blue, as dawn draws back its curtain on the world. The streets are empty and shiny with frost and I drive with a renewed sense of urgency. A renewed sense of what has to be done.

I turn into my grandparents' road and pull up outside their house. It's almost light now. There's birdsong when I open the door to get out. It hasn't sunk in yet, this thing I'm going to do. I'm still living as if I don't know the truth of what I am. What I'm capable of. The morning world is about as new and shiny as it's ever been.

I let myself inside, take off the Crombie and dump it over the bannister. Not like me not to put it somewhere tidy but I've other things on my mind. I go upstairs to the kitchen, careful to avoid the treads that creak, I don't want to wake Babcia. Not yet. Lucky for me, what's left of the moon provides enough light to go by.

I tiptoe across the kitchen. Babcia's bag is where it always is, on the sideboard, next to her puzzle books. I open it without thinking and pull out her purse. It feels fatter than normal and when I open it, I see why. It's full of the crisp new notes she's withdrawn from the cashpoint. The silly woman will only deal in cash even though I'm always telling her it's not safe, that she could be mugged. But she won't have it, she won't be told. She doesn't trust credit cards and that's that. She's the only person I know who only believes in spending what she has.

I take what I think I need. Then, flicking through what's left, take a little more. Careful, I'm not too greedy. But my wage packets are fuck all compared to this, I could never earn this much in a week. It's why this stealing from her is becoming a habit. A habit I need to feed, now I've weaned myself off the pills. Because my life is changing and I need the extra money more than ever. I need to be seen as more than someone who wields a mop for a living. And I'm becoming more cunning by the day. Look at me – sneaking in here when they're asleep, I'd never have dared anything like this before.

I rezip the purse and return it to her bag. She'll be none the wiser, it's obvious the daft old bat's losing her marbles. The last time I was here, she spent the whole afternoon hunting for her reading glasses. It was hilarious. I didn't tell her, I never let on, even though it was plain to me where she'd put them. I waited until she went to the bathroom, saw herself in the mirror and found them on top of her head. She wasn't happy with me, I can tell you, but she never is, so there's nothing new there.

I whack my skull against the enamel colander Babcia insists on hanging above the kitchen table. It clanks against the row of pots and pans that are suspended alongside it. The sound is ultra-loud in the stillness. Then comes a rattling from the room below.

I grab Babcia's marble rolling pin from the box of utensils. Wait with it heavy in my hand, for whatever it was to rattle again. But nothing does. The house settles back into the quiet. I exhale and feel my expended breath bump against the foggy subfusc of dawn that's found a gap in the kitchen curtains. I'd best clear out of here before she wakes up, and I slot the rolling pin away again.

But I'll be back, I think, scanning around for anything else I can nick. I like it here when she's out of the way. She's always on my case: nag, nag, nagging with her damn questions. I tap the pocket of my jeans and am reassured by the wad of cash now nestling inside it. I might be able to jack in my rotten jobs if I can keep this up. And if not, then I'm going to have to think of another way to get my hands on what's mine, aren't I?

I feel myself smile. The levels of what I know I'm capable of fizz in my brain.

Dangerous.

Like the sound a kettle makes when it's boiling dry.

FORTY

'You didn't need to return the dress, my dear girl. I told you to keep it.' Zofia smiled and handed Angela a cup of tea. 'And did you have a wonderful time? I want to hear all about it.'

'I didn't actually get to the party.'

'You didn't? Oh dear, what happened?'

'I had to work in the end.' Angela couldn't bring herself to tell the truth, she just wanted to forget it. Falling out with Rhiannon, and now Anne-Marie, there was no way she was risking falling out with Zofia too.

'You poor dear. I bet you were cross. You'd have been the belle of the ball.'

'I'll have the chance to wear it again, I'm sure. Thank you for saying I can keep it. And the shoes too?' Tentative, she held her breath for the reply. If Zofia said she wanted them back she wouldn't know what to do, the shoes were ruined. She took them to a cobbler in town but they told her they were beyond repair and she felt dreadful about it.

'Absolutely, you must keep them. No good for me with my arthritis. But what a shame about the party.'

'I do have some good news.'

'Really?' Zofia's face opened like a flower.

'I got chatting to that guy from college the other day.'

'I guessed something. *You*, with your rosy cheeks, you look so happy.' Zofia, beaming, perched on the edge of her chair, offered up a plate of biscuits.

'I am happy.' Angela grinned. 'We spent last Thursday afternoon together.' She took a ginger nut and bit it in half.

'*And?* How did it go?' Zofia, eating no biscuits herself, stirred the usual sweetener into her tea.

'Really well. He's lovely. I mean, it's too soon to know but—'

'*Ooh*, you know when you know. You're in love, I can tell.' Zofia jiggled about on her chair. 'This is so exciting. Are you going to see him again?'

'I hope so. He said he'd text me.'

'Where did you go?'

Angela told her about their walk around the park. The meal afterwards in the pub. She avoided all mention of her awful argument with Rhiannon. 'He's so easy to talk to, to be with.' A shy little look at the floor. 'I really like him.'

'And I'm sure he's just as smitten with you, my dear. How lovely for you.'

'I did a drawing of him. Would you like to see it?'

'Very much.'

'I'll just drink this, then I'll go and get it.' Angela looked around. Realised what was missing. Oskar wasn't there. His chair at the kitchen table was empty. 'Where's your husband today?' She took another biscuit when Zofia offered the plate again.

'He's come down with a bit of a cold, poor darling. I sent him to bed this afternoon. He's not been feeling well for a few days. Complaining of aches and pains, which isn't like him; my Oskar never complains.'

'I'm sorry to hear that.' Sounds of crunching. 'Can I get you anything for him? I mean, I could nip out now, the chemist along the high street should still be open.'

'He's okay, I think. He's had a couple of aspirin. He's sleeping now.' Zofia's fingers journeyed the purple petals of a flower stitched on her apron. 'I'll call the doctor if he gets any worse.'

'If you're sure? Because it's no trouble.'

'Don't worry, child. You finish your tea, then go and fetch me your drawings.'

When Angela nipped next door, she returned the dress to its hanger. Bending into the bottom of the wardrobe, she took out Zofia's shoes and stroked their satin toes. Not the only things she'd ruined, were they? Her mind spinning to Rhiannon again.

Minutes later, sketchbook under an arm, she was back in her neighbour's cosy kitchen. She stood by the door waiting for her to finish washing up the tea things, wondering whether to ask Zofia if she might draw her and, if it was decent enough, she could frame it and give it to her as a thank you.

'Would you like me to dry up for you?'

'No, my dear.' Zofia wiped her hands on her apron, then cleared a space on the tabletop. 'You put your book there. The light's better in here.'

Angela lay the sketchpad down and waited for Zofia to find her reading glasses.

'I can't think where I put them. Oh, look, not to worry, I've got a spare pair in here, somewhere.' She rootled the drawers of the sideboard, under table mats and photographs Angela would have liked to look at. 'They're here somewhere. Trouble is, there's so much junk. I really should have a good tidy-up. Oh, would you look at that—' She mumbled to herself as she lifted out a key with a tag which read: BOWEN. 'I thought I'd seen the last of that. I can't think who could've moved it.'

Angela, lost in thought, didn't hear Zofia or see what she was doing. She had moved to stand at the window and had drawn back the nets to reveal a full white moon that was silvering the city below. 'Going to be a hard frost tonight,' she predicted while Zofia looped the key on a hook by the sink then returned to the sideboard.

'Got them.' Smelling of hairspray and face powder, Zofia was at her side again. Reading glasses in position. 'Come on then,' she giggled, 'don't be hiding your light under a bushel.'

Angela opened her drawing pad, turned a page, then several more.

'My, they're good.' Zofia, glimpsing what Angela wasn't quite ready to show.

'Here. This is it.' She found her drawing of Leon and lay the flat of her hand on the sheet of paper to turn the pad around.

Zofia scrutinised it and Angela thought she looked impressed with her work.

'I'm pleased with it. I've really caught him.'

Because there he was, drawn as clearly as if he'd stood before them now. That slightly crooked smile, that sleepy look. His hands folded in his lap. The dark cotton shirt he wore beneath his smart overcoat. Everything down to that V-shaped crease between his eyebrows: a downward arrow to his eyes.

She heard Zofia swallow: a peculiar, dry sound.

'Do you like it?' She was now half afraid and unsure. It was the same feeling she always had when she showed her drawings to anyone. 'It's how I see him, anyway. Honestly, I think it's exactly like him. He's good-looking, don't you think? It's his eyes, he's got the loveliest eyes.'

A sudden noise from the room below.

'Oh, that'll be Oskar.' Zofia leant over and snapped the covers of the sketchpad shut. 'Please excuse me, I really should go and check on him.' And she gave a weak smile Angela didn't understand, before disappearing downstairs.

FORTY-ONE

The park is deserted this afternoon. There aren't even the usual dedicated dog walkers or joggers I usually have to share this space with. To tell you the truth, I'm glad there's nothing but the pale sky reflecting in the crinkly-skinned lake to see me do my warm-up exercises. The ones I remember from PE at school. I'm not much good at running yet but I'm getting better. This is my third attempt and I set off at a steady pace. Breathing in through my nose, out through my mouth. Dodging the puddles, the discs of duck shit littering the path. I spot a bench on the other side, under the dripping trees and aim for it. When I get there, panting, sweating, I know I'm not supposed to cool down too quickly but I'm boiling, so I tug my sweatshirt off over my head and knot it around my middle. My T-shirt is wet with sweat. The material's stuck to my back. I'm completely knackered but I'm glad I pushed myself.

I'll have a little rest here for a minute, then try jogging on again. No point overdoing it, no point crippling myself. I sit down and read the little brass plaque that, screwed to the bench, commemorates someone's life. I like that people think of honouring lost loved ones this way. We should've done something like this for Mum, she loved this park. She told me she used to push me around in my pram in here.

I stare down at the toes of my trainers. But before I have the chance to feel sad about Mum, a sudden burst of fierce flapping makes me look up at a rush of white taking shape on my periphery. I can almost feel the weight of them as they hit the water and skim to a halt. Two swans. I watch the waves that slow to ripples, as they glide in perfect synchronisation across the water, folding their pure, white wings away.

Too beautiful for words.

But seeing these swans brings a memory I'd rather forget.

New Year's Eve. A day of freezing winds and post-Christmas blues. Me and my sister – I was thirteen, Yana was seven – buttoned to the chin by Babcia and sent off with a bag of stale bread to feed the ducks in this very park.

'Look after her.' My father's warning. He was only ever concerned with Yana's well-being and thinking this, jars me even now.

But I didn't look after Yana, did I? Once I'd stumbled across my mates, all thoughts of my little sister's well-being were dumped. Yana ran back to Babcia and Grandpa's. I should have gone after her but I didn't.

I was useful with my bag of bread and coaxed the unsuspecting waterfowl out of the water and onto the tarmac path that surrounds this lake.

'Swans are the best, don't bother feeding the other fuckers. It's a swan I want.' I can remember my bloodthirsty battle cry and my friends' spiked excitement. 'They burn really good, just wait and see.'

I made my promise and tugged off the plastic nozzle on the lighter fluid I'd filched from my father. Squirted it over the swan's plumage.

'You've got to keep them busy. You've got to feed them. It'll give the fuckers the chance to bite you if you piss about.'

This was how I kept the momentum going. How I kept my friends hanging on my every word. I can see them now, immobilised by awe, as they did as I told them. My fingers dipping in and out of the bread bag, passing it over to the demands of the orange-beaked swan.

And then one of them lit the match. Egged on by me, because it was all my idea, I take full responsibility. I remember the small square of folded black card that was almost too pretty to use. They hadn't looked like matches at all, the casing as shiny as Babcia's patent leather shoes. The Flamingo Club, it read, in pink swirly letters.

I don't think any of us had been ready for the sound. A heart-stopping whoosh, like when my father had bonfires out the back and doused them in petrol. The speed of the blaze was shocking, fizzing along the tarmac path where some of the fuel had spilt, it ignited the swan's white breast feathers in the blink of an eye.

It nearly had me. Frighteningly huge, the S-curve of its neck fully extended and its vast breast and black legs stretched taut in panic, the creature had seemed as high as a house. Frantic, the serrated snapping of its beak through the choke of smoke, the swan spread its huge wings and flapped back into the water with a massive splash, instantly dousing the flames before swimming to freedom.

Thinking about this now, it's hard to imagine that no one saw five youngsters tormenting a swan in broad daylight. Why hadn't my father been suspicious? Or Babcia? I remember being in the doghouse for letting Yana find her way back to Coracle Road on her own, but no one bothered to quiz me about my filthy hands or clothes. Why didn't somebody stop me?

I lift my head and watch the majestic swans floating out on the water. If you were to ask me why I committed such atrocities when I was a kid, I wouldn't be able to tell you. But what I can tell you is that off the drugs like I am, I'm not so different now. And the thought doesn't scare me as much as it ought to. The problem is that I'm not sure I have a conscience. I don't have the same concerns as ordinary people. I wish I could say it makes me feel queasy to think I was capable of doing such a thing to a defenceless creature but I can't lie, not to you. It's all about speaking the truth to you.

I'm not telling you this because I'm proud of what I am. I'm telling you because you need to know what I'm capable of. For you to understand that I will kill you if you get in my way or threaten my liberty. I would have killed my father. A man who's always known me and what was simmering beneath the veneer of my childhood, waiting to hatch. Waiting to burst out and grab him by the throat.

I shiver a little, it's getting cold and it's also starting to drizzle. I'll do another ten minutes running, then that'll be enough for today. They shut the park at sunset and going by the tawny light in the sky it's not far off. After a few minutes of stretching, I leave the bench behind, untying my sweatshirt and tugging it on over my head as I jog. I can smell my sweat, it's not unpleasant, it shows I'm pushing myself.

The cold air is sharp, it burns my lungs but I keep putting one leg in front of the other. I should've brought my headphones, I usually do. I always run better when I've music to motivate me. I find the likes of Nina Simone is good for keeping up the momentum.

Then it is music I'm listening to. The ringtone on my mobile. I pull it from my pocket as I run and check the screen.

It's Marvin.

Fuck.

'*Hi-ya,*' I answer, remembering in time not to sound too chirpy.

'There you are.' He's his usual bumptious self. 'I've been trying to get hold of you all day.'

'Have you?'

'You know I have. You must've seen you had missed calls?'

'I've been busy.'

'Why are you panting? What are you doing?'

'I'm running,' I tell him, then instantly regret it. The likes of me don't go running.

'Running? Since when did you go running? Are you feeling all right? You're not keeping anything from me, are you? Changes in your behavioural patterns are not a good sign. I know we saw each other last week but I think we need to fix up another appointment for you to come and see me again. You're due a blood test. What d'you say?'

I stop. Wipe rainwater and sweat from my face. I must catch my breath. I've got to think carefully about how I answer this.

FORTY-TWO

Angela tied a final knot in the bin bag and opened the front door. Darker than she realised, the drizzle she'd walked home through from the bus stop had gathered momentum and she listened to rainwater gurgle along the guttering. The light from the hallway was enough to guide her to the metal gate at the end of the path. Following her shadow, she lifted the lid of the wheelie bin and dropped the rubbish inside with a thump, releasing a puff of rotting sweetness. She was closing it again, when something jolted against her shin and, glancing down, she saw a black, cat-sized shape dart between her and the gatepost and bolt for freedom.

'Bimbo!' she squealed, realising her mistake. And before Bangles was tempted to copy his brother, she leapt up the path to close the front door.

'Puss, puss, puss... Come on, boy, where are you?' Calling ahead, she charged into the murky night-time street, the gate swinging back on her heels.

Visibility was poor and, scanning around, breathing in the syrupy, silent world, she started to panic. The meagre glow dispensed by street lamps was scarcely strong enough to penetrate the gloom as she set off along the pavement. Passing houses and imagining their high-ceilinged interiors flickering beyond bay windows, they offered no illumination either. Any light from within had been firmly shut off by curtains drawn tight against the night. How was she supposed to find the cat in this? She blinked through the thickening rain and hastened her pace. Lin and Greg's warning, *never let the cats out in the street,* swirling in her head.

'Bimbo! Bimbo!'

Within a few short paces, her socks had slipped down inside her sheepskin boots. They rubbed the heels that were still sore from the battering she gave them in Zofia's shoes. Thinking of Zofia reminded her of Oskar, and she wondered if he was feeling better today. She should have called over and checked they were all right. They were so old, the pair of them, and it didn't sound as if they had visitors unless it was the persistently elusive grandson. Perhaps she could nip over when she'd found the cat... *If* she found the cat, she reminded herself miserably.

'Puss, puss... Bimbo.'

By now a sob had invaded her voice and out in the cold and the rain Angela was frantic. Supposing she never found him, that he never came back? That he liked this new-found independence she'd accidentally given him. She couldn't think like that, she had to keep trying. But searching the length of pavement, the wet seeping through the stitching of her boots, she worried she'd seen the last of him.

'I know you're out here somewhere, silly boy. Come on, Bimbo, *please?*' She pushed her wet hair out of her eyes and listened to her feeble entreaty ring around the deserted street. 'Come on, come inside, it's bloody freezing out here.'

Despite the muffled quality of the night contained within the terrace of high Victorian houses, Angela could sense the restlessness of the city beyond. But here, in Coracle Road, all was still and eerie in its quietness. Trapped in some kind of bubble that was about to blow. Agitated, she rubbed her arms through the sweater she'd slung on before taking the rubbish out. The sleeves were soggy and the T-shirt beneath it felt damp. This was impossible. She shivered, her mood spiralling down further when she reached the bottom end of the street and there was still no sign. She spun around to head back along the curve of tarmac, now and again crouching to check under the row of parked cars.

'Oh, this is crazy. Come on, boy, show yourself.' Angela, bobbing upright again, wrung her hands in desperation. 'Trouble is,' she mumbled, 'I can only see your eyes in the dark. Come on, boy.'

She knew this was hopeless, that, unlike dogs, cats didn't come when you called them, but she couldn't give up... Didn't dare give up.

'Bimbo. *Please*, come back.'

When she reached the top of Coracle Road again, she crossed to the other side and was about to head back, when something moved on the rim of her vision and she realised, in an instant, that she wasn't alone. That the deserted street was not as deserted as she first thought.

Something was out there. She could hear its footfalls and ragged breathing pulsating through the dark. Whatever it was, it was gaining on her and she pressed the flat of her hand to the fear that was sharpening to a spike behind her ribcage.

'Who's there?' Her anxious plea was little more than a whimper, as her scalp beneath her damp hair constricted in alarm. 'Who's there?'

She flung her head from side to side, hunting the shadowy pockets that fell between the bands of tangerine street light.

Nothing.

But the sense that something was gaining on her through the dark wouldn't go away.

Then she saw it. A human shape. Big and tall and moving towards her with a steady determination.

Closer, closer... Their actions were as rapid and rhythmic as her quickening heart. She slapped a hand to her mouth to trap the trepidation fizzing in her throat.

It was that kitchen porter. He'd hunted her down... He was coming to kill her like he'd killed Toni.

She narrowed her eyes and peered through the haziness at the advancing figure.

Closer... Closer.

A jogger.

Just a jogger. Not the kitchen porter at all.

She relaxed her shoulders and exhaled her relief. Told herself off for being irrational and silly; the brute didn't know where she lived and she had to get a grip, she had to stop letting her imagination run away with her.

Then, when the jogger emerged into the indeterminate light, she saw who it was. The realisation came just as a drop of rain slid down inside her collar. Icy and shocking, making her gasp.

FORTY-THREE

'Cat got out, has it?' Leon, panting heavily.

Angela jumped at the sight of him. 'What are you doing here?'

'I've been for a run.' Jogging on the spot, he dragged an arm over his forehead.

He certainly looked as if he'd been running – glistening with perspiration, she saw there were wet half-moons under his arms and a dark triangle on the back of his sweatshirt.

'But you don't live round here.' She swallowed what remained of the anxiety she'd been holding on to. There was nothing to worry about, it wasn't that horrible kitchen porter, it was Leon and he wouldn't hurt her. 'Fagins-on-Sea, I thought you said?'

'Yeah, I do.' Still panting. 'But I like the park.'

'The park? Roath Park, where we went?' Angela flicked a strand of wet hair out of her eyes.

'Yeah.' He breathed through his mouth and she saw he was sucking a sweet.

'You never said.'

'Didn't I?'

'No. But you can't run in there at night, they lock it up.'

'Whatever. I like the streets here better than where I live. Nice and quiet, I get to have them to myself.'

Angela stared at him, trying to fathom why he was here.

'Anyway,' he said, his breathing returning to normal. 'I'm sort of killing two birds with one stone.'

'How come?'

'I'm visiting my grandparents 'n all. They live along here.'

'In Coracle Road?' she yelped her shock. 'What number?'

'Eighty-six.'

Angela followed the line of his finger.

'No way. You mean, Zofia and Oskar?' Bimbo had been temporarily forgotten while she unravelled the news Leon just gave her. 'That means... You're their grandson. God, this is weird. They, I mean, Zofia... she talks about you all the time. God, Leon, talk about a small world. Honestly, this is incredible. I don't believe it. And you're not going to believe me when I tell you I'm cat-sitting next door. At the Bowens'. Number eighty-four.'

'Yeah? What are the chances of that?'

Angela gazed up at him, she didn't think he sounded particularly surprised. 'I know, it's nuts. The coincidence is amazing.'

'I'll tell you what it is,' he grinned down on her through the orangey street light, 'it's incentive for me to visit them more often.'

'Bimbo!' Angela, remembering the cat again, swung her head around to search the shadows. 'Come on, boy, where the hell are you? He snuck out, Lin and Greg will kill me if I don't get him back. The cats aren't supposed to be out the front,' she explained to Leon.

'Wily little buggers though, aren't they?'

'I know, and so slinky and quick. I can't tell you the number of times they've tripped me up on the stairs in that house. Puss, puss, puss. Bimbo!' she called again.

'Try not to worry.' Leon put an arm around her. His breath was strangely reminiscent of childhood sweetshops. 'You got any cooked chicken? They love chicken. Well, my neighbour's cat used to love it. It was the only way I managed to get hold of it.'

'Oh, look. There he is. Quick, grab him.' Angela, talking to herself, sprinted across the road and scooped the fugitive Bimbo up in her arms. '*Ooh*, you're a naughty cat.' She nuzzled his fur and kissed his head. 'You nearly gave me a heart attack, you little sod.' She looked up at Leon who was hovering by the gate. 'I'd best get him inside. D-do you want to come in for a coffee, or something?'

'I hate coffee.'

'Oh, okay. I just thought—' Looking at him, she still couldn't believe he was Zofia and Oskar's grandson, it really was the most astonishing fluke.

'But we could go for a drink at the pub at the end of the road if you like?' he suggested.

'The Pear Tree? Yes, okay, it's really nice in there.'

'Give me a moment to freshen up. Meet you back here in ten, yeah?'

'Great. I'll go and smarten myself up too.' Angela cuddled Bimbo tighter when he wriggled to get free. 'See you in a minute.'

'I've never actually been in here before,' Angela admitted as she scanned the ochre-lit interior, the oak-panelled walls and weighty furniture.

'I thought you said it was nice.'

'I always thought it looked nice, from the outside. And it is, isn't it? Nice and quiet and cosy.' She snuggled into him, her damp hair against his shirt. 'I reckon, if you're up for it, we should try the food in here one night. They've loads of offers on.'

'Or better still, you can cook for me?' Leon sipped from his bottle of alcohol-free lager.

'What makes you think I can cook?' She flung back her head.

'Just a hunch.'

'You can have a proper drink tonight, can't you?' *Did he know she was a chef? Had he been asking around about her, in the same way she'd been asking about him?*

'Me? No, I'd better not.' She watched him draw patterns in the condensation on his bottle: his movements seemed erratic. A little nervous maybe.

'But if you're staying over with your grandparents.'

'Who said I was staying over?'

'Oh, I just thought.' What had she thought? That with his key to their house, he used the place as if it was his own?

'No, I'd better get on home after this. They don't like me staying. And anyway, I've an early start in the morning.'

'Me too.' Drinking her vodka and tonic, she looked at him over the rim of the glass. He looked nice. He'd changed into the same shirt and jeans he wore the last time they were together. The dark-purple shirt suited him, suited his eyes. 'I still can't believe you're Zofia's grandson. Honestly, Leon, I can't get over it.'

'Yeah, it's weird all right.'

'But great though?'

'Oh, yeah, it's great.'

'I really like your gran. I think she's one of the kindest people I know.'

'You can't know many people then.' He laughed a laugh she couldn't tell if he meant or not.

'I showed her that drawing I did of you.'

'You did?' She felt his body stiffen on the bench beside her. 'What did she say?'

'She loved it. But I don't think she could've recognised you.' Angela accidentally swallowed an ice cube. It made her face ache like when she ate ice cream too fast. 'You're really lucky to have them as grandparents,' she said when she could speak again. 'They're the loveliest people.'

'You reckon?' Neither his tone nor his expression gave anything away.

'Without a doubt. Zofia's been a real friend to me since I moved in. Which is nice, as I've managed to just about piss off everyone I know.' The vodka was making her head swim. She must stop drinking on an empty stomach, it made her say things she shouldn't. 'All my fault,' she raised the flat of her hand, 'I've brought it all on myself.'

'How d'you mean?'

'It doesn't matter.' She picked a hole in the already soggy beer mat and laughed too loud, too sharp. Listened to it reverberate around the near-empty pub.

'It's obviously bothering you. Might do you good to share it.'

She loved it when he cuddled her. Wrapped in his arms, her head on his chest, it felt the safest place on earth.

'Okay.' She sprung upright to dig through her purse for the ten-pound note she knew was in there. 'If you go and get us another round in first.'

He pushed her money away and rose to his feet. Sitting back to watch him, she returned the money to her purse and drained what was left in her glass. Watching Leon was fast becoming her favourite pastime. And watching him tonight, something stirred inside her. A liquid ache spread under her skin and made her heart beat faster. She didn't want to feel like this, it gave her that exposed feeling she didn't like, but even though she tried to tell herself to go slow, that she'd been hurt this way before, she couldn't help it. She was safe with him, wasn't she? Yes, look at him talking to that pretty girl working the bar, there's not so much as a flicker of interest. She didn't know why she thought she could trust him when she had such a disastrous track record with men, but something about Leon told her he was one of the good guys.

Angela liked the idea of fidelity. With everyone else either dying or deserting her, Leon, along with Zofia, could be the only people she had. And from the moment she clapped eyes on him, he seemed different. For a start, he wasn't half as sure of himself as other blokes less attractive than him were, and that had to count for something. She could trust him, couldn't she? He wasn't going to hurt her. No, come on, he didn't seem capable of hurting anyone with that bruised look of his, he was as vulnerable as she was.

'So, d'you wanna fill me in?' Leon was back at the table with their drinks. 'I'm a good listener.'

'Thanks for this... I don't know where to start.' After a fortifying gulp of vodka, she slid her gaze to his and felt a quivering in her chest.

'From the beginning?' he suggested, giving her the trust-me blue of his eyes along with his hand to hold.

She talked, now and again scanning his expression for signs she had said too much. But his face didn't change from one revelation to the next and she took it as a sign to keep going, even though it was the vodka doing the talking now. She hadn't eaten anything since breakfast and there was nothing inside her to soak up the alcohol. But he asked her, didn't he? He wanted her to share her troubles. And if there was going to be anything longer-term between them, he needed to know what had gone on.

When she looked up again, Leon was smiling. Good, she thought, it was worth the risk. And carried away by the deliciousness of the moment, she gripped his hand tighter.

'That's why I can't leave it alone. You can see my dilemma, can't you?' Eyes petitioning, believing herself justified in her mission to clear Mark's name. 'They're going to send the wrong man to prison if I don't stop them. He didn't do it, you see. He couldn't have, he's too gentle.' Her voice dropped away.

She looked down at their fused hands, liking that she could hardly tell where hers ended and his began. She felt comfortable with Leon; it was as if she'd always known him. He demanded so little from her and this made her want to give all of herself. She was his, she decided; she decided it the moment she knocked her tray against him in the college canteen. Some things were just meant to be and who was she to question it? She'd not been as content in anyone's company since Robert and it wasn't just the booze, she'd felt it in the park on their first afternoon together.

'You seem very sure. How come you know this Mark guy so well?' She felt Leon's fingers tighten further over her hand. 'Because in my experience, none of us truly know what someone else is capable of until they're pushed.'

'*Pushed?*'

'Well, yeah. She got rid of his kid without telling him, didn't she? I'd have had something to say about it if a girlfriend did that to me.'

'How d'you know Toni had an abortion?' Angela tugged back her hand.

'I dunno.' Leon scrunched up his lips. 'Must've heard it on the news.'

'I hear what you're saying but I'm still going back to the

police. This is new. It proves that the kitchen porter had motive. Toni got him the sack, for God's sake.'

'I know you said you'd talked to them before, but are you saying you're going back again?' Leon frowned.

'Yes. And I'm going to keep on until they arrest the right person and let Mark go.' She picked up her drink and sipped it, tried not to guzzle it too quickly. 'I meant to go last Thursday but I wanted to meet up with you. I haven't had a chance since.'

'So, let me just get this straight. You still haven't told them you think this bloke could've had a motive for killing your friend?'

'Not yet, no. It's been too full-on at work. I'm planning to go Wednesday. I've finally got an afternoon off.'

'Wednesday. The day after tomorrow?'

'Yep.' *Why's he so interested?* Angela hunted Leon's expression for the answers that weren't there.

'But what if it wasn't him? You've not got any proof. Aren't you worried about making a fool of yourself?'

'Okay, say it wasn't him,' she accepted, reluctantly; the last thing she wanted was for Leon to give her the cold shoulder too. 'All I know is that it's not Mark. So whatever I do, it'll help catch the real perpetrator. And I don't care what anyone else says, I'm going to make sure that happens, even if it kills me.'

FORTY-FOUR

Sitting here, drinking this disgusting fake beer, it was beginning to dawn on me how blithely careless most people are about their lives. I hear it in the way people speak and see it in the way they live. I suppose what it is, in a word, is that they're free. I want some of that, I want to live like I have no secret I'm trying to keep under wraps. To live like there is no poison at my roots.

Angela has this innocence and openness. The way she happily talks of private worries, shares her fears, her theories on this and that. It's quite foreign to my nature – or, if I had been like it once, then it's been eradicated by the fogginess of time. Buried under layers of grief and bewilderment. The years when I had those antipsychotic drugs in my bloodstream. The mumbo-jumbo I've been fed under the pretence it will make me well. The way I've been talked at, and talked out.

On the subject of talking, I wish she'd stop going on about Mark bloody Fairfax. I really like her and I think I want to make a life with her; it's why it's a shame she's hell-bent on clearing his name. She doesn't know it but she's going to spoil everything. Why can't she leave things alone? They've got it all wrapped up, it's going to trial in a month or two.

Yeah, Angela could be the one I've been waiting for all my life and bumping into her like that in the college canteen was a message from Mum. Funny to think we both worked at the Lloyd George without knowing it. But I told you, didn't I? No one notices us lot in pot wash. We're the invisible people, we don't even notice one another, and this proves it. Because I don't know that bloke she's been banging on about, if he was working the pot wash then he must've been on different shifts to me. Anyway, whoever he is, I can well imagine Toni having a go at him. She had one hell of a mouth on her. She shouted at me that time in front of everyone, not that it bothered me; because of the drugs I was on in those days, it just washed over me. Granted, it didn't exactly help my situation there, it was another nail in my coffin so far as Chef was concerned, but because of my poor attendance record, I would've been given the sack eventually. I've decided I won't tell Angela that I used to work at the same hotel, it might spoil things if I admit I didn't notice her. But in my defence, you wouldn't, would you? Chefs – whether they're men or women – all look the same in those hats and whites. But at least I now know why she was familiar when I saw her moving into the Bowens' place that afternoon.

While we're on the topic, cheffing, in my opinion, doesn't suit Angela. She's too nice. Too sweet. Chefs are vile people, I hate them. Yes, I know she told me she worked in hotel management but I know different. Funny, how we're both starting on a lie. I mean, accountancy – where did that come from? Clever though, I'd just finished with my mop and bucket, popped into the canteen... Well, why couldn't I have been a student? Nothing to show otherwise, and she bought it. But going back to the subject of cheffing, she can't be doing it because she likes it. Same with the horrible jobs I do, it must just be a means to an end. Trust me, whatever plans she thinks she's got sorted for her future; she's deluding herself. She doesn't know it but she needs rescuing. By me. Because, as I said before, there's no way I'd tolerate any woman of mine going out to work, mixing with others… Other men. I've got to keep her close, I've got to keep her all to myself.

But listening to her talking this way worries me. She does seem set on clearing Mark Fairfax's name. And if she does, where the hell does that leave me? In danger of being arrested and charged, that's where. If the cops give up on him, if they realise they've made a mistake – which they will, if she goes back there stirring things up – they're going to find the real culprit, aren't they? They're going to trawl through the evidence with a fine-tooth comb next time around. And then they might very well find something they missed the first time.

Like my DNA.

Inside that flat.

Because if it's not Mark – and we all know it isn't – then it's me they're going to come after. Because in the same way we know it's not Mark, it isn't whoever this other kitchen porter is either. Angela's dead wrong on that count. But if I let her go back to the cops with this new information, it could threaten me big time. I thought my father was enough of a thorn in my side, but Angela's worse.

Those things she was saying about Mark: how they've been speaking on the phone, going on about visiting him at the remand centre. Well, I'm not having that. I don't want her seeing him, he might give her more ammunition to pass on to the law. Hearing her talk about him like that, it made me a bit jealous. Jealous and scared. Because if she keeps on, she's going to destroy me.

I've got to work out a way to stop her. How long have I got? When did she say she was going? Wednesday afternoon. Damn it. I've got an appointment with Marvin on Wednesday, and if I cry off, he'll go ape.

What the fuck am I going to do?

This is dangerous.

She's dangerous.

It's all getting too close for comfort. I've got to do something. I've got to stop her from talking.

Hey, now here's a thought, perhaps there's another reason why the two of us met. Perhaps Mum was showing me what needed to be snuffed out before it snuffed out me?

I stare down at Angela's head as she cuddles up to me. How fragile she is. How easy it would be to hurt her. Is knowing how easy it would be the same as wanting to do it? I'm confused. I'm confusing myself. Layers of wanting and not wanting to do it, reflecting off themselves.

Just my hand over her nose and mouth would be enough.

Snap.

Break her neck.

I focus on her pulse banging away in her temple, and it makes me dizzy to think how easy it would be with her curled up against me, trusting me to hold on to her. Her instinct, telling her she's safe – safe with me.

Yet instinct can be wrong. We all know that. Isn't it awful? I bet I've got you worried that she's no idea who she's entrusting herself to. Especially as you know what I'm capable of.

FORTY-FIVE

'Change of plan, Spike.' The following day, Tyrone at her shoulder needed to shout above the usual racket, the periodic shouting. 'I know you were supposed to be having the afternoon off tomorrow, but Chef wants you and me to work a double so we're on top of it for that party coming in.'

'Oh, the thing is,' Angela sighed, 'I had plans and I can't put them off any longer.' She was thinking about the promise she'd made herself to go back and see DS Varrius. 'And it's not like I can do it today. I'm working until eleven tonight.'

Tyrone threw his gaze to the clock, then back to her. 'Can you do what you need to do now and be back here for six?'

'I suppose. When can I knock off?'

'Just finish up what you're doing there, then you're free to go.'

The road outside the police station had been cordoned off to traffic. Red-and-white tape flapped around in the rain. Within its confines, men in hard hats were forced to holler at each other over the din. Their fluorescent-orange tabards were the only things of interest amidst the otherwise drab surroundings. Walking in and up to the reception desk, the sound of a pneumatic drill made it difficult to think, let alone be heard.

Her parka, zipped up over her whites, dripped rainwater on the floor. Angela asked to speak to DS Varrius, explaining who she was and the nature of her visit. She watched as his extension was dialled. The listening lips of the third-party puckering against the receiver.

'If you'd just like to wait, DS Varrius says he'll be with you soon as he's free.'

Angela wandered over to the window that looked out over the back of the building. Outside, darkness ruled. The area beyond the night-blackened car park was a wasteland. A dead zone of featureless tarmac and a forest of spindly steel lamps. She stared out at the rain that was coming in sideways. Millions of silvery lines were brought in on the gusts of wind and clarified by the amber hue of street lamps and sporadic car headlights circling the city.

'Miss Billigan.' DS Varrius appeared and she left the dismal scene behind. 'What is it I can do for you this time?'

'Sorry, it's... it's *Milligan*. Angela Milligan.' She emphasised the *M* of her surname.

'Yes, yes.' A stressed-looking Varrius led her into a nearby interview room, where they sat across from each other.

'Did DC Thompson tell you I phoned?'

The detective shook his head. 'No, I don't believe he did.'

'Never mind. I've found something out that you need to know.' She hesitated to assemble what she wanted to say. 'That kitchen porter I told you about... It turns out he's got a motive for killing Toni Perry.'

'Is that right?' The rustle of fibres as Varrius adjusted himself inside his clothes.

'According to my friend in HR… it's all on file if you need to check,' Angela rushed on, 'Toni reported him for moonlighting. It was because of her he got the sack, and that's what they must've been arguing about. And—' she took a breath, 'Toni had accused him of stealing, only it turned out he hadn't—'

'If I could stop you there,' Varrius said, cutting her off. 'This isn't news to us. We've been aware for some time that Mr Kowalski was sacked on Miss Perry's say-so.'

'You've spoken to HR?'

A terse nod.

'I'm sorry, I didn't know.'

'*Ah*, but it isn't me you should be apologising to, is it?'

'Pardon me?'

'This man you've been harassing, this Mr Kowalski – he's the one you should be apologising to.' Varrius made a steeple with his fingers. 'I say, harassing, Miss Billigan, when what I think we're dealing with is rather more serious.' The gleam in his eye made her uneasy. 'I think you'll find, that in the eyes of the law, what you've been doing would be classified as stalking. And stalking, as I'm sure you're aware, is a criminal offence.'

'I'm sorry, I'm not sure I understand what you're saying.' *So that's his name, is it? Kowalski.*

'You keep saying sorry but somehow I don't think you are. You've become rather too fixated on this man. Too fixated to see how wrong you've been. Somehow, you've managed to convince yourself that he was involved in Toni Perry's murder. Am I right?'

'Well, yes, I do think that.' Angela listened to the rain pummel the exterior walls of the building.

'I think the grief you've suffered from the loss of your friend has somehow,' he tapped the tapered ends of his fingers against his lips and mumbled, 'How to say this… How to communicate the seriousness of the situation without hurting feelings?' He took a long, deep breath. 'I think what I'm trying to say, is that you must be suffering from some kind of delusion. And please, believe me, I don't use this term lightly. It's why I'm pleased you've come to see me today.'

'You are?' Angela, brightening a little.

'It gives me the opportunity to warn you,' he raised an eyebrow, fixed her with his gimlet eyes, 'that if you persist in harassing this gentleman, then it won't be a civilised little chat we'll be having. You'll be facing criminal charges that could well lead to prosecution.'

'Prosecution?' she echoed, swallowing hard.

'Good, I can see I'm getting through to you at last.' He raked a hand up through his thatch of black hair, making it stand up in tufts.

'Who told you?'

'*Ah*, so you don't deny you've been following him?' A thin smile.

'I've never denied it.' Angela stared at her lap. 'I told you I followed him, and why I did it.'

'And are we talking just the once?' She could tell he knew there'd been other times, so there was little point lying.

'No, more than once.' She looked up and met his gaze.

'Good, this is good. Thank you for your honesty.'

'But who reported me?' Angela was half-wondering if it could have been Anne-Marie or even Rhiannon.

'He did. The complaint came from Mr Kowalski. He knows you came asking questions about him at his place of work. He says he's been aware of you and your unhealthy interest in him for some time. The thing is, you see,' Varrius spoke through lowered lids, 'he remembers you from when he worked at the Lloyd George. He says your fixation with him started there, and that it was long before Toni Perry died.'

'That's a lie. I don't know any of them working the pot wash.

There's such a high turnover of staff, none of them last long enough. I'm telling you, I never clapped eyes on him until I saw him and Toni arguing. And the next thing, she'd been killed. You can't blame me for being suspicious of him.'

'But I'm afraid, it is a case of his word against yours.'

'And he got his complaint in first,' her turn to mumble, 'and you're never going to believe me.'

'Sorry? I didn't quite catch that.'

'Nothing.'

'Mr Kowalski isn't stupid, Miss Billigan.'

'No, I'm sure he's not.' Why did he persist in getting her name wrong? To show she wasn't important enough to get it right, she answered herself.

'But then again, you've hardly been discreet, have you?'

'I don't know what you want me to say?' Angela, shamefaced and uncomfortable, just wanted to get out of there.

'You need to say it stops here. That you stop harassing Mr Kowalski and let him get on with his life.' Varrius tapped his biro against the table, impatient, irritated. 'Look, I really shouldn't be discussing this case with you, but for the sake of enabling me to hammer the point home – Mr Kowalski has a watertight alibi the night of your friend's murder and we have absolutely no evidence to suggest he was anywhere near her flat, or anywhere near her. So, can we please agree, that this will be an end to it?'

'So, you have talked to him?' Whatever this detective thought, Angela was still convinced that creep of a bloke murdered Toni. And what worried her now, was the idea the weirdo knew who she was.

'We have indeed.'

'And you really don't think he's got anything to do with it?' She picked at an imaginary thread on her chef's trousers.

'No, we don't suspect him of anything.'

'I do find it a bit unsettling that he knows me. You haven't told him where I live, have you? Supposing he comes after me?' Her mind spun to the previous evening when she was out after dark hunting for Bimbo, thinking the man had found her. But it wasn't him, she needed to remind herself, it was Leon, and there was nothing to fret about.

'Why on earth would he do that? Dear me,' a croaky laugh, 'I think you've been watching too many crime dramas on the television.'

'That's what my friend Anne-Marie said,' she admitted.

'You've got a good friend there; I suggest you listen to her.' He smiled a small smile. 'All right?'

'Yes. I'm sorry if I've been a nuisance, but I was just trying to help.' Angela pretended to go along with it. She couldn't tell him that Anne-Marie had lost patience and as well as Rhiannon, wanted nothing more to do with her. He would probably say she deserved it.

'I have no doubt your intentions were honourable, and I thank you for that. But please, don't go concerning yourself with this anymore.'

FORTY-SIX

I found out today that Angela's been asking after me at college. My fault, I shouldn't have lied about the accountancy course but I didn't know she'd already seen me around there before. She probably won't want anything to do with me, now she knows I clean toilets for a living. It serves me right. But compared to the other lies I've told, it's bugger all.

I know I should've been straight with her but I suppose it's because I've been brought up on a diet of lies and this is how I think the world works – my world, anyway. But we all lie, don't we? Lying is good. It must be because she does it too.

I notice there are no lights on at the Bowens' place next door. There rarely is, Angela always seems to be working. Her message said she was doing a double shift today, which is good for me because while she's at work, she's not down at the cop shop causing me trouble. I'll try and forget about it, for now, just get tomorrow's meeting with Marvin out of the way, then I'll sort things with her. But tomorrow will be too late, won't it? Fuck, I'm stupid. I've got to act tonight if I'm going to stop her blabbing. And I think I may have just worked out a way to do it.

I slide my key into the lock of number eighty-six and climb the stairs. I really can do this in one these days, I'm not out of puff at all.

'There you are.' Babcia is waiting for me on the top landing, hands on hips. 'Oh, I am glad to see you're getting some wear out of that coat.'

'I sure am.' I push past her into the kitchen.

'Good. You're taking your gloves off without being told for once.'

'Yeah.' I flex my fingers. 'My circulation's been loads better.'

'I told you it was nonsense, didn't I? Now get out of that wet thing before you drip water over my nice clean floor.'

'Where's Grandpa?'

'He's gone to bed early tonight.'

'*Again*?' I take the Crombie off and let her hang it over the stove to dry.

'He wasn't feeling all that bright. We shared a little supper and then he said he wanted his bed.'

'He's not been right for days; don't you think you should call a doctor?'

'I would if I thought they'd come out. But the surgery doesn't do home visits anymore. I'll ring them in the morning. Oh, look—' she lifts and drops the curtain, 'the rain's stopped for a minute. Want to come and see the bunnies with me?'

We go out into the dark to feed the rabbits. I love the way they twitch their noses through the wire mesh. Hopeful of treats. Or whatever constitutes treats in the rabbit world. The reason why Babcia keeps rabbits is one of the few family mysteries that has been explained. And out of all the things that weren't explained, it puzzles me why it was this one. These rabbits, well, the great-great-grandparents of these rabbits, belonged to Mum. And since she died, Babcia's made it her life's work to continue the line.

I like helping to clean them out. Making hospital corners with the newspaper she saves to line their cages with. Neat and orderly, it's about the only thing Babcia ever compliments me on. I stand back to watch her worm a finger through the hexagonal netting to stroke the soft fur between their ears. Wet-eyed creatures, with fear shimmering behind their eyes, they live on the tips of their nerves.

I look away to the west. See how the sky has crept forward into the darkness.

'Tea?' Babcia suggests, and we go inside.

Kettle on, I watch her busy herself with dressing the tray. It's a strange ritual, I've no idea why she bothers, it's only ever the three of us. And only two of us this evening.

'Shall we do a puzzle?'

Babcia's an expert puzzler, she thinks it keeps her brain sharp. Not only the ones in her daily newspaper but the periodical that falls with a thud on the front doormat. A puzzle book she will work through methodically from start to finish. Her handwriting is as neat as her embroidery, and she uses a fountain pen with real ink as if she will be marked on it afterwards. I pull up a chair and sit beside her at the kitchen table. Lean over her arm as she makes a start on the first of her cryptic crosswords.

'Fifty-one cats to the rescue.' She taps her pen against her bottom teeth. '*Mm*, don't know... What about four down?'

'Hang on.' A lightbulb moment. I've been having rather a lot of these since I stopped the meds. '*Lifelines*,' I say, with confidence. 'The answer is, lifelines.'

'Get you!' She slides her eyes to me. 'Who's got his brains back all of a sudden? I didn't know you knew how to do these.'

'There's lots about me you don't know.' Deliberately mysterious, even though I wish I could tell her I'm as surprised by my ability and lucidity as she is.

'There's something different about you. Are you all right?' Babcia squeezes my arm – I told you she was clever; she sees the change in me too.

'I'm fine, never better.' On the tip of my tongue, the words that would convey how, in a few short weeks, I've gone from someone who'd lost all sense of himself, to discovering what joy is... What living is. That I have a kind of fluttering elation quivering inside. A sense that something good is about to happen if I could just clear the way ahead.

'Are you in love? Is that what it is?'

I remember Angela saying that she showed Babcia her drawing. Did she recognise me after all? Why won't she confront me with what she knows? No wonder I've turned out the way I have, brought up by people who won't speak plainly. I sometimes wonder, if I'd been born a girl, then perhaps Babcia would've talked to me, instead of leaving me to catch the drift of things, because I know she talked to Yana. Yana – who claimed she was so afraid of me, she upped sticks and moved about as far away as she could, as soon as she could.

'I might be.' I'm not the only one who can skirt around the elephant in the room. And I could be in love. But not just with a girl. I'm in love with life. Colours are brighter, sharper – the world is in full focus like never before.

'Well, you want to have a proper shave. Whoever she is, she isn't going to want to be seen out with Grizzly Adams.' She turns away as if disgusted by me. 'Have you been losing more weight?'

'A little.'

'What's wrong, you're not ill, are you?'

'Of course I'm bloody ill. I've been telling you all my life, I'm ill.'

'I don't mean like that; I mean properly ill.'

I have nothing to say, so I drink my tea. Decline the biscuits she's trying to foist on me.

'There's something up. You're not yourself at all.'

'Because I turn down a biscuit?' I smack the arms of the chair and watch her flinch.

Then, up on her feet, she carries her cup and saucer to the sink. Fingers the green-looking bananas in the bowl on her work surface. 'I'll just nip down to see if Grandpa needs anything. Won't be a tick.'

I watch her go. My eyes bore holes in her as she picks her way over my feet. I don't bother to move out of the way. I wait until I hear their bedroom door open and close before I get up. I've been eyeing her handbag since I arrived. And now's my chance. I've bugger all left until payday. I'm getting through it loads quicker, even with what I've already nicked from here, it doesn't last five minutes now I've got Angela to pay for. It's not that she doesn't offer, she's always pushing money onto me but I don't like taking it. I suppose I'm old-fashioned like that.

With my back to the door, I open Babcia's handbag. Convinced I can do this quickly, I pull out her purse and flick open the press stud and undo the zip.

Easy-peasy, lemon squeezy.

I'm getting nifty at this. I pull out a couple of tenners. There's not so much in here tonight but it'll tide me over for a while. But I'm overconfident, I drop the purse before I've had the chance to zip it closed again. Coins spill over the floor and roll under the sideboard. I must get down on my hands and knees and stretch an arm into the cobwebs and dust to retrieve them.

Something shifts on my periphery. I turn my head and see Babcia's stockinged calves, inches from my nose.

Fuck it.

FORTY-SEVEN

It was raining so hard Angela's parka was soaked even before she joined the queue at the bus stop. Slotting in behind a couple who couldn't keep their hands off each other. Her thoughts spun to Leon as they had been doing on and off all day, and if she concentrated, she could feel the press of his lips against hers. Smiling a secret smile, she caught the unwanted attention of a grey-haired man and was forced to look away. She couldn't help smiling, she didn't think she'd ever felt this happy, not even when Robert was alive. She wished she still had Rhiannon and Anne-Marie in her life. She would have liked to talk about Leon with them. But in the same way she tried not to agonise over their fallings out, she tried not to brood on why Leon hadn't replied to either of her text messages that day.

His silence didn't have to mean anything ominous. It didn't have to mean she'd been wrong to share her woes with him last night. Or did it? Doubts crowded in. Had she said too much, gone on too long about wanting to clear Mark's name? A pledge, that after her conversation with DS Varrius earlier, she doubted she'd be able to honour. Why did she have to go drinking too much and waffling on? Leon probably thought she'd lost the plot too, in the same way Rhiannon and Anne-Marie did. *Oh, please, don't let me have screwed things up with him as well.*

The experience at the police station was excruciating but Angela wasn't sorry she went. If anything, she was angry – angry with that kitchen porter because she'd worked out what he was up to, even if the police hadn't. He was getting his accusation in first. It was called *throwing them off the scent*. And if she could see it, why couldn't they? Granted, they said they'd spoken to him but she doubted it would have been an in-depth probing; not when they already had Mark Fairfax behind bars. She may well have left the station with a flea in her ear but Varrius wasn't going to deter her. Not when he and his team of detectives were making the most monumental mistake.

That Kowalski bloke killed Toni; he had murderer written all over him and her trip to the police had made her more determined than ever to prove Mark's innocence. At least now she was armed, she knew the creep was onto her. Although, she should have guessed it from the look he gave when he trapped her in the courtyard in her party dress – a courtyard she doubted she'd be able to find again. But he certainly knew his way around the city, didn't he? And in her opinion, this made him doubly dangerous. If she did get lucky and clap eyes on him again, she needed to ensure he didn't see her, because if he did lead her down some blind alley, she was sure he wouldn't let her escape a second time.

The bus lurched away from the kerb to join the traffic. The air was heavy with a wet wool smell and she wiped a hole in the condensation and looked out on the rain-drenched city, the blur of lights. Mindful of the diesel stink and tortured throb of the engine through the floor.

Her mobile beeped.

Leon?

She lunged for her bag, too enthusiastically, and her elbow caught the woman sitting beside her. She apologised, then looked at her phone to see Mark's name on the screen. His text was only short but reading between the lines she could tell he was distraught. His message was only to convey the address of the remand centre where he was being held in custody. The train she would need to catch to Bristol Parkway. The strict visiting times. How he was only permitted two, one-hour slots, every four weeks, and that the first available slot was Thursday. *What, this Thursday?* She held her breath and counted up the days. It was okay, today was Tuesday, she only had to work tomorrow then she had Thursday off. Earned it too, working two doubles on the trot this week. She stared at the screen. She wanted to reply now but stopped herself. Supposing they had changed the rota without telling her? Better to wait and message him when she knew for certain.

When the bus slowed at a stop, a young woman embarked, dripping rainwater from her umbrella. Angela recognised her from college. Her name was Gina and she worked in the admissions office. Gina had been especially helpful when she went to enquire about accountancy courses. Exchanging shy little nods, Angela wondered if Gina might join her on the seat opposite but she chose to sit just behind the driver. She hadn't wanted to doubt Leon, but she was so sure she'd seen him around college before finally getting to talk to him. There was no way he'd just signed up for a course, not mid-term – he hadn't been particularly clever with his lie. So what? He was a cleaner. It wasn't such a great surprise; she'd guessed from the state of his hands that he didn't count money for a living. He probably only lied to impress her, embarrassed about the job he did and, in a way, she was flattered he'd cared enough about what she thought. And how could she mind? She hadn't exactly been straight with him either. Saying she was in hotel management and making out she was doing better than she was. What's good for the goose... Anyway, her feelings for Leon meant she would probably forgive him anything. Identifying his sense of loneliness and latching onto it, because this was how she felt herself. His desire to belong, to be acceptable to society, all echoed her own needs because she'd bet, that like her, Leon had always found himself on the margins of things too.

She stared at her washed-out reflection in the darkened window as the bus juddered on. *I think I love him...* Her thoughts butting up against the spent breath of fellow passengers. *He needs looking after and I'm going to be the one to do it.* She would cook him pasta and casseroles, Angela decided, her plan taking shape. She would make him happy in the way he would make her happy. Was it as ridiculous as it sounded? She tried to push the thoughts away but they kept jogging back. She smiled again, she couldn't help it, there was something comical about the way she was feeling, it was bordering on the absurd.

The bus wheezed to a standstill at the bottom of Coracle Road. The rubber-skirted doors hissed apart and she twisted away on her heavy shoes, clomped down the metal steps and onto the rainy street. Feeling happier than she supposed she had a right to after a twelve-hour shift and more of the same ahead of her tomorrow.

FORTY-EIGHT

'I'm sorry, Babcia.' I'm still on my hands and knees but I make sure I get my apology in first. 'Really, I am. But I'm desperate. Things are tough now Dad's buggered off and left me again. I can't afford to run that house on my own.'

She doesn't know this is a lie, that my father pays the mortgage, the utility bills. That he's set up countless direct debits to ensure I always have a roof over my head. But she's caught me with my fingers in her purse and I've got to lay it on thick if I'm going to win her round.

'It won't happen again. I'm really sorry.'

'Sorry you got caught, or sorry? If you're short of money, you only have to ask.'

'I didn't like to.'

'Have you ever done this before?' Abandoning whatever dark visions had momentarily distracted her, she refocuses on me.

'Never.' I shake my head emphatically, enthralled with the idea of my honesty.

'I've always thought I can leave my purse anywhere in the house and you won't touch it.'

'No, I've never taken money from you before.'

'It's just—' She looks away. 'I just thought I had rather more in my purse when I went to the post office to send Yana's birthday present.'

'You must've spent it.'

'I suppose I must have.' She steps up to me, reaches out to stroke my lengthening hair.

'Do you like it longer?' Still on my knees, I look up at her for a change. I want her approval.

'Not really.' Babcia is always blunt. Sometimes I wonder, if there was a little more in the way of compromise, it would have made our lives more comfortable. 'Is there anything worrying you?'

'No, nothing. Apart from having no money.' I make my eyes as honest as I can and haul myself up off the floor.

'Anything you want to get off your chest?'

She gives me a look that makes me think she can smell my treachery. I'm convinced she knows. Knows about Toni. The fact that another man is about to be sent to prison for the rest of his life for something I did. The plans I've got for her and Grandpa. For shutting Angela up.

'When were you going to tell me about Angela?'

So she did recognise the drawing after all. Okay, I can deal with this.

'You're not going to pretend you don't know her, are you?'

'Why not? You lie to me all the time.' Good, this is good. Throw it back to her. What I'm doing with Angela is none of her business.

'Lie to you? Dear me, about what, for goodness' sake?'

'About Poland. About the life I could have had there.'

'You're being silly and romantic. If you'd been born when me and Grandpa were, Poland would've sold you out too. People we thought were our friends, they all turned against us when the chips were down.'

'It doesn't mean it would've been like that for me. I know Mum wanted to live there. She said so when we went to Gdańsk for a holiday.'

'I'm sorry, but why are we talking about Poland all of a sudden?'

Because I don't want to explain about Angela – I might inadvertently give something away, some clue that means you stop me from doing what I need to do to her.

'It's important. It's important to me,' I say instead.

That look again. 'You wouldn't have been born if it weren't for Britain. So think yourself lucky you weren't our generation because look where your precious heritage got you then.'

I don't see it. I love Poland. Mum loved it too. No doubt she had the same conversations with Babcia that I have. I know I'd feel more at home in Poland than Cardiff, and who is she to tell me otherwise? I fix her with my eye. Words of violence burst in my mouth. I hold them there, bloody, like loose teeth.

'Don't you dare look at me like that. I don't know how you've managed to turn this back on me. I've just caught you stealing from my purse.'

Angela seems to have been forgotten, thank fuck. I can't have Babcia sticking her oar in there. Not now I've hatched this brilliant plan. Look how gullible she is, the silly old bat. My slyness pleases me. She must either be losing her touch, or I'm firing on all cylinders like never before. I can't usually get one over on her.

'Can I stay tonight?'

I watch her mull this over.

'I think I'm coming down with something. I might have picked up what Grandpa's got.'

Babcia tries to test my temperature with the flat of her palm against my forehead, in the way she would when I was small. But unlike when I was small, I bat her away.

'What about your medications?' I flinch from her gaze. 'Don't you need to take them regularly? Isn't it dangerous to even miss a single dose?'

'It won't hurt for one night.'

'I think it would.'

'Oh, please, Babcia, I'm not well enough to drive. You wouldn't want me to have an accident, would you?'

'All right.' A defeated sigh. 'I'll go and fetch you a pair of Grandpa's pyjamas.'

'And a toothbrush?'

She nods but I can tell she's not happy.

I go downstairs to the bedroom that used to be Mum's. Scoop out the coins from my pocket and make a stack of them on the bedside table beside my mobile. The sheets are cold when I slip between them and I lie here listening to the voices of my grandparents, the toilet flushing, sounds of life filtering through the thin dividing wall.

The single bed is piled with soft toys, there's barely room for me. I'm not sure if they were Mum's or things Babcia bought because she had no toys as a child. I pick up Pooh bear. Finger the little red tank top that doesn't cover his tummy. I remember playing with this as a child. It doesn't bring happy memories, so I put Pooh down again. I can't sleep. It often happens, although not for a while, not since the chemicals have been out of my system. I wonder if there are others like me, or does everyone else wake up refreshed and well-rested? Nights like this are when I think of death. My own death and how I might eventually leave this world. It's something that has concerned me since I was small. A fear of never being found, of not mattering to another living soul. But at least death is certain, it's something we can bank on. I turn over onto my side. I don't like looking at that tailor's dummy, it's always creeped me out, the thing's too human, which is probably the point but I still don't like it looming over me. I stare at Mum's old posters and the fussy wallpaper that, lit by the street lamp filtering in from outside, shows me a pattern I know by heart.

I must have drifted off at some point but I'm awake again now. Wide awake. Which is good because I've got to work out what I'm going to do. It's later than I thought, it's nearly midnight. The house is quiet. Babcia and Grandpa have gone to bed. All the lights are out but the street lamps give enough to go by. I'm thirsty and kick off the bedcovers and head up to the kitchen. It feels nice to have the place to myself again, I like the cool feel of lino beneath my bare feet. I find a glass and turn the tap. Run it until the water makes my hand ache from the cold. I drink it down. I'm hungry, my insides feel unpleasantly hollow but there's nothing in the fridge worth having, the fruit pie is long gone. I dip a hand inside the bread bin, hoping something remains of yesterday's batch. I'm lucky and, locating the block of butter from beneath its chequered cloth, I scrape the corners of a crust into its salty yellowness. Chewing and swallowing, I lift a free hand to my hair. I'm glad I haven't given in and shaved it. Babcia might not like it but I know someone who does. And I need to keep her sweet, at least for the time being.

The fear that Angela could ruin things for me rears its ugly head again. I've got to stop her from going back to the cops. I know I should've confessed at the time about Toni but it's too late for confessions now. The questions Angela asked about me at Hafod College prove how tenacious she is, and her dogged determination to clear Mark's name scares me.

Why's she doing it? Has she got the hots for him? Whatever her reason is, it's a serious threat to me. And just when I've got a real chance to get my life together. With my father finally out of the way, things are good, so I'm sorry if I sound callous but I can't stand by and let her ruin everything. Even though I think she's the one, I love my freedom more than I could ever love a girl. Because they will lock me up for good next time. Lock me up and throw away the key.

I'm going to have to kill her. She's left me no choice. It's her own stupid fault.

Rain thrashes the window and I part the nets and peer out on the night. Then, checking and rechecking the taps are off, I find a key on a brass hook next to the sink. I lift it down and read the label, bounce it in my hand: dice I'm about to cast. Serendipity strikes again. This is fate. This is Mum guiding me.

I go back down to the bedroom to dress. Transfer the key to my jeans and fold Grandpa's pyjamas on top of the bed, after I've tidied it. Then I creep along the landing and push open the door of my grandparents' room. A bar of light from the hall cuts across the bed and shows the shapes of their bodies beneath the duvet. The room is cold, colder than it should be because they sleep with the window open. I see the curtains flap against it and shiver a little inside my clothes. I see Grandpa's watch on his bedside cabinet. The watch he doesn't need because he can't see to tell the time. Far better for me to have it; it'll come to me one day, so it might as well be now.

I listen to them sleeping. The faint rattle of Grandpa's bad chest and Babcia's soft snores. She really shouldn't sleep on her back. It's dark in here, but gradually the street light permeates the room, allowing me to pick out the skeletons of furniture I've known since childhood. I see Babcia's dressing gown hanging over the back of the wicker chair. The one she found in a second-hand shop and altered and dyed. She finds bargains everywhere; she hardly buys anything new.

By the side of the bed are Grandpa's trainers. Placed neatly together, their soft tongues tucked inside. He takes care of everything; they hardly look as if they've been worn. Which I suppose they haven't, he doesn't go anywhere. I look at the watch again, then pick it up and fasten the strap to my wrist. It would be so easy to finish them here.

I look at the velvet cushion on the seat of the wicker chair. Lift it up and hold it in both hands. I struggle with the buzzing that is louder than ever. It's too loud for me to think. Too loud for the rational voice of self-preservation to find me and change my mind. I haven't the strength to quell it, I'm going to have to give in to it... I can't stop myself. Look at them sleeping, oblivious to me standing over them in the dark. The power to end their lives in my grip.

I hear the sound of a faraway police siren as it weaves through the city. Then the banging of a car door and voices in the street. Cushion poised; I wait. I'm not sure what for. Sudden rain pelts the window. If I could just ask her, talk openly about how she would like to leave this world, she might say she was grateful for this. That it's a relief not to have to end her days in a nursing home, sitting in a chair with dribble down her chin, being fed through a straw.

Yeah, come on, I'd be doing her a favour. Doing them both a favour. I take another step closer.

I think my head's going to explode.

Do it. Do it.

That voice. The bad one that tells me to do bad things.

I've lost the fight; I can't wrangle against it anymore, the drive is too strong, too loud, it's taken me over. I'm thinking about the money... The money it will save if they don't have to sell this house and use it to pay for a nursing home. More money for me. Because let's face it, it's all I've ever been interested in. It's the only reason I bother with them.

Thoughts of my inheritance battle for room alongside the soaring din between my ears, as I lower the fat velvet cushion down over Babcia's face.

At least this wasn't the end Hitler had in mind for her.

For them.

FORTY-NINE

Angela unlocked the front door and pushed the time switch on the wall. It flooded the stairwell in a yellow glare. Quickly, before the light ran out, she whipped off her wet parka and hung it over the bannister. Little point trying to dry it out upstairs, she'd be putting the thing on again in a few short hours.

Pausing at the foot of the stairs, she glanced at her face in the mirror hanging at shoulder height. It told her what she'd already guessed. Damp hair, plastered to her forehead, the skin around her eyes, purple and thin-looking – she looked worn out and was glad there was no one around to see her. The house was silent. The rain going on in the street was little more than a muffled whisper against the exterior walls. Accompanied by plans to raid the fridge and change into her big, fluffy dressing gown, she dragged her weary body up to the top floor. But after the allotted two minutes, the light snapped off. The timer had run down and she needed to climb the final section in the dark. *But the dark is never as deep as you think.* Her thoughts as she braced herself for the ventriloquist's dummy on the turn of the second landing. And although prepared, the sight of its sinister stare still made her jump.

'*Uch!*'

Something soft had yielded underfoot and, reaching the kitchen to grope for the light switch, she turned back to look at what she'd trodden on. Found a small brown rabbit stretched out on its side. Stiff with death.

Then it was Leon she was looking at.

Seated on a kitchen chair, one leg crossed over the other.

'Bloody hell!' she shrieked and slapped a hand to her quickening heart. 'How did you get in?'

'I've been watching it.' Leon ignored her question and pointed to the nugget of brown fur. 'It was the tabby what caught it. Playing with it for ages, it was.'

'They're buggers, they bring mice in all the time. Never seen them bring in a rabbit before.' She nudged the poor dead creature with the toe of her boot, still wondering how Leon had got in. 'Where d'you think they found it? They've only got access to the roof garden.' Then she remembered Zofia's little brown bunnies. 'Oh, no, it's not one of your gran's, is it?'

'Afraid so.' Leon, from his chair. 'And she's not gonna be happy.'

If he saw it happening, why didn't he stop it? Rescue it? She stared at him and realised with startling clarity just how much space he claimed. The fact he was here, uninvited, it unnerved her.

'So, how did you get in?' She frowned.

'The door was open.'

She threw a look over his shoulder, working out a way to clear up the rabbit remains without touching it.

'You can't have locked it.'

'I think I did. I'm always careful about stuff like that.'

'It was open. How else d'you think I got in? You can see I haven't *forced* anything.' When he said the word forced, he narrowed his eyes and jutted out his chin. 'Anyway,' he jingled something in his pocket, 'aren't you pleased to see me? I thought it would be a nice surprise. But if you want me to go?' He looked hurt and got to his feet, making for the door.

'No. Don't go. Course I'm pleased to see you.' A self-conscious hand to her hair. 'It's just that I look such a mess.'

'You look beautiful to me.' He sat back down again.

'Huh, you old charmer.' She smiled, shy under his interest. 'But I don't believe you. I stink of kitchens.'

'*Oh*,' he leant forward over his knees, 'you're admitting you're a chef now?'

'Yes,' she groaned. 'I'm a bloody chef. Guilty as charged.'

'I knew you were telling fibs.'

'Did you?' Sheepish from under her long, damp hair. 'How?'

'I dunno. I just sort of guessed. The hours you work are a bit of a giveaway.' His gaze was unflinching. 'Aren't you going to say what you found out about me?'

He can't know, surely? 'What's there to find out?'

'That I mop floors and scrub pans for a living?'

'Oh, that.' She flapped a hand. 'I don't care about that.'

'Others would. Kitchen porters are the lowest life form in most people's books.'

'Well, I'm not most people.' She crossed the kitchen to take the hands he held out to her.

'You had a tough day?'

'It's been a long one and I've got another double shift tomorrow.' She jigged his hands up and down. 'Chef switched the rota.'

'But I thought you had tomorrow afternoon off?' His expression brightened; she could think he was relieved about something. 'Can that boss of yours even do that?'

'The bastard can do whatever he wants.'

'But you were going back to the police tomorrow?'

'You what?' She was thinking she should go and have a bath and wash her hair. Smarten herself up.

'The police. Tomorrow? You said you had an appointment to see them Wednesday afternoon.'

'I didn't have an appointment. But it doesn't matter, I had a couple of hours off today, I nipped over to see them then.'

'You went today?' He gripped her hands like a punishment.

'Yes. It's not a problem, is it?' Troubled by his expression, Angela saw his face had become suddenly pinched and drawn.

'What did they say?'

His brow was filmed in sweat. Why was he so agitated? What was wrong? Had she done something to upset him?

'They were very grateful I'd come forward.'

'And?'

'They said they'd look into it. Well, actually, the detective I spoke to said they might have to reopen the case.'

'They said that?'

'You don't have to look so surprised, it's obvious they would. That bloke having a motive; it changes everything.' She lied to Leon to save face. How could she admit that Varrius had warned her off? That he said she'd be facing charges herself if she didn't leave things alone. She was feeling bruised enough. 'Now—' she took back her hands, 'I suppose I'd better dispose of this poor thing.' Grateful to change the subject, she crouched to inspect the rabbit. Was saddened by the glazed look in its button-black eyes. 'Your gran's going to be so upset, how am I going to tell her?'

'Don't tell her.' He gave her a wild look. 'She doesn't have to know everything that goes on. There's loads of stuff I don't tell her.' His blue eyes were especially piercing tonight, and his look was cold and hard.

Angela didn't want to, but she was remembering things Zofia told her about Leon's sister needing to up sticks and move to the other side of the world because she was scared of him... Something dark happened during their childhood and she wished she'd pressed Zofia for specifics.

'I'll just go and find somewhere to put it.' She tore off a square of kitchen towel and used it to pick the rabbit up by its hind legs. Stepping around Leon's feet, she reached for the key from the windowsill, before reminding herself the door was already open. It had started raining again, so she dropped the dead rabbit onto the back step, she would deal with it in the morning.

Bimbo trotted inside and jumped onto the work surface. He lifted his leg and proceeded to lick his back end with an urgent fervour.

'God, that's disgusting.' Leon pulled a face. 'You shouldn't let them do that. Not on there. It's unhygienic.'

'They're cats,' she laughed; uneasy, jerky, 'they do what they want.'

'If you ask me the whole place is bloody stinking. I was surprised, I had no idea it was such a dump. You'd never know it to look at the pair of them.'

'Who?'

'The Bowens.'

'Oh, right.' Angela stifled a yawn, all she wanted was her bed: the soft counterpane, the frilly pillowcases.

'I must say, I'm a bit disappointed in you. Don't you want to give it a good scrub?'

'No. I like it.' She ignored the *disappointed in you.* 'My mother's obsessive about cleaning, I've got better things to do with my life.'

'I couldn't stand having animals in the house. Look at the hairs. They're on bloody everything.' He wet the tip of a finger and slid it over the velour-covered seat of his chair. Pulled away a clod of grey fur. 'Isn't there a vacuum you can use?'

She shrugged; she was too tired to defend herself. 'Want to go and see what's on the telly?'

'If you like.'

They went down to the floor below, where Angela busied herself by turning on the lamps, drawing curtains, making it cosy. Leon wandered the room, randomly picking things up and putting them down. He opened the lid of the piano, picked over the keys.

'Do you play?'

'Nah.' And he snapped the lid shut.

He seemed different tonight. Edgy. Wired. His eyes were disconcertingly bright. She watched the muscles in his jaw twitch as he looked around him, his reflection bouncing back to her from the walls of mirrors. She hated to admit it but she was a little afraid of him.

'I usually watch a bit of telly before bed. It helps me unwind.'

She switched the television on and they dropped onto the couch with a leathery creak. The cats were nowhere. Usually, they joined her – one on her lap, the other beside her – she wondered if it was Leon making them nervous in the way he was making her nervous.

'Would you like something to drink?'

He shook his head. 'Might catch something from that stinking kitchen.'

'Aw, come on. It's not that bad.'

He gave her a look that told her he thought otherwise and she wondered again what he was doing here. Why he'd bothered to come over when it was obvious he wasn't in the mood for company and had nothing to say? It was odd. He was odd. But because she couldn't bear to think she'd got him wrong, not before they'd had the chance to see if they could be good together, she ignored the corks of doubt that had bobbed to the surface of her mind.

They sat without speaking. The film they had missed the beginning of – some high melodrama with excessive shooting and car chases – wasn't holding her. Conscious of the dwindling time and her need to get some shut-eye, she was relieved when Leon yawned. Then, looking sideways, she saw he'd kicked off his trainers. *Was he staying the night?* She didn't think she was ready for that.

He dropped his head on her shoulder and the minutes ticked by. Another look to see he'd closed his eyes, had her turning the television off. She sat in the silence, waiting for him to wake but he didn't, so she eased his head onto a cushion and rose to her feet. She looked down at him, wanting to check he was asleep. He was slumped in a spill of light from the lamp, saliva shining at the corners of his mouth. He looked asleep to her. The room was chilly, so she went down to fetch a pillow and duvet from the room Toni had been going to stay in that time.

Toni.

She wouldn't have left her boyfriend sleeping on the sofa, she'd have taken him to bed. But Angela wasn't Toni, she didn't rush into things. She was someone who thought everything through, picked over every detail, looking for pitfalls even when there weren't any.

She took the opportunity to change into her nightclothes and knotted her dressing gown around her middle. That expression on Leon's face. The chill of his sudden, angry silence. It curled up in her mind like a question mark, but there was no way to explain the change in him.

Returning to the living room, relieved to find Leon was still asleep, she slid a pillow under his head. Felt him shift under her hand. He made a small noise but he didn't wake. She dropped the duvet over him, feather-light, and tucked it carefully around his socked feet. She was about to cross to the landing, her hand on the door, debating whether to close it or leave it ajar, when his eyes snapped open.

'Going to bed without me?' It sounded the most honourable accusation but there was an undeniable menace beneath it. She hadn't wanted to hear it but now she had, there was no unhearing it.

Angela looked at him. *Why's he acting so weird?* She didn't like it; she didn't like him. This wasn't the Leon she had come to love; this was someone else. She couldn't put her finger on what the change was, she just knew she wanted him to go but was too frightened to say.

Then there were sirens. An ambulance. Ice-blue lights splintering the night. A series of shouts went up from outside. She rushed to the window and threw back the curtains. Raindrops glinted on the glass.

'Leon! They're going next door!' Her nose pressed to the cold windowpane. 'To your grandparents' house. Leon! Quick! For God's sake, quick!'

When he eventually joined her, he peered down onto the action. His eyes were dark with fatigue.

'I think you're right.' Leisurely, unconcerned.

She twisted her incredulity to him. 'Don't you think you'd better get over there? Find out what's happened?' She couldn't believe she was having to spell it out.

'I suppose I should.' He scrubbed his eyes with his fists, then yawned and stretched, abandoning himself to the yawn with a judder.

'D'you want me to come with you?'

'Nah. You stay here. I'm sure it's nothing.'

'But you'll let me know what's going on?'

'Yeah, I'll let you know.'

It was then she noticed the watch on his wrist: designer, smart, not something she remembered him wearing before. Yet there was something familiar about it. Then she realised where from, and who had been wearing it.

Oskar.

Was the ambulance for him?

Had Leon hurt him?

And thinking he could have done made her mouth go dry and her heart beat faster.

FIFTY

There's nowhere to park and I've had to drive around the block four times. When I do eventually find a space, it's a full three streets away from where I need to be.

I'm meeting Angela tonight. We're going to see Grandpa. She was working all day yesterday so, up to now, I've been going to the hospital on my own. That ambulance, late Tuesday night, was for him. He'd taken a turn for the worse, so it was lucky Babcia woke up and was able to call for help. She went looking for me first, apparently, but I'd already gone next door to Angela by then, hadn't I?

I'm nervous about leaving the car this far from my grandparents' road. Especially after dark. It's got a bit of a bad reputation around here. What used to be grand Georgian houses when I was a kid, have been carved up into student flats: unkempt hedges, blankets for curtains, rubbish piled up in weed-riddled driveways, dubious goings on all day and night... I'm quoting Babcia here. I'm only nervous because there's been a spate of car break-ins along this stretch and I can't afford anything to happen to the car. When it comes to my personal safety I've little to fear. There aren't many who would be stupid enough to try anything on, my size is usually enough of a deterrent. I weigh up my options and decide the car should be safe enough, the thing's ancient and I doubt anyone would bother to nick it, and with Grandpa's watch safely stowed in the glove compartment, I'm hardly asking to have a window smashed by leaving it on display.

Once I've locked it, I search the shadows the measly street lamps can't penetrate. I've got that uneasy feeling I'm being watched again but there's no one around, the place is deserted. I button the Crombie to keep out the fingers of cold and shove my hands into the pockets. I've left my gloves in the car. I don't need them; I haven't needed them for some time.

I know all the shortcuts around here and take the first right into a brick-walled alleyway. Listening to my footsteps, I imagine the frowsy gardens going on beyond the high timber gates. It's an oily dark along here, the lights from the backs of the houses are too far away to be of much use. But, hang on, what's that? The lights are useful enough to illuminate something big and baggy up ahead. Something my instinct tells me shouldn't be there. Loitering where the alleyway opens onto Coracle Road. I stride towards it, struggling to identify its precise shape from the shadows.

Then I see what it is.

It's him again.

The same homeless man I've been seeing on and off for months. I recognise the stinking grey blanket he's wrapped in.

It's a shock when he rears up in front of me. Blocking my way. And now he's upright, I see he is easily as tall and wide as me. I swallow the sudden rush of apprehension and feel my pulse thump in my neck.

The flash of a blade. Long and thin. Drawn from the filthy folds of his blanket. It glints in the limited light. I gasp in horror.

'You still don't know me, do you?' The voice is deep and thickened by an accent I can't place. 'I follow you all over the city and you don't know me. I get a job at the place you work and you still not know who I am.'

He says this while he brandishes the point of the knife at my jaw. He is playing with me. Enjoying himself. The madness in his eyes has me fearing for my life.

'Man, I tell you, you are one stupid fuck.'

His accusation is thrust in my face along with the smell of his blanket: putrid, rotting, like the contents of a wheelie bin left to stand in a hot August sun.

'But you are knowing me now, yes?'

An evil laugh before he flings off the stinking blanket and beanie hat and, along with his shorn head, I see the wizened stump of gristle – all that remains of his left ear.

An explosion of that night ten years ago. The brawl in the pub over a girl who meant the world to me at the time. The metallic taste of his blood in my mouth. His ear was between my teeth as I bit through the cartilage.

I was wild back then. Perhaps I'm wild now.

I shove him off me and run. Run for my life. I think I am shouting… Shouting and screaming for help. I'm quick but not quick enough. He is gaining on me. The bastard is faster, he's on my heels as I rush out into Coracle Road.

Then it feels as if I'm being punched in the back. Hard, swift movements that force the air from my lungs. Three, then four. A hot, tingling sensation ripples up between my shoulder blades and I'm down on the pavement. A cold wind sweeping up through my body.

The world goes quiet for what seems to be the longest time. Then a swell of sudden commotion that I'm not part of, as lights go on and people spill from their houses to circle me in slippered feet. I look past them at the street. It looks strange sideways up and I see my grandparents' gate swinging on its hinges.

'Oh, my God!' A shout goes up close to my head. 'He's been stabbed. Look at the blood… Look at the blood.'

'Quick, get an ambulance. He needs an ambulance.'

Someone else, I don't know who, reaches to cradle my head in their hands.

'Don't move him. Don't touch him.' Another voice attached to a pair of black boots advances, authoritatively, along the pavement. 'Wait for the paramedics.'

Eased down again, I'm aware of a small circle of cold where my cheek presses against the pavement. I focus on this circle while my eyes follow a crack in the paving stones and I listen to my mobile beeping from a pocket that I haven't got the strength to reach.

This is it… I roll onto my side and close my eyes. This is where I am going to die.

FIFTY-ONE

It was dark by the time Angela got off the bus in Roath. Asked to stay for an extra hour meant she was late leaving work and worse than this, she was late meeting Leon. She tried his mobile again. *Why won't he pick up?* Surely, he'd have waited. He'd made such a big deal about them going to the hospital to see Oskar together, she couldn't imagine he'd gone on his own. *Stop worrying, it will be okay.* She was nearly there, the turn into Coracle Road was just up ahead.

A siren. Rising clear and sharp through the winter air and ceaseless traffic sounds. She turned to see an ambulance bouncing down the road. Its wide, suspended backside rocking slowly. A blue light spinning on its roof. Then another siren whizzed up behind it. A patrol car.

Something was going on.

When the ambulance swung into her road, she began to run. Turning the corner into Coracle Road with a dreamlike slowness, she saw a collection of blue flashing lights and that whatever had occurred had drawn a considerable crowd.

The bubble of panic in her throat grew bigger.

As a child, she and Robert were told not to look at accidents.

You didn't watch when a person was shunted out of this world into the next. But in the same way these onlookers were, she was greedy and curious to find out what had happened.

Too dark to see much beyond the cluster of emergency vehicles. Their headlamps and revolving blue lights, criss-crossed in ugly patterns against the brick façades of houses and up into the sky, blocking out the moon.

She stood still and felt the shiver of the wind as her eyes flicked from face to face, plucking snippets from the discourse she wasn't part of.

'I hope they got here on time.'

'There was so much blood.'

'God, yes... So much blood.'

'D'you think they can save him?'

'Don't reckon on his chances.'

Catching the tail-ends of people's sentences, she stared into their wide-eyed shock. Until it was Leon she was looking at. Ashen and limp on a stretcher.

She screamed and charged forward but the way ahead was barred by the hefty arm of a police officer.

'Keep back, please.'

'But I know him.'

'No further forward, please, Miss.'

'But you've got to let me through. He's my boyfriend.'

The police officer threw her a look, then beckoned one of his colleagues over.

'What the hell's happened? Why's he covered in blood?'

The hard, dull thumps of her heart were so loud, she could hardly speak over them. *Why won't they say? Why won't they let me see Leon?* A hot panic flooded her and the wind slapped her face.

An image of Leon in the park. As he looked when she drew his portrait. How it felt to hold his hand. The weight of his thigh against hers. His mouth on hers. Warm and full of life. She held the memory of him there. Determined he would live. She must hold on to it, or he would give up and she would lose him too. Lose him like she lost Robert.

'Miss?'

The pressure of a hand on her arm and Angela spun to a uniformed policewoman.

'What the hell's going on? Is he dead? Oh, God, please don't tell me Leon's dead.'

'He's going to be okay. You must stay calm.' The hand gripped her tighter. 'He was attacked.'

'Attacked?' Angela listened to her echo. 'What? Who... Who attacked him?'

'We're not sure yet. It was a knife attack.'

'Oh, my God. Oh, my God. Leon! Leon! Let me see him.' She struggled against the hand that held on to her sleeve. 'Let me— Let me through.'

'Please try and stay calm. Someone will drive you to the hospital. I just need to clarify a few things with you first. Do you think you can do that for me?'

Nodding her consent, her mind elsewhere, Angela answered the stream of questions, automatically and without fully engaging. The policewoman, close at her side, kept writing things down. Angela looked at her feet. *Blood... So much blood.* The words skidded around her head and she wondered, appalled, if she could be standing in it. Standing in Leon's blood.

Something made her look up. Big and dark and emerging from the knot of spectators. It jolted against her, making her jump. She couldn't believe it and needed to look once, then twice more. Unwilling to trust what her eyes were showing her.

She watched him stroll towards her as if in slow motion. Saw how the crowd of people stepped aside as if they were afraid of him. He carried his body as if he was climbing uphill. As if negotiating, in his menacing and clammy way, the steep and greasy slopes of life.

Angela's stomach heaved with frostbitten butterflies and she clutched her bag to her body as if in need of protection. The shock of seeing him thumped in her chest and whatever else the policewoman asked was lost to her.

It was the kitchen porter.

The Mr Kowalski DS Varrius said had complained about her.

He passed by close enough for her to smell the unpleasantness of his shabby clothes, the filthy grey blanket he carried tucked under his arm.

Was that blood on his sleeve?

Staring up into his face, she didn't care if he saw her. But not a flicker betrayed him. Without his usual bandanna or beanie hat, his shaved head was exposed and looked knuckle-hard in the cold blue flashing lights.

Then she noticed it.

She recoiled in horror.

The nub of gristle was like something you'd find in a meat pie. Something that had been chewed and spat out.

His mutilated left ear.

FIFTY-TWO

My bed is by the window. I suppose it's a position that's in high demand but you'd hardly say I was lucky. Stabbed four times in the back. Once in the thigh. Another stab, a surgical incision, deep enough to insert a draining tube into my lung.

I heard the nurses whispering about me. Using the word lucky. Lucky to be alive. Lucky the knife didn't go in a few millimetres to the left. Lucky I was wearing a decent coat because although the blade was sharp enough to pierce the cashmere, it didn't penetrate me as deeply had I not been wearing it. I'd like to ask them: Had I been zipped inside my bomber jacket, would I have been a goner?

There are other things I've been overhearing too. Like, despite recovering from the emergency surgery they needed to perform when I was rushed in last night, I'm not out of the woods yet. Complications that come from having a punctured lung and severe internal bleeding mean it's still touch and go. All in all, the butcher did a pretty good job on me. Calling it payback for what I did to him, and going on about finishing what I'd started. Talk about bearing a grudge – I chewed his ear off years ago.

I avert my gaze from the ward. I'm not interested in the distress of others; I'm not interested in engaging with anyone. Making eye contact isn't my business. Instead, I look out the window, to a square courtyard with a few withered shrubs and what might have once been a fountain but now is choked in brambles.

I close my eyes. Listen to the beeping monitors they've hooked me up to. Between the beeps, it's quiet enough to hear the wheeze of air, in what's left of my lungs. There's no real pain as such, I'm doped up to the max, but I can feel the damage he's done to me if I move; so I try not to move, I try not to breathe too deeply. I try not to dwell on the attack either, but you can't stop yourself from raking over bad stuff, can you?

Some irony here, I feel, recalling how close I came. How I stood, knife in hand, ready to stab my father.

I must have been mad.

Was I mad?

Has anyone told my father what's happened to me? I imagine him taking the call, packing a hasty bag and hurrying to the airport to catch the first available flight to Cardiff. And is this what I'd like? I can't decide. The only person I know I want to see is Angela.

My Little Girl Blue.

And if she comes, I've decided, I'm telling her. Telling her straight. I'm done with lies and secrets, I'm going to own up about what happened with Toni that night and what I did to her. Even if she ends up hating me, I can't live with the guilt anymore, it's eating me up inside. The truth must out. I thought I could keep it hidden but I can't. As things turned out, I'm not so ruthless after all. If the cops do open the case up again, and Angela seems to think they will, it's only a matter of time before they put two and two together and she should hear it from me first. I know I've got some explaining to do but I'll just have to face the music. I'm disgusted with myself. As if it wasn't bad enough letting an innocent man go to prison for what I did, to think I could've killed Angela to save my own skin... I must have been out of my mind.

Talking of being out of my mind, reminds me to tell you that

Marvin's been. I heard him chatting to the surgeon moments before I was wheeled down to theatre on the cusp of floating off on the pre-op meds they injected me with. Marvin was one of the first people they called. I don't know how, or who told him, but I suppose they got his number off the card I have to carry. Him being my acting guardian, in case something was to happen to me – and something has happened to me. And the upshot of that is – yeah, you've guessed it, I'm back on the drugs. That as well as the painkillers and whatever other shit they're giving me, I've got the serotonin reuptake inhibitors, the anticonvulsant mood stabilisers and the antipsychotic ones to swallow too: medication only my psychiatrist can prescribe. So, what I'm saying is, don't go expecting too much from me anymore. I'm back to my dumbed-down, accepting self; but it was fun while it lasted. Not that anyone knew I'd stopped taking them, that's my secret. But I've got to thinking, perhaps it's better I'm back on them. Perhaps they do help me. I certainly don't have that anger inside anymore, and that infernal buzzing has stopped. I don't have the urge to kill either. And I doubt, if and when I get out of here, I'll be going around with death on my mind. Because I came so close to killing my grandparents too, didn't I? I mean, what was that all about? I couldn't imagine wanting to hurt them now.

The light changes. Someone is here. I can feel them shifting around at the foot of the bed. Too hesitant to be a nurse. This is someone unfamiliar with their surroundings.

I eventually work up the necessary impetus to open my eyes.

Angela.

Her heart-shaped face, framed in that mass of red hair. She looks so pretty. I must have been crazy to think I could live without her.

'There you are.' She smiles and I watch her drag over a chair and sit close to the bed. Her expression is empty, serene; but seeing a flicker from behind those green eyes of hers tells me the steady look is for my benefit. 'Hello.' Her voice is gentle, lower than normal. 'How are you feeling?'

I know I'm crying. That I'm making that raw belly sound men like me make when they cry.

'Don't get upset, Leon. It'll be all right. You're in safe hands.' She strokes the inside of my arm. The cool tips of her fingers finding a sliver of skin between the IV and bandages. 'Has your gran been to see you?'

I give a feeble nod and listen to the croak of my voice as I struggle to speak. 'But she's… she's got enough…' my mouth is claggy, 'with Grandpa.'

'You mustn't fret about your grandpa; he's doing well. He'll probably be out of here before you are. And I'm sure you'll be allowed to go home soon.'

The curtain Angela has drawn around my bed for us to have privacy is abruptly pulled aside. And a nurse, one of the whispering ones, with a pinched face and a pixie haircut, appears.

'You're not to wear him out,' she warns Angela as she busies herself: checking my monitors, my drip, testing my blood pressure, the bag that is steadily filling with fluid from my punctured lung.

We wait for her to go before speaking again.

'I came in to see you last night but you were sleeping.' Angela pulls the curtain around us again. 'It's lovely you're awake now. I've been so worried about you, Leon. You're so brave. They're saying you put up a hell of a fight.'

I suppose I must've done, going by my bandaged hands but I can't remember much. I turn from her inquisitive face to watch the sky. See fast-scudding clouds over a clear plate of winter blue. Despite everything, I feel calm, at last.

'Have the police been to interview you?' There's a fragile look in her eyes now.

I return my gaze to hers and croak, my lips ungluing themselves.

'Gave them...' it's a struggle to speak, 'his name... said about his missing ear.'

'His missing ear?' I hear her gasp and feel the weight of her hand intensify so that my arm feels uncomfortable under its grip.

'Call him Van Gogh. B-but his real name's...' I swallow and wince in pain. 'Bruno Kowalski.'

Angela tugs back her hand. 'How d'you know him?' She looks alarmed.

'Ten years back... was eighteen. A fight... Went too far. Bit his ear off.'

'Leon, that's awful.'

'He's been pretending,' I fight for breath, 'pretending he's homeless... Going on about working with me.'

'Really? Where?'

'Dunno. I work so many places.' It's difficult to speak, I've hardly any air in my lungs but I want her to know.

'He's been stalking you?'

'For months... years, maybe...' My mind drifting, my eyes closing, I can't go to sleep, I have to tell her everything. 'Think... me not knowing him pissed him off more... Was testing me... made it sound like... like some kinda game.'

'D'you think?'

'Yeah. If I'd recognised him... showed he'd been important...' I have to stop to catch my breath. 'Might not have stabbed me.'

'But how come you didn't recognise him?'

'Never got a proper look at his face... that night in the pub. So long ago. All a-a blur.'

'I suppose if it was ten years ago, that's hardly surprising.' The feel of her hand stroking my skin is soothing, lulling me to sleep. 'D'you remember anything about it at all?'

'You what?' I open my eyes, try to focus on her face.

'I just wondered, if you remembered anything about that night?'

'Was probably pissed. Used to drink too much back then... All I remember was getting back from the toilet. Finding some bloke chatting up the girl I was with. Then me and him fighting.' I can only speak quietly, in short spurts. Any effort – and it is an effort, despite the morphine I've got swimming around in my bloodstream – hurts like hell. 'Can I have... water?' I wait until she's guided the beaker with its jolly yellow straw to my lips. It's agony to swallow and I see my pain reflected in her gaze. 'Don't worry... The cops will have picked him up by now... There's loads on file about him.'

'That's a relief,' she says but she doesn't look it. 'It's a shame you didn't recognise him if that's what he wanted.' Angela stares at something beyond the window. 'If it meant you could've saved yourself all this. I mean, Leon – that man meant to kill you.'

'I know.' I'm drifting off again. So tired, all I want to do is sleep. I can hear her talking but she sounds a long way away.

'I might've been able to save someone else too. I always knew he was a vicious bastard. You won't know it, but that man who attacked you, he's the kitchen porter I've been going on about. He's the one I think killed Toni.'

I force myself to wake up. 'There's something I've got to tell you.'

'Yes?' A gentle smile.

'It's really important.' I take a breath and push myself. It takes everything I have.

'Oh, don't talk if it's too hard, Leon, please.' She frowns her concern. 'Whatever it is can wait, can't it?'

'No, I've got to tell you now... Should've told you...' I heave down more air, even though it's agony. 'I did something... Something terrible.' The words lodge in my throat like shards of ice. 'Please say you'll forgive me?' I stretch my fingers over the starched white hospital linen wanting her to hold my hand. But she doesn't.

'Forgive you? What are you going on about? You're frightening me.'

'It's about Toni.'

'*Toni*? What about her? I didn't know you knew her.'

An unexpected flurry of doctors and nurses burst through the curtains. Urgent. Officious. Crowding the bottom of my bed and cutting between us with clipboards and explanations about blood tests and scans that have flagged up a serious problem.

I think I hear, 'Clot on the lung' and 'Urgent surgery,' but can't be sure. All I can unravel from this sudden intense activity is that they need to do a CAT scan immediately. Something about, 'Acting now' and 'No time to waste.'

'Only a window of half an hour.' The pixie nurse is at my shoulder, her stiff polyester uniform brushing my arm. 'The scanner's free now. Got to get you down there immediately. You're not to worry, Leon. Everything's going to be fine.'

The nurse's platitudes are directed at Angela too.

Angela who is hovering, awkward. Her anxious fingers pressed to her lips as I'm wheeled away.

FIFTY-THREE

It took the cab driver a while to find a space to pull over.

'Will here do ya, luv?' He squeezed to a stop on the far side of Bristol's remand centre.

'Yes, this is fine.' Angela peered out at the day through the taxi's windows. 'I don't mind a walk now the rain's eased off.'

'S'pposed to cheer up good this afternoon.'

'Well, that's something.'

She avoided the man's gaze in the slice of driving mirror and once she'd paid, the central locking system was deactivated with a violent clunk. Out on the tarmacked forecourt, sniffing the stink of exhaust as the taxi accelerated away, Angela adjusted herself inside her parka and stared up at the ominous building that rose before her.

She was doing the right thing by coming to see Mark, wasn't she? A flutter of nerves made her think she should have stayed with Leon, that she shouldn't have left the hospital. Angela checked her phone for messages. The action was automatic. No one at the hospital knew how to contact her. She hoped Leon was going to be all right. At least Zofia would be with him and

Angela didn't suppose she would be here long. What had he been about to tell her about Toni? It sounded important. Why didn't he say whatever it was that night in the Pear Tree? It was odd, Angela wasn't aware Leon even knew Toni. Could whatever it was have something to do with his peculiar behaviour on Tuesday night? Because although she'd tried not to dwell on it, something had obviously been bothering him.

Coming home to find him in the house was enough of a shock, but it was his mood that scared her. He was weird, unreachable somehow. He'd frightened her and she wasn't sure she had wanted to see him again. If it hadn't been for Oskar taking a turn for the worse and needing to be rushed to hospital, she probably wouldn't have. But today things felt good again. Despite his horrific injuries, Leon had seemed calm and content; as if a great weight had been lifted. Perhaps it was the painkillers chilling him out because that wild look in his eyes had gone and he seemed more like his old self in the days she would see him around college before they got talking. Laid-back and cool-looking – the things which first attracted her to him.

Angela had reached a large set of sliding doors and, with a final glance at the sky that seemed to be clearing, she stepped into the dismal reception area. It reeked of floor polish and fear and the smell hurled her back to the gym at her old school. Nervous, she barely noticed a couple scurrying outside, umbrella at the ready.

'Sorry,' she apologised when she accidentally bumped against them.

Acutely uncomfortable, she dithered at the entrance, as unsure of her chosen outfit as she was about being here. *But you're here now*, she told herself; *you've come too far to back out.* Mark was expecting her and she couldn't disappoint him. This was just something that had to be got through and she hoped when she'd had the chance to explain, Mark would understand how hard she'd tried to help him.

Asked by the woman behind the safety screen if she had any photographic ID, Angela handed over her driving licence. Fiddled with her hair while she waited for it to be scrutinised.

'That's all fine.' The woman nodded. 'I'll just telephone through if you wouldn't mind waiting.'

Chilly, Angela shivered and zipped her coat as high as it would go. It couldn't be a more hostile environment if it tried. Hollow and barren, the few chairs that were scattered about looked as if they'd been screwed to the floor and the only windows were positioned well above head height and barred to the sky. She looked up to watch the dark shape of a bird fly over it. Freedom, she thought, had to be the most precious of things and coming here hammered it home. To have your liberty taken away if you were guilty of committing a crime was one thing, but if you were innocent like Mark...

Angela could have done with going to the toilet but there was no one to ask; no one kind-looking anyway. She questioned herself again as to what she was doing here. Thirsty and tired, it wasn't as if she'd come bearing good tidings and she couldn't imagine the sight of her would lift Mark's mood. A mood, going by his latest text, that sounded desperate. But, she reminded herself, he had no family and all his mates had forsaken him and she was here to give him moral support, as much as anything else. She was being a friend; the poor guy had reached out to her after all.

Ushered into another room, she was patted down by a woman with brown bobbed hair and goggle specs, behind which swam pale, suspicious eyes. Her uniform of black trousers and stiff white shirt looked as if it was held together by the shiny black belt fastened around her chunky middle.

'We ask you to please leave all personal belongings in the lockers, then to wait in line.'

Angela did as she was told and then joined a lengthy queue of people who stood in single file. No air. No natural light. Only a dim fluorescence above, which gave a corpse-like tinge to the brightest complexions. She realised other visitors had carrier bags of what looked like toiletries, magazines and confectionery. It hadn't occurred to ask if Mark needed anything and now it was too late.

A door banged somewhere behind her and she watched a male prison guard, towed by a wagging liver-and-white spaniel, weave along the crocodile of visitors. She knew the dog was here to sniff out drugs and, facing the front, she flushed a guilty red even though she hadn't smoked a joint since sixth form. The dog snuffled around her ankles, the floor by her feet, then moved down the line. Seconds later, aware of a spurt of activity behind her, she turned to see the dog had stopped at the feet of a young man in ripped jeans and trainers. Watched as he was steered away through a set of swing doors at the rear.

The guards bristled inside their uniforms and looked fearful of their safety. Herding visitors in to see the guilty until proven innocent was clearly dangerous work, and Angela heard them grunt as she was touched and jostled through into a huge, bare-walled space with tables set out like an exam room.

Angela failed to recognise Mark to begin with and walked straight past him. The man with the shuddering white face and dark mop of greasy hair was a stranger to her. He'd put on weight and had a tired, pulpy look, not unlike the chefs she worked with. Mark wasn't handsome anymore. Along with his liberty, this horrible place had robbed him of his looks.

'I miss her, you know.' He dropped his head on his arms and began weeping as soon as she sat down across the table. All she could do was stare at the top of his head. The guy was a quivering mess.

Unsure what to do, she scanned around in the hope of catching someone's eye. But the prison guards, sporting identical uniforms and removed looks, would not be drawn. With hands clasped over their belt buckles, they were as impervious as the invigilators at her end-of-year exams and, puffing out their bulk, they patrolled the vast linoleum floor in pairs, validating their bonds, inch by squeaking inch.

'I know we used to fight. Fight like cat and dog.' Mark lifted his bloodshot eyes, and she saw his face was soaked in tears. 'But I did love her.'

'I know you did.' A waft of unwashed armpits she did her best to ignore.

'We used to have some fun, me and her.' He sounded weird, choked – far worse than the times they'd spoken on the phone. 'It weren't all bad.'

'I know it wasn't.' She squeezed his arm, wanting to comfort, but he shrugged her off. 'I'm really sorry, I've done everything I can to get you out of here. The police warned me off in the end. They said I was stalking that kitchen porter and if I didn't stop, I'd be facing charges myself.' She'd been weighing it up on her forty-five-minute train journey and decided it was best to be honest. To give false hope would be beyond cruel.

Angela sat on her hands; she couldn't trust herself not to reach out to him again because he didn't want it. Now she was here, she wasn't sure he even wanted to see her. She could cry herself, she felt so sorry for him in his regulation grey sweatshirt and jogging pants. If she'd been asked to describe what he looked like, she'd have said he looked like a man who'd given up on life. And who could blame him? He was about to be put away for murdering his girlfriend. He was facing a prison sentence that would probably mean he would never get out. And how was that fair, when Toni's killer was still free? The only chance she could imagine there being for Mark, was when Kowalski was questioned about assaulting Leon, and the police somehow discovered his alibi for the night of Toni's murder was false, as she still believed it to be. Thinking about it, there was a pretty good chance of this. She'd been saying all along how dangerous Kowalski was and how could Varrius argue with that now? Should she tell Mark any of this? No, best keep quiet, she didn't want to go raising his hopes in case it came to nothing.

'She was all dazed and weird when I went back to the flat.' Mark was talking again. Talking through his sobs. Angela abandoned her thoughts to concentrate on what he was saying. 'She was stumbling around the living room, holding her head... Going on about some bloke from the hotel who'd given her a lift home after you'd stood her up.' He paused to scrub a hand over his face and gave her a black look. 'She was supposed to be staying with you that night, weren't she? She weren't even supposed to bloody be there.' Then he began to cry again. His whole body shaking.

Powerless to help, she turned from him to watch a family at a nearby table. The woman in jeans and T-shirt, her bleached-out hair pulled back from her face in a high ponytail. Two little girls swinging their socked legs were looking bored. The father, dressed the same as Mark, was trying to make them smile, to engage them in conversation. The woman caught her looking and Angela threw her gaze to another set of prison guards who had moved to stand side by side. A pair of heavyweights, big as bouncers and undoubtedly trained to step in should they need to.

'Hang on...' Something Mark said had filtered through and she returned her attention to him. 'I know you told me you bumped into Toni outside the flat when you were moving your stuff out, but did you just say you went back there again that night? That you went back to the flat a second time?'

'Yeah.' He wiped snot from his nose on the cuff of his sweatshirt. 'And she was all groggy. She had this cut.' He flapped a hand at the back of his head. 'There was blood in her hair, on the carpet... She kept going on about a bloke who'd been there. Something about him coming on to her. She said she'd fallen, smacked her head on the table.' There was now a faraway, almost dreamy look, in his eye.

'Sorry, Mark, I don't understand.' Angela shook her head; unsure if she'd heard him correctly. 'What did you go back for?'

'She still had me mum's ring.' He'd dropped his head on his arms again and was sobbing so hard, it was difficult to understand all he was saying.

'What d'you mean?'

'I'd given it to Toni. Sort of an engagement present. You know the one. She wore it all the time.'

Mind spinning. Then Angela remembered it. The blue-and-green gem on Toni's right hand. 'I didn't know it belonged to your mum.'

'Toni did. And she knew it was all I had left of her. But she still wouldn't give it back to me. And after everything she'd done: killing me kid and betraying me like that. And, as if that weren't bad enough, I go back to the flat to get the ring, and find she's just had another bloody bloke in there.' Mark lifted his head and she saw his eyes – eyes that, although swimming with tears, looked piercing and cold. 'All I wanted was me mum's ring. I didn't mean to do it.'

'Do it? What didn't you mean to do?' She leant over the table, strained to pick out some kind of meaning.

He scrubbed his hands across his face again. A frantic gesture to clear a way through his tears, as if hoping there might be a different truth concealed beneath. 'I didn't mean it, honest, I didn't.'

'Didn't mean what? For God's sake, Mark, you're scaring me.' She gripped her face, her fingers digging into her jaw. 'You're not making any sense.'

'I just wanted the ring back but she flew at me. Clawing and scratching, like some banshee. You knew what she could be like, so don't look at me like that.'

Angela was looking, she was looking at the scratch that had heeled into a scab on the left-hand side of his face. 'I had to do something to stop her.' He smacked his hands against the tabletop, making it rock on its spindly legs. 'I didn't mean it, it just happened. I just wanted her to shut up. But the next thing was, me hands were round her throat,' he hiccupped through his sobs, 'and then she went all limp. I didn't mean it... I didn't mean to kill her.'

The pair of prison guards Angela had been watching, suddenly swooped on their table. One of them thrust out a meaty hand and seized Mark's wrist and hauled him to his feet.

'I didn't mean it. Honest, Spike. I didn't mean to kill her...' He was shaking and crying as he was manhandled from the room.

She stared after him aghast. Her incredulity wheeling and flapping around her. She couldn't move. Couldn't speak. The bitter taste of bile on her tongue. How ugly he was. It was as if she could see right down to his evil core. Even the dimple on his chin, something she used to think enhanced his looks, seemed only to highlight the threat of a lurking, manic violence. A sort of contained cruelty she hadn't noticed before.

'*Please!*' Mark wailed through his tears before being dragged beyond a reinforced door. 'You've gotta believe me...'

The other prison guard, smelling of cheap aftershave, touched her shoulder. 'If you'd like to follow me, Miss.'

Dazed and bewildered, the guard's feather-light touch at her back, Angela allowed herself to be ushered into the lobby where she collected her coat and bag from the locker, before being steered out into the unexpectedly sunny afternoon.

Listening to the doors slide shut behind her, she stood in bemused silence and tried to process what she had just been told.

It was him all along.

Mark killed Toni.

He strangled her.

The papers had never revealed how she was killed. The bastard did it with his bare hands.

'And there's me defending you to everyone. I've pissed off my friends, the police. I nearly got myself into real trouble over you.'

She was remembering the ear-bashing from DS Varrius who, as things turned out, wasn't a fool after all.

'It's me who's been the fool,' her thoughts spilling into words, 'a stupid, stupid fool.'

What risks she took. Dangerous risks. All of them for Mark. She must have been mad to follow that Kowalski bloke back to his house that night and to think the blonde head she saw at the window was Toni when it was probably his wife. Then that other time, tearing around town after him the evening she should have been at Rhiannon and Geraint's engagement party. Anne-Marie was right all along. Why didn't she listen? Angela was determined to make it up to her and tell her she was sorry. With Rhiannon, too. Although she feared things between them had gone too far and too much had been said. But she would try. They had been good friends once.

Angela tilted her head to the beautiful blue sky. It had cheered up just as the taxi driver promised. She took it as a sign of happier times and pulled her mobile from her bag. Despite all that had happened and the horror of what she'd just discovered about a man she had been prepared to jeopardise everything for, it was the idea of speaking to Leon, of hearing his voice and the chance they had of a future together, that brought a small, slow smile to her face.

FIFTY-FOUR

THREE YEARS LATER

Roath Park was teeming with sunbathers. Their pale limbs spread like beached starfish over the grass that, newly mown for the season, felt as springy as a sprung dance floor. The air was alive with chatter and laughter, along with the intermittent chilly chime of an ice-cream van that cruised the block, garnering children beyond the high black railings.

The weather forecasters had promised a fine weekend, and for once, they were right. Temperatures were warm enough even for Leon – who never showed his legs unless at the gym or out running – to pull on a pair of shorts. Looking relaxed and happy, he was barely recognisable. Although his recovery had been long and arduous, the months of physio and rehabilitation therapy had paid off – he was back to his former self. There were those who claimed Leon was even better than his former self, especially as he was now on the right cocktail of drugs and under the care of a new and sympathetic psychiatrist who had adopted a more holistic approach to treating his illness.

Leon had his daughter tottering alongside him today. Already two but still unsure if she should trust her chubby legs to hold her upright, little Kristina stooped now and again to pluck a daisy and check on her new pink shoes. Given the name of his late and much-missed mother, the child's face was familiar, as was her tumble of red hair. Father and daughter crossed the park together, moving steadily down towards the trees and the lake Leon had known since his own childhood. The still stretch of water his mother liked to push him around in his pram until he was old enough to explore its perimeter on his bike with his friends. Pleased with how his life had turned out, Leon had lost the look of the hounded, the haunted... the guilty. When it was revealed that Mark Fairfax was the murderer of Toni Perry and not him, a burden lifted from his shoulders. Without the need to live in fear of impending punishment, rather than walking beneath a weight of cloud expecting to be rained on, he was free. And more than this, the future had become somewhere he wanted to be part of.

A sudden scuttle of excited voices, sharp through the air. Leon looked up to see two women emerge from the trees and join the path at the water's edge. They waved to him and Kristina, calling out their names. One older and stout, in a chilli-red cardigan and orthopaedic sandals. The other, young, with the same headful of glorious red hair as her child, was pushing an empty buggy. She looked pretty in the bold floral print of her summer dress, and the sight of her made Leon's heart soar.

'Look! There's Mummy.' He raised his hand to wave as Kristina ran forward, her arms outstretched. Leon watched her, poised for her cry to come and rescue her when she fell down with a bump on her nappy. But no cry came and before he reached her, she was on her feet again. Leon bundled the child into his arms and, grinning, jogged the rest of the way down to the path where he joined the women. A quick kiss for his grandmother, Zofia. Another for his wife. Loving, lingering, their child squashed between them until, bubbling with excitement, Kristina demanded her daddy set her down.

The younger woman was Angela. But, as it was with Leon, this was not the Angela of before. Stressed and tired, with no time for anything other than college and work, she never used to look like this. While they organised themselves and fell into step beside one another, Angela's hand swam out to press the material of her dress against the swell of her unborn baby. As a gesture, it expressed an utter completeness and easiness that only those of us who are truly loved could feel. Aware that Leon was observing her, she knew she looked beautiful. That happiness made you beautiful. Finally able to put the trauma in her past behind her, and accepting the death of her friend, sad and violent as it was, Angela was the happiest she had ever been.

Before too long the little family reached the lake, which, smooth as silk, shimmered under a high, bright sun. It reminded Leon and Angela of the illustrations of Cinderella's sparkling evening gowns in the Ladybird book they took turns reading to Kristina before lights out. The ducks and geese were cheeky and quite tame. Stretching their necks and chivvying for the bag of food they could see swinging from Leon's wrist. They made Kristina giggle. Smacking their bills together and making a similar sound to the castanets she played with at her toddler group, they were impatient for her to distribute the sweetcorn she scattered in the way she'd been shown. But too slow for their liking and increasingly intimidating, Leon was forced to lift his daughter up and out of their way.

The noise they made was raucous and Kristina, now balanced aboard her daddy's shoulders, had tired of their quacking demands. It was the swans she'd set her heart on and had done as Leon advised by retaining a handful of corn, hoping he would tempt them over. But the swans remained strangely evasive. Floating serenely as white-sailed ships on the far side of the lake. Kristina's eyes filled with tears when she realised how, despite her daddy's best efforts, the magnificent waterfowl insisted on keeping their distance. It was as if instinct had made them wary of the child – Leon's child. And that the harm her daddy caused one of their ancestors had been passed down through the generations, and no matter how hard Kristina cried, they would never swim near.

ACKNOWLEDGEMENTS

Special thanks must go to Betsy Reavley and the wonderful team at Bloodhound Books, especially Ian Skewis for his enthusiasm and expertise and Tara Lyons for her commitment and efficiency. But most of all my thanks must go to my darling husband Steven, for his indomitable belief, love and creative inspiration.

Rebecca Griffiths grew up in mid-Wales and went on to gain a first class honours degree in English literature. After a successful business career in London, Dublin and Scotland she returned to rural Wales where she lives with her husband, a prolific artist, their giant black cat called Mouse, and writes full time. *Little Girl Blue* is her sixth published thriller.

A NOTE FROM THE PUBLISHER

Thank you for reading this book. If you enjoyed it please do consider leaving a review on Amazon to help others find it too.

We hate typos. All of our books have been rigorously edited and proofread, but sometimes mistakes do slip through. If you have spotted a typo, please do let us know and we can get it amended within hours.

info@bloodhoundbooks.com

www.ingramcontent.com/pod-product-compliance
Lightning Source LLC
Chambersburg PA
CBHW031304210726
48287CB00005B/1412